They
that money could buy...
And passion could win

Favors of the Rich

WHITE STAR OIL—One magnificent man, FONTAINE DURAND, created it and gave it to Cimarron, the woman he cherished. But this beautiful, vulnerable woman is under siege as a corporate raider swoops down to steal her company and her heart.

KAMNICK OIL—A hard, dangerous oilman, LAZ KAMINSKI, made it the biggest corporation in the Southwest and made money his passport to power and to pretty women... especially Raye, the shopgirl who could be a millionaire as long as she belonged, body and soul, to him.

LAREDO OIL—The wild, rough-and-ready motorcycle cowboy, NICK KAMINSKI, decided to buck his rich father and the oil establishment with a company built on his daring alone... a daring that makes him risk everything for a woman named Cimarron.

"The multi-faceted talent of Sara Orwig gleams as bright as gold in her absorbing new novel. From its pastoral beauty, Oklahoma springs to life abounding with a wealth of interesting and vivid characters. This gripping story will capture your imagination and steal away your heart."

—Rave Reviews

Also by Sara Orwig

FAMILY FORTUNES

Published by
WARNER BOOKS

FAVORS OF THE RICH

SARA ORWIG

A Time Warner Company

Thanks to: Albert Lukken, Nancy Hermann, Jan Deatheridge, Ginni Stein, Jim and Beth Jameson, Jerrell Reed, Joe Brown, Jim Jewett, George Dawes, Joe Kneib, Jim Patton, Gordon Combs, Mary Lou Combs, Casey McBride, Herb Orwig, Ann Brown, C.A. Cromwell II, and Jackie Meyer. Also thanks to my editor, Jeanne Tiedge.

WARNER BOOKS EDITION

Cover design by Jackie Merri Meyer
Make-up by Laura Geller Studios
Cover photograph by Mort Engel

Warner Books, Inc.
666 Fifth Avenue
New York, N.Y. 10103

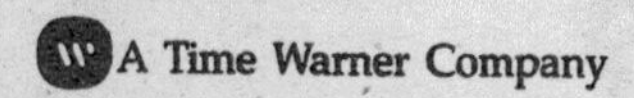

Printed in the United States of America

First Printing: March, 1991

10 9 8 7 6 5 4 3 2 1

PROLOGUE

APRIL, 1980

Remote and cold, a thin slice of a white moon shone high over Tulsa. The stars were obliterated from earth's view by city lights below, and by a fire more brilliant than any sunset. Along with a siren's distant wail came the deep-voiced yell of a fireman as orange flames danced in a sleek high-rise. Dark hoses, like slumbering engorged snakes, lay across the landscaped grounds while men in yellow slickers fought the blaze. More trucks arrived, their sirens shrieking when they turned off the freeway into the suburban business district bordered by expensive residential areas. Police cordoned off the block, pushing the ring of spectators back.

Cimarron stood as still as one of the tall oaks lining the curb. In spite of the full-length mink coat that was pulled high beneath her chin, she shivered. Her auburn hair tumbled loosely over her shoulders and the diamond on her finger sparkled in the fire's glow, but her face was pale, her eyes translucent. The glittering building, so unlikely to be consumed by fire, was a raging inferno whose acrid smell made her nostrils flare. Streams of water spewed in silver arcs only to be swallowed by flames. The glistening mirrored windows popped from the heat, glass shattering and crashing on the concrete walks below. Shards fell within yards of Cimarron, but she paid them no heed.

As she watched the building slowly crumble, she experienced the demolition of years of labor in one dark night. A part of her felt like walking into the flames; she saw her life was going up in smoke within that building.

She was surrounded by strangers: the idle spectators, those who thrived on disaster, and others who sympathized. Another siren screamed and died as a truck stopped behind Cimarron. She suspected all the south-side and east-side trucks in Tulsa had been summoned. Men burst into action around her, hauling more hoses toward the fire.

Her wide green eyes shifted from the mesmerizing flames to the crowd, futilely searching for a head of curly hair. Instead she saw a broad-shouldered man whose profile was unmistakable and whose presence she abhorred. Her anger flared, as she wondered how he knew about the fire. Soon his revenge would be complete and he would surely get what he wanted. The triumphant smile now curving the corners of his mouth made her draw a deep breath. She hated him with an almost blind rage. He was using her to get what he wanted: she was simply a means to an end.

Freedom appeared at the edge of the crowd. He turned his head as if he too were searching for someone, the flames highlighting his thick, golden hair, a frown creasing his wide brow. He hadn't seen her yet, but his gaze rested on her enemy.

At the sight of familiar faces, Cimarron felt a hysterical laugh threaten to burst forth. It seemed impossible that they had learned about the fire so quickly, and yet here they were, witnessing her destruction. Once again she slowly scanned the crowd, expecting any moment to look up and see the one man she wanted to be there. Disappointment and hurt surfaced, something tangible and forceful and demanding more of her emotions than the fire. She felt more alone than ever before in her life.

Those who would suffer the greatest loss and gain the biggest reward from this night were present—except one. And that one was conspicuous in his absence, for if the others knew of the fire, then so must he. *Why hadn't he come to see it?*

Emotions churned in her when she glimpsed a tall man

with tousled locks; her heart seemed to stop until he turned. It was a stranger.

She was too numb for the tears that would surely fall later.

The alchemy of fire had changed her life three times before. As she considered and remembered each, she decided four was a more accurate count. Four fires had transformed her life. Four times she had felt charred and broken.

The first had been on a farm, when she was eighteen years old, and its memory burned as brightly as the conflagration in front of her. She wondered if she could, like the phoenix, rise one more time.

1

JUNE, 1971

Beneath a June sun hot enough to scorch the earth, Cimarron Virginia Chisholm gripped the wheel of the green John Deere tractor as it rumbled along a narrow section line, its rattling motor shattering the silence. A floppy red umbrella patched with faded denim gave her some shade. Her thick auburn hair was bound in two braids that hung over her shoulders and faded coveralls. She loved summer even when the temperature climbed over a hundred as it had for the past six days. Her nickname "Sunny" fit her perfectly. Satisfaction came when she glanced to her left where hundreds of acres of ripe, golden wheat, pale as honey, was ready for harvest, spread as far as the eye could see. Dad was pleased this year—the crop promised to be bumper. With the past lean years, the mortgage payments that had to be met, and a new baby on the way, Peter Chisholm would need a good yield.

She headed home, unaware of the heat or the dust dancing in her wake. It was blazing hot, a drought year, yet farmers were hopeful because the ripened wheat was ready to harvest. Thursday the combines would start and work straight through the next three weeks.

She turned up the narrow road leading to the two-story, white frame farmhouse that had been built by her grandfather, Gerald Chisholm. Megan was her young, twenty-nine-year-old step-mother, the wife her father had taken six years ago when Sunny was twelve. Her mother, Eileen Chisholm, had died of cancer when Sunny was ten, and Peter Chisholm was not a man to live without a woman. Sunny loved Megan almost as much as she had her own mother. She still missed her mother, and sometimes the hurt came unexpectedly, but Megan had come into their lives with love and it would have been impossible not to love her in return. Now she was expecting a baby. Excitement gripped Sunny every time she thought about it.

She drove the tractor into the shade of the weathered barn and climbed down, smiling at her father who so often made her think of Vikings. When he stood, his height, broad shoulders, and tangle of golden hair stirred images of ancient warriors even though as far as she knew, there had been no Vikings in the Chisholm family.

Peter Chisholm pushed his hat back to wipe sweat off his brow. His blue eyes held a twinkle when he glanced at Sunny. "I thought you'd be back an hour ago."

Freedom, her twenty-one-year-old brother, turned off an electric drill. "Bet you've been making out with McClendon!"

"Freedom!" She grinned, thinking about the stolen hour spent with Homer McClendon at the creek. They had discussed their plans for the big dance on Saturday night. "I got my jobs done."

"Yeah," Peter said. "Well, run and give Meggie a hand, because she's tuckered out."

"Sure, Dad," Sunny said, giving Freedom a swat. He jumped, but too late. When he swung to retaliate, Sunny ran. She hurried inside, the screen door slapping shut behind her. The cool kitchen was a welcome relief, and one of Sunny's favorite places. It had the original high ceiling, long glass-fronted cabinets, and the wide porcelain sink that was big enough to hold three watermelons.

Megan sat at the round oak table snapping green beans. Her black hair hung limply in a braid, strands escaping to lie against her neck. In spite of the coolness of the house and the fan turning slowly overhead, perspiration beaded her brow.

"I'll do that, Megan. You go sit down in the other room where it's cool."

"Thanks, Sunny. I'll accept your offer without any argument." She heaved herself up out of the chair and left the room. It was cool and quiet in the kitchen as Sunny washed her hands and went to work. An hour later, she rang the bell and in minutes they were all seated, heads bowed while Peter Chisholm prayed. Then, deep voices rose in conversation about the harvest, the heat, and the cracked adapter plate on the small tractor while they passed blue china bowls of mashed potatoes and golden corn, and a platter of thick chunks of roast beef. Sunny was happy with her world, listening, participating occasionally.

"If we have a good harvest this year and next, I want to get a new tractor," Peter said, and Sunny glanced at him, knowing all the money from this year's harvest was going to pay off a second mortgage on the farm. Peter was pushed to his limit with debt and bills. His skin was burnished the color of pecan; his forearms bulged with muscle. With thickly lashed blue eyes, he was one of the most handsome men Sunny had ever seen. Her friends commented about it, and during the two years before he had married Megan, women had bustled around him like flies around meat on the grill.

Sunny glanced at her brothers, seeing a young replica of Peter in his oldest son Pierce. Twenty-three, Pierce had graduated last year from college with a degree in animal husbandry and was going to work for Peter until he could buy his own farm. While he wasn't as thick through the shoulders as his father, Sunny could imagine him in fur capes with a broadsword in hand as easily as she could Peter. Her gaze moved to the middle brother, and all images of Vikings vanished. Short, slender, as dreamy as the others were practical, Tim was twenty-two. Because of Peter, Tim majored in animal husbandry in college, yet Sunny suspected he would have preferred English literature as a major. Her gaze moved to the brother closest to her in age—twenty-one-year-old Freedom. Tall, and as handsome as Peter, he was far too practical to have roamed anywhere as a Viking conqueror. Freedom would have stayed home to watch over the treasures left behind. He studied accounting, detested the straits they were in, and late at night during the past winters, she could hear him arguing with Peter. Once she had tiptoed down the stairs to listen, learning that Freedom wanted to sell land and raise cash, while Peter argued vehemently, saying he was willing to risk all their futures to hang on to the land. Freedom was the only one who planned to turn his back on farming, something impossible to conceive of as far as Sunny was concerned.

Even with his practical ways and quieter nature, Freedom attracted women almost as easily as Pierce. Sunny could quickly name at least three of her friends who had crushes on Freedom, about five who had crushes on Pierce, and none who ever questioned her at all about Tim.

"What about the pickup?" Freedom asked. "I don't know how many more times we can wire it together and keep it going."

"We'll have to do a little at a time," Peter said, his gaze intent on Megan. As soon as they finished eating he left the room with his wife beside him, his arm around her waist.

The next morning began the day the dance was to be held and Sunny rushed through chores. Halfway through the afternoon when she was cleaning a chicken, Megan yelled. Sunny raced up the polished wooden stairs to the big bedroom where Megan lay in the middle of the four-poster bed. Her fingers gripped the sheets, and her face was as pale as the white lace curtains.

"Get Peter. The baby's coming!"

"Lordy, Dad's not here. The boys aren't here either. I'll find him!" Sunny added in the same breath.

Outside, to her relief, she saw Peter approaching in the pickup.

"Megan says it's time," she told him as soon as he reached her.

"Lord," he said, glancing up at the second story. He sprinted past Sunny as if he were thirty-one instead of fifty-one. Excitement bubbled in her while she rushed behind him.

"Get the van, Sunny. Write a note to the boys."

Sunny's heart pounded as she sat on the edge of the seat

in the van and timed Megan's contractions until they were a minute apart. They whipped into the emergency entrance of the Enid hospital where Megan was rushed inside while Peter and Sunny went upstairs to wait.

"The boys are repairing a fence and the pickup blew a tire," Peter told her. "I was coming in to see about Meggie and then planned to go back for them. They'll have to walk to the house, but they should be here in a couple of hours."

"I better call Homer and tell him where I am," Sunny said.

Peter caught her hand. His face was ashen and for the first time since her mother's illness he looked frightened. "I want you to stay here with me."

"Of course I will," she said without hesitation. His fear alarmed her, because Peter was the strength of the family. As she hurried to a pay phone, she remembered the blue dress laid out on the bed for the big night that she had looked forward to for months, but a baby took precedence over that. She called Homer, then hurried back to wait with Peter.

The boys arrived two hours later as Peter predicted. They tried to engage Peter in conversation, but he barely heard them. Then a nurse appeared to take Peter to the delivery room. In another twenty minutes he reappeared in the doorway. He wore a hospital gown and held a small baby whose head was covered with wisps of red hair.

"Peter Gerald Chisholm," Peter announced proudly. "Seven pounds, four ounces. We'll call him Gerald." All of them came close to peer at the new baby who smelled of talcum and had his eyes closed.

"He's the most beautiful little thing I've ever seen," Sunny murmured, feeling a knot form in her throat. One brother put his arm across her shoulders and another slid his arm around her waist. They all stood in a close circle, awed and curious about the newest member of their family. Sunny glanced at Freedom. "Isn't he the prettiest baby in the whole world?"

"Yes, he is," Freedom answered solemnly, looking at his

tiny red-faced half brother wrapped in a nubby blue blanket, his rosebud mouth puckered.

"It's time to take him to the nursery," the nurse interjected.

They moved away, discussing the baby's features until Peter joined them. "Boys, why don't you take Sunny home. I'll be along later. Megan's worn out, and you can see her tomorrow. Leave the pickup for me."

"Sure, Dad," Pierce answered, dropping his arm across Sunny's shoulders to steer her toward the door. They drove home in the van, the boys singing, talking about getting a football and putting up a new basketball goal for Gerald, who was already called Jerry.

They stopped and bought beer. Then Pierce drove, singing lustily, and the boys shared a beer with her, another first in her life. The windows were down, so Freedom lolled in the back with his long legs stuck out the window. Fields of alfalfa sweetened the night air as wind whipped against her face.

Once during a lull, Freedom sat forward. "Hey, y'all, our little brother isn't going to know any of us very well. We're old enough to be his parents and we'll be gone from home."

He was shouted down instantly. "You baboon, I'm home," Pierce said, "and I'm going to buy land as close as I can and live there all my life and he can come stay at my house any time."

"You think Mary Clemens is going to like that?" Freedom asked.

"I think Mary will love him and anyone else in my family."

"Think Mary would love me?" Freedom asked with a leer in his voice.

"You're the exception. We'll lock you out of the house."

"Okay," Freedom persisted. "Sunny's going to college. I'm going to college and—"

"Sunny will marry Homer and live right here too," Pierce answered firmly. "Tim will come back here to farm." For a few minutes they were all silent, because they knew about Freedom's determination to be an accountant and move away. Then Pierce started singing again, the moment forgotten.

On Wednesday, Megan came home with Jerry. The next day harvest started, the big, red Massey-Ferguson combines coming in from the highway, their motors rumbling, men filling the yard, anticipation running high. The Chisholm future depended on the ripened wheat, and Sunny could feel the tension growing in each member of the family except Megan and her new baby who were insulated from worry.

That Friday afternoon, Sunny drove the pickup into Enid to get groceries. As she sped the hour's drive home on the narrow country road that stretched straight and flat for miles, she had no fear of being alone because she was in familiar surroundings. And Pete's loaded .22 was beneath the front seat of the pickup. She passed the McClendon place where combines were harvesting, the sickles and reels working, spilling golden grains into an auger and then elevating them into a bin until full. Then the grain would be dumped into a waiting truck. Straw and chaff were thrown out the back to fall to the ground, spewing up a cloud of dust around the combine.

Waves of heat made the yellow fields shimmer. Heat pressed down, all pervading, blasts of hot wind taking her breath. Yet it was summer; she was eighteen, and wheat would get the family out of debt. "Raindrops Keep Falling on My Head" played on the radio and Sunny tapped her thumb to the beat while a south wind whipped across the land. The pickup rocketed over a creek, the wooden bridge rattling above a caked stream bed devoid of water. A bang followed, power diminishing swiftly. Sunny pulled off the shoulder to a shady spot in a draw with cottonwoods flanking the road.

When she raised the rusty hood, she spotted a hole in the block, and glared at the engine because she would have to walk home and get someone to tow the pickup. She rearranged cold packages into two sacks to carry with her. As she worked, she heard a roar.

Heat waves rising from the pavement made the seven black Harleys a wavering apparition. Like jets coming in to land, they sped down the road toward her, and she was frozen with fear because of her vulnerability. She climbed inside the pickup as they whipped past. Riders waved and whistled and grinned. They raced down the narrow asphalt and diminished in the rearview mirror. One of the bikers turned around.

Her chill of apprehension returned; the pickup offered little protection. The .22 pistol was the only safeguard. A roar seemed to envelop her as the Harley approached.

The rider's long, curly brown hair blew back from his face. He sped past, turned, and came back, slowing down to stop beside the pickup. The stranger was burned brown by the sun; his chest was bare, and faded tight jeans hugged his hips. Dusty boots showed beneath the frayed bottoms of the legs of his jeans.

"Trouble?" he asked.

"Nothing I can't handle, thank you."

An eyebrow quirked in amusement. "Yeah?" He went around to peer beneath the hood. In seconds he was back beside her, standing a few feet from the door, his feet splayed, his hands in his hip pockets, an animalistic wildness radiating from him in spite of the stillness of his quiet stance. "Good at fixing thrown rods?"

"I'll manage," she answered coolly.

"Maybe you ought to accept my help before someone comes along who doesn't have help in mind."

"I don't need your help," she replied.

"You shouldn't be here alone."

"I'm not. Dad and my brother are working over there," she motioned toward the field. He didn't look around. Her heart began to beat faster as he stepped up to the door of the pickup until he was only inches away. She could smell the odors of sweat and grease and tobacco while she gazed into smoke-colored eyes that held absolute confidence.

"You need a ride home."

"It's all right. I can walk home," she said with a rising sense of panic. He exuded power, and she wanted to reach for the .22, to force him to leave her alone. She was accustomed to big, muscular men—this one was as tall as

Freedom, but far more lean, honed down to hard muscle and bone, looking fierce and rebellious instead of reliable like the men she knew. He stood so close she could see the beads of sweat on his brow and shoulders, smell the tobacco on his breath. He frightened her with his hard gray eyes, his implacable stance.

"I'll take you home." He yanked open the door.

Heart pounding, she grabbed for the pistol. He moved faster than she expected, catching both her wrists in his, searching for the gun with his left hand. She tried to stomp his hand, and he released her wrists to clamp his hand around her ankle in a vise that was unyielding. His strength stunned her; his speed was impossible to match. He withdrew the pistol and grinned at her.

"Baby, you're a mean momma," he said softly, turning the pistol.

Her heart thudded, roaring in her ears. He flicked out the cylinder, gave it a spin, and snapped it shut. He placed the pistol back under the seat and stepped away. "If I hadn't come back, one of them would."

Relief settled like a cool breeze on a hot day, because he wasn't going to hurt her—he'd had every chance when he held the pistol. Her curiosity stirred. He was as alien to her world as if he had dropped from the sky. He stared at her. "You're stranded."

"My brothers will be along here any minute now," she said, hoping she sounded casual, reminding herself he hadn't used the gun when he had had the opportunity. His gaze flickered over her.

"I'll take you home." It wasn't an offer. He glanced at the groceries. "Got cold beer in there?"

"As a matter of fact, yes." He rummaged in the sacks and got two beers. When she climbed out and turned, his gaze was moving up her legs. The assessment stripped her and speculation was plain in his eyes. It gave her a peculiar tingle.

"Bikers don't usually take this road because it's a back road."

"That's why we chose it," he said, handing her a beer.

He snapped the lid and tilted it to drink, the prominent Adam's apple in his throat working as the cold beer went down. A drop spilled out and ran over his jaw and down his chest. Unable to take her eyes away, Sunny watched the crystal drop slide over burnished skin that covered sleek muscles, down across the flat washboard belly beneath low-slung tattered jeans. She looked up and met his gaze. Her mouth was dry and for a moment curiosity fanned white-hot like the summer sun while she wondered what it would be like to touch him. The thought made her insides quiver, and she drew a deep breath.

Amusement showed in his eyes. "What's your name?"

"Sunny. What's yours?"

He shrugged. "They call me Reb."

"For Rebel?" she asked, wondering what caused the rebellion—society, family, crime?

"Yeah, sure," he answered. He reached into his pocket and pulled out a joint, lighting it.

He held it out to her and she shook her head quickly. "No."

That seemed the end of the conversation. He studied her and it made her intensely aware of herself. "How far do you live?"

"Not far at all."

"Come on. I'll take you." He put the roach away carefully and moved to the Harley. It was a massive, customized Harley Davidson with chrome and skid bars. He looked as if he didn't have ten cents, yet the bike appeared to be in mint condition.

She climbed on awkwardly behind him. He tossed the beer cans in the ditch where they rolled out of sight in the underbrush. "You live in town?"

"No. On a farm. Straight down this road, the second dirt road on your left, turn west."

He kicked the motor to life and it thundered in her ears. They whipped up on the road, and she had to cling to him. She had hugged brothers, her father, Homer. But he was leaner than any of them, and rock hard, his waist narrow, his flesh smooth, heated. She should be repulsed by him, frightened of him, yet she felt neither. Beyond that, she wouldn't assess her reactions. His hair was long enough to curl over his shoulders. She wondered if he ever knew fear or loneliness or love—if he had a woman in his life.

They roared down the road, hot wind assailing her until her senses warped and the familiar became unknown. Trees and fences blurred as tears stung her eyes, sounds changed to an incessant roar like a never-ending storm, and she wondered how fast they were traveling.

They took the turn to the dirt road in a swooping curve that made her heart skip as she expected to spin off across the hard, sun-packed ground. Ocher dust spiraled behind them while her gaze swept over the visible part of the thousand Chisholm acres.

Where all had been golden wheat meeting a wide blue sky, now was a black cloud smearing the horizon and her heart lurched. He glanced over his shoulder and slowed.

"What the hell? Have I taken the wrong road?"

His question barely registered until she realized how hard she was gripping his shoulders, her fingers digging into them. He jerked his head. "What's that?"

Panic came because of the enormity of the cloud. "Fire. The wheat field's on fire," she said, her voice seeming to come from a distance. "In this high wind . . ."

"What do you do when that happens?"

"Contain it and put it out. Try to save the house and barn and whatever else you can. Can we go?" Her last words came out in anguish, because she knew how close the fire was to the house.

"What would start a fire? There hasn't been a bolt of lightning—"

"Sparks from the combines; sometimes bearings burn out and fall apart, dropping into the stubble. The wheat is as dry as paper. We haven't had rain in weeks. Dad keeps a tractor and disk to plow a fire guard, but in this wind that won't be enough. Section lines will help contain it, but there's six hundred and forty acres in this section. *Let's go.*"

He revved the motor and they lurched forward, skidding crazily, the big Harley sliding on loose rocks, smoke filling her nostrils as they sped along. When they drew closer, she glimpsed the line of flames above the ground. They could hear the dull rumble of the fire, the crackle as flames swallowed the wheat. The acrid stench of smoke came; sparks blew overhead, the clear sky darkened with smoke in spite of the wind that merely fanned the smoke over a wider area. She could hear their wheat burn. Men shouted and motors roared as they tried to move combines and trucks out of the way. Heat radiated to the road; unless the fire was controlled soon, the Chisholm house would be in its path. The road was lined with cars belonging to neighbors who had come to help.

"Dante's *Inferno*," Reb said.

"Let me off here." As she crossed the bar ditch, she was aware of the biker striding beside her. A red rural fire truck moved along the edge of the fire with a fireman standing on the bumper behind the guard rail. He held a short hose with the nozzle aimed at the fire as water poured from the big tank on the truck.

As the fireman battled the blaze, men beat isolated burning spots with wet gunnysacks, others trying to smother the advancing line with shovelfuls of dirt while Peter drove the orange Case tractor, plowing a path next to the road, the disk turning straw and chaff and dirt. A pickup was in the field, a man passing out shovels and gunnysacks. As they ran toward him, she spotted her brother.

"Freedom!"

"Sunny, get to the house!" he shouted. "Get Megan and the baby out."

He tossed keys to her, and she raced to their truck, glancing again at the fire that was inching closer to the road, men struggling frantically to control it, the biker working alongside Freedom.

The rebel, Nick Kaminski, beat flames with a gunnysack, wondering why the hell he had stopped. Heat came at him in waves like a boiling ocean; sweat streamed off his body. He hadn't wanted to go back and help the girl. She was green as grass and looked sixteen years old, but if he hadn't gone back, Cheeter would have. Then she would have been in trouble for sure.

Nick ran his arm over his brow, shaking his hair back from his face, glancing at men who were puffing with effort. The place felt like a furnace, and he was tempted to turn and walk away. These men didn't mean anything to him. In fact, if they met him under ordinary circumstances, they'd urge him to get out of their town. He swung the soggy gunnysack, beating back flames while sparks escaped and ignited wheat inches beyond his reach, the line slowly edging forward in spite of everyone's efforts. He glanced at the blond guy next to him. She had called him Freedom. Freedom and Sunny. Brother and sister. Their chins and green eyes bore a resemblance.

When the wind changed direction, smoke billowed over him and made him cough. Suddenly, there was a roar like his Harley, and a dark shape emerged from the inferno. A truck, horn blaring, barreled through the flames. It burned, its load of wheat a cargo of fire, the driver barely discernible.

"God!" Freedom said, loud enough for Nick to hear. "Pierce! Jump!"

"Pierce!" another man yelled, throwing down a shovel and running for the truck. There was an explosion that knocked Nick off his feet. He fell on flames, yelled in pain and rolled, beating out a spark that caught the frayed edge of his jeans. He shook his head and stood up. Only the bent metal frame of the truck was standing, fire burning all around it and men leaned over a body stretched on the ground.

Swinging at the flames savagely, Nick turned back to fight the fire, swearing under his breath from the blistering heat, wondering if all their efforts made the slightest difference in the course of the blaze.

He watched men bear a body away, heard snatches of conversation, and realized a man named Pierce had died. He caught enough remarks to know he was Sunny's brother and had been trapped in a ring of fire, trying to drive a truckload of burning wheat through the blaze to safety. These were tough people. Cheeter called them hayseeds, but Cheeter couldn't have fought this fire as these men and boys had. The one named Sunny was a green kid, but she was probably as tough as the men. He thought about the pistol. Cheeter had wanted to go back and get her. Had he tried to rape her, she might have been able to hold her own with him. Nick backed up, beating at the flames. They were yards from the road, but no sparks had blown across the road and as the yards narrowed to feet, he saw they might contain the fire and the field beyond might go untouched.

It was late afternoon when it was finally under control. Nearby, two men engaged in conversation, gray smoke rising from smoldering fields behind them.

"Thanks, Mr. Sorenson, for your help."

"Sure, Freedom. Damned sorry about Pierce."

Nick headed in long strides for the Harley to get the hell away. His hands were raw, he was burning from heat, and thirsty.

"Hey, mister!"

Nick turned, walking backwards.

"Thanks," Freedom yelled.

Nick waved and broke into a run for his Harley. In minutes he was roaring down the dirt road. He spun out onto the asphalt highway and pushed the engine to full speed, letting wind beat against his body, trying to forget the past hours. His throat burned, his breath wheezed, his nostrils and lungs stung from smoke. He wanted a chilled Dos Equis, a cool shower. His blistered hands ached. Trying to ignore the pain, he lifted his chin, absorbing the wind as if it could soothe his mind and drive out all thoughts.

At dusk, he passed a sign welcoming him to Miller's Bend, Oklahoma. It was a wide place in the road, only a few street lights up ahead lining the highway. He wondered where the others in the gang were. He knew they would wait for him.

Slumbering houses were dark, yet lace curtains blew in open windows. White frame houses with front porches and swings were set back behind flower beds. The street widened when he reached the two blocks of businesses: a store, a gas station, a post office, and a bank. Kids gathered around a lighted drugstore, and Nick felt as if he were dropped back in time. He hadn't been in a town like this in years. At the opposite end of the street, there was another gathering. Nick saw his friends pull away from the curb, peeling away with a deafening roar, racing down the main street. He yelled, accelerating to catch them, and then he saw a sheriff's car, a highway patrol car, and a shiny black car with no markings.

"Jesus." As Nick spun the bike around, he heard the motors roar behind him. The sheriff's car and the highway patrol car passed him on either side, drove ahead, and slammed on their brakes, blocking him. The black car raced beside him. He would have to crash or stop. He stopped.

Four men in dark suits spilled out of the black car to surround him. One had his hand beneath his coat. By this time the sheriff approached, hiking khaki pants up over his paunch.

"I don't want no trouble, y'hear?" the sheriff said and spat a stream of tobacco that splattered against the curb.

"Come with us," one of the men in suits urged Nick. "We'll take you back willingly or like last time."

He looked at them, rage welling up in him as heated as the blaze he had fought earlier. He clenched his fists and turned. The sheriff stood between two of them.

"We don't want no trouble here," he said quietly. "You're going with them."

"They don't have a right to do this!" Nick ground out the words, his ears roaring as fury pulsed in him, his words directed at the lawman.

"They can do it. I ain't going to stop them. We can search you for pot, fine you for speeding . . ." He shrugged, indicating his indifference. Then he walked back to his car.

"Come on, Nick," one of the men said, smoothing black kid gloves over his knuckles.

Nicholas Lazlo Kaminski turned to face him. Rage boiled inside him. His father, Laz, had a knack of finding him anywhere he went, and he wasn't a man to give up. He had the wealth to get what he wanted. "I must be getting tougher," Nick snapped. "There's four of you this time."

"Your father said we can put you in the hospital, just don't kill you," one of them said, moving a step closer.

Nick looked from one to the other, trying to assess the weakest link, trying to control his rage enough to think. He saw one move in close and he swung, smashing his fist into the man's jaw. He had to fight all of them and he swung his fists, his anger erupting as he slammed another one on the jaw, then took a blow on the back of the head that sent him staggering. Hands grabbed him from behind, trying to pin his arms. Something crashed against his skull, and the world seemed to explode.

He opened his eyes and focused on blue carpeting. When he tried to move he groaned. Pushing against the floor, he raised himself and stood up, swaying.

"You smell like a sewer," came a sharp voice, and Nick knew where he was.

A man stood in front of a plate-glass window gazing into the dark Dallas night. His shoulders were broad, his hair a thick mat of brown curls streaked with gray. His suit fit to perfection, the navy pinstripe adding to his aura of wealth and well-being, yet the suit and his stillness didn't hide the determination in his stance.

Memory and rage returned as Nick regained consciousness from the beating. The men had brought him home to Dallas, Texas, to his father's house. Fighting waves of pain, Nick staggered, leaning on the desk for support. "Why the hell don't you let me go?"

Lazlo Nicholas Kaminski turned to stare at Nick. They gazed at each other through eyes that were the identical gray color of ashes, and filled with rage.

"When will you be my son?" Laz asked.

"When will you learn you can't force another human being to fucking obey you like a puppet?" Every breath hurt. Nick's eye was puffed shut, his lip swollen, his head and leg throbbed with pain. "If you don't get off my back, I'll put out a contract on you."

"Yeah. You and how many others? I'm not afraid of a

hit." Anger tinged Laz's face as he strode across the room and struck Nick with the palm of his hand. The blow slammed Nick into a chair.

"Damn you. I offer you the world! All I want is a son."

"You have a hell of a way of showing it," Nick said, wiping blood from his mouth.

Laz opened a drawer and tossed money on the top of the desk. "Here. One hundred big ones. Come back to work. I'll give you a division and let you run it."

"You know what happened when we tried that. A fucking geology degree, just like you wanted. All my high school and college summers working in the oil business like you wanted. My first two years out of college working my ass off for Kamnick like you wanted. Everything you wanted down to the smallest memo. It's only been a few months since I quit, so you should remember."

"I swear to you—I'll let you run it your way." The words were ground out in a rasp.

"I've heard that promise before, and then the first order I give that counters yours, you sabotage me. No, Laz. We've tried and it won't work. You'll keep paying your goons to bring me back until you understand I won't do it your way."

"Yes, you will." Laz leaned over the desk. "I'll make your life such a hell you'll do it my way. I want my son to take over Kamnick Oil. Someday you'll be grateful. Someday you'll wake up and realize you're my blood. My only blood. I should have let you rot in that jail in Texas longer."

"Yeah—to make me love you more."

"I'll win, Nick. I always do."

Nick leaned forward, facing his father, their strong jaws both firm, each pair of eyes mirrored by the other. "No, you won't win if you mean you'll own my soul. How old will you be before you learn that if you love someone, you let them go?"

"I'm willing to let you go—take over this division and you can go to the ends of the earth on your vacations. And you can take long vacations. Don't you know half the men in the world would jump at this?"

"Vacations! They wouldn't jump if they knew it meant

eating, breathing, fucking, the way you want them to. No." He turned to walk out.

"Nick," Laz said, his voice even, commanding in spite of its quietness. "I'll play rough. If you won't be my son, you're not worth a damn to me. You step in or you're dead."

"If I become your son, I sell my soul. I'm dead either way."

With a flash of his wrist, Laz tossed a bundle of money across the room. Nick acted reflexively and caught it with his left hand.

"You're not particular where you sleep, the street, the beach, a car. Sleep here tonight and you can have your Harley back in the morning."

"Always you add the threat. Some time you should try just asking." Nick bounced the money in his hand and slanted a glance at his father without raising his head. "But then I suppose you'd always be turned down." Nick walked out of the room, closing the door behind him. He didn't think the old man would shoot him, but he wouldn't put anything past him just short of murder. Never in Nick's adult life had they understood each other or been able to communicate, so he didn't know why he expected it now.

Two hardbodies dressed in white shirts, dark ties, and slacks moved in beside him. Deltoids and biceps bulged even when they were relaxed, their walks a rolling gait, their white collars tight around thick, tanned necks.

"We'll show you to your suite. Mr. Kaminski said you'd stay the night."

Nick shook his head, staring at the one who spoke. "Shove it. I know where the friggin' guest rooms are."

Nick could imagine the debate grinding in the muscle-bound mind. The guy shrugged, and both returned to their seats. Nick moved down the hall, the sound of his steps absorbed by the white carpet. Gilt-framed oils hung on the walls that were lined with marble columns. Over the bannister, Nick glimpsed the marble floor, tall, potted palms, and a fountain of splashing water. His silken prison. Daniel Webster should have been so tempted. Money, power, women—Laz

Kaminski always offered it all. His only requirement was that you forfeit your soul.

After closing the door behind him, Nick felt bittersweet amusement as he viewed the one-of-a-kind bed handcrafted in Italy with Italian marble posts and a golden satin spread. How different from a bench in a park or a doorway on the street were the bed, the Carrara white mantel, the nineteenth-century French fruitwood furniture, and the thick white carpeting that showed each footprint. He guessed the maid had backed out of the room when she vacuumed, leaving a pristine surface as smooth as wind-swept snow. He was torn between the urge to smash the porcelain jardinieres or to run his hand over the polished fruitwood. As much as he hated to admit it, he liked the comfort and luxury of the room.

He walked across the carpet to the window to peer outside. The room was on the east wing that angled out so he had a view of the swimming pool and cabana—as calculated as anything else Laz did. Lights gleamed beneath the aqua surface. Nick dropped the curtain in place. Weariness made him exhale in a long breath. He went to the bathroom, peeling off his ragged, burned clothes, dropping them on the floor. Tonight he was going to relax in a soft bed and wear clean clothes. He lifted the receiver in the bathroom and punched the number to the maid downstairs.

"Yes, sir?" came a prompt, cheerful answer.

"Who is this?"

"Hilda, Mr. Kaminski."

So Laz had told them about his guest. "Hilda, would you get me some clean clothes. Size fifteen-and-a-half shirt, thirty slacks—"

"They're in your closet, sir. Unless none of the clothes is satisfactory—"

"I'm sure they'll be fine. I didn't look in the closet. Send up dinner and a bottle of Chivas Regal, ice, and soda, please."

"Of course, sir," she answered as if anticipating his needs.

"Thanks, Hilda." In the mirrored wall across the spacious room, his reflection stared back at him, the startling white strip of flesh across his loins a contrast to his deeply bronzed skin. Skirting a potted palm, he climbed down into the tub, thinking that some motels had hot tubs that weren't as big as this one. The water made him relax and sigh with relief. Soon he heard the call of a feminine voice and turned the faucets.

"Just set down the dinner. Thanks." No tipping. Gratis on the house.

The door pushed open and he glanced up straight ahead in the mirror at the reflection. In the doorway behind him stood a woman in a white satin gown, her black hair falling over her shoulder. In her hands was a tray with two glasses, an ice bucket, and two bottles. She smiled at him in the mirror. "Hi." Her voice was deep and throaty.

"Hi." The gown clung and she wore nothing beneath it. His mouth went dry and he forgot his aches. "Hilda, you're wasting your time working in the kitchen," he said so softly that he didn't expect her to hear.

Her smile widened. "I'm not Hilda. I'm Christie."

"Christie? Did the cook change since I called downstairs?"

She crossed the room to sit on the edge of the tub, making an elaborate ceremony out of mixing his scotch and soda and handing it to him. "I'm a friend of your father's. He thought you might like some company tonight." Her fingers brushed Nick's as he took the drink. "I'm here to keep you from getting bored."

She poured the second drink and held it out to him. "Here's to an interesting time."

Nick touched her glass and drank, watching her over the rim. He took the drink fast, letting the scotch hit his stomach and start its own fire.

She sipped, her ruby lips leaving a clear lipstick imprint on the glass as she lowered it. All her movements were slow, sensual. With a shrug of one shoulder a strap fell. She did the same with the other shoulder. When both straps went down, she wiggled as if to shake free of the gown. It slipped lower, yet remained in place because of the upward tilt of her full breasts. Nick reached out and hooked his finger in the satin to gently pull the fabric over the barrier. It fell to her hips and he drew a deep breath, his chest expanding.

She stood up and the gown slipped to the floor. With enticing deliberation, she stepped out and moved down the steps into the tub, Nick watching her all the time, his blood heating. As she sat down beside him, he took the drink from her hand and set both drinks on the marble shelf behind his head, then he turned to face her, his aches and cuts forgotten.

"The night just got infinitely better," he said in a husky voice and wrapped his arms around her slippery, wet body.

He woke when the sun's golden rays slanted over the edge of the earth into his window. Christie lay sleeping beside him, quiet now, all her passion spent. She had tried twice to talk him into staying longer than overnight, and he could imagine the bonus Laz would give her if she succeeded. She lay with one arm flung across the pillow; her smooth skin was the color of alabaster. Nick peeled bills off the stack that had been tossed to him and let them flutter down on the bed beside her. He smiled, remembering, knowing she had enjoyed herself or been one hell of an actress.

He moved quietly, his body aching, his hands blistered from the fire, his ribs hurting with each deep breath. He pulled on new jeans, his old boots, and a new white cotton shirt. He opened the door to the hall and no one was in sight. Holding the key to the Harley, he went downstairs without making a sound. In minutes he roared down the gravel drive, letting some of the twenties fly away behind him. He kept most of the stack of bills, but let enough go so that Laz would find them or hear about them.

2

The light burned brightly above the kitchen table, the golden and red hair of the Chisholms shining in the yellow glow. The grandfather clock ticked steadily in the background while Peter Chisholm gazed at his children.

"I've been trying to figure what I'll do," Peter said. "Mortgage payments are overdue. I'm going to have to come up with money or lose the farm." His words slowed. "I can sell half the land. You become self-supporting. That way, I can still hang on to enough for Megan, the baby, and me to survive."

He ran his hands through his hair as they sat in silence. It was tantamount to dissolving the family, and Sunny knew what a price it would cost Peter.

"We're on our own?" Tim asked. "What'll we do for a home? Are you just kicking us out?"

"Tim! Dad's doing what he has to," Freedom snapped. "We're all eighteen and older. It's time we stood on our own two feet."

"Sorry, son, that's the only solution I can find."

"You can try and borrow some more money," Tim said, and Sunny hurt for Peter. Only in desperation would he have made such a suggestion.

"I've borrowed to the limit. Some of our equipment that was used as collateral burned in the fire."

"Dad, why don't we all earn money for payments?" Sunny asked, and the men looked at her. It seemed simple enough to her. "We all get jobs in Enid. We live here, commute the hour's drive to town, and give the money to you. That way you can continue to make your loan payments."

"I can't ask you to do that," Peter Chisholm said, and she realized he had already considered the alternative she proposed.

"Of course you can! Next year you might have a whale of a wheat crop—it's only one year."

"If we do what I proposed, you and Tim and Freedom can get loans, and get your education."

"We can put that off one year—"

"I can't allow you to do it," Peter said with a look that warmed her. He was grateful for her offer even though he was refusing, and it made her love him all the more.

"I think it's a damned good idea," Freedom said. He stared at Tim whose face flushed. "I won't stand in the way."

"Dad, you've given us everything," Sunny said, her slender fingers lying on Peter's work-roughened hand. "Let us do this."

"I hate to do this," Peter said, but he sounded so relieved Sunny hurt for him. "You're all young and you don't realize what time means."

"Don't worry about us," Sunny declared emphatically. "We'll make it. The important thing is to keep the farm."

The boys echoed her sentiments, but none of their remarks brought the glimmer of a smile to Peter Chisholm. "Very well. Get jobs in town—no college this year. If we can pool your wages, grow some of our own crops to put up for the winter, I can make mortgage payments and buy seed, rent the pastures out for cattle to graze until next spring. I'm blest to have all of you," he said, his voice becoming hoarse as his eyes misted over. Abruptly, he pushed away his chair. "I'll go see the young'n now." He left the room, his broad shoulders slumped forward for the first time in Sunny's memory.

"Well, tomorrow morning, we all start job hunting," Freedom said, "but, dammit, someday I'm going back to college."

"I thought you were so all-fired in support of his plan," Tim snapped.

"I was, because that's the only way he can hang on to our land. It would kill him to lose this farm."

"Well, damn, you don't really want to give up college next year any more than I do."

"You both promised," Sunny reminded them.

"You have the least to lose," Tim told her.

"She'll lose as much as any of us," Freedom said. "It's a good idea, Sunny."

"Thanks, Freedom," she answered, pleased by his praise.

"But we've only promised a year," Freedom added solemnly. "On a farm things can go bad so damned fast—I want out of here and I want to finish college so I don't have to come back ever!"

"You don't feel the same about it as we do."

"It killed Pierce. How long will you love it, Sunny? It turns women old before their time, it wears men down."

"It gives you roots and a place for a family," Sunny persisted, wishing Freedom didn't want to move away.

"Farming is the only thing I ever want to do," Tim declared. "I don't want to punch a clock or answer to a boss."

"Instead, you're at the mercy of hail and tornadoes and flood and drought and sometimes all in the same year! We need to plan what we'll do," Freedom said. "The pickup isn't running, and we can't afford to get it repaired, so we'll have to take the van."

"We'll all ride to town together and meet when it's time to come home," Sunny said. "We should be there at eight in the morning," Sunny said, determined to put a smile back on her father's face as soon as possible.

"Okay by me," Freedom said, heading toward the door. "I'm going to see Janie."

Freedom sped down the dirt road as if he could hurry away from grief and loss. For two years Janie Winters, a classmate of Sunny's, and Freedom had dated. Janie's family had founded the second bank in Enid, and her father was president. Freedom's thoughts were on Janie's lush, golden body that she occasionally offered to him like a treasured gift. And he accepted her offer in the same manner. He was awed by her passion, drawn to her beauty. Tonight he needed her warmth and laughter and comfort. He hurt over Pierce with an ache he thought would never stop, and it made him want to hold Janie, to feel someone so full of life it pushed away the specter of death.

An hour later he parked in front of the Winters's Victorian frame house with rectangles of light showing in the long windows. The air held the fragrance of summer roses and a newly mown lawn. Janie came out on the porch, her chin lifted high; the sight of her long, tanned legs in the brief cutoffs stirring his desire. She paused a few feet from him as he closed the door to the van.

"I had to see you. Come ride with me and we'll talk."

"Let's just talk here, Freedom," she said. "We can sit on the porch. The folks are inside."

He took her arm, gazing down at her, running his fingers across the nape of her neck. She drew a deep breath and leaned back to tilt her head and look up at him.

"Come on, Janie," he cajoled softly, tugging on her arm. She went with him, climbing into the van. He drove out of town, stopping on a country road. He didn't have any place else to take her, and he had to hold her and kiss her. He moved to the middle seat of the van and pulled her back into his arms.

She sat stiffly, resisting him, gazing at him and biting her lower lip. Carefully, she reached up and unfastened a pearl drop around her neck.

"Freedom, you gave me this and said it would be replaced with an engagement ring. I'm giving it back to you."

Stunned, he watched her. "Why?" He ran his fingers along her throat and across the nape of her neck. He was intensely aware of her full breasts and slender body, and he wanted to feel her arms around him badly.

"I'll be going to college in the fall and I think we should both start to see other people." Her words slowed as his hands played over her.

"Janie, wait," he said, but she went on relentlessly.

"I think we should stop seeing each other," she said, her

voice growing more breathless. In spite of his shock, he wanted her. He leaned forward, gazing into her eyes until he saw her resolve disintegrate. Her eyes darkened with passion and her lips parted. His arm tightened around her waist and he pulled her to him to kiss her deeply, stopping her protests, trying to smother the tight knot of sorrow in his chest that he feared would unravel into tears. He kissed and stroked her and gradually his fear and sorrow succumbed to passion.

Janie yielded to him eagerly, and he took her quickly. When passion was spent, they lay sprawled together across the seat while he kissed her throat and breasts and murmured endearments. "I need you, Janie. Oh, sweet Jesus, I needed you tonight!"

She pushed him away. "I shouldn't have done that!"

He blinked, her words sinking into his consciousness while he denied them at the same time. He sat up, buttoning his jeans. "You wanted to as much as I did."

"No, I didn't!"

He caught her arm and turned her to face him. "Now tell me no," he said, staring into her brown eyes.

She bit her lip and looked away. "You always affect me like that, Freedom!" she snapped and fumbled on the floor of the van, finding the drop and shoving it into his hand. "I'm not ready to settle down yet."

"You were ready to only a few weeks ago," he said, and his chest began to hurt again, the familiar knot reforming. "We're practically engaged. What changed your mind?"

"I just feel like dating others. I'm too young to settle."

He turned her to face him again. "Last month you were talking marriage and house building and plans. You weren't interested in college, only marriage. What happened?"

"Just take me home or do I get out and walk?"

He stared at her, trying to understand what had happened. "Ten minutes ago you gave yourself to me completely—"

"Don't remind me! I didn't intend that to happen."

"Oh, hell." He moved to the front seat and started the motor, jamming his foot down on the accelerator. The van lurched forward, rocks spitting out behind the back tires. He clenched his jaw, hurt and anger gnawing at him. He had spent a lifetime with a family that always brought everything out into the open, and Janie's oblique answers frustrated him. Suddenly, he braked as abruptly as he had started. "There has to be a reason. There's another guy," he persisted, knowing he should let it go, but the tension of the past weeks had wound him tight and he couldn't drop it.

"No," she snapped, losing her temper. "You can't afford to get married. Your father is losing his farm; you can't go to college—I'm accustomed to things in life."

Astonished, he stared at her. "This isn't forever! It's Dad who's in financial trouble. I have a whole lifetime before me."

"You don't know if you can support me. Are you going to college this fall?"

"No, but that's temporary."

"You don't know how temporary it'll be. I want to go home, Freedom. I know what I need."

Trying to hide his hurt, he swore, starting the motor to drive her home. It was over an hour later when he climbed out of the van to find Sunny on the screened porch.

"What are you doing up?"

"I couldn't sleep. How's Janie?"

"She's okay."

"You don't sound as if you're okay."

He sat down and propped his elbows on his knees. "She doesn't want to date anymore. Guess why?"

"Because the wheat burned, the house is mortgaged, you're not going to college—" she said, aching for Freedom.

"How in hell did you know?"

"I've gone to school with her, Freedom," she answered frankly. "Janie Winters is a snob. If you're somebody and have money or something else important, she'll be your friend. If not, she won't. It's pretty simple."

"I didn't realize I was so wealthy before. We're just farmers."

"If the wheat had come in, you know we would have been well fixed this year. Dad could have paid off the second mortgage, bought some new equipment, and you would have gone back to college. All this year she's bragged about dating a college man. If it's any consolation, loads of girls in my class would like to date you."

"Sure thing, Sunny," he said. "Damn, but it hurts."

They sat in silence unable to assuage each other's grief, or his pain. "I expected to marry her. She's all I want."

"It's coming at a bad time," she said, angry with Janie.

"Yeah. We better get some sleep if we're going to be fit for any job tomorrow."

"I know." She stood up with him and Freedom draped his arm across her shoulders. She slid her arm around his waist, hurting for him. There would be someone else.

With her lack of experience, Cimarron expected it would take a long time before she could find an office job. To her surprise, because of her classes in shorthand and typing that had given her skills, she was hired within the week to commence work as a secretary at the refinery office of White Star Oil. The office was a small frame building in front of the giant gleaming pipelines, steel treatment towers, and the catalytic cracker on the north side of Enid. Freedom became a salesman for an Enid tractor company, and Tim worked selling and tending plants at an Enid nursery. Most of the time they could coordinate their hours and ride to town together, leaving one vehicle at the farm for Peter's use. On days their hours were different, they took the van and the pickup. Within a month she was moved to the office in downtown Enid to become secretary for the assistant distribution coordinator, James Curtis. Short and brown-haired, Curtis was as affable as he was forgetful, a willing instructor. Learning to file tariffs, Cimarron would handle a new stack every day, replacing the sheets in the tariff books.

When she received notification of tank-car shipments, she typed up forms, passing out a copy to each of the men in distribution: the distribution coordinator, Curtis, his assistant, the railroad man, and the traffic supervisor. She got out transfer documents, pipeline tickets that told how much product was bought or sold. She learned about the underground storage in Kansas, and the facilities in Mont Belvieu, Texas.

From the first week, she heard rumors that her department would be moved to Tulsa, but she dismissed speculation. She tried to avoid thinking about Homer in college. They had parted with promises to see each other every weekend; Cimarron soon realized it was a bigger separation than she or Homer had thought. To cope with disappointment, she tried to immerse herself in her job, working overtime to keep busy.

During May in the following spring, James Curtis was promoted to manager of gas-plant processing, still in the Enid office. Cimarron was promoted to managerial secretary and given a part-time high school assistant to do typing and photocopying, leaving her free to handle salary administration for Curtis, and to assist in scheduling product distribution.

Cimarron dated little and worried often about Peter. She knew it ate at him to take money from his children, but by doing so Peter was making the loan payments regularly and Freedom and she were saving for college. Freedom did the best of all; he was a good salesman and his commissions were steadily eating away at the debt Peter owed the bank.

In a momentary lull, Cimarron stared out her office window. From her window on the west side of the three-story White Star building, she overlooked a body shop and a new convalescent home.

She swiveled around to look at her new office with all the transportation files, a telex machine to receive notice from the railroads of which tank cars were shipped, and three windows with a view out the back of the building. Picking up a stack of tariffs in front of her, she started to the tariff room to place them in the blue books.

"Morning, green eyes," came a cheery greeting from Tory Manning, an engineer from the district division that shared the building with the distribution people. With a smile, Tory strode down the hall toward her. His black hair was combed smoothly in waves, his tweed blazer far more conservative than he was. His gaze drifted down over her blue cotton blouse and skirt, causing her to want to pull her collar higher beneath her jaw, but she resisted the impulse. "Where you going? Down to the files?"

"To the copy machine and then the tariff room."

"Want some help? That's a dark room."

"It has lights, thanks," she said dryly. To her relief he winked and disappeared into his office.

When she returned to her office she had a stack of filing. As she stood at her file cabinets, Tory reappeared.

"Ah, boss in?"

"As a matter of fact yes," she said, glancing across her office at the closed door. "He said he didn't want to be disturbed unless it was urgent."

"Okay. What I want will keep," Tory said, moving too close. He propped an elbow on the file cabinet and watched her work. "Blue looks good on you."

"Thank you."

"This is Friday. Want to go out tonight?"

"Thanks, Tory, but I already have a commitment."

Tory touched the gold chain around her neck, his fingers brushing her throat. "Did he give you this?"

"No, he didn't," she said, becoming exasperated when he wouldn't let go of the necklace. "Tory, please."

"Hey, baby, what's wrong? This is a beautiful necklace," he said, leaning closer to study the chain that was like a million others. She moved in front of the next row of drawers, and he stepped behind her, reaching around her. "I'll help you open the drawer," he said, his breath fanning her ear.

"I can manage. Get away before Mr. Curtis comes out of his office. I need to do my work," she said, moving behind her desk. He followed, and she flipped out a lower desk drawer.

"Aw, come on, baby. Loosen up," he said, rounding the desk and bumping his shin hard on the drawer. "Goddamn."

"You heard the lady," came a deep voice. A stranger stood in the doorway. He was over six feet tall with black hair touched with gray above his ears. His broad shoulders appeared relaxed, but his stance and direct gaze were commanding.

"I was just kidding around, sir," Tory mumbled, heading for the door. "Sorry." Tory left.

"Does he do that often?" the man asked, entering her office.

"I hope not. I've only worked here a few weeks," she replied, wondering who the stranger was. "I'm Cimarron Chisholm, Mr. Curtis's secretary," she said, curious about the man who had caused the transformation in Tory. "Do you have an appointment?"

"No," he said and smiled, his features rearranging in a manner that was as warm as a spring thaw. His white teeth were even, creases bracketed his mouth, but his most arresting feature was his dark eyes that were as compelling as they were friendly. "I didn't expect to be in town. This turned out to be a stopover, so I thought I'd come by the office. And maybe it's a good thing I did."

"Oh? Because of Tory? That's all right. I can manage."

"I see you can, young lady. Miss Chisholm, you said?"

"Yes," she answered, laughing.

"Something I said was amusing?"

"Yes, as a matter of fact—that 'young lady' business. You're too young for that," she said frankly. "May I tell Mr. Curtis you'd like to see him?"

"Of course," the man replied, his smile becoming warmer. "I'm Fontaine Durand," he answered, and for the first time Cimarron realized she was talking to the owner of White Star Oil.

She pressed the intercom. "Mr. Curtis, Mr. Durand is here."

The door opened and Curtis emerged, offering his hand. The two men disappeared into the office, and Cimarron stared at the closed door. She shouldn't have told the CEO of White Star he was too young to call her 'young lady.' And he wasn't at all what she had pictured; he was younger than she had imagined the owner would be, startlingly handsome, charming.

They emerged within the hour, Curtis pausing at her desk. "We're going to lunch. I'll be back by two o'clock."

"Fine," she said, glancing at Fontaine Durand who smiled in return, but she wondered if he really saw her. She was curious about his life. All she knew was that he owned the company.

Curtis returned alone, picking up memos of phone calls. At ten until five, Tory appeared, his usual cheer absent. "Jeez, did you complain?"

"About what?"

"You know, making a pass—sexual harassment, I believe it's called. I've got a bruise on my shin like a plum."

"I didn't complain. And you walked into my drawer."

"I've been called in to see the boss. Jeez. Why didn't you tell me the big man was coming?"

"I didn't know it. It's the first I've ever seen him. Is he here often?"

"No. He's probably in town because of the field they've discovered near Hennessy, but of all times for him to appear—damnation." She informed James Curtis that Tory was waiting, and Cimarron left for the day. The next day she began to pay closer attention to office gossip. Unable to forget Fontaine Durand, she listened avidly to talk about his marriage, his travels, company acquisitions. Occasionally, his picture was in the paper or a magazine and she couldn't resist studying him, clipping a picture to put away in a drawer at home.

She didn't see him again until June. A meeting had been planned with men flying in from three offices, the manager of maintenance and measurements, the business manager of products, the manager of supply, and the vice-presidents of marketing, business operations, and products. The following morning a meeting was scheduled with the engineers. Although the company had started in Enid, the White Star headquarters and Fontaine Durand's home were now in Tulsa, Oklahoma. Cimarron knew they were going to look at wells in a new area they had recently leased and that's why they had chosen to meet in Enid rather than Tulsa.

Trying to look her best, she wore her navy skirt and a new white blouse, piped in navy. Fontaine Durand arrived with a vice-president and an engineer, and they were immediately ushered into Curtis's office. Through the closed door, she listened to the deep resonance of Fontaine's distinctive voice. After hearing office gossip she knew he was married to Lissa Morant, the actress; there were no children. His grandfather, Arnaud, had founded the company that was growing into a giant corporation under Fontaine's direction. Cimarron couldn't understand her reaction to him, but she assumed he had that effect on every woman he encountered, because there was a magnetic charisma about him. Commanding and attractive, he seemed aloof until he smiled, and then charm radiated from him like rays from the sun. She learned he had a villa in the Caribbean, a home in Beverly Hills, and the home in Tulsa. His wife was stunningly beautiful, a Hollywood sex symbol, and Cimarron wondered what their lives must be like—far removed from anything she knew.

Cimarron had caught up on her ever-present tariff filing, and she gazed outside, watching storm clouds gather. It was tornado season and she prayed they wouldn't have a devastating storm, because just as last year, the wheat crop looked promising, and they had already started harvest.

She glanced down at the body shop where a man was half-hidden beneath the hood of a car. Next door, several elderly people in wheelchairs sat on the patio while overhead, clouds dark as slate accumulated.

Yellow street lights turned on, and her unease grew. A big gust hit, limbs of trees bending beneath the onslaught, papers and leaves blowing down the street. The body shop worker ran inside and nurses wheeled the elderly into the convalescent home.

Cimarron wondered about the farm. They were two days into harvest, but they needed every grain of wheat to get Peter out of financial difficulty. A volley of heavy drops of rain spattered against the glass while a limb snapped on one of the elms. The eerie high wail of the tornado sirens sounded.

"Let's go to the basement," Dana Whitedove said, thrusting her head into Cimarron's office, her brown eyes wide with concern. "I've got a radio. There's a funnel above the ground five miles south of town. It's headed this way. I don't intend to blow away while I'm filing papers."

Cimarron rapped lightly on the conference room door, then entered the paneled office. "According to the radio, a tornado is approaching. It's suggested we take shelter," she said to Curtis, yet all the time she was aware of Fontaine Durand's dark eyes watching her.

"We'll be there in a minute," Curtis said with the casualness of a native who has endured hundreds of tornado warnings. Cimarron closed the door and rushed down the hall. It was five before five on Friday afternoon. Many of the staff were gone; geologists were out on wells. Downstairs, a nurse stepped inside when Cimarron passed the front door.

"I'm Jean Coats from the convalescent home. We don't have a basement. Can we use yours for our patients?"

"Of course," Cimarron said, appalled the home didn't have their own basement."

"Can some men help us move patients? As many as you can send over, because we have so little time."

"Sure, right away."

A phalanx of men came down the hall. It was Curtis and the men who had been in his office. Cimarron faced them. "The convalescent home asked if they can bring folks to our basement. They need help to move patients."

"Okay," Curtis said. "Mr. Durand, no need for you to come along. Cimarron, show him where the basement is."

"It's in the bottom of the building," she told Fontaine abruptly, accustomed to men who acted in an emergency. "Ask the men down there if they'll help." Turning toward the door, she said, "Mr. Curtis, I'll help."

Fontaine Durand's hand closed over Cimarron's arm, and she looked up into amused eyes. "You go to the basement and get volunteers," he ordered. "Take my coat," he added, shrugging out of it and handing it to her.

She was aware of the casual touch of his fingers on her arm. He ran out the front door, bending forward against the wind, his thick black hair tangled by a gust. She looked down at the coat in her hands, running her fingers across the soft wool.

Placing Fontaine's coat over a basement chair, she returned to hold the front door. People came, the elderly wrapped in shawls and blankets, some in wheelchairs. Fontaine Durand assisted an elderly man while one of the engineers argued with a small elderly lady who refused to let him push her wheelchair onto the elevator.

"I won't ride in that contraption."

"We need to go down to the basement where it's safe," he said patiently. "That's the only way I can get you down there."

"Nosiree, sonny. You just leave me right here in the hall."

"If you'll hold this door—" Cimarron said to the engineer. "Ma'am," Cimarron said quietly, kneeling down to pat the woman's thin, blue-veined hand. "It's safer downstairs. Close your eyes and you won't know you're in the elevator," she said gently.

The woman stared at Cimarron, her chin jutting out. When she didn't answer, Cimarron said, "Please. Just close your eyes. I promise, you'll be all right. I'll ride down with you." Wrinkled eyelids closed, and Cimarron wheeled the chair into the elevator while the engineer grinned and shook his head.

"Keep your eyes closed. I'll tell you when to open them," Cimarron said, winking at Fontaine who stood beside the elderly man. Fontaine pushed the button, the doors sliding shut while Cimarron patted the woman's shoulder.

"Here we are," Cimarron announced cheerfully when they reached the basement. She found a place for the woman and went back upstairs. The nurse raced inside and grasped Cimarron's hand. "That's all. We've moved everyone."

"Do you know how widespread the storm is?" Cimarron called, tugging the door closed, a cold torrent of rain sweeping over her before she ran for the stairs to the basement.

"It's south of us heading northeast, the usual pattern."

The farm might be safe because it was west of town. Cimarron's mind jumped to the problems at hand. With concrete-block whitewashed walls and myriad pipes overhead, long rows of filing cabinets at the back, the basement was crowded with the elderly mixed in between the White Star people. Cimarron helped pour coffee into paper containers. Once, Cimarron looked up and discovered Fontaine watching her, his dark eyes filled with dancing light and for a moment when their gazes met, she seemed caught as if they shared some special knowledge just between the two of them. Flustered, she turned, going back for more coffee.

"Here, dummy, take this to Mr. Durand, and then give the old folks some," Dana whispered.

"Mr. Durand looks healthy enough to get along without hot coffee for a few minutes. Some of the old folks may need it."

"You want to keep your job?"

Cimarron laughed and passed out more coffee to the elderly, finally taking two cups and weaving through people to Fontaine Durand who was still watching her. She handed one cup to James Curtis, and then moved to Fontaine, who had been sandwiched between two men in wheelchairs. Fontaine stepped forward to accept the proffered cup.

"You were laughing. I'm glad you're not terrified."

"We're safe enough. Sorry, there's no cream or sugar."

"It doesn't matter." The lights flickered and then went out, and a few people gasped. Two people produced flashlights that gave off beams in a far corner of the basement, leaving it dark where Cimarron and Fontaine were. A radio could be heard in the momentary hush of conversation. They listened to the weatherman and realized they were directly in the storm's path, yet in the basement, the sound of wind and rain was muffled.

"Ever been in a tornado?" Fontaine asked her, his voice a deep rumble as conversation resumed around them.

"They've touched down on the farm. It's too crowded to find a place to sit."

"Why don't we just sit down where we are," he suggested. "No one is walking around to step on us."

"You're right," she said and lowered herself to the floor, bumping against him. His fingers closed on her arm and steadied her and another flash of intense physical awareness of him came from his touch. "I hope I didn't bump your coffee."

"No. You live on a farm?"

"Yes, an hour from town," she said. "We raise wheat."

"I hope you're not having this storm at home." The building seemed to groan, and someone gasped.

'Oh, Lordy," an elderly woman muttered near Cimarron. Cimarron reached up to pat her hand.

"We should be safe here in the basement," she said. Others began to talk again, breaking the momentary quiet, and Cimarron shifted, bumping Fontaine's knee. "Sorry."

"Sounds as if the weatherman's predictions were correct," he said as if he hadn't noticed her touch. "I imagine my evening flight is cancelled."

"Were you making connections in Oklahoma City?" she asked.

"No. I fly my own plane. Cimarron's an unusual name."

"So's Fontaine." Instantly she said, "I'm sorry, I shouldn't have said that to you."

He laughed softly and it was a nice sound that she wished she could hear again. "You can say whatever you want. My name is French. My grandparents were from France." He spoke softly when he talked, and she leaned close to hear him. The basement was growing warmer, but Cimarron wondered if it was Fontaine's proximity that heated her.

"My name came from the Cimarron River," she replied. "My grandfather made the Run when the government opened the land in Oklahoma for settlement."

"Ah, a Boomer who came in 1889."

"Actually, he was a Sooner who slipped in before the time for the race and he staked out his claim for land early. Later he moved to this area."

"He's a match for my great-grandfather who was a pirate and raided English ships."

"I wonder if they would be disappointed in us and how civilized we are," she said, gazing into Fontaine's black eyes that seemed to draw her closer. The moment was suspended in time, and for a few minutes she could forget that he was married to a beautiful actress or that he owned a huge conglomerate or that he was much older than she. Another crash came and the door flew open. A shaft of gray light gave a dusky illumination.

She stood up abruptly, moving away from him. One of the engineers climbed the stairs. "There's a tree through the front doors," he called. "You guys come help. We'll have to shove it over to get it out of the way."

"Mr. Durand," Cimarron said, "here's your coat."

His fingers brushed hers, and he gazed at her solemnly. She climbed the steps, staring in amazement at the wreckage in the front hall. Wind had smashed the double glass doors, and an elm had been uprooted, falling through the doorway. She climbed over branches and went outside. Trees had been denuded, their branches stripped bare, honed to points as if thrust into a giant pencil sharpener; windows were broken. A roof was pushed off a nearby clothing store and debris lined the streets.

After helping move the elderly to their home, a horn honked as she returned to the office, and Freedom pulled to the curb. She ran to him, and he squeezed her against his side.

"Thank God, you're okay."

"Do you know about the farm?"

"No. The phones are knocked out. Let's get Tim and go." She climbed into the pickup to look back at Fontaine Durand standing beside the White Star building watching her.

3

JULY, 1972

Enid, Oklahoma

The days when equipment was purchased or loans paid off were special in the Chisholm household, creating an undercurrent of excitement. Peter drove faster than usual, the radio turned to country western, his big fingers tapping on the steering wheel while Cimarron sat beside him. The May tornado missed the farm and the wheat crop was bumper, forty-five bushels per acre, putting Peter back on his feet. When he paused in front of her building, he reached across the front seat of the shiny new Ford pickup to hug her. "If it hadn't been for your suggestion, I wouldn't have the farm now."

She buried her head against his shoulder, feeling the strong muscles in his arm that held her. "I'm so glad." She kissed his rough cheek before she stepped out and watched him drive away. The past year had been hard on him; she knew he still grieved for Pierce, and Freedom's wildness had become a worry. Thankful that Peter could pay off the loan, she entered the White Star building, her thoughts shifting to work.

She tried to keep up with the oil industry, aware of talk about decline in domestic production and soaring oil imports. Often there were meetings to deal with charges by Congress that oil companies were conspiring to create artificial shortages.

White Star was one of the twenty companies involved in a government study of reserve crude production capacity and distribution. The Enid office was to compile data for their division, and Cimarron's tasks increased. She worked overtime, staying late in the afternoons and returning to the office on Saturdays. The last week before winding up the study, Fontaine Durand worked in the Enid office. He was to take the information they compiled to Washington to present to an energy hearing.

The Monday he was to arrive, Cimarron's nerves felt raw. Every man that walked through the office caught her attention, because each time she expected to see Fontaine Durand. With an effort, she tried to concentrate, wondering why Durand was so disturbing, why was she more aware of herself as a woman than an employee in his presence?

Her fingers danced over the keyboard when she glanced up to see Fontaine standing in the doorway.

"Sorry, I didn't want to startle you. Is James in?"

"No. He's at the refinery. He thought you'd join him."

Fontaine nodded. "Have you been in any more tornadoes?"

"No. That was the last."

"I'm glad your farm wasn't hit."

Tiny shock waves reverberated from his words. "How'd you know about the farm?"

He shrugged, his dark eyes unfathomable. "I heard from James. Your wheat crop came in bumper."

"We're thankful it did. This has been a good year."

"Yes, it has," he answered, still studying her. "Except you're leaving us this fall, but I can understand your wanting to go to college." As if he realized he had more urgent things to do, he said, "I'll be at the refinery. I'm expecting calls. Tell them I'll be here after one o'clock."

"Yes, sir."

During the next week she worked closely with Fontaine and James Curtis, spending hours typing and verifying tables and figures with them, ordering sandwiches brought in and eating with them while James dictated statistics to her. All along she was acutely aware of Fontaine Durand. Thursday afternoon he dictated figures for a file to her. His head was bent over a chart, his thick dark hair brushed with gray along the temples, and she could imagine how it would feel to touch.

"Read the last column, Cimarron," he said as he raised his head, looking directly into her eyes. Embarrassed to be caught when she was imagining running her fingers through his hair, she blushed. For just an instant something flickered in his eyes, a look of curiosity surging.

She read aloud, a breathlessness to her voice that soon vanished as she concentrated on the figures. Later they ate sandwiches and their conversation shifted from business to fishing, and Cimarron listened to the two men discuss lures.

"My brother uses a Lucky-Thirteen lure," she said during a lull. "He caught a seven-pound bass this summer."

"Where?"

"On a farm pond. We fish close to home."

"Have you ever used that for bait?" Fontaine asked James, who shook his head.

"Neither have I, but if your brother caught a seven-pounder with a lure, I'll try next time I go fishing. The best catch I've had this year was a catfish. I was using minnows." He continued talking and Cimarron listened. The more she worked with him, the more her admiration increased. He was intelligent and competent. He worked decisively, far more so than James Curtis, who was slower to discover solutions to problems.

In James Curtis's office Fontaine sat back in a leather chair. He had until a quarter past ten tonight to catch the TWA flight from Tulsa to Washington. Cimarron finished typing the last report and carried it to Curtis. She was aware of crossing the room under Fontaine's steady scrutiny. He was businesslike, and she tried to be as cool and intent on matters at hand as he, but she couldn't ignore the fact that he was an appealing, handsome man.

As she placed the papers in front of Curtis, she glanced over her shoulder and felt a ripple of surprise, because she caught Fontaine's gaze drifting down over her.

Startled, feeling a flush creep into her cheeks, she asked James Curtis if he needed anything else.

"No. Thanks, Cimarron, for getting this out for us."

"Thank you, Miss Chisholm," Fontaine added in his deep voice. "Now I can walk into the meeting on time and prepared."

She acknowledged their thanks and gathered her things to go home while she listened to their deep voices engaged in discussion.

The next morning James Curtis finished dictating and gazed at her across his desk. "You go back to college soon."

"Yes. I'll be giving you official notice in a few weeks."

"I've heard you say you're going to be a teacher. You've got a good mind for business. I hate to lose you; give some thought to majoring in business."

"I've been thinking about it," she admitted, knowing that he held an engineering degree from Texas University. "I like working here."

"Good! I'd like to have you work here vacations, next summer."

"I'd like that," she said, surprised.

"Give me notice when you'll be available. Another thing, Cimarron, although it hasn't been officially announced—it won't be a surprise to anyone—the distribution office is moving to White Star headquarters in Tulsa. We can be far more effective there. The only reason we're here is a carry-over from Mr. Durand's grandfather who started in this area. As it is, I work there half the time now. The move may change your situation, but I'd like to have you with us next summer."

"Thank you."

"Contact the railroad man about the tank cars," he said, returning to the business at hand. "I'll be out of the office until two for a dental appointment and lunch with Tate Winters."

"Yes, sir." She nodded and left, her thoughts swirling over her future.

The next month Peter's older children went to college. Cimarron hated leaving her job at White Star Oil and leaving little Jerry. Deciding to major in business, she went to State University, agreeing to work the following summer at White Star even though it would be in Tulsa and necessitate her renting an apartment.

In college, in spite of the taunts of her roommate who knew her status, Cimarron was too old-fashioned to casually lose her virginity. The fumbling of Homer when she had been in high school and the caresses by the boys she dated in college never led to consummation until she signed up for a class with Dr. Sean Banks, professor of philosophy.

One afternoon in early October after a discussion about Kant, she stayed to ask Dr. Banks a question and he told her to walk with him to his office. In a cluttered, book-lined room, Dr. Banks offered her coffee, pausing once to study her with his thickly lashed blue eyes. "You're one of the most intelligent coeds I've ever had in my class, Cimarron."

"That's the nicest compliment I've had," she said, "but I'm sure I'm not. Some of this is difficult to understand," she said, thinking that was the understatement of the year. A discussion of Nietzsche or Kant at dinner at home would last only long enough for someone to ask, "Who're they?"

"*Au contraire*," Dr. Banks protested. "Don't underestimate your own mind, my dear. You don't agree with Kant?"

"I don't understand categorical imperative." She searched her notes, read a paragraph, and then listened while Professor Banks simplified it. When she left his office, she was smiling. Glancing at her watch, she was amazed to see it had been two hours and she would be late for dinner and a date.

After the next philosophy class as she was starting out the door, he called her back. Sean Banks was thirty-nine, only an inch taller than Cimarron. He had a deep, mellow voice, classic features, a sensual mouth, and an insatiable craving for young, nubile females. Since fourteen, he had possessed one hundred and forty-eight women, but all Cimarron knew was that Dr. Banks was a handsome, intelligent older man who was her professor. Sean Banks was polite, considerate, and leisurely while discussing various philosophical theories. From his window she could see a broad view of the campus, the willows with iron benches beneath them, the maples that turned from green to yellow and red as the days passed, their long branches spreading above curving walks that lead across the landscaped grounds.

Gradually, she became aware of him as a desirable man. She had listened to girls talk about his sexy eyes, his wavy blond hair, his sensual way of looking intensely at whomever he was talking to, but her fascination in Sean Banks was with his mind more than his body. And then one Thursday afternoon in November while he talked about Kierkegaard's arguments that there were no reliable guidelines for men's actions, she noticed Sean Bank's gaze linger on her legs. They talked until twilight when she glanced at her watch.

"I should go. I didn't realize how late it is."

"Why don't we go to dinner? Do you already have a date?"

"No, but—" She paused, seeing complications from dating one of her professors. "Maybe—"

"Cimarron," he said in his quiet voice, his eyelids drooping in a sensual manner. She was captivated. He was handsome and interesting and more sophisticated than any man she had dated. "I don't have a previous commitment either," he said, using the smile and voice that had melted more experienced resistance than Cimarron's. "Come to dinner with me."

"Yes, I'd like that," she replied quietly.

They drove north along the Interstate to a restaurant on the highway where they ate pasta primavera by candlelight. While they ate, he reached across the table to take her hand.

"Such slender fingers—I can't believe you've grown up on a farm." His fingers moved lightly tracing her.

"I haven't driven a tractor in months," she said, laughing, feeling excitement bubble, unable to ignore his tactile investigation of her hand. He ordered another bottle of Lohr Chardonnay, pouring the dry pale wine into her glass.

The wine relaxed Cimarron; she was bemused with Sean's attention, charmed by him. When they left the restaurant and stepped into the darkened parking lot, he leaned back against his car, opening his coat to pull her to him. "You've brought something new into my life," he whispered.

"Dr. Banks—"

"Oh, never! Call me Sean."

"Sean. I know so little about you. I haven't even asked if you're married."

"Do you think I would be here?"

She gazed into his blue eyes that studied her with languor. "No, I guess you wouldn't . . ." she whispered as her words trailed away. He kissed her with an expertise she had never known. His hands moved under the coat in tantalizing caresses, no fumbling sophomore touches, but the leisurely, heated caresses of an experienced man.

"Come to a motel with me," he whispered. "I don't want to wait."

He kissed her before she could answer. When he slid behind the wheel and started the engine, his hand moved to her leg, remaining only inches higher than her knee, and in her aroused state, it was torment. She gazed at his profile and realized he was as handsome as all the girls said. His nose was straight, his mouth sensual. Her pulse raced when he smiled at her. He registered at an old motel set back from the highway.

The room was in an early-sixties motel with plastic furniture and yellow decor. The painting on the wall of a bullfighter had a hole punched in the center, but as soon as the door was closed, Sean Banks pulled her into his arms and she forgot the surroundings.

Wondering if she were doing the right thing, yet wanting to be in his arms, she responded eagerly. His hands jumbled her thoughts as he made her aware of carnal delights. She was sexually awakened, slowly, a sweet torment. His hands moved over her, a magic that she hadn't dreamed possible. Their clothes fell away and he gazed at her with a look that made her feel as if she would melt. His chest wasn't broad, and he was a small man, barely taller than she, but his arms were muscular from weight lifting and his legs muscular from running, his body fit and strong. He picked up her hand and placed it on his thigh, the short, crisp hairs sensual against her palm.

Slowly losing inhibitions, she lost her virginity, learning passion, clinging to him, their bodies heated from lovemaking.

She was in a cocoon of bliss during the next weeks, her infatuation mushrooming. Leaves turned brown, and then winter winds came sweeping across the campus. They went back to the same restaurant and motel two more times. He told her it might start a scandal if he took her to his home. For the first time in her adult life, Cimarron accepted everything she was told without question. She was in love with Sean Banks, in love with love.

She didn't worry about breaking the news to Megan and Peter—there was such a difference in their ages, they would accept Sean easily—but Freedom was another matter and he was the person she saw the most. She avoided mentioning Sean to him. Tim would accept it as well as Megan and Peter, but Freedom wouldn't.

On a snowy Monday in November, two days before she

was to leave for Thanksgiving vacation when she planned to tell all her family about Sean, she had to buy cookies for a dorm party. As she placed packages in a cart, she heard two women behind her.

"Vickie, hi!"

"Jan. How are you?" the other asked while Cimarron carried another handful of cookies to dump into her cart.

"Fine. How's the handsome professor husband of yours?"

"I'll tell him you said that. Sean's busy as ever. How's Michael?"

Beneath the grocery's bright fluorescent lights Cimarron froze, bags of cellophane-wrapped cookies clutched in her hands while a moment in time became suspended in unforgettable clarity. She told herself there could be a hundred men in town named Sean. Or at least a dozen. Or even two. Her ears seemed to grow points and she felt hot all over and intuition made her heart face the truth before her brain began to accept it. She never heard the other woman's answer. The two talked about a party while Cimarron put the packages in the cart.

The woman who had answered about Sean was an attractive, petite blond. Dressed in jeans that hugged a trim figure, she looked Sean's age, and a small diamond glittered on her left hand. When the women parted, the one called Vickie moved toward her, and Cimarron gazed into brown eyes.

"Excuse me," Cimarron said, the words tumbling out without forethought. "I have to get cookies for a party. How many packages should I get for one hundred girls?"

"Looks as if you have enough there," the woman replied, running her long red nails over the packages.

"You look familiar. Are you a professor?"

The woman smiled, revealing crooked teeth. "Oh, no. My husband, Dr. Banks, is the professor. Perhaps you've seen us at a party."

Cimarron mumbled an answer and pushed the cart away. *"I've fallen in love with your husband,"* is what she wanted to shout at Mrs. Banks. He's married. *Married*. Driving straight to his office, she hurried inside, her navy wool jacket swinging open, yet she was unaware of the cold. His secretary let her in immediately. Dressed in a thick blue sweater that matched his eyes, he was seated at a desk, and he smiled.

"I just met your wife," she announced.

He closed the door behind her and faced her, taking hold of her upper arms. "I was going to tell you."

"When? A year from now? Why did you do that to me?"

He moved away and sighed, running his hands through his hair. "You're an adult. You didn't ask for a commitment."

"I asked if you were married," she snapped, aghast at his reply.

"Well, now you know I am." He wasn't apologizing or making excuses—or even looking ruffled, and it dawned on her that he was accustomed to such a scene. He had used her; she meant nothing to him except another conquest. A knot formed in her throat and tears welled up, spilling over unheeded.

"Oh, come now, not tears! I thought you were more sophisticated than that. I didn't expect a virgin. Perhaps if I had known—"

"You don't care at all," she whispered. "Not at all."

"We had a good time. You can't deny that."

"Damn you," she said, thinking how blind she had been, captivated by his lofty conversations and then his sensuality.

"Cimarron, for God's sake don't be a gauche farm girl!"

The words stung. "I am a gauche, trusting, *gullible* farm girl!" she flung back at him. "That's all I've ever been. You know I wanted you to meet my family, that I thought there was a commitment."

"I always told you they wouldn't like me. I never offered anything lasting."

"You said they wouldn't like you because you were so much older than I am."

"You know I didn't want to meet them. I have an appointment," he stated flatly, gathering up papers. "You'll have to go."

Dumbfounded, conceptions shattering, Cimarron stared at

him while tears coursed down her cheeks. "Does your wife know?"

"She's an understanding woman," he said in a level voice. "Don't try to interfere with my marriage." As he snapped his briefcase closed, she fled. She had been as gullible as he accused, handing over her heart along with her body while he had given nothing of himself except physical pleasure.

She sat down on a bench and fumbled in her purse for a tissue to wipe her eyes. Half an hour later she went back to the dorm.

Through Christmas vacation she tried to hide what she felt. Even though she knew she was doing a poor job of it, her family didn't pry. During the long vacation, she went to stay a weekend with a friend in Tulsa and while there, she made an appointment to see James Curtis.

As she parked in the lot, gazing at the solid red-brick building that was the corporate headquarters for White Star Oil, all she could think about was that Fontaine Durand was somewhere inside the building. James Curtis's office was on the sixth floor. It took only an hour to get a job as his secretary. To her relief, he hadn't found one who had worked out successfully since he had moved to Tulsa. The last had worked two weeks when her husband had received a transfer to Colorado and her predecessor had quit because of pregnancy. Cimarron enrolled in night classes at Tulsa University and already knew a friend who was happy to share an apartment.

The next task was to break the news to her family. They sat at the dinner table when she made her announcement. "I have some news from my trip to Tulsa." She gazed squarely into Peter's eyes. "I have a surprise."

She had everyone's attention. "I'm transferring to Tulsa University. I'll take night classes. I'm going back to work at White Star full time."

"I'd like to see you get your degree," Peter said with a cautious note in his voice.

"I would too, Cimarron," Megan added. "I couldn't have gotten my job without one."

"I will. It may take a little longer and if I don't like this, I'll go back full time to college."

"Where'll you live?" Freedom asked.

"With Amy Baker. She transferred because she didn't like a big state university. She just graduated and got a job as a flight attendant. You remember—I brought her home with me last October," she said with a sense of relief that her family seemed supportive.

Later after dinner when she was striding back from the barn, Freedom came outside. "You really want to work and go to school at night?"

"I think so. If it doesn't work out, I'll go back to the university."

"That's a sudden change," he said, studying her.

"I need a change. I'll start at twelve hundred a year more than I earned before."

"Wow. They must want you. Just don't drop your classes. I'll help you move."

"Thanks, Freedom."

Within a month she was thankful she had made the change. While it was a longer drive to the farm, almost three hours now, she was happy with her work and liked the classes. Aches caused by Sean Banks began to fade, but she was determined to keep her dating casual and avoid any deep involvement. She had seen more of Fontaine Durand in Enid than in Tulsa, never seeing him in the hallways or parking lot as if he were nonexistent. He was present though on an upper floor and she wondered about his life. White Star had purchased land and would someday start construction on a new office building, a high-rise in a suburban area of Tulsa.

Halfway through the summer of 1973 James Curtis called her into his office one afternoon at four o'clock and asked her to close the door. When she sat across from him, he picked up a pencil, twirling it between his fingers while he talked. "I know you're taking night classes."

"Yes, sir."

"You've done a good job here."

"Thank you," she said, pleased. "I've enjoyed it."

"I have an offer—give it some thought, because it's a big decision. I'm offering you a job as my assistant—assistant distribution coordinator, to be specific."

Shocked at the unexpected offer, she smiled at him. "Thank you!"

"If you take the job, you'll have to give up night classes, because you know the work that would be involved. Frankly, I'd like to see you get into some of the public relations work. If you accept, it'll mean forgetting your formal education, but there are big opportunities right now in this business and you'd be getting in at a good time. There are few jobs like this open to women."

"I'm astounded, frankly," she answered, knowing there were almost no jobs like that offered to women.

He gave her a lopsided smile and shrugged. "This is an opportunity or I wouldn't try to lure you from college."

"Thank you, Mr. Curtis. I'm pleased you made the offer."

"You've done a good job and I think you can handle this. A lot of it is public relations, and you deal well with people."

She thought of all the entertaining he did, lunches, dinners, ski trips to keep the contacts so necessary for the business. She realized she was dismissed and stood up. "Thank you, sir. I'll think about it and let you know soon."

She left, finishing the last hour in a daze, finally deciding to drive home that weekend and discuss it with Peter, knowing already that she preferred to work at White Star. The possibilities of a career there dazzled her.

At home, in his usual quiet manner, Peter listened and finally let her make her own decision and tell him that she was going to take James Curtis's offer.

Monday morning she told Curtis and the change was implemented immediately. She moved into another office and tasks were delegated to her that Curtis had performed. She had been assistant three weeks when Curtis appeared at the door to her office.

"I just talked to Wakefield Oil. We have a million-dollar

invoice. Make arrangements to fly to Chicago and pick up the check for us."

"Yes, sir."

"We'd like to get that money in the bank drawing interest as soon as possible. You're going to need a credit card for expenses. Here's an application. Since you don't have a card now, let me know your expenses, the ticket price, and I'll get the cash to you."

She nodded, picking up the phone to make flight arrangements, and then made a rush back to her apartment. Within an hour and a half, she was on her way to Chicago.

Three weeks later she faced him across his desk. "My credit card application was turned down. I don't have a credit record."

"Well, damn. Hand me the application and let me call those people. You can't carry cash every time you have to leave town."

"There are moments like this when I'm clearly reminded that it's unusual for a woman to be doing this."

"You're doing fine. We'll get you a card."

Cimarron casually dated, but there was never anyone who really held her interest. Friday night she watched Amy get ready for a date.

"I wish you'd go out with the guy Chet wants you to meet," Amy said, brushing her long, black hair.

"Thanks, but I want to get this done to take back to the office Monday and I'd just as soon work on it tonight."

Amy turned to face her. "You work too hard."

"The job is interesting. It might not seem so to you since you're a flight attendant."

"No, what you've told me sounds interesting. All you work with are men, men, and more men!"

"A lot of good it does," Cimarron said with a laugh.

"That's your own fault." The doorbell rang and Amy whirled around.

"There's Chet. Don't slave all night." She winked. "And don't wait up for me."

Five minutes after she had gone, Cimarron was lost in thought over the papers spread in front of her.

4

AUGUST, 1973

Nuevo Laredo, Mexico

The smoky Nuevo Laredo cantina reeked of fried meat, tequila, tobacco, and marijuana. Two guitar players sang with gusto while a parrot squawked and conversation rose in decibels. A waiter in baggy white cotton pants slammed a shot of tequila on the table, capped the drink with his hand when it foamed, and tipped Nick's head back to pour it down his throat in one long gulp as onlookers shouted "*Ole!*" While the waiter swished Nick's mouth with a dingy white rag and turned to the man across the table to see if he should repeat the process, Nick grinned.

His head spun as he pulled Chiquita to her feet to dance. Watching her breasts jiggle beneath the flimsy cotton blouse, he peeled off his shirt, the gold chain around his neck glinting as he swayed his hips, moving in time to the music. When the song ended, they wound back to the table, and he sprawled in the chair, gazing at his new-found friend, Vicente.

"Come on, Nee-ko. *Vamos!* We find something better," Vicente said in a thick Mexican accent, his teeth stained brown, yet still a contrast to his chocolate-colored skin.

Nick nodded, slipping his arm around Chiquita's waist. The three staggered outside where there was a faint breeze. With the cool air, Nick's head cleared a fraction. He glanced down the curving street that was lined with cantinas and small shops, men lolling in doorways, small brown-skinned boys selling "*Cheeklets*." In spite of the crowd,

Nick noticed two men approaching him. They wore white shirts and jeans, looked no different from others, but wariness broke through the fog in his brain. Without a word he spun around and ran toward the Harley, shoving aside the kid he had paid to guard the bike as he kicked the motor to life.

Ignoring Chiquita's shouts, he glanced over his shoulder and saw the men running, waving at someone behind them. Vicente blocked them, and all three went down.

Nick swung into an alley and whipped past trash cans, spinning out into the street. In minutes a car roared behind him, and he cut across a vacant lot toward the highway. They followed, headlights dipping and rocking over the rough field while he swore and clutched the bike when he sailed over a drop in the ground. He landed and spun around, then suddenly a ditch loomed up. The bike hit something solid, jolting Nick loose; he sailed through the air, landing with a crash that brought unconsciousness.

He stirred, groaning as memory returned. Crickets chirped and a faint sigh of wind was heard, but no other sounds. His leg and shoulder ached, his head throbbed. Something warm ran down his cheek and he swiped at it, his hand coming away with a dark smear of blood. He was at the bottom of a shallow, cactus-filled bar ditch, splashed with moonlight. Hurting, Nick stood up, swayed and groaned, clutching his side. His father. Always Laz was after him.

He climbed out of the ditch at the edge of a highway; in the distance were city lights and yards beyond him was the meandering Rio Grande that divided Laredo and Nuevo Laredo. A tire lay by the side of the road; a few yards away was another one. A taillight. A cam cover. A shock absorber. A tachometer cable. The Harley littered the highway.

Laz would never let up. He had gotten where he was in life by bullying and beating and overpowering obstacles and opposition. Studying the pieces—the foot pegs, the muffler, the smashed brake caliper—Nick kicked out, hitting a gas cap and sending it spinning across the pavement with a metallic clatter. He didn't want Laz running his life.

He was fed up with fighting Laz. And he hadn't forgotten the last beating, or the luxury of his father's mansion.

He sank down on the side of the road, rage making him shake. He didn't know how long he sat there, but while he did, he decided to fight Laz. And he would fight in the one way Laz would understand—through business.

He walked across the border into Laredo, sinking down in a dark alley to sleep a few hours. Early the next morning he hitched to Dallas where he went to a bank.

There was a small trust fund, set up by his mother, money lying there building interest because he hadn't touched it. It became available on his twenty-first birthday, but he hadn't needed the money because in college Laz had given him a generous allowance and he had worked summers. After graduation, on the payroll at Kamnick he had a far better income than most first-year geologists. Savings from his too-generous salary along with bonuses from Laz had earned him a tidy sum that had been drawing interest. Once on the road, drifting from town to town, he hadn't cared about the money. It was a mindless existence, blotting out the past. Now he would need cash and plenty of it to get started. He had some available and he was confident he could interest investors.

Two days later he had cash in his pockets, and a six-year-old Ford pickup. He bought two pairs of slacks, three new shirts, four ties, shorts, three pairs of shoes, and a suit. He drove east, angling across Texas to Oklahoma to the Indian Nation Turnpike, north up to Tulsa.

Nick knew men in the oil business—he had known them all his life, so he knew whom to see. A week later he had three job interviews with men he knew. The first was Ed Johnson and within two minutes after Nick sat down to talk, disappointment began to grow.

"Laz has everything you could want waiting for you."

"I want some independence."

"Listen, I've known you a long time." He peered at Nick over gold-rimmed spectacles. Only a little over five-feet tall, pale in coloring and sandy haired, his physical appearance gave no indication of the sharp mind and abundant energy he possessed. Ed Johnson was Nick's first choice, but he could see the door closing in his face. "Go back to work for him. You'll have the whole company someday. Look at John working for me."

"You and John have always had a good relationship. You're reasonable with John."

Ed laughed and ran his finger along the edge of the desk. "I know Laz has his own ideas, but you can't give a new graduate a lot of authority."

"I don't think I expected an unreasonable amount," Nick said gently, standing up and offering his hand, because he knew it was useless to discuss a job further. "Thanks, Mr. Johnson."

"Sure, Nick. Go back to Kamnick. You'll be glad. Just be patient."

"Yes, sir. Tell John hello."

"I'll do that. After you get settled, we can all have lunch sometime."

"Yes, sir."

Ed Johnson walked him to the door of the outer office and Nick strode down the hall after saying goodbye. He wondered if he would have to interview strangers and get farther away from Dallas than Tulsa, Oklahoma, but right now Oklahoma had some booming fields and the prospects looked good.

Ten minutes later in Dallas, Laz settled back in his chair, greeting Ed Johnson over the phone, wondering if he planned to be in Dallas soon.

"Laz, I thought you'd want to know. Nick was just here."

"That right? Last I knew, he was in Nuevo Laredo." Laz brushed a tiny bit of lint off his soft brown woolen trousers.

"He wants a job. I told him no one could give him the kind of job you can. Maybe he'll be in to see you soon. I thought you'd want to know."

"Yeah, I do. Wonders never cease. Thanks for calling."

"When are you coming up this way? It's been a long time since the last game of golf."

"I'd like to, but I'm busy as a cranberry merchant now."

"Yeah, so are we."

"Thanks for calling, Ed." Laz replaced the receiver and swore, causing Jenks Wilson, Kamnick's comptroller, to lower the report he held in his hands and had been reading before the phone interruption. Laz pushed back his chair, moving impatiently to stride to the windows.

"Dammit to hell! That was Ed Johnson. Nick's hunting a job in Tulsa."

"Better than drifting down through Mexico," Jenks said quietly.

"The hell it is." Laz spun around to stare at him. "How would you like your son going to friends asking for a job? Why the hell if he wants to work for an oil company doesn't he come home?"

Jenks's long-standing relationship with Laz allowed him to say most anything he wanted to his boss, but he knew when it was best to keep quiet, so he studied the folder in his lap. "I'll come back."

"No. We'll get this done, and then I'll worry about Nick. The good thing—no one will hire him. I've got friends."

Jenks gave a snort. "You've got a strong right arm," he said in a cynical tone.

"That too," Laz agreed. "And it pays. Right, Jenks?"

"Right," he answered, his dark-brown eyes staring into Laz's smoky ones, both men understanding the use of force, Laz remembering the early days and how Jenks would wade right into a fight alongside him. Jenks could play as dirty as anyone, yet he had always given Laz loyalty. And Laz had always rewarded him for it.

"I have friends. And the others are afraid of me. Good enough. But I don't know everyone out there. New companies start up every day." Laz strode to the desk to punch the intercom and the moment his secretary answered, he snapped, "Get Anderson up here."

He looked at Jenks, but his mind was on Dee Anderson, another employee who was listed on the payroll as a bookkeeper, but who actually gathered information for Laz whether it was about an oil field or about a person.

"Damn him to hell! Go back to where you were."

Jenks opened the folder and began to read and Laz made the effort to drop all thoughts of Nick. He could get back to that problem soon enough. He tugged at the collar of his shirt. Rage made him hot and he wished Nick were in the room with him now. He wondered what Nick would do when he found he couldn't get a job anywhere.

As swiftly as the thought came, Laz realized someone new in the oil business would hire Nick. If so, he could deal with it. Nick wouldn't be a good employee to have. He would cause high risks to a company.

Jenks read figures, his dark head bent over the folder in his lap. His hands were large, scarred from fights in early days. Gray streaked his hair now, but his body was hard and fit, kept in condition by jogging and racquetball. He paused at the sound of a rap on the door. It opened and a man entered.

Laz was briefly struck again as he looked at Anderson. Of all his most trusted employees, Dee Anderson looked the least like what he actually was—Laz's hired man who did detective work, supervised the bodyguards and muscle men, and did any tasks for Laz requiring muscle. About five feet, eight inches tall, he had mousy brown hair and features that wouldn't be remembered an hour later. Dee was an innocuous appearing fellow who could handle bad situations with efficiency and who never talked about his work. He had a passion for crime novels, carrying one with him constantly. The only indication of the strength beneath the nondescript brown suit was in the width of his wrists, the thickness of his knuckles and neck.

"Just a minute," Laz said to Jenks. Laz stood with his back to the windows, light filtering around his broad shoulders. He had shed his coat.

"It's Nick. He's in Tulsa, Oklahoma, trying to get a job. I want to know what he's doing and where he goes to work. He's not going to work in the oil business unless it's Kamnick."

"Right," Dee replied, nodding his head. He waited a moment as if to see whether Laz had anything else, and then he left without another word. Laz turned to Jenks. "You were reading about the Anadarko field."

"Right," Jenks said, continuing reading figures while Laz concentrated on what he was saying, all thoughts of Nick gone for the moment.

After the third unsuccessful job interview, Nick sat in a darkened bar. Surrounded by happy-hour revelers, he quietly sipped a beer until he heard someone behind him.

"Hey, Nick?"

He turned to see Kevin Pitman, a friend from college. They shook hands, both men the same height, Nick thicker through the shoulders, his skin burnished in comparison to Kevin's pale complexion. "Sit down. Are you with someone? Is Laura here?"

"No," Kevin answered, sliding onto a barstool next to Nick. He loosened his tie. "I'm divorced now."

"Aw, sorry. I didn't know. I've been in Texas."

"I've heard about the wayward son."

Both of them laughed. Kevin ordered a beer. "So what are you doing here? Looks as if you're in the corporate rat race," he observed, his glance raking over Nick's navy suit and tie.

"Job hunting."

"Same here."

"Oh? Because of the divorce?"

"Right. It doesn't pay to work for relatives. At least, it wasn't smart to work for *my* in-laws."

"Sorry."

"Oh, John would have let me stay. He was more than nice. Actually, they're not happy with Laura and the divorce. They've been as good to me as if I were the son and she was the daughter-in-law, but it's shit to work there. Everything's in a turmoil. Every move is colored by the divorce. I wanted out." He grinned. "So I'm out. I'm job hunting too. I go back for a second interview at Sinclair tomorrow."

"My situation's different. The answers are no to me because of Laz. I've been thinking about it."

"Try another field."

"Yeah, sure. Would you?"

"If I couldn't find work. Or go farther away."

"I want to be in oil. Right now Watergate has people's attention more than oil, but the Arabs are getting complete ownership of companies."

"To control world prices."

"They have control. Algeria nationalized more than half the oil operations. Iraq nationalized oil. OPEC boosted oil prices. They have the embargo."

"Prices up twelve percent," Kevin said.

"You're an accountant. You should know all the figures," Nick said. He paused to take a long swallow of cold Coors. "We've got an energy crisis. I think there's money in oil."

"Did you try White Star? I don't think Fontaine Durand holds hands with Laz."

"No. I mistakenly thought some of the men who knew me might want me. I forgot they also know Laz."

"And work with him. Or they're scared of him. Or he has them conned. They probably haven't seen him with you except socially. I have. I wouldn't apply at Kamnick Oil if it were the last possibility. And if I were his son—" He drank his beer.

"What I'm thinking about is going on my own."

Kevin studied him and grinned. "You're crazy. You've always been crazy. Laz beat all the sense out of you when you were a little kid."

"No, listen. I have a small inheritance. My mother set it up. She got along with Laz worse than I do."

"You never told me that." Kevin shrugged. "I don't remember you talking about her at all."

"I guess it didn't come up. She died when I was in middle school. Anyway, I have some capital. I've worked on rigs all those summers. I started with Abe Lowery out on a rig. I've done lease work, was at Kamnick two years after graduation, and have a geology degree."

"You think you have enough capital?"

"No one has enough capital in the oil business. You know the risks," Nick answered flatly.

"That's why I'm an accountant."

"I can find investors."

"You don't mind the gamble?"

"No."

"That's a stupid question to ask a man who flipped off Kamnick Oil. Want another beer?" Kevin ordered two more.

Nick shifted on the stool to study Kevin, looking at his long, slender fingers, yet Kevin had worked at Kamnick one summer along with Nick.

"If I get it going, want to work for me?" Nick asked, becoming serious.

Kevin turned his head, his hand pausing as he raised the longneck. Blue eyes studied Nick. "You need an accountant?"

"Hell, no. Not now. I don't have anything to account. I will eventually though."

"I might. Come see me then."

"You'll be moving up the corporate ladder at some big outfit by the time I'm able to offer you a real job."

Kevin shrugged. "Give me a call if the time ever comes. I've been sitting in bars at night, doing anything to avoid going to the empty apartment. Right now women don't look too good to me." He took a long drink and lowered the bottle and Nick could barely hear him as he talked. "The divorce was bad, Nick. I didn't know it was coming. I was happy and thought she was too. There was another guy." He took a drink, tilting the bottle.

"Give me your number."

Kevin withdrew his wallet and gave Nick a business card. "My new number is on this card."

"Let's find a booth and get something to eat."

"For once, I'm beginning to feel hungry."

"C'mon." Nick threaded his way across the smoky, dimly lighted bar down three steps to the restaurant that was decorated with a fishing motif; nets adorned the walls, potted palms were placed at strategic spots around polished oak tables. Nick felt better every moment he thought about working on his own. It was his ultimate goal anyway.

Ten minutes after the geologic library opened in downtown Tulsa the next morning, Nick walked through the doors. With his past experience he had spent time researching given areas and working in certain locales. He went back to areas he liked. The summer of his junior year in college he had responsibility for mapping the Seminole area for Kamnick. The next summer he had been in the Oklahoma City area, one where he knew he would have to go deeper and it would cost more. The central part of its basin looked inviting, but it would be costly because he would have to go eighteen- to twenty-thousand feet. The old Seminole area appealed to him the most.

He studied his maps looking for Cromwell and Wilcox sand oil traps.

The Cromwell was the number-one producer he was looking for in the Seminole area. By far the most lucrative would be the Wilcox sand, some four hundred feet deeper. He made economic and reserve evaluations. He had maps drafted for a prospectus. Along with the maps, the prospectus would contain a geologic report with an economic rundown of the potential of the area where he planned to drill.

On Monday of the following week he made a record check at the courthouse to determine the mineral ownership of the lands in his area of interest. For ten dollars an acre and one-eighth royalty interest, a farmer, Cyrus Brannigan, leased the oil and gas rights.

About this time he became aware that he was being followed. He couldn't catch a glimpse of the man's face and he was certain it was a hired tail from Laz. He wasn't surprised Laz knew what he was doing, and could imagine his curiosity.

When the prospectus was finished, Nick had a list of potential investors and he began to make appointments to call on them. Some were old acquaintances from college, some men he had known through business and country-club contacts. He called Hiram Baedeker, a physician whose son had worked with Nick at Kamnick. During his first call he had presented the prospectus, outlining the potential, offering percentages in the royalty of the well.

On the second visit, Nick sat across the desk from Dr. Baedeker, who was now bald, and slightly overweight. Nick wore his new navy suit as he leaned back in his chair. "I think the possibilities are excellent, Dr. Baedeker."

"Review me, Nick. I seem to have lost touch. How long did you work at Kamnick?"

"When I was sixteen I started work for Lowery Drilling, working for Abe Lowery."

"What could a sixteen-year-old kid do on a rig?"

"Get in the way," Nick answered with a grin, and Baedeker smiled. "I worked four summers for Abe, the next summers for Kamnick between years in college and as soon as I graduated with a degree in geology, I went to work as a geologist for Kamnick."

"I never did know your father. What's he think of this?"

"He doesn't approve. He wants me back at Kamnick."

"I see. Well, that's old ground. I can afford an investment. I guess I'm doing it out of sentiment. If you were a total stranger, I might be more cautious, although you present a good prospectus here. So, Nick, as you should have guessed when I called you to come in today, you have my support. I think the terms are agreeable and I'm interested in one-sixteenth percentage."

"Good, Dr. Baedeker. I'll do my damnedest to see that you're glad you did this," Nick said as he placed a briefcase on his knees and withdrew a contract to place on the desk. "I have a contract ready.

Hiram Baedeker laughed. "You don't want to waste any time, eh?"

"No, sir." Nick sat quietly while Hiram read through the contract and finally signed it, taking out a checkbook to write Nick a check and hand it to him.

"Thanks, Dr. Baedeker. I don't think you'll ever regret it."

Baedeker smiled. "I've known you about seven years now and I know what George thinks about you. As a matter of fact, he's interested and wants you to give him a call. Here's his new number in Akron. You two were close friends for several years there."

"Yes, sir." Nick tucked the paper and contract with the check in his briefcase. "Thanks again."

"Good luck."

A grin didn't break out until Nick left the building. As soon as he was in the car, he opened the briefcase and withdrew the check, staring at the money as if he had never before seen such a sum, while in reality, he had turned down larger sums offered by Laz to get him to come back to work for Kamnick. This check gave a sense of reality to his dreams and plans. It was the first investment in him as an oil man and he gazed at the check with joy. He tucked it into the briefcase and whistled as he backed out of the parking place.

Next he went to Abe Lowery, the drilling contractor, a tall somber man with droopy brown eyes like a bloodhound's, and long brown hair that hung to the top of his collar along the back of his neck. Nick had known him since he was ten years old.

Abe slouched behind his desk in the metal building that served as his office. "So you're in business for yourself. Laz know?"

"Sure. Lurking somewhere out there near your driveway is my shadow who probably sends him daily reports on my activities."

Abe shook his head. "Your father's an unusual man."

"I've given you all the information. If you supply the rig and bear the drilling costs, you can have twenty-five percent. Are you interested?"

Abe stared into space, rubbing the back of his neck. "You suddenly got struck with ambition. I guess blood shows after all. I heard you were traveling the country on a bike."

"I was, but not any longer. Ambition," Nick repeated.

Abe scratched his thigh. "Any reason I shouldn't work with you? Any usual hazards?"

"Laz?" Nick had a tight feeling in his stomach, but he remembered one time in the summer of his junior year in high school, Laz had appeared at the rig and chewed him out. Abe had stepped between them, talking to Laz, leading him away from the rig, and it was the end of the problem. Nick didn't want anyone who was afraid of Laz. He gazed into sad brown eyes. "He could cause trouble. He demolished my bike."

Abe nodded. "I've known Laz longer than I've known you."

Nick waited in silence. Abe studied him. "Right now I'm up to my hairy head in jobs. You'll have to wait your turn."

"I'll wait. What kind of time are you talking about?"

Another silence followed. "Seven weeks."

Nick wanted to groan, but he kept silent and nodded. "Seven weeks it is."

Abe put his feet on the floor. "I think we can do business."

"Good!" Nick exclaimed quietly and meant it. He could count on Abe Lowery, and he didn't think Laz would relish tangling with Abe.

"Abe, we're set on the deal. I want to ask you something, but if your answer is no, it won't change our deal. I've worked on your rigs before. I'm on a shoestring with this and I'd like to be up on that rig. It'll take me two more weeks to get preliminary work done. In two weeks can I go to work for you, work with a crew that will be on my well?"

Once again a long silence came.

"I know it would mean insuring me, the whole thing," Nick said, encouraged when Abe hadn't flatly refused. He waited, giving Abe time to think about it.

"Okay, Nick. You're part of the crew. You want to be geologist, roughneck, and operator of the well?"

"This one time."

"Should be interesting. You're back on my payroll. How old were you last time? Eighteen?"

"Nineteen."

"You'll have to fill out forms, all the crap."

Nick nodded. "Thanks, Abe. You'll get your percentage and a hard worker."

"That's why I agreed. I'm going to call Laz. We might as well know right at the start what his reaction is."

"That's fine, Abe."

"I'll put you on daylight tour," he said, pronouncing it *tower*. "You'll be with Mole Reindorf and Hap Grenoble. Hap's about twenty-five, white-blond hair, looks like a Cowboy linebacker, and has dimples that you don't mention unless you're tired of living." Lowery called his blond secretary who smiled at Nick when she entered the room. His gaze raked over her as she turned to Abe.

"Mary Jean, this is Nick Kaminski. Nick, meet Mary Jean Smith who will give you the proper job application forms and tells you what's necessary to become an employee."

"Thanks, Abe," Nick said, standing up and smiling.

As he followed Mary Jean, Abe called him back. Nick turned, saw Abe waiting, so he crossed the room to the desk.

In a voice too soft for Mary Jean to hear, Abe said, "You forgot to ask about salary."

"No, I didn't, because you're doing me a favor this time. I won't be your employee forever."

"Okay, Nick. Report in two weeks from today."

Two days later Nick got a permit to drill from the Oil and Gas Commission. He found the final partner he needed in Hob Brownbear, who would supply pipe for a percentage of the well. As he drove away from Hob's office, Nick slowed for a light, glancing in the rearview mirror, seeing the familiar black Chevy two cars behind him. His gaze shifted to a slender woman crossing the street, her golden, shoulder-length hair bouncing with each step. His gaze raked over her figure and desire heated him. He had been too busy to date and he missed it. It had been a long time since the last night with a woman. He stared hungrily at her as she took the curb in a quick step, her bottom jiggling slightly, hips swaying as he mentally undressed her. He had Mary Jean Smith's phone number and a date with her Saturday night, and for a few hours he intended to forget about rigs, pipe, and oil.

The light changed and fantasies vanished. He had time, so for the hell of it, he decided to give his tail a chase and cut swiftly across lanes, accelerating up the ramp to the freeway.

When he arrived at his motel that was temporarily home, a black Cadillac was parked outside. The familiar surge of anger came because of Laz's interference. Smoky windows hid the interior of the Seville from view, but Nick knew at least one man waited in the car. The door to his room was ajar.

He pushed it open and went inside. A man sat on a straight chair across the room, another behind the door. Laz stood at the windows looking out. He nodded at the men and they left.

"So you came all the way from Dallas," Nick said as he entered and tossed his briefcase on the bed.

"I had business."

"How much do you pay the tail?"

"Enough. What the hell are you doing?"

"Going into the oil business like you always wanted. Come to congratulate me?"

"Screw you, Nick. If you want to be in the oil business, come to Kamnick."

"The words have been said too many times."

"I won't let you succeed."

Nick shrugged. "We'll see."

"If I get rough, it's because you've forced me to."

"C'mon, Laz. Cut the crap."

"I can never understand why. You hate me—is it that simple?"

"I've explained it—how many times since I resigned at Kamnick? At Kamnick I couldn't take a leak without permission."

"I'll change that."

"Yeah. We went over that about four months after I went to work for you. And over it and over it."

"Blow your money on a dry hole."

"Maybe."

"You were warned." He crossed the room to Nick. His hand lashed out, slapping Nick. Nick's fists clenched, his muscles tensed, but he held himself in check. His ears roared with rage, and he wanted to double his fist and smash Laz in the face, but he held back.

"You're a coward, Nick. I'd have belted my old man for that," Laz said contemptuously.

"My mother instilled in me a damned misguided sense of respect for you, you son of a bitch," Nick said in a raspy voice, fighting the urge to swing.

"Someday you'll fight me or you'll do it my way."

"Because you're sure you'll never change," Nick answered bitterly, stepping back to control his fury.

"She was a coward too," Laz added with a sneer and closed the door behind him.

Taking a step after Laz, Nick stopped, shaking with rage. Three men burst into the room. They had shed their coats and ties and shades. Nick almost welcomed them to vent his anger. He shifted his back to the wall as one swung a meaty fist. Nick ducked, taking a glancing blow. His own punch connected, sending the man spinning into a table.

A second man waded in with an uppercut that slammed Nick against the wall. He pivoted to throw a quick left and then a solid right to the middle that knocked down the second man. The third jumped Nick. Both crashed against a lamp and fell on the bed, rolling to the floor. Nick swung his fists, alternating right and left until a chair crashed over his head.

Pain was hot and sharp as Nick spun around, tackling the man, taking him down with him. He jerked his knee, catching him in the groin, hearing a grunt of pain when the man doubled.

Nick staggered to his feet, striking out with a solid right that smashed into a man's face. The force of the blow spun him around, and he sprawled across the bed, no longer moving. The third man was struggling to his feet and Nick yanked him up, running for the door with him, slamming him into it full force. He yanked open the door to shove the man outside. He toppled over the curb.

Nick's head swam, blood ran down his cheek, and one eye was fast swelling shut, but he had worked off some of his rage and he felt like giving a Tarzan yell for the benefit of the occupant of the darkened Seville. Instead, he heaved the second inert body out, turning to face the last man who was on his feet.

"Step over this way," Nick directed.

The man stepped out into the sunlight and swung his fist. Nick sidestepped and took his time, slugging the guy who then staggered back. Nick followed, swinging one more punch to send him reeling. The man spilled across the hood of the Seville and slumped to the ground. Nick raised a finger to the darkened windows of the Seville before he turned and entered the motel, closing the door. The flimsy lock wouldn't do any good if they wanted to get back inside. He crossed the room to the bed, peeled back the covers and slid his hand down at the head until he found the slit he had cut in the mattress. He worked his hand inside and withdrew his snub-nosed Chief's Special. He tucked the .38 caliber, small-frame Smith and Wesson into the waist of his pants and moved to the window, stepping over a broken lamp and pieces of a chair. A glance through thin curtains showed an empty space where the Seville had been parked. Nick pulled on a jacket and strolled to the office to pay for damages and move to another room.

Two weeks later his preliminary work was done. He went to work for Abe on a well in southwestern Oklahoma, starting on the seven to three shift, meeting Mole Reindorf, the driller, who gazed at Nick as if he had found something slimy under a rock until Nick realized that was Mole's usual expression. He had lost two fingers in an accident and his spiky hair gave the appearance of constant shock. As the driller, he handled the machinery necessary to control the rig and was in charge of the morning tour. He was the smallest man on the rig, only five-six and wore a size-six shoe, but Nick had seen the tools he could lift and noticed men took his orders without question. Nick thought the odds on the well coming in a producer were more likely than a smile from Mole.

One of the roughnecks was Hap Grenoble, as big as Abe had described and mild and affable. He was from a wide place in the road in west Texas and had worked in the oil patch since he was seventeen.

The derrick man was Freddy Kleinschmidt, a sandy-haired man from Louisiana who worked on the racking board sixty feet high above the rig floor, disengaging and reengaging the long pipe. As soon as he was off duty, Freddy would head for the nearest bar. He carried his own round fiberboard target and a Bowie knife that he could put in the bull's-eye by either an overhand or underhand toss. As long as he was sober, Nick enjoyed his company, but Freddy drunk was an unpredictable man.

Nick was the worm, the new man, and he worked the worm's corner. He didn't know if anyone knew about his connection with Kamnick Oil, but men on rigs usually judged a man by the work he pulled and not by who his daddy was. Within two weeks Nick's muscles began to adjust, and he fit in with the crew as if he had worked with them for months instead of days. He began to feel better about himself than he had since the early days at Kamnick after graduation when he had been filled with expectations for his future. The thought of his own company, his own wells excited him. As each day passed, his determination to succeed grew.

The crew had a week to go to finish, and another man replaced Nick, freeing him up to go to his own site in the Seminole area. The next morning Nick was the first at the site. The pickup bounced along the new road; overhead the sky was pink with dawn, a fresh smell in the air and meadowlarks springing up ahead of the truck. Nick parked and stepped out, walking around the ground, his pulse racing with excitement. He kicked up a puff of dirt and wondered if his geological interpretation would be right, if the gamble would pay or cost him. He climbed to the roof of his pickup to sit and watch for a sign of trucks or men.

The sun slanted above the horizon when the first rumble of an engine came and Nick spotted plumes of dust rising. Three trucks came down the road carrying the drill pipe, the derrick, the draw works, engines, and other equipment. Following them was Abe in a pickup. As men went to work, he stepped out and crossed to Nick.

"Sorry, I was delayed about an hour."

"I was here early."

Brown eyes studied him. "Anxious, Nick?"

"Yeah, I guess I am. I didn't think I would be again," Nick said, his hands jammed in his back pockets as men began to rig up over the staked location.

"This should be more fun than being a bum."

"Sure."

"I have thirty rigs going now. I hope the boom times go on forever, but they never do."

"I better get busy," Nick said. "Shall we go to work?"

Abe's crew rigged up, drilled the rat hole and mouse hole, and were ready to spud the well.

Nick pinned his hopes on the first well to give him a start. He was impatient to get what he wanted, impatient to succeed.

5

As they drilled at one minute per foot, the rotary table stopped turning; Mole waved his hand. "Don't pull! We're stuck!"

"Work it up and down," Nick said.

"If we have circulation, we can jar it free," Mole added. In minutes, Nick felt the pipe come free, and they pulled it up to make the connection. His muscles strained as Nick hoisted it clear to screw on the new length of drill pipe in the mouse hole, the smell of mud and oiled machinery pervading the air.

"Hold it," Mole said, standing over the rotary table as he worked. "Now, go ahead." Nick followed Mole's instructions, knowing Mole Reindorf was a natural on a rig. He could fix anything mechanical and had a sense for anticipating trouble.

"What the hell?" Mole said, gazing beyond Nick. With a glance over his shoulder, Nick swore. A shiny black car with smoky windows approached the rig, mud spattering on the gleaming metal as a Cadillac bounced and slid along the rutted road.

"It's not a bit salesman this time," Mole said dryly. A stretch limo followed the Cadillac.

"All of you stay out of it," Nick ordered. "I don't want anyone hurt." Stepping to the doghouse to get his Chief's Special, he crossed to the edge of the rig.

The cars slid to a halt, four men in suits stepped out of the limo and stood beside it. A man in a chauffeur's uniform emerged from the Cadillac. Only the width of his shoulders indicated that he might be more than a chauffeur. Pausing at the foot of the rig, he gazed up at Nick. "Hi, Nick. Laz wants to see you."

"Okay, Timmie." Nick turned to hand the revolver to Mole and went down the steps. Laz sat in the back corner of the limo and motioned to Nick to get in. Knowing he was tracking mud into the expensive car, Nick sat on the soft gray seat.

"Your thought processes are as tangled as your mother's. What are you doing? You going to compete?"

"Oh, hell," Nick murmured. "If I had something one hundred times as big, it wouldn't be competition. I'm trying to earn a dollar. Be my own boss," he said with quiet emphasis.

"Bullshit. You're trying to start something. You're becoming an embarrassment. If you won't work because you want to drift, people shrug, give me sympathy. If you're working your butt off in competition—"

"Competition! One fucking well, Laz. There's no way in hell you can call this competition."

"Everyone sees it that way. Work on a Kamnick well."

"Hell, no. I wouldn't be in control."

"Yes, you would, Goddammit!" Laz snapped, slamming his hand on the glass. "You can be in total control. I'll give you all the wells you want."

"No. I tried it your way."

Laz leaned back. "I'm not going to let you. A well is machinery like a Harley. You can't protect it all the time."

Nick stepped out, slamming the door and striding past Laz's men. He expected to be jumped at any moment and his muscles tensed. He went back to work without a glance toward the cars.

Sounds of the big Waukesha motors drowned out the noise of car engines revving, but in minutes Hap pointed and Nick turned to see the cars leaving.

Nick plotted the drilling time and made a sample log. He watched samples for the Cromwell sand and the Wilcox sand. Tuesday his excitement mounted; they had been drilling a foot every three minutes and they got a lucky break. They began to drill at one minute per foot, indicating it might be the porous sand he was looking for.

The roughneck brought him a sample bag of drill cuttings every ten feet so Nick could examine them. As he worked, he realized how desperately he wanted this well to produce. He had gambled on it, emotionally, financially, and for the first time in years, he cared about the outcome of his actions.

They were into a pay zone, and when he gazed at the sample, he saw it was bleeding with tiny drops of oil. They went in the hole with the test tool and opened the tool to flow the well. When the flow was good, Nick's spirits soared. He decided to run pipe on the well and attempt to complete as a producer. According to the agreements, the investors were to be notified of the results of the test, so Nick took copies of the log back to Tulsa to distribute to the partners.

They ran pipe, cementing the bottom three hundred feet of casing across the formation from which they would attempt to perforate and produce. The cementing necessitated waiting for twelve hours to dry and the evening tour was on duty.

Nick, Mole, Freddy, and Hap climbed into Nick's pickup. Hap was riding in a rodeo and the others were going to watch. After working night and day on the well, Nick wanted to forget about it for a few hours. He drove too fast in the smothering heat of a September Oklahoma evening, the sun still high and waves of heat shimmering above the highway. At a roadside tavern, the dark stuffy interior was cool enough to soothe Nick's sweaty body. He lost count of longnecks and drove with bleary-eyed caution to the country arena.

Cars were scattered over a hard-baked field, people sat on planks set on concrete blocks. A flat-bed trailer held the judges and loudspeakers. Hog wire surrounded the simple arena that had wooden chutes on the north end.

"Here we are," Freddy said. "Gonna watch ol' Hap ride the bull."

"He's gonna have to wake up to ride him," Nick observed, glancing in the rearview mirror. Hap was passed out in the back of the truck and no more in view than when they had left the tavern. They parked and tried to get Hap on his feet while the roar of the crowd rose and fell. "Mole, withdraw Hap's name."

Nick found a water spigot, filled a bucket, and threw cold water on Hap, who still didn't move. Two ladies on the bleachers watched as Nick waved. "Honey, com'ere and fan some life into my friend."

After a momentary consultation, the two jumped down and Nick swayed as he watched the taller one saunter toward him. She was a long-legged, big-eyed blond wearing tight cutoffs. He grinned at her. "Thank'ee kindly. Ol' Hap's had a few too many."

Hap sat up, and Nick hunkered down by him. "Your name's off bull riding."

"No!" Hap squinted at him, the crowd roaring behind them.

"You aren't in shape to ride a bull," Nick pronounced solemnly.

Hap, who was as mild as a sunflower on the rig, had a personality change with beer. He grabbed Nick by the shirt and slammed him to the ground.

"I can ride!" Hap bellowed. "You friggin' sand sniffer can't tell me about a bull. It's more'n you can do!"

"Hell it is!" Nick replied, standing and weaving.

"Money where's your mouth. Sign up to ride, bullshitter."

"They won't let me."

Hap guffawed and slapped his thigh. "They got an exhibition ride at the end. You hard-ass rockhound, see you ride."

"I'll do it," Nick declared owlishly. "And put your name back on the list."

Hap threw his arm around Nick while Freddy and Mole cheered and the two women applauded.

"Give me a kiss for good luck," Nick told the blond. She laughed and tossed her head, the shimmering fall of white-blond hair shifting like a silken banner in a breeze. "What's your name?" he asked as she walked up to him.

Nick didn't ask why she was called Cricket. No cricket ever had such long legs or big tits. She kissed him and in his befuddled state, it was a scalding kiss. The two staggered away to the officials. Nick entered the exhibition ride and Hap was reassigned. Hap led him behind the chutes where he was given resin, a grass rope, and a leather glove. Then Hap showed him how to get his gear ready. After he was bucked off in the first second he came out of the chute, Hap came back to help Nick. The exhibition ride began after the last cowboy was bucked out in the regular event.

"They put a flank strap on him in the alleyway," Hap told Nick. "Now put your knees down on him real easy," Hap instructed, clinging to the fence as Nick gingerly slid down on the broad back of a Brahman bull. Hap and other cowboys helped him wrap the rope, all the time giving Nick instructions while he sat there grinning. "Keep your eyes on his hump," Hap said. "You drew a big'un. If he spins, it'll get you points. Tell us when you're ready. Remember, keep your right hand high, and don't let it touch his back."

"Don't think I can worry about my right hand. Powder Keg." Nick said the bull's name aloud. "Okay."

The buzzer sounded, the chute opened. One ton of animal leaped into the air and came down with a jolt that seemed to unhinge the bones in Nick's body and bring instant sobriety.

The next lunge felt as if all his disjointed parts were being pulverized into bits of gravel. He couldn't focus his eyes on anything; his head snapped back and forth as he clung for his life and listed to port like a wallowing ship.

He sailed through the air, torture momentarily suspended. He slammed into the ground with a force that stunned him, unable to move until he looked up to see the bull coming at him. Life surged in his limbs and he jumped up to clamber over the fence.

He heard laughter and Nick gazed at his friends. "You son of a bitches almost made me commit suicide in the messiest way possible!"

"You were great, darlin'," Cricket said, smiling at him. Nick grinned back.

"You almost rode him one full second," Mole said, chuckling, one of his few moments of humor, revealing snaggleteeth.

"One second?" Nick said. "I thought it was more like ten minutes. That was the longest one second of my life," he said in awe. "Let's celebrate." Nick draped his arm around Cricket's shoulders. "How'd you ever get a name like Cricket?"

"I used to be a little-bitty thing, darlin'," she said, leaning against him. "You were brave. They said that was your first bull ride."

"Yes, ma'am. Indeed it was," he said, blissfully aware of her hand slipping down to his hip.

They drove to another tavern and he spent the evening in euphoria. He took Cricket to the pickup, climbed into the back, and had a far better ride than on the back of a bull.

The next day he wanted to die. Every muscle ached and work was torture. The rotary rig was moved off. Nick coordinated the completion of the well, hiring the completion unit, telling them where he wanted the well perforated.

When the well started to flow, they pulled the swab to kick it into the tanks, and Nick let out a whoop of pleasure. The brownish green oil flowed, gas with it, at four-hundred barrels a day. Nick had made his start.

* * *

By spring of 1975 Nick was acting geologist, he hired a landman to do title research, and he was able to leave the rest to the drilling contractor and other crews. With more money to invest, he rented one side of a red-brick office building in suburban Tulsa, and the men he hired were as eager for a chance as he was. Kevin Pitman became his accountant. Along with Kevin came Moss Maddox, over six feet tall with wheat-colored hair, an engineer who had left a corporate giant to take a chance with Nick. Charlie Leonard, a prematurely bald attorney and one of Nick's close friends, went on Nick's payroll as soon as the offer was made. Nick suspected that they all felt Kamnick would back Nick if he ever got into a tight spot, yet he hoped they went with Laredo Oil because they had faith in him.

6

MAY, 1975

Dallas, Texas

Newspaper fluttered to the floor of Laz's office as he stormed out in the middle of the morning. He drove to Alexa Reubens's office. Dark-haired, twice-divorced, Alexa had her own real estate business and had dated Laz for two years. She was an inch taller than he, a lusty woman who had as little use for marriage as Laz.

He took her to his downtown apartment to bed, finally able to forget his anger as he thrust into her in a frenzy. When he rolled away satisfied, she studied him. "What made you so angry?"

"You want to bring it up again?"

"I'm ready when you are," she said in amusement, leering at his swollen member.

He laughed. "Get dressed, Alexa. I'll take you wherever you'd like for lunch."

"I'll do that," she said, smoothing her black hair into a chignon.

He drove her to a recently opened restaurant nestled in a new cluster of expensive boutiques. Over Norwegian grilled salmon with cucumber sauce, she asked, "Ready to tell me?"

Laz set down his martini. "Nick's opened an office in Tulsa."

"Is that all?" She laughed. "So how many employees does he have? Six, seven?"

"Damn him. He'll make me a laughingstock."

"Don't be absurd. Everyone expects him to eventually join Kamnick. He'll grow up, become embroiled in earning a dollar—and he'll come back."

"You think so?"

"Darling, am I a businesswoman or am I a businesswoman?"

Laz studied her, considering what she said, knowing she was a damned good businesswoman. Suddenly he felt better. He smiled at her. "I'd still like to gobble up that shitty company of his, Laredo Oil, but maybe you're right."

"You'll see. You're letting emotions get in the way on this one."

He smiled at her. "For that, baby, I'll buy you a new dress after lunch."

"For that? Ah, Laz, I must be slipping. A year ago you would have bought me a dress for what I did before lunch instead of what I said during lunch!"

He laughed. "That too. There's a new shop right across from us. We'll go there."

After lunch Laz steered her across a lane past a fountain sparkling in the hot August sunshine into a cool, boutique. Red carpet was thick, soft music played in the background.

"Pick out whatever you want," he said.

"How nice!" Alexa exclaimed, her dark eyes sparkling.

He knew she loved expensive clothes and jewelry and it would keep her happy to give her something. It would also keep her available at his slightest whim. With two martinis under his belt he felt better.

"May I help you?" came a low voice from a slender young woman in a blue cotton dress.

"I want to get the lady a dress," Laz said, his gaze sweeping over the clerk.

"Of course. If you'll have a seat," she said, leading them to two comfortable chairs and looking at Alexa. "What type of dress would you like?"

"Something for a party," she answered with a twinkle, and Laz knew this hour was going to cost him. Alexa had expensive tastes. "Something in red silk."

"I'll see what we have," the clerk said and vanished behind a curtained doorway. Alexa smiled. "You're a generous man, Laz."

He stroked her arm. "You're worth every penny," he said, an undercurrent of irritation still plaguing him. Alexa helped, but she hadn't completely erased his anger. He shifted impatiently while the clerk hung half a dozen shimmering dresses on a rack and showed one to Alexa. Laz watched the young woman move around. Her bust was too small to be interesting, her waist tiny, too broad in the hips for the rest of her; in spite of her shortness, she had long legs. He mentally undressed her, idly watching her, glancing up at her face. The color of her cheeks had deepened in pink, and he realized he was making her blush. Amused, he watched her and couldn't catch her giving him so much as a fleeting glance, yet he felt sure she was blushing because of his blatant study. Her lips were sensual and full, a mouth that pouted when in repose, a round face. There was no wedding ring on her finger and he wondered what she would be like in bed.

"It'll only take a minute," Alexa was saying to him. He nodded, paying little heed as she disappeared behind a closed door with three of the dresses. Moving to the counter, the clerk carefully avoided glancing his way. Willing her to look at him, he wondered how long she would avoid meeting his eyes. Slowly, her head raised and she met his gaze. He stared boldly at her, indifferent as to whether it made her uncomfortable or not. Her lashes came down and she turned her back to rearrange jewelry. Bored, Laz enjoyed disturbing her. He crossed the room.

"What kind of bracelets do you have?"

She waved her hand at the jewelry tray. "Do you see anything you like?"

Wondering if she would flirt or if she were as shy as the blushes indicated, he paused in answering until she looked up. "Yeah, I see something I like," he said softly, watching her and not looking at the jewelry.

She drew a sharp breath and suddenly laughed, catching him by surprise. Her teeth were tiny, white, and even. Her smile softened the harshness of her long nose. "Which bracelet, sir?" she asked, amusement crinkling her eyes.

He was curious now. She had more spunk than he thought.

"Laz, how's this?" Alexa called behind him. She wore a moss-green silk that clung to her full figure; it was severe yet eye-catching.

"It's gorgeous, Alexa," he said truthfully. She smiled in satisfaction.

"Wait until you see the next one."

"Nice clothes," he said when he turned back around.

"Thank you. I'll tell the manager you said so, Mr. Kaminski."

"Smart lady. I don't remember telling you my name."

"Your friend did."

"Now I'm at a disadvantage. What's your name?" he asked.

"Raye Honeywall. Are you interested in a bracelet?"

"Show me one you like."

She withdrew a band of gold leaves. He picked it up, looked at it, and dropped it into the palm of his hand, holding it out. "Nice, but I don't think I'm interested."

Her short fingers brushed his palm. Instantly, his hand closed over hers and he looked into her eyes. "Go out to dinner with me tonight, Raye," he asked softly on impulse.

"I don't know you."

"I'm Laz Kaminski. I own Kamnick Oil." That sufficed for an introduction to women. He ran his thumb over her knuckles.

"All right," she answered.

"What time do you get off?"

"Half past five."

"I'll pick you up here."

She nodded as Alexa called to him again. His good humor restored, anticipation exciting him, he watched Alexa pirouette, a black skirt swirling around her full calves. It was another simple, yet dramatic dress that would flatter just about anyone. Laz would remember *Van Loring's* as a store he could trust to select gifts for him when he didn't have the time.

As soon as Alexa was gone to try on the third dress, he turned his attention back to Raye Honeywall.

"I've changed my mind. Let me look at that bracelet again."

She removed it and he pulled out his billfold to purchase it. "Put it in a box and I'll carry it in my pocket," he said. She boxed the bracelet and handed it to him and he slipped it out of sight. The transaction was completed in a minute, done before Alexa returned, and he suspected Raye was fully aware the bracelet was not intended for Alexa.

"Do you wear things from here?"

"Sure," she said. "I get an employee discount."

"Is this store a chain? I don't remember the name."

"No. It's locally owned," she answered, watching Alexa emerge in the third dress.

"They're all beautiful. You pick, Laz."

He shrugged. "The green."

"Good taste, darling," Alexa said, and he guessed he had picked the one with the highest price tag. Raye followed Alexa into the dressing room and emerged with the green dress and once again he pulled out his billfold.

"It's nine hundred, sixty-eight dollars."

He counted the bills and dropped them on the counter while she got out a box and tissue and carefully folded the dress. Her arms were slender and muscular and he wondered if she worked out or had a hobby that kept her muscles well toned. Her fingers were as short and as blunt as a man's; he hoped he wouldn't be bored with her tonight.

"How long have you been in this location?"

"Six months," she answered. He let his gaze drift down to her breasts, staring at her.

"I didn't expect such a find when we came in here," he said in a low voice, flirting with her. She drew a deep breath and the cotton strained over her figure.

"Until tonight," he said, finally raising his gaze.

Her cheeks were pink, her eyes darkened, and he had the feeling she would go to bed with him with eagerness.

At five, Raye stood in the dappled shade beneath a tall sweet gum tree and watched the tan Rolls Silver Shadow II turn into the lot. Butterflies danced in her stomach, because she knew a man like Laz Kaminski could be interested in her for only one reason. She had to admit there was more than one reason she was interested in him. Kamnick Oil was enough reason, but the man had a sensual appeal that drew her like a moth to flame.

She settled against the soft beige Connolly leather and tried to give her attention to Laz Kaminski instead of the fanciest car she had ever ridden in. They drove to a small Italian restaurant with soft lights and quaint musical entertainment from a guitarist. They faced each other across a flickering candle.

"Where do you live, Raye?"

"In Wind Run, an apartment on east One Hundred and Eleventh."

"Alone?"

She nodded. "Yes."

"You're from here?"

"No. My family is from South Dakota. Farm people. I left home when I was seventeen. I tried acting, but for the past few years I've been working in retail sales."

"That's what you want to do?"

"Yes. Well, I want to have my own shop sometime. Deborah Van Loring, the owner, is good to let me run things, so I'm getting experience."

"Everyone wants his own business," he echoed in cynical tones, thinking of Nick.

"What's that?"

He shrugged. "Never been married?"

"No. I came close, but it didn't work out. Now I want a career."

Laz was accustomed to hearing such conviction from men. But the women he knew were either already well established like Alexa or didn't care about business. He wondered if the little clerk realized how far out of reach her own store actually was, what an investment inventory would take.

She looked more relaxed here than she had in the store. Laz ordered an appetizer of porcini mushrooms in a thin soup and a bottle of Ruffino Chianti.

She seemed lost in conversation when the waiter appeared, placing before them a first course of angel hair pasta with shrimp and mussels in a wine sauce, later bringing entrees of *astice ai carciofi*, flaky white lobster with artichoke hearts in lemon and butter sauce.

She ate with a zest he found erotic. Her tongue flicked lazily over her lips, she licked her fork, she sipped and savored her wine with deliberation while she asked him about his background. He gave his standard fabricated answers he had told people a hundred times over.

"I'm Polish. I came to this country right after the war and hitchhiked across the land." While he talked he shifted so his knees caught her knee between them. There was the faintest flicker to her lashes, but otherwise she sat quietly listening to him. He slipped his hand beneath the table and fondled her knee. Still she was quiet, neither responding nor rejecting him, yet her breathing had quickened and grown more shallow.

"I went to work in the oil patch and here I am today."

"Were you a soldier in Poland during the war?" she asked.

"I was too young. I helped guerrilla fighters in my home town."

"Oh? How'd you do that?"

"Stealing ammunition, serving as sentry, odd jobs."

"Selling black-market goods?" she asked suddenly, tilting her head to one side.

Startled, he glanced up. "Maybe occasionally," he answered, temporarily distracted and moving his hand away from her knee, wondering how she had guessed. No one else ever had. "How'd you guess?"

"You were too young to fight, old enough to do some things. You look tough."

He laughed softly, and she smiled at him.

"What about you? What kind of background do you have?"

"Nothing unusual. I grew up in a farm family with six younger sisters. We were poor, always eking out a living. There wasn't any chance of college. When I was seventeen, I quit school and went to California for two years to be an actress. Then I went to Kansas City to stay with an aunt and work in a department store, and last year I got a job with this company. Occasionally, I'll get a bit part in local theater to keep in touch with my friends and acting."

"And the guys?"

She shrugged. "There's no one in particular," she said, leaving huge gaps in her history. He wondered if he had misjudged, if she would be dull and coy and cold. The women he took out usually had better bodies, better faces too. Raye Honeywall wasn't a knockout and for a moment he was impatient with himself for getting tangled up with her for a whole evening, but then he thought about taking her to bed, and his interest rekindled.

"I'm surprised you're not married," he said over steaming cups of cappuccino while she finished a chestnut semifreddo in chocolate sauce. His questions usually caused women to tell him why they weren't married.

"It never worked out. You must have been married sometime."

"Oh? What makes you think that?"

"It's standard. You know women well."

"Yeah. We married young when I first came to this country. She was seventeen, I was eighteen. She's no longer living."

"Sorry. Any children?"

"One son. He's probably your age."

Her laugh made her appealing. "You're not that old!" she exclaimed.

"Oh, yes, I am. I'm forty-eight. Nick's twenty-nine."

"And I'm twenty-six. Where's Nick?"

"Gone." He reached into his pocket to hand a box to her. "I bought this for you."

Removing the bracelet he bought earlier, she smiled. "You knew I was buying it for you."

"The thought crossed my mind. Thank you. It's my favorite."

Laz wanted to make her laugh again. It took more of an effort than with most women, but it was more rewarding. After dinner he intended to take her to his apartment, but when they stepped outside, she placed her hand on his arm. "Some friends gave me tickets to *H.M.S. Pinafore* in the park. They're performing, and it's a nice night. Would you like to go, Mr. Kaminski?"

In half an hour he was seated on the hard rocky outcropping that served as an amphitheater in a local park while Gilbert and Sullivan was acted out on a lighted stage across a curving stream of water. It was a cool pleasant night and Raye had suggested they stop and pick up cold beer so they sat and sipped the beer while watching the performance.

Afterwards as they clapped, she caught his hand. "I know the actors. Come on and we'll meet them."

Laz couldn't remember when an evening had been out of his control and he was surprised because she seemed quiet and unaggressive, yet without more than a few words, he found himself at a local restaurant for an after-the-show cast party. He was one of the few men present over forty. He watched Raye who was animated enough with her friends, laughing easily, including him in the conversation. And he had a good time. It was relaxing; he liked music, and Raye was beginning to interest him.

He still intended to take her back to his apartment, but wasn't surprised when she said she had to go home.

"I work early in the morning. It was fun tonight, Mr. Kaminski."

"Laz."

"Laz. Thanks. I'm glad you didn't mind going to the party. This was the first night for them and some of them were nervous."

"They did a good job. How about dinner Saturday night?"

"That would be nice."

He turned into a crowded apartment complex. She told him good night at the curb.

"I enjoyed the evening. Thanks."

He wanted to kiss her, to see what she felt like. The only reason he asked her out Saturday was to get her into his bed. He caught her arm and pulled her to him, tilting her face up to his. It was too dark to see her expression, her eyes were in shadows. He bent his head and discovered her lips were incredibly soft, parting beneath his eagerly. She felt slight in his arms, dainty, young, and responsive. He let his hand slide over her hip and buttocks and she didn't protest or make him stop, finally moving away to tell him good night again and then she was gone, the door closed behind her.

Saturday night after dinner she had tickets to a performance of *As You Like It*, appearing in Dallas one night only. He had intended to order tickets and take Alexa and had forgotten until they were sold out. Again Raye knew someone in the cast, and they joined the actors in an after-play party at a Tulsa home.

Gazing at her Monday night while their dinner was cooked before them on a hibachi, he asked, "What have you got tickets to tonight?"

"I'm so glad you asked! I wasn't going to say a word, but since you asked, Mrs. Van Loring at the shop gave me tickets to the baseball game."

"Are we going to an after-game party?"

She laughed. "Would you like to?"

"Not particularly."

"You didn't have to go to those other—"

"I enjoyed them. Let's go to the ballgame."

She was an enthusiastic fan and he lost himself in the game, aware he was having fun when he was with her. She was a good listener, giving him her full attention. At first he asked her for dates impulsively, taking her out on nights he didn't already have a date with Alexa or Bea, the women he regularly dated. And then he began to ask Raye instead of them, taking her to the season opening of the opera, knowing word would get back to Alexa and she would be furious, but he wanted Raye at his side. He realized he was being manipulated, something that hadn't happened to him in a long time. It amused him at first that she had tickets to plays, parties later, with her show-business friends always clustered around her. His sole purpose in asking her out the first time had been to take her to bed, yet one month later, he was no closer than before because something always came up or kept them busy until she had to be home to go to work the next morning. And after the opera, he intended to change that.

He took her to dinner at Old Warsaw in Oak Lawn, dining in elegance. They attended one of the Dallas summer musical programs and he held her hand, stroking her short, thick fingers, running his fingers lightly over her palm. She gave him a level look in the darkened theater; her hand rested on his knee. It was the first time she had touched him in such a manner and he felt an erection from nothing more than her faint touch. He shifted in the seat, catching her hand in his, trying to concentrate on the performance.

When it was over and they started up the aisle, she said, "I know one of the singers."

"Do you know every actor and singer performing this year?"

She laughed and squeezed his arm. "No, of course not, but I have been in shows and I've performed here with various groups. You know most of my friends are actors and actresses. Let's go backstage to speak to her."

Actually, Raye had to hunt through actress friends to find someone who knew a performer in this show, but she prevailed upon her friends for a favor. When she went backstage and congratulated Aeriel Gino on her performance, Aeriel slipped her arms around Raye and hugged her as if she had known her for years. "Thank you."

"I want you to meet Laz Kaminski. Laz, this is Aeriel Gino."

"So happy to meet you," Aeriel murmured. "Darlings, come to the party we're having."

Laz wanted to groan, but he kept a smile on his face. In the car, he turned to Raye. "Can we make this party short?"

"We don't have to go at all if you don't want to. I thought you enjoyed the actors and singers."

"I do—"

"I'm relieved! For a minute there I thought you meant you hadn't liked going. It's at the Fairmont."

He wanted to swear. All he had to do was say no, but Raye looked at him with wide, expectant eyes, and he found he didn't want to disappoint her. He wanted to get her alone. He was beginning to think of her constantly at work, something no woman had done to him in years.

At the Fairmont as they entered the hotel, he pulled her into the narrow empty alcove where the pay phones were located. He slipped his arms around her waist and caught her to him roughly. Startled, her hands flew against his chest and she looked up at him.

"I want you, Raye. You're going to be mine. And I'm not going to let you go."

His gray eyes seemed to envelop her and a tingle coursed in her. She wanted to tell him to forget the senseless party, but she suspected Lazlo Kaminski's conquests came far too easily.

"Shall we go?" she asked in a quiet voice.

He went and nursed a stiff bourbon and water while he watched her talking to people. They were in a suite near the top floor and he stared angrily outside at the lights of Dallas sparkling below. When an hour was up, he moved to her side.

"Ready to go, Raye?"

She glanced up at him and nodded. "Sure. Let me speak to my friend and I'll meet you at the door."

Lingering with Aeriel, Raye leaned close. "Thanks for tonight. I appreciate it."

"Sure. He's a handsome man."

"I think so too." She moved past Aeriel to say farewell to other singers she had met, taking her time, knowing she was goading Laz to a limit, but she refused to be a pushover; she wanted things from Lazlo Kaminski. Being easy wasn't the way to get them.

Raye's heart pounded with excitement as she moved toward him. Laz stood at the door, his smoky eyes raking over her, his searing glance peeling away every inch of clothing. She wondered what the night would be like. He looked as if he had the energy of a twenty-year-old. And he looked like the type to be impatient, taking what he wanted swiftly. He was handsome. Even though he was old enough to be her father, he made her pulse race and she had felt the powerful muscles in his arms and shoulders when he held her. She toyed and played a game with him, but beneath all that, she was attracted to him.

His blood thundering in his veins, Laz took her arm. He led her inside his downtown apartment, turning lights low, his pulse racing, feeling as if he had waited a year to get her here.

She was dressed in a simple deep-green cotton, her hair pinned in a bun on top of her head. He mixed martinis, crossing the room to stand facing her while they sipped their drinks. They were twenty stories high, the lights out with only the splash of moonlight through floor-to-ceiling glass doors that opened onto a balcony overlooking the city. He pushed open the door and stepped outside with her to look at the view.

"Tonight was fun," she said, gazing over a high, brick parapet. "It's a beautiful night."

He set down his drink, taking hers out of her hands. "I've never seen you with your hair down," he said softly. In deft strokes he removed pins and long locks of black hair uncurled, far longer than he had guessed. When the last pin was out a thick mane of glossy hair fell to her waist. He shed his coat and tie, dropping them negligently on a chair, fighting his need for haste.

"This is what I've been wanting to do," he said gruffly. His hands slipped to the zipper at the nape of her neck and when he tugged, she protested.

"We're outside."

"We're twenty stories up. It's private," he said and pushed the dress away. He thought his heart would burst as he gazed at her. When he undressed her, he discovered she was more amply endowed than he had guessed, dressing so she would look less buxom. Her breasts were full and conical, dusky tipped.

As he kissed her, he pushed her down on a wide, padded chaise lounge, standing beside her to shed the last of his clothes. His body was compact, his chest covered in thick brown curls that were a mat across his chest, tapering down darkly over his belly. Wind blew across them, sounds of the city drifting up from the street below, cars, horns, an occasional roar of a plane overhead, but Raye was lost to Laz's demands, giving to him, trying to bind this powerful man to her, doing anything he wanted, using him in the same manner he used her as she straddled him and leaned down to lavish kisses across his bare skin.

Laz carried her to his mirrored bedroom, turning the lights on full so he could watch her. Near dawn while he lay holding her in his arms, he felt his strength renewing, a hunger for her that surprised him.

He tilted her face up to his. "Raye. I have to be honest. I'm not a marrying man. I did it once and it was disastrous."

An enigmatic, sleepy-eyed amusement curved her thick lips. "I'll be honest too, Laz. I'm not a marrying woman. I almost tried it once, and it was disastrous."

He had had women tell him as much in different words before, but as he gazed into Raye's golden-brown eyes, he believed her. If he could judge human nature at all, she told the bald-faced truth. To his surprise, it should have brought relief. Instead, he had a strange feeling of regret. He shoved the thought aside, relieved a sticky matter was out of the way. He lowered his head to kiss her and forgot the conversation.

She insisted she had to go home because she sang in the church choir the next morning, so reluctantly he drove her home, returning to his empty apartment and wishing she were still there. Images of her floated in his mind, causing his body to respond, desire flaring to life in him when he thought he would have been satisfied.

He wanted to take her out Sunday night and called her after church. She wasn't home all day. Images of the night before taunted him; she had an insatiable appetite for sex, an energetic body that made up for her slight figure. He wiped his sweaty brow and dialed her number again, swearing as he listened to the unanswered rings.

When he called her Monday and asked her to dinner, she had a date. She had a date Tuesday, Wednesday, and Thursday, and Laz's temper frayed. She was playing a game with him, suddenly busy when she had been totally and instantly available before. He mentally called her every name he could think of and decided he was through with her and it was just as well.

He didn't call her for the next two weeks, but he had lost interest in the women he knew and he had dreams of Raye at night that made him wake trembling and sweaty, staring into the darkness with his heart pounding, his penis hard and throbbing.

"I'm too old for this," he grumbled, throwing back the covers and dressing early Friday morning. He drove to her apartment and rang the bell.

She opened the door and gazed at him, her brows arching. A pink and purple flowered robe was fastened to her chin and her feet were bare, glossy hair tumbling down over her shoulders. She looked scrubbed and sleepy, about fifteen years old, yet his body was aching for her right now.

"I need to see you."

"Now? Come in," she said without waiting for his answer.

He stepped inside and she closed the door. "When can I take you out?"

She shrugged. "When do you want to?"

"Tonight." Startled, he had come prepared for an argument.

"Fine. What time?"

"Dinner." She looked sleepy, dishevelled, marvelous. His body was heated, responding to his need for her. He reached out to take hold of the zipper at her throat. Watching her, he tugged it slowly down.

"You're a little bitch. You've been toying with me, Raye."

"What are you talking about?" she asked, her eyes going wide. Her heart slammed against her ribs, because she hadn't expected to be confronted like this. He looked as if he could lock his finger around her throat and squeeze. In a tug of wills, she fought panic and gazed back coolly. Better to lose him now or else win him on her terms. Here he was standing in her doorway at seven in the morning. A little flicker of triumph came, and she stroked his cheek as he pulled the zipper to her waist, revealing her bare skin beneath, the full curves of her breasts showing.

"God, I've missed you," he breathed, stepping the last few inches to take her into his arms.

7

SEPTEMBER, 1975

Tulsa, Oklahoma

"Did you get the telex on the shipment out of Shreveport?" Ted Levitts, the tank car coordinator, stepped into Cimarron's office. Shaking straight brown hair away from his face, he gazed at her expectantly.

"I did, but it's not being shipped because of rain on the tracks."

"Dammit! We have to get ninety thousand gallons to Georgia." He punched the wall, yelped, and shook his hand in pain. "See what you can do."

"Sure," she said, knowing she couldn't do anything about railroad tracks that were under a foot of water.

He left, but in seconds he thrust his head back in the office. "If I promise to be on good behavior, how about lunch?"

She smiled. "Fine, if you promise. Walt's already thrown his stapler across his office and cracked a windowpane."

"Did he? I gotta go look. See you at twelve."

She stared at the door thinking about lunch with him. A graduate of Texas University, he held a degree in engineering, was thirty-three-years-old, and had a temper, but not as bad a temper as Walt Ferguson in transportation. Glancing down at the forms on her desk, she sighed and went back to work. She pulled the list in front of her, checking which plant she was calling. She phoned Jiggs Larson, plant foreman, in Pierre, South Dakota.

"Jiggs, this is Cimarron Chisholm. How are you?"

As he answered, Ted appeared in her doorway again, waiting.

"How are the twins?"

Ted made a face and she waved her hand at him, turning her chair slightly so she faced the wall while she listened to Jiggs Larson tell about his boys winning a relay race.

"That's great. How's the weather in Pierre?" she asked. "Wow, thirty-eight degrees last night! I hate to tell you it's in the seventies here." She glanced around to see Ted seated in the chair looking at papers in his lap. She talked to Jiggs another five minutes before she got to business, pulling the form in front of her.

"Jiggs, how many gallons did you make?" She wrote in the figure and moved to the next line. "How many did you sell? Eighty thousand? How did you sell it? How was it shipped? Okay. I'm sending over forty thousand gallons of C-three by truck. It should arrive this afternoon by four."

She filled out the form, talked to him another three minutes about the twins, and finally said goodbye.

"How're the twins?" Ted asked when he looked up.

"They're fine."

"You're pretty good with the bs."

"He's off by himself. I can't just call and start asking how many gallons he's sold and then hang up."

"No. What about Shreveport?"

"I can't get water off the tracks."

"Trucks?"

"I'll call."

Ted stood up and grinned. "He cracked the hell out of his window."

She picked up the phone to make the next call as Ted left. Her morning was spent on calls as she tried to regulate the product, getting shipments recorded. At noon she met Ted in the lobby of the building.

They ate a hurried lunch in a cafe around the corner from the office and rushed back to work because the day had become busier, but as the weeks passed they began to eat more lunches together and finally he asked her for a dinner date.

She had fun with Ted; they could talk about business together. She learned he ran every year in the Boston Marathon, lived in an apartment in south Tulsa, and owned a Saint Bernard.

Over a candlelight dinner in November she told him about her promotion. "Ted, it'll be announced right away and in the company paper. I got a promotion today."

"Congratulations! It's the time of the year when they move people. That's great. You tell me all about it, but let me say one thing—I got promoted too!"

She gave a yelp of excitement and squeezed his hand. "Wonderful! Tell me about yours."

"No way until you go first. And I'll order us a bottle of champagne to celebrate. Just a minute and I'll get the waiter." As soon as Ted ordered and the waiter left, Ted turned to her. "Tell me."

"I'm distribution coordinator!"

"That's great, Cimarron. What about Curtis?"

"He's executive vice-president."

"Congratulations! I think that's really great."

"I move into Mr. Curtis's office right away, and he moves upstairs."

"In a few months we'll move to the new office, Star Tower. Anyway, what'll you do now?"

"A lot of what I've been doing. Plus more entertaining."

"Poor thing, have to take people to lunch and all that."

"We have to know the people we work with," she said blandly, still keyed up over her promotion. "Tell me about yours."

"I'll be transportation manager."

"Wonderful! We'll still work together."

They paused while the champagne was uncorked and poured, and when they were alone, Ted held up his flute of clear, pale liquid. "Here's to the new distribution coordinator. May it be all you hope and fun besides."

He clinked his glass against hers and they sipped, and then Cimarron held hers out again. "And here's to the new transportation manager—may it be a grand future!"

They clinked glasses and drank, laughing together. And later that night as he held her and kissed her in her apartment, she knew he wanted to possess her, but it was for reasons that had far more to do with White Star and excitement over his promotion than over any strong feelings between them, so she gently extricated herself.

"Ted, I have fun when we're together, but I can't take a relationship—"

"Aw, hell, Cimarron. I understand, but—" He stood up and moved away, picking up his shirt. "Honey, you ought to learn to relax and enjoy life. You're too much fun to shut yourself away from a good physical relationship."

"I can't give my body easily without getting my emotions all entangled."

"Well, at least you're honest," he said with a sigh. He came back to the sofa to stroke her cheek. "And beautiful. But you're sure missing out on a lot of fun in life."

"You're nicer about it than most."

"Yeah. Maybe I understand. My problem's the reverse. I'm scared of the emotional entanglement. I can have a roll in the sack with the greatest of ease, but anyone starts talking marriage and I want to run."

"I feel like I've spoiled your day."

"Oh, hell no. I wasn't forced to ask you out," he said, and she wondered how many times he had had this conversation. "See you Monday, Cimarron."

She followed him to the door and leaned forward to kiss him. His arms tightened and he kissed her passionately, released her, and sighed. "Good night."

She locked the door behind him. Amy was gone the next two weeks on flights, and Cimarron had the place to herself. She turned on some of the lights, feeling let down, a little guilty over sending Ted home, yet she couldn't give herself lightly. It wasn't her nature, and while she had fun with Ted, he never really excited her. She dated others and knew he did too, but he was the one she saw most often over the longest period of time. The moment she got off work she had called home to tell Peter about her promotion. Tomorrow morning she would call Freedom, who now had an accounting job in Tulsa.

She moved into her new office, but every morning she followed a routine that included some tasks she had been doing as assistant. Usually her lunch hour ran from half past eleven until one, because she had to take customers she called on to lunch.

By Christmas 1976 she still occasionally dated Ted Levitts in intervals between the other women in his life. He asked her to the White Star Christmas party. A few minutes before time for her date with Ted she took packages to Freedom's apartment. Freedom held the door and tried to help.

"When you go to the farm tomorrow, take these," she said.

"No wonder you can't cram everything in your car. What did you get them?"

"Wait until Christmas! And don't shake the packages," she said, taking a package from him.

"I'm getting ready to go out. Come talk to me while I put on my shirt," he said, striding back to his bedroom.

"Okay, but I just have a minute and have to get back, because Ted is picking me up." She followed, leaning against the door watching Freedom pull on his shirt. Tilting his head back, he knotted a gray tie.

"My, you're fancy tonight," she said.

"We have a party to go to."

"Who's the latest woman?"

"Tonight is Miranda Smith," he answered, struggling with his cuff links. Cimarron helped him, taking his bony wrist, noticing how much a thinner version of Peter's it was. When she finished, Freedom went back to the mirror again, adjusting his shirt collar. His golden hair was tousled, damp from his shower. He was startlingly handsome, with his angular face and his height.

"Have I met her?"

"I doubt it. You said you have a date?"

"Yes, Ted Levitts asked me to the White Star Christmas party."

Freedom smoothed his tie, and put his billfold and handkerchief in his pocket.

"Why haven't any of us found the right person?" she asked him suddenly. He paused, his green eyes meeting hers in the mirror. "I'm too young," he said and gave her a cocky grin, but she couldn't smile back.

"I mean it, Freedom. Tim doesn't date anyone special. I never have. You never have."

"I did once," he answered solemnly, and she drew a sharp breath.

"You still care for Janie?"

"You've never really been in love, Cimarron. I hate to run, but I'm going to be late," he said, escaping to the living room to get his coat. She followed him, smoothing the folds of the tailored green woolen dress she wore.

"I have to go anyway. Ted will come for me in half an

hour. Think this dress looks okay to go dancing?" she asked, slipping off her coat.

"You look gorgeous."

"You didn't even look at me," she accused lightly.

"Sure I did," he said, bending his knees and squatting down enough to see in a mirror to comb his hair. The thick waves sprang back as he raked the comb through them.

"At least you date all the time," she said, slipping back into her black coat. "Tim just lives at home and stays there."

"He has a built-in family. He has Dad and Megan and Jerry."

"That's not the same. I thought we'd all grow up and marry and live close to each other. Mom and Dad married young." She smoothed her hair, repinning a strand. "They want you to come back and work, don't they?"

"Don't you start on me, Cimarron."

"I'm not. I just wondered if they had given up."

"Nope, but I'm not going to farm or keep books for the farm or settle out there like Tim who acts like an old married man. No sir." He glanced at his watch. "When's Tom picking you up?"

"It's Ted! I don't even know a Tom."

Freedom grinned and shrugged into his charcoal-gray coat and she walked to the door with him. Outside she paused. "Tell everyone at home hi for me and I'll be there in a week."

"Sure. Have fun."

"You too, Freedom. Thanks for taking the packages." She headed for her car and drove to her empty apartment. Amy was on a date, and Cimarron sat down to wait for Ted, her thoughts on Freedom, worrying that he still loved Janie who was now married to someone else. She knew Freedom had been wild in college, but he kept his grades up, graduated, and got a good job. She worried about him, wishing he would settle, hoping he didn't turn into a man like Sean Banks.

The Petroleum Club was fourteen stories high with a view of twinkling lights of refineries across the river to the west, the Osage Hills beyond them in the dark. After a buffet dinner, couples filled the dance floor. The deep-green dress swirled around her knees as she walked to the dance floor with Ted. He faced her while they twisted and turned in time to the fast beat. Her hips swayed, her hands making small circles in the air while she danced, lost to the rhythm, simply enjoying the tempo. She glanced beyond Ted into the dark eyes of Fontaine Durand.

The beautiful blond dancing with him wasn't Lissa Morant, the actress. Fontaine moved easily with a lithe grace, his coat swinging open. The same appeal still existed for her, and the evening changed from ordinary to important.

The music ended, and Ted held her hand while he talked, words she barely heard because she was as aware of Fontaine as she was of herself. Ted watched the crowd, and she tried to avoid looking at Fontaine again, but the pull on her senses was impossible to resist. And then he was there, walking up to them, looking only at her. He shook hands with Ted, greeted her, chatted a moment, and finally asked her, "May I have this dance?"

She moved into Fontaine's arms for a slow number. She couldn't understand the sparkling chemistry that made her react to him. Why was it always older men she responded to? This one was as married as Sean Banks. And far more appealing, darkly handsome, his black eyes holding a tempting warmth.

"Hello, young lady," he teased.

"You're still too young to call me that. And I'm well over twenty-one."

"Well over?" he asked with amusement.

"Twenty-three now," she answered, smiling at him.

"Is it serious?" he asked with a tilt of his head, and she knew he was asking about Ted.

"No, not at all. Is your wife here tonight? I don't see her."

"I'm divorced," he said and the words were like an electric surge, a warning, a relief, welcome and frightening at the same time. *He can't feel what I feel. C'mon, Chisholm, hang on to good sense,* she urged herself. *Don't be taken in again.* But her silent cautions held little meaning because Fontaine's black eyes conveyed an unmistakable invitation.

"You've been doing a fine job for the company."

"Thank you," she replied with amusement.

"I see skepticism in your eyes."

"I don't think you can know what everyone who works for you is doing, but thanks."

Now he looked amused. "Maybe I don't know about everyone," he said softly, "but I know about your department, Cimarron. I've heard about your work, seen the results of it. You're good at getting your expensive sales in early in the month."

"I learned that from Mr. Curtis. He always stressed how slim our profit margin is," she said, pleased Durand did know.

"The way you're handling them makes us more money. I know your family farms, you read Faulkner, your favorite color is blue, you wear Chanel, and you love children."

Dumbfounded, she stared at him. "How'd you know?"

"Observation. Reasonable deductions," he answered. "Go to dinner with me tomorrow night, Cimarron."

Reasonable deductions. His answer echoed in her thoughts. The invitation hung between them, invisible, only words, but her heart beat faster. Since Sean Banks, she had been more cautious with men and had never become intimately involved with one again, pulling a protective shell around her to avoid another foolish mistake. There was not one shred of logical argument for accepting Fontaine Durand's invitation. It could be a repeat of her relationship with Banks, only this time would be far more devastating, she knew intuitively, because she suspected she would love this man deeply, and she couldn't imagine holding his interest or love. Older, more experienced, he moved in a glittering world with women who were as dazzling as his first wife.

The thought of an evening spent in his company seemed the most exciting thing she could contemplate, dressing for him, learning about him. At the same time, logic said no.

"I'm sorry, I've got plans," she said quickly, avoiding

looking him in the eye, for once in her life turning coward. When he didn't answer, she looked up.

His black eyes were unfathomable, and she didn't know if he was disappointed or not. She wondered if he ever had been rejected before. Already a little voice inside her was yelling, and she wanted to say yes, but the answer was given and it was the wise one.

"You're right, of course," he said softly. The music ended, Ted appeared from nowhere, and Fontaine was gone, saying goodbye swiftly and moving through the crowd to the beautiful blond who smiled eagerly at him. For a moment while she watched him go, Cimarron wanted to call him back and tell him she had changed her mind. She would rather go out with him than anything else on earth.

"You're right, of course." He had gone against his own logic or he wouldn't have answered her that way. I should have known better was his unspoken meaning. She glanced back at him and saw him headed for the door.

The first of February she received a phone call from Brad Crown and she remembered instantly when he had been a White Star employee and James Curtis's supervisor. He said he was with Van Horn Petroleum, asked her to lunch, and said it was about business, so she agreed to meet him the following noon.

Stocky and blond, Brad Crown stepped forward, offering his hand. "Miss Chisholm, it's been almost two years now."

"That's right. Time goes past in a hurry."

"Let's get our table and we can talk."

No more was said about business until after they had ordered, but as the waitress left, Brad Crown said, "How are things at White Star?"

"Busy. It seems to get busier all the time."

"It's good times right now. I guess you're wondering why I called. I have a business proposition. I'm a vice-president at Van Horn Petroleum, which isn't nearly as large as White Star, but we just acquired another company in Texas this past year, Daily Petroleum. We're moving our headquarters to Dallas. I know from working with Curtis and indirectly with you at White Star that you're good at your job."

"Thank you."

"We'd like to offer you a job with us as manager of supply and distribution."

Shocked, she stared at him while her mind raced. It would mean moving from distribution primarily to sales and another facet of the business, a move she hadn't dreamed she could make this soon.

"We're a smaller company. The same job at White Star is held by Ron Baker—assistant supply manager. I think we can offer you some real incentives to make the change."

Stunned, she ran her finger along the edge of the table. "Common sense said this was why you wanted to meet with me; even so, it surprises me."

"I've heard a lot of good things about you and I remember your work from when I was with White Star," he repeated. "While we're not as large as White Star, this acquisition will increase our size, and we can offer you a good salary, a stock-sharing plan, a better chance at promotion. You probably won't move up the corporate ladder for a longer time where you are now."

The waitress brought Cimarron a bowl of crisp salad, and red beans and rice to Brad Crown. While they ate, she listened to him present his offer, the salary named was a twenty percent increase, the opportunities in the company seemed good, and by the time they finished lunch and headed toward the door, she told him she would give serious consideration to his offer.

"We'd like to fly you to Dallas, have you meet Jason Burnam, our president, meet some of the other vice-presidents."

She stood in the sunshine on the sidewalk, a brisk wind sweeping against her. "I'd like to think about it."

"Sure. I gave you my card. If you want to see the office, give me a call. Come look at our office and meet some of the men before you make a decision."

She nodded and held out her hand. "Thank you for the offer."

"We've tried to make it a good one. Give it some thought."

They parted and Cimarron climbed into her car. The first thought that came was if she accepted Crown's offer, she would no longer see Fontaine Durand.

Ultimately, the fact that she wouldn't see Fontaine Durand was a contributing factor to the change. Knowing he had a keen mind for business, she discussed the move with Freedom. She discussed it with Peter who, after his children were grown, always withheld personal opinions, thinking they should make their own decisions. Finally, she flew to Dallas to meet the men who ran Van Horn Petroleum.

Jason Burnam was different from Fontaine Durand. Jovial, sandy haired, overweight, he put her at ease at once. She met three vice-presidents, looked at their new office in a red-brick building, and before she left, she told Brad Crown she would give him a decision soon.

She waited two more weeks, weighing pros and cons, deciding she might like Dallas and the challenges offered at Van Horn Petroleum. She needed to get away from a company where the CEO could start her heart palpitating.

She called Brad Crown and accepted, the next day going to James Curtis to give him her resignation.

He leaned back in his chair and smiled. "I hate like hell to see you go, but if you think you have more opportunity at Van Horn Petroleum—you have to do what you think is best for your future."

"I can't tell you how much I appreciate all you've done."

"It helped to have a good co-worker. You won't be here to move into the new building. Good luck. Keep in touch."

"I will. I'll be here awhile anyway."

"I know. We'll get your replacement in as soon as we can. If you can give us at least a week after we get someone in your spot, it would be good. I'll pass your resignation along channels."

As she walked back to her office, she wondered how long it would be before Fontaine Durand learned she wasn't an employee.

The last day at White Star, she received an envelope marked personal. She tore it open and read a flowing scrawl: "Sorry to lose you to Van Horn Petroleum. Good luck on your new job and thank you for your years with White Star. Fontaine Durand."

She stared at it with a mixture of feelings. She was surprised to receive the note, surprised he would take the time, but deep down there was a flicker of disappointment that he hadn't sent for her to appeal to her to stay. He let her go with what amounted to a pat on the back and a handshake. She tucked the note in her purse, knowing she should shred it and try to forget Fontaine Durand when she walked out of the White Star building for the last time.

After she found a small Spanish-style apartment of white stucco with tiny enclosed areas in front and back, Freedom helped her move her things. For the first time she would live alone. Van Horn Petroleum's office was only a mile from her apartment, and her office was on the third floor, giving her a view of downtown Dallas, trees, houses, and a busy freeway. Her boss was Brad Crown, and since he had trained James Curtis, he had similar methods, so by the end of April she felt at ease in her job and had begun to meet people outside of work. Freedom had a friend, Deke Payton, who took her out a few times, but she felt he was doing it to be nice because of his friendship with Freedom. Ted came one Saturday, but when she kissed him that night, she suspected it would be goodbye, because she didn't think he would be back.

The first week in May she attended an annual Liquid Propane Gas convention in Houston, Texas. In the ballroom of the Sheraton, she had seen a report about the convention and knew there would be twelve hundred in attendance. She counted four women in the room filled with men who were in distribution and supply, sales, and engineering, as well as vice-presidents and company presidents. Brad Crown was present as well as James Curtis, and she had spent a few minutes chatting with Curtis when she arrived.

The president of White Star, Ralston Taylor, stood beside James Curtis. A large man with a high, wide forehead,

Ralston nodded his head as he greeted her perfunctorily. His eyes were slightly popped and as prominent as his bulbous nose, his lips thick beneath a bushy brown mustache. Cimarron knew she was dismissed from Taylor's attention almost as swiftly as he said hello. In the group was another White Star executive, Peyton Phelps, an engineer and vice-president in charge of transportation. Phelps was soft-spoken, blond, and handsome, looking more like a model than a corporate executive, with a genuine warmth in his hello. As he asked her about Dallas, Ralston Taylor moved away, leaving Peyton and James Curtis to talk to her.

Within the first hour she became friends with the women, learning that Bea Klein worked in Houston, Bev Adams was in supply with a company in Oklahoma City, and Katie Brown was in sales in Baton Rouge, Louisiana, as was Nan Jones in Kansas City.

Cimarron milled through the crowd, felt compelled to turn around, and saw Fontaine Durand standing in a cluster of men, listening to a man talk. She blinked as if wondering if he were a figment of her imagination. CEO's didn't attend this LPG convention. His gaze met hers, his unforgettable, burning dark eyes held her gaze, and she drew a deep breath, smiling slightly in a silent greeting, watching him say something to the men and move toward her.

"Hello, Cimarron." His voice was as deep as she remembered, his gaze as unsettling.

"Hello," she replied with shock, barely able to say the word, a tight constriction doing something to her breathing. "I didn't expect you to be here."

"I don't usually attend." His voice lowered. "But I did expect you to be here, so I came this time. I'm not here for the convention. How's your job?"

She wondered if she had heard him correctly as she answered his question.

"Have you registered?"

"Yes."

"I know the social side of this is important to you, but in another hour, everyone will break up to eat. And now we're no longer with the same company. Will you go to dinner with me tonight when you're through here?"

It had been a shock to see him; now she was surprised by his invitation, but this time she didn't weigh pros and cons before she answered. "That would be nice," she replied, her voice softer than usual.

Pleasure shone in his eyes, the faintest lift to a corner of his mouth. He kept his features impassive, probably a characteristic that helped him in business, yet his eyes seemed expressive to her, emotions revealed in their dark depths. Feeling a bubbling eagerness, she couldn't resist smiling at him, and he smiled in return.

"We can talk over dinner, Cimarron," he said and moved away. She drifted to a cluster of men including Brad Crown who gave her a curious glance and later when he was standing beside her, said, "It's damned unusual for the CEO of White Star to be here. Durand never attends these things."

"He said hello."

"I hope he doesn't try to lure you back."

She laughed. "I'm quite happy with my job," she replied, her thoughts swirling around Fontaine, wondering why he was present, unable to imagine he would be here solely to ask her to dinner, and yet that was exactly what he had indicated.

At half past eight Fontaine appeared at her side. "People are leaving. Can you get away now?"

"Yes. Any time."

"Good," he said, taking her arm to steer her toward the door. As they stepped outside into a warm night, he asked, "How do you like Dallas?"

"I like it fine, so far. I have an apartment not too far from work."

"No one man in your life yet?"

"No. I wouldn't have accepted the dinner invitation otherwise," she answered, looking up at him, aware of his height.

"I wanted to hear you affirm what I surmised. Here's my rental car," he said, opening the door to a gray Lincoln. As he drove, he glanced at her. "Is the work about the same as you did at White Star?"

"I'm in sales now and I'm just getting started meeting people in this area. There's a lot of socializing."

"James Curtis said you're the best."

"That's nice," she answered with a smile, "but do you know how many supply managers were in that ballroom tonight?"

"Not really as many as you might think. There were hundreds of other executives. And do you know how many *women* supply managers were in that room?"

"Two," she answered.

"Two out of twelve-hundred executives," he said with emphasis as if settling the matter. "I understand you like Chinese food."

"Yes," she said, turning to study him. "You *understand*?"

He laughed. "All right, I asked Curtis. I wanted to take you to a place you'd like."

"I'm not difficult to please," she said, thinking any place with him would have been fine and wondering what else he had asked James Curtis.

"Here we are," he said, turning into a curving drive to a building set back on landscaped grounds. He stopped at the canopied entrance to a Chinese restaurant that had winged chimeras flanking the door. A valet parked the car while Fontaine spoke to the maitre d' and they were led to a table. The rooms held exotic tropical flowers in large vases, deep oriental rugs on the polished floors, and white linen tablecloths on ebony tables.

Over cups of hot OO-Long tea, they talked while they waited for appetizers of shrimp toast.

"Thanks for sending the note when I left White Star."

"As I said, Curtis hated to lose you. He said you are good with customers and you have a real mind for math."

"I like people. My brother is the math whiz of the family," she said, trying to change the subject.

"How many brothers do you have?"

"Two now. My oldest brother was killed five years ago. Do you have brothers or sisters, Mr. Du—"

"We're no longer with the same company; you're no longer an employee. Now you're an executive with another company. Call me Fontaine."

"Fontaine," she said, and felt as if a barrier had dropped.

"Sorry about your brother," he said. "It must be nice to have a big family. I was the only child."

"I've heard White Star is a family business."

"That's right. My grandfather started teaching me about White Star back as far as I can remember."

"Did he groom you to take charge?"

"In a sense. In a way, he didn't," he paused while plates of shrimp toast were placed in front of them. As they ate, he continued, "I think my father was such a disappointment to him, that he was afraid to expect anything from me. He started taking me to work with him when I was seven years old. He'd take me on rigs, and later, when I was in high school, he began to teach me things about running the business. He'd let me go over the accounts with him and he gave me stock on my birthdays."

"So you knew you'd do this someday."

"I did. He didn't. He always said, 'If you ever decide to step into the business, Fontaine, you remember this and it'll help.' And then he'd instruct me in some phase of the business, but he never said, 'When you're in charge—' Not one time."

"Is he still alive?"

"No. He didn't live to see me take over and I wish he had. He loved this business. He built it from nothing. He hit oil with a wildcat. That was back in the days of the old wooden rigs, steam-powered rigs, fishtail bits. My grandfather slept out at the rig and he kept watching one bright star. That's where the name White Star came from. He was a blustery old man, but down deep he was sentimental. I wish he could have lived to see me take over. I never considered doing anything else."

"You must love it."

"I love it," he said, his black eyes intense, his deep voice a coaxing rumble that she could listen to endlessly. "I want to build it into one of the country's largest companies, to protect it. It's my lifeblood."

"That's why you're so meticulous about your projections each year."

"How'd you know I'm meticulous?"

She shrugged. "James Curtis has said so. I have a father who's the same way. The farm is his lifeblood and he always looks ahead. Even when times are bad, he looks ahead."

"I've heard the wheat crop is good this year."

"It's expected to be, but you can never be sure until harvest. Too much can happen."

They talked as bowls of Peking hot-and-sour soup were served, and finally the entrees. Cimarron ate steaming moo shu pork served with mandarin pau bin, and all the time they ate and talked, her emotions boiled like a stormy sea. She couldn't believe she was actually having dinner with him. Their meeting hadn't been accidental. He had singled her out, asked her to dinner, and left her alone until time to leave the ballroom. He looked relaxed, content, yet his gaze lingered on her longer than necessary, more intently than necessary when they talked. He gave her his full, undivided attention, barely glancing away except with the arrivals of the waiter.

"So you gave up on your ambition to be a teacher and decided you like the oil business better."

"Yes, although I still want to marry and have children," she said while she spread plum sauce on the thin pancake wrapped around shredded pork, bamboo shoots, and stir-fried vegetables.

He laughed softly, and she cocked her head to look at him. "You find that funny?"

"I'm amused because I can't recall ever hearing a woman say it to me. Absolutely not one."

"I'm sure some of the women in your acquaintance wanted to marry and have children."

"I'm certain they did, but they wouldn't announce it."

"Well, it may scare some men away, but if it does, I might as well know."

"You want to see if it'll frighten me away?" he asked in a soft tone that made a blush heat her cheeks.

"No! I just answered your question honestly."

"You don't care if it frightens me off?" he asked with a tinge of amusement in his tone.

She laughed. "I gave a frank answer. We're not sufficiently well acquainted for you to be scared or anything else."

"Not anything else?" he asked, lowering his voice, gazing directly into her eyes, searching for her reaction, because she couldn't mistake the innuendo in his question, and she knew absolutely why he had appeared at the convention tonight.

"I don't know," she said breathlessly, her gaze meeting his, and he could all but see the question in her eyes.

"No, it doesn't scare me," he answered. "Go ahead and ask. When you want to know something, Cimarron, don't be afraid to ask me."

"I'm not afraid," she replied, mesmerized by the coaxing look in his black eyes.

"I really didn't think you were," he answered. A waiter appeared and the tension between them eased.

They lingered, talking about White Star, about Dallas, and she forgot his position, his affluence and power. He was charismatic, exciting, and she was drawn to him.

Cimarron didn't want the evening to end. When they left the restaurant, she was aware of Fontaine's hand holding her arm lightly as they walked to his car. He tipped the attendant and held the door for Cimarron. When he went around to the driver's side, Fontaine paused to shed his coat and drape it in the back seat, something so casual, yet it removed some of his businesslike appearance and made her more physically aware of him. He drove past tall, darkened buildings with lights in store windows, mannequins staring back impassively.

"Want to drive to Galveston and look at the beach?" he asked.

It would mean two more hours with him, and she agreed eagerly, giving no heed to the hour, knowing her time was her own until ten o'clock the next morning. He was headed in the right direction along the freeway, and it seemed only minutes before they were coming off the long causeway, passing tall palms. Fontaine turned on Sixty-first Street to Seawall Boulevard, driving west until the sea wall was gone and flat dunes stretched from the highway. He turned on a sandy road to drive close to the beach. Moonlight shimmered on the water and Fontaine cut the motor. "Want to walk along the beach?"

"Yes." She kicked off her high heels and climbed out of the car. They were on a windy, deserted beach, yet she felt safe with him, unable to imagine a situation where he wouldn't be in control. Their voices were low, the steady splash of waves the only other sound as they strolled to the water and he turned to face her.

"Tonight has been fun," he said softly.

"It has for me too," she replied. She enjoyed his company more than she ever had anyone's, finding him the most exciting man she had known. "I'm glad you came to Dallas."

He touched her throat beneath her ear as lightly as a breeze playing over her, and Cimarron drew a sharp breath. When she gazed into black eyes that seemed to have their own irresistible pull, her pulse quickened.

His arm slipped around her waist and he drew her to him. He was the most handsome, exciting man she had ever known. Her lashes dropped, sight gone, hearing obliterated by the roaring of her pulse. Only her tactile senses were left, the brush of his warm lips on hers, the taste of his mouth, the clean cottony smell of his shirt. His arm tightened, crushing her to him. One tiny part of her was stunned with surprise, the tiny part that was still a young farm girl. The rest of her responded, the poised young woman in her, the purely woman part of her. Sensations bombarded her as he bent over her, molding her to his length, his hand coursing down her back.

She wound her arms around him and kissed him with abandon, relishing his arms around her, his mouth on hers. The world became a dream, yet his demanding mouth was reality. It was Fontaine kissing her! Fontaine holding her!

"Fontaine," she said, finally pushing away. They both were breathless. How long they had stood and kissed, she didn't know. Wild kisses that made her want more, infinitely more.

"I know you'll be busy with the convention," he said, his voice husky. "Next Friday when you're home again in Dallas, will you go to dinner with me?"

"Yes."

"And Saturday?"

"Yes," she answered eagerly and they both laughed. He reached for her and their smiles vanished. He crushed her in his arms, kissing her passionately, and she clung to him, responding, thinking she had waited so long.

He raised his head. "There's a car coming on the highway. We better get back." He took her hand and they returned to the car. She brushed sand off her feet and climbed in. As he drove back, he stretched his arm across the back of the seat while they were on the deserted ribbon of highway by the black waters of the Gulf. While they talked, his fingers toyed with her hair, brushing the nape of her neck, stirring little tingles of pleasure in her.

In traffic as they drove back to Houston, he shifted, placing his right hand on the wheel. Finally he slowed to a stop in front of the Sheraton.

"I'll tell you good night here, Cimarron. Next Friday at seven."

"Thank you, Fontaine. It's been"—she paused, gazing into his black eyes that were filled with warmth—"wonderful," she said softly and saw his chest expand as he inhaled deeply.

She closed the door and stepped back, turning to enter the bright lobby and take the elevator to her room. Later, when she was back in Dallas, she barely remembered anything that happened at the convention after that night with Fontaine.

8

MAY, 1977

Dallas, Texas

Fontaine called every night and they spent hours talking. They couldn't discuss business because they were competitors, yet there were endless topics. Finally, Friday night, she opened the door to face him, her breath catching as her gaze swept over his navy suit and white shirt. He came into her apartment, closing the door behind him, stroking her cheek lightly.

"How beautiful you look," he said softly, his gaze lowering, lingering as it drifted down over her teal dress. He looked beyond her. "This is your apartment."

"Come look around." She took his hand and they moved through the tiny apartment that had one watercolor on a living room wall, plants, white wicker furniture, and family pictures in the bedroom. Fontaine paused to study them.

"Which one is Pierce?"

"The tallest. The shortest is Tim, the other is Freedom."

"Pierce was a good-looking boy."

"Pierce was special. Our family has never been quite the same without him. A part of us is missing like a chunk out of a tire and when we roll along, it's not as smooth as before."

Fontaine turned to look down at her. "We moved into White Star Tower three weeks ago. I thought you might like to have dinner in Tulsa and see it."

She laughed. "Fly to Tulsa?"

"I have a license. Would you like that?"

"I'd like anything you'd like," she answered frankly, and he drew a sharp breath.

"Dear Cimarron," he whispered, leaning forward to kiss her lightly. He took her arm and they left. Fontaine flew them in his single-engine Bonanza that bore the White Star logo on the side. They ate steaks in a secluded corner of a restaurant in Tulsa, and afterwards, Fontaine drove farther south to show her the new headquarters.

"We celebrated the move to Star Tower last month," he said, speeding along a divided four-lane expressway until he turned into a new suburban area. Beyond blocks of businesses fronting the busy street were shingled roofs of expensive homes, but Cimarron merely gave them a glance, her gaze sweeping over the strip mall, the well-landscaped single-story office buildings to the tall building dominating the others. Hidden lighting on the grounds reflected on long glass windows; a fountain splashed at the front steps. Yellow flowers bloomed in well-tended beds, and an expanse of green lawn swept from the street to the parking lot in back.

"Here it is," Fontaine said casually, yet she suspected he was as proud of it as Peter was of the farm. "I'll show you my office."

"Something I didn't see when I worked at White Star."

He laughed. "Then it's high time we remedy that."

In the marbled lobby they passed a security man and took an elevator to the twentieth floor. Fontaine ushered her through a reception area into his office, which occupied the northwest corner. The only light was a low one at a bar behind oak doors. Fontaine turned on recessed lights and she strolled across a thick beige carpet. The office was as unique as Fontaine, attention given to details from the goatskin-and-stainless-steel desk to the bronzed three-foot derrick on a pedestal near a wall. She moved soundlessly around the room, seeing the adjoining bathroom and another room for entertaining that had a wide wood-burning fire-place, deep maroon calfskin sofas, glass tables, and a view of the city from the floor-to-ceiling windows. Both rooms had bars and electronic equipment, a television, and a stereo. She gazed out at the view to the north, the river and downtown Tulsa in the distance. In one corner was the only incongruous piece of furniture, a small wooden desk, and she ran her finger along the nicked surface. "Was this your grandfather's?"

"Yes. Care for a drink?" Durand asked, opening a bottle of cognac. He handed her a drink and touched the desk. "I spent hours sitting at his side at this desk. I wanted it here as if I could bring a little part of him here with me. Foolishness."

"It's nice," she said, smiling at him. "Your office is marvelous."

"I enjoy it. Come look at the view."

She moved toward the windows and he switched off the lights except the small one over the bar. He moved to her side, his shoulder almost touching her, and she could feel the heat from his body. Lights twinkled in a panorama below, but all she was aware of was Fontaine.

"It's beautiful," she said softly.

"Very," he answered in a husky voice, kissing her nape.

Her heart felt as if it had stopped beating and then started again at a swifter speed. Fontaine set their glasses down and turned her into his arms, pulling her close.

She came into his arms with an eagerness she didn't try to contain. He gazed into her eyes a moment before he kissed her and the longing she felt was blatantly mirrored in his expression. Gone was the man who could be so impassive and reserved, the controlled businessman, the quiet, powerful oil man. Instead, he shook with need as he groaned and crushed her to him, his mouth covering hers, his tongue touching her lips that parted.

Cimarron was lost in a giddy spiral of sensation, returning his kisses that made her faint and at the same time, made her strain toward him for more, wanting so much more. His hand drifted over her nape, down her back while she clung to him and let go all reserve, unafraid of being hurt because she trusted him completely.

Fontaine's heart pounded with hers, her softness pressed

against him, his hand moving across her shoulders. He couldn't get enough of her; he wanted to be lost in her warmth, to possess her. His erection throbbed painfully as he released her and held her away, one hand on her shoulder, the other stroking her cheek. Her lids raised in a languorous, heated manner that almost made him lose his resolve. She was his whenever he wanted; he could see it in her eyes and it made him shake with flaming desire.

When she finally pushed against him and moved away, their breathing was as ragged as if they had been running.

"We should go now," she said quietly.

He wanted her badly, gazing down at her, trying to be patient and exercise control. He nodded and set their glasses on the bar, turning out the lights and taking her arm. He flew her home to Dallas, kissed her again at her door, and said he would see her Saturday night.

The next night he took her to dinner in Dallas, and at her door as he held her in his arms, he asked her out the following weekend.

"I've promised I'd go home to the farm on the weekend. I have to leave right after work, because it takes me over four hours from here."

"How about dinner Friday night in Oklahoma City, and then I'll fly you to Enid and rent a car and drive you to the farm."

"Oh, you can't do all that!"

"I can if you'll say yes."

He watched a sparkle come to her eyes and she said yes eagerly, sliding her arms around his neck. He groaned with desire that fanned through him and he kissed her again passionately before releasing her and telling her good night.

Monday after work she received a dozen red roses and read the card that made her heartbeat quicken: "Cimarron—The weekend was fun—F."

He called each night and they spent hours talking during the week and once again on Friday, she hurried with bubbling anticipation when her doorbell rang. As she swung open the door, he stood leaning against the jamb watching her, his gaze moving with smoldering deliberation that set her aflame, drifting down slowly over her simple blue cotton dress.

"You're beautiful. I think I've told you that before."

"Thank you. I won't ever tire of hearing it from you." She wanted to walk into his arms. He waved his hand. "Shall we go? There's a hint of rain to the north, coming down across western Kansas, so we should get started."

They flew to Oklahoma City, ate jambalaya in a rustic restaurant, and when they stepped outside, a cool wind whipped against them.

They flew and in a short time he landed on the Enid runway. A rental car was waiting, but before they climbed in, she placed her hand on his arm. "The air smells like rain and there's lightning all across the north. Freedom or Tim can come get me."

"I won't run any needless risks. I've reserved a room at the Holiday Inn in Enid."

"You can stay with us."

He caressed her cheek. "Thanks. I already have a room."

"That's an hour's drive back to town."

"Get in the car," he said lightly, "before it rains on us."

Laughing, feeling as if she had had too much champagne when she actually hadn't had any, she sat down in the rented Lincoln. They talked about books while lightning flashed in the distance, illuminating banks of storm clouds. Open country smelled sweet and fresh. Gusts of wind flattened sunflowers caught in the glare of the headlights along the side of the highway. Halfway to the farm, they encountered rain.

It was after ten o'clock, the rain gone, when they swung into her drive and parked. It was Friday night and she saw Freedom's car, Tim's car parked by the garage, as well as the Sorensons', Megan and Peter's close friends. At the sight of the cars, Cimarron knew her family was entertaining company, so she placed her hand on Fontaine's arm.

"My family has company. They're probably sitting on the back porch visiting. Come meet them."

"Thanks. I don't want to intrude."

"You won't intrude. Come on." She took his hand.

"If you insist, Cimarron, but I can't remember when I've dropped in on someone unannounced."

"My folks are used to people dropping in unannounced. That's not unusual for my family and their friends."

He was introduced to the Chisholms and their neighbors and sat down next to Cimarron. Cool breezes smelling of damp earth and wet grass blew across the screened porch as they talked about an outbreak of pinkeye in the Sorensons' cattle, and then they discussed the best local fishing spots. Freedom gave Cimarron a Coke and Fontaine a cold Coors. Peter asked Fontaine if he worked for Van Horn Petroleum and Fontaine merely answered he was with White Star, but within minutes of talking with Freedom, he realized Freedom knew exactly who he was. Other than Freedom and Cimarron, Fontaine didn't think any of the others knew he owned an oil company. Talk went from wheat to guns to fishing. Fontaine draped his arm across the back of Cimarron's chair, aware his hand was only inches away from her shoulder. He had removed his tie and unbuttoned his collar. He relaxed, enjoying the Chisholms and their friends, interested in hearing the talk about crops and wells being drilled in the vicinity.

Suddenly, clouds opened and rain poured, glistening in rivulets across the yard when lightning flashed.

"Folks, we've got plenty of beds and I think all of you better stay the night."

"Lord, we don't mean to crowd you," Jeb Sorenson said.

"I have a room in town," Fontaine said.

"Jeb, you and Irene know we have room." He turned to Fontaine. "Son, you might as well bed down here. Jeb's being polite, but he knows as well as I do, you can't get out now. You forded a creek coming in. This kind of rain, you have to stay."

"We have plenty of room," Cimarron added, and Megan Chisholm seconded the offer.

"We have people all the time," Freedom said quietly. "They wouldn't ask if they didn't mean it."

Feeling foolish, Fontaine consented, wondering when the last time was that he had not only dropped in unannounced, but stayed overnight unexpectedly with strangers—a first in his adult life. Tim brought him another beer while Peter went to the kitchen to get cheese and crackers.

"Folks, y'all visit as long as you please, but I'm tuckered out," Irene Sorenson said.

"I'll show you your room," Megan said. "Peter, would you carry Jerry to bed? He's been asleep for an hour."

"Do you know much about Walker Able Company?" Freedom asked Fontaine as the women left.

"It's a good one. I've used their accounting services in the past."

"I've interviewed with Walker."

"You're changing jobs?" Cimarron asked in surprise.

"They contacted me. I'm happy with Dun, but Walker has an interesting proposition. I just wondered about the company."

"How long have you been with Dun and Holt?" Fontaine asked, listening closely to Freedom. "Why don't you come by my office? I'd like to talk to you about it if you're thinking of changing."

"Fine," Freedom answered, soon changing the subject from himself. "Think the Yankees will lead the league?"

"I think they'll come in near the top. My favorite team is Cincinnati."

"Pat Zachry will give them a boost. For a rookie, he's super," Cimarron said, and Fontaine glanced at her in surprise.

"A baseball fan?"

"We all are," Freedom answered. "All the kids. Peter and Megan aren't interested, but all of us played baseball. Cimarron played at home with us. She's a good shortstop."

"Freedom," she threatened, laughing at the same time.

"I hope I get to see that," Fontaine said.

"I don't play baseball anymore."

"Not since last month," Freedom said cheerfully.

"My brother has a bad habit of exaggeration."

"The Reds have Joe Morgan, too," Peter said.

Jeb Sorenson stood and stretched. "I'm going to turn in. This is way past my bedtime."

"I'll go up, too. Good night, Fontaine," Peter said easily.

"Good night, sir," Fontaine answered politely, coming to his feet. "Thanks for taking me in."

"Glad to have you. Any friend is always welcome here. Night, Cimarron." He picked up the sleeping Jerry and carried him into the house while Jeb followed.

"It's getting late," Fontaine said, feeling foolish for staying over and amazed he had allowed them to talk him into it when he usually was in control of everything around him. "And it's only a fine, gentle rain. Surely, the creek goes down as quickly as it rises. I have a room at the Holiday Inn."

"If you go now, my father would think we ran you off. You can't imagine how much company we have at this house."

"My sister doesn't have a habit of exaggeration," Freedom said dryly.

"No, she's into the bald-faced truth at all times," Tim added, and Cimarron wrinkled her nose at them.

"See what you missed by not having brothers?"

"How about one more beer?" Freedom asked, moving to the small refrigerator they kept on the back porch.

"Sure," Fontaine answered easily and in minutes he was deep in discussion with the three Chisholms about President Carter's announcement concerning the energy crisis, about movies, and television. They talked until two in the morning when Tim stood up and stretched and told them good night. Freedom followed, leaving Fontaine and Cimarron.

"I imagine this family rises early, so we should"—he paused, gazing at her and she heard the change in his voice—"go to bed too." She knew what Fontaine was thinking and it made desire burn in her. She wanted him to kiss her, to hold her again, but she stood up and moved away. "You'll be in Pierce's old room. C'mon. I'll show you the way."

As he entered the big kitchen, watching her turn out

lights, he said, "I can't remember when I've dropped in and spent the night, or spent an evening like this. It's been fun, Cimarron. You have a wonderful family."

"Thanks. They love company. It would be lonesome out here if they didn't."

"This house looks older than your family."

"It is. Grandfather Chisholm built it."

"The Sooner?"

"That's right. Do you ever forget anything?" she asked lightly.

"Not if you've said it," he answered, his voice changing to that melting warmth that became at once personal and sensual.

She wondered if he had the slightest idea what effect he had on her by mere words and glances. She led him down the wide hall. "Here's the family room where we spend most of the time in the winter," she said, motioning her hand toward the room with braided rugs, comfortable chintz-covered furniture, shelves filled with books and memorabilia, Peter's gun rack, a mounted bobcat, and Jerry's tricycle near the fireplace. Cimarron thought of the pristine elegance of Fontaine's office in comparison. "It's pretty lived in," she said, glancing up at him as he paused beside her, his gaze shifting from the room to her.

"That's a good way for a house and a room to look," he said softly. "How fortunate you are."

"I think so too," she answered, barely aware of what she said, because desire was as obvious in Fontaine's black eyes as the steady beat of rain on the roof. He touched her shoulder lightly, a hesitancy to his gesture.

He wanted to slip his arms around her, but tonight with her family he was taken aback. When he saw how warm and giving the Chisholms were, he felt as if he were an intruder. Cimarron should have someone her own age taking her out. He suspected in the light of day when Peter saw the gray in his hair, he would quit calling him "son" and be less receptive.

More importantly, Cimarron should have someone who could offer a permanent relationship and Fontaine had never intended that. The family had made him realize how much she would want that. Not since his marriage had he made a lasting commitment and after the divorce, he decided he never would again.

He curbed his impulse to take her in his arms, and she moved away. "I'll show you Pierce's room."

She gave him clean towels, showed him Pierce's room, which was right next to hers. Fontaine paused in her doorway, gazing at her room that looked like a high school cheerleader's with its bulletin board filled with mementos. He walked around, looking at everything to learn more about Cimarron.

She knew she would always remember this moment. It seemed the most unlikely thing to have Fontaine Durand, collar open, coat and tie negligently hooked over his shoulder by his fingers, walking around her bedroom, gazing at her old teddy bears, touching a wilted corsage she had worn years ago.

"I'll say it again. You have a terrific family. Mine wasn't like yours. My father was an alcoholic."

"I'm sorry."

Fontaine shrugged. "They're all gone now. I'm alone," he said quietly, thinking she filled a void when he was with her. That aching loneliness he had experienced more and more lately, a restlessness and dissatisfaction with old friends was gone when he was with Cimarron. He gazed into her wide, guileless eyes, seeing that she was attracted, knowing if he tried to kiss her, she would respond eagerly and he almost reached for her. At the last second, his hand shifted and he straightened her collar, wondering when he had been thrown into such a turmoil by a woman—probably not since he was thirteen years old. Lissa had been exciting, but he had never had any inner battles over her, any doubts about what he should or shouldn't do.

He moved away to the door. "And I'm next door."

"Yes."

"Call me in the morning."

"Unless you have to be somewhere at a certain time, you might as well relax and enjoy yourself. I'm sure we'll wake you all too early. Dad gets up before five and he's not quiet."

"That's fine. Don't go to any trouble for me. I'm accustomed to coffee and juice."

She laughed and shook her head. "You won't get that here—at least that's not all you'll get. Dad is a breakfast nut—he thinks that's the most important meal, so we always have a big one."

"Good night, Cimarron."

"Night," she said quietly and closed her door.

Fontaine stretched out in bed, moonlight splashing over the room. He gazed at his surroundings, looking at Pierce's belongings that filled the room. Trophies, old pennants on the walls, football posters, family pictures, as if Pierce were merely away at college, not gone for eternity. Tonight, included in the family circle, accepted by her brothers, he had enjoyed their companionship. They all treated him as openly as Cimarron. Nice. The word fit her family but it was far too inadequate for Cimarron. She was a heady wine, filled with anticipatory pleasure, sensual, inviting. When she had first seen him at the convention in Houston, he remembered the expressions crossing her features, that startling awareness the first moment they had looked into each other's eyes.

How could she make him feel weak in the knees? He was too experienced, too cynical and jaded, yet she did.

His body ached for her as erotic images danced in his mind. He hadn't ever shared his life with anyone. Always, he had been alone and for years he had thought that was the way he functioned best, but now he felt so damned alone. He felt alone in a crowd of familiar people, as if part of him were missing.

He groaned and got up to cross to the window and gaze out over the yard, the barn, the fields spreading flat and endlessly, but all he could see was Cimarron. He wanted her and he didn't want to wait.

The next morning she was cooking when he entered the kitchen. She flashed him a smile over her shoulder and he sat down at the table with her brothers. She wore jeans that fit like skin, a T-shirt with short sleeves, and her hair was pinned on top of her head.

"If you're watching your cholesterol, you came to the wrong place to eat," Freedom drawled dryly.

"Mine's fine so far," Fontaine replied, "I'm going to indulge myself. Where are the Sorensons?"

"Left long ago with Peter," Freedom said with a grin.

Over an hour later Fontaine thanked them all and told them goodbye, telling Cimarron he would see her the following Friday night as he walked to his car with her beside him, trying to slow his stride to match hers.

"Your family is marvelous."

"Thank you. They liked you."

"Can you go to dinner next Friday?"

"Yes."

"Good. I'll be there around seven." He turned to look down at her, and as she gazed up at him, she thought he looked as if something were worrying him.

"Is something wrong?"

His brows arched, and he stared at her. "I've been watching you with your family. You should be dating someone your age."

She laughed. "Back to the *young lady* business! Fontaine, look at the difference between Peter and Megan."

He watched her laugh, seeing that age was no barrier to her, wanting to reach for her, afraid if he did it would embarrass her because her family might see. He wondered at himself. When had he been torn with indecision, worrying over age and commitment? Never before. He thought to hell with it and pulled her to him to kiss her. After the first startled moment, she clung to him for a few minutes and then moved away.

"I'll call you tonight."

She nodded, watching him until the car was out of sight down the road. When she entered the kitchen, Megan looked up from helping Jerry build a model plane. "Fontaine's nice. And incredibly handsome!"

"He said he'll call tonight."

"Oh." Megan tilted her head to study Cimarron. "Have you dated him long?"

"I've known him since that first spring at White Star."

Megan nodded and moved a tiny piece of wood that Jerry's pudgy fingers grasped. "Peter said Fontaine is an engineer, but sometimes he doesn't get things right."

"Fontaine is an engineer. And he owns White Star."

Megan paused, her eyes round. "*Owner* of White Star Oil Company? I gave the owner of White Star Pierce's bed with the old frayed blue blanket?"

"He had a good time here."

"Cimarron, I hope—" Suddenly she closed her mouth.

"What Megan? You can say what you want with me."

"Nothing."

Cimarron started out of the room. "Cimarron," Megan said. "Older men are nice."

Freedom's reaction was different. He came back at five, dusty from helping Peter, stripped to the waist, his blond hair tousled, muscles glistening with sweat, his boots dirty. Lounging in the doorway, he held a cold beer and a bandanna that he swiped at his sweaty forehead. "Megan says you're going out with Durand regularly."

"That's right." A slight shock buffeted her when she saw Freedom's stormy eyes.

"He's old enough to be your father, Cimarron!"

"Not quite. I'm twenty-three and he's only forty-one. And when I'm with him, I don't notice age."

"You're going to get hurt. What are you looking for? A second father?"

"No, I'm not," she answered quietly. "I don't think of my father with Fontaine."

Freedom muttered an expletive. "He won't marry you."

"I don't expect a proposal from every man I date. I know he won't marry me. You don't just date women you expect to marry."

"He's handsome, enormously wealthy, worldly. He was married to a movie star. Do you think—"

"No, I don't think he can be fascinated with me, but he seems to enjoy my company and I enjoy his."

"Durand's just using you. He'll use you and dump you."

"What do you do with the women you date? Where are your fine motives?"

"Aw, shit." They glared at each other as she brushed her hair, angry spots of color showing in her cheeks.

"He was really slumming last night."

"Our family and our home isn't 'slumming'! He had a good time here. Maybe we have something he doesn't have."

"If you believe that, you're a fool."

"I'm grown, Freedom. I enjoy being with him, and he enjoys being with me."

"For how long?" Cynicism laced his question.

"It doesn't matter. You haven't set an example, you know."

"I'm not going to get my heart broken again," he said with so much bitterness, her anger evaporated.

"Oh, Freedom. There are so many intelligent, beautiful women in the world. How can you just see Janie?"

He pushed away from the door, his gaze raking over her. "If he hurts you—"

"I'll be all right."

"Said the mouse one second before the cat's paw came down," he replied and disappeared down the hall with a clatter of boots against the floor. She sighed, staring at the empty doorway, concerned for Freedom, who was so in love with Janie it blinded him to the rest of the women in the world.

That night when her family and visitors sat on the screened porch and talked, she lay on her bed, her door closed while she talked to Fontaine on the phone.

"Your father knows I own White Star now, doesn't he?"

"Yes, I told him."

"Why do I have a feeling that he won't approve of me?"

She laughed softly, conjuring up images of Fontaine, thinking his question the most ridiculous thing she had heard, yet she realized it did make a difference to Peter.

"He approves. Unless you have a sinister side to you that you've kept hidden."

"Cimarron, does your family approve?"

She thought of Freedom. "They like you."

"That wasn't what I asked. You're the only people I've met who hold it against me that I'm the owner of an oil company."

"We don't hold it against you!"

"Your brother Freedom doesn't?"

"Well—it's a different world than ours."

"I'm just an ordinary man."

"No, you're not, and you never have been," she said. She was drawn to him as she had never been to any man.

"Maybe I'll win them over."

She laughed again at the tone in his voice. "Fontaine, has there ever been anyone you couldn't win over?"

"Of course. When you ask something like that, I want—" He broke off abruptly. "I won't hurt you, Cimarron, I promise," he heard himself say, wondering why he was making such a damn fool promise. "Next Friday is a hell of a long time. Any night this week you can go to dinner?"

She thought about her schedule. "Monday I have dinner with a salesman."

Fontaine groaned.

"It's business!"

"That makes it only slightly less odious."

She stared at the phone. How could he *care*? Fontaine Durand who had married an actress, a beautiful, sexy woman. "I'm free Tuesday and Thursday and the weekend."

He swore again. "I'm not. I have meetings. I'll be there Friday. Do you need to be with your family now?"

"No. They have company and everyone's talking and they won't miss me. I'm looking at your picture."

"You have a picture of me?"

"It's years old—that first year I was with White Star. It was in a magazine and I saved it."

"*The first year,* Cimarron?"

"Yes. It's a good picture," she continued quickly, "I cut

you out so I just have you and not the woman you were with."

"Good thinking. Whoever she was, she wasn't important."

She could hear the lightness back in his voice and she relaxed, yearning for him, relishing every word with him. They talked for an hour and finally said good night and after she replaced the receiver, she stared at his picture, remembering, longing for him, wondering what he really felt for her.

Fontaine replaced the receiver and strode across his bedroom, his emotions seething in turmoil. She was so young, so damnably trusting. He was astounded at his reaction to Cimarron.

He yanked off his tie and threw it down, swearing in anger. His gaze followed the tie to the bed and instantly he had a clear vision of Cimarron stretched there, arms lifted, waiting for him.

He swore and spun around to go to the window and stare outside. Marriage could be so sticky. He hadn't wanted to marry again. The divorce from Lissa hadn't been costly simply because she was wealthy and they had parted in an agreeable manner, but that wouldn't happen again. Yet he couldn't imagine an affair with Cimarron and then walking away and leaving her. He stormed across the room, peeling off his shirt and tossing it aside. He didn't have to marry her. Let things happen as they happened. Then he realized he was standing over the bed again, staring down at it, seeing Cimarron there.

If he wanted her that badly, sleep with her. The lady was willing. She had made that plainly evident.

"*I want to marry and have children.*" The words seemed spoken aloud in the empty silent room and he thought about sitting on the porch with the Chisholms, enjoying their company, relaxing completely and losing all his loneliness that had haunted him so often lately.

The lady is old enough to do as she pleases. She dates, she enjoys men. She doesn't have to have marriage, he argued with himself and swore viciously.

"You don't have to decide anything tonight," he said

aloud, running his hand through his hair. He changed to shorts and went downstairs to his exercise room. He started on a treadmill, setting the speed so he had to jog, feeling sweat pour off his body, trying to work himself into exhaustion while he wondered if Cimarron was blissfully sitting on the back porch with her family, perhaps with men she had grown up with, had dated. He tried to think about business and failed, turning up the speed to run faster, thinking the week was going to be long, his business was being neglected, and he would have to make some decisions soon about Cimarron.

The following Friday she was ready, more eager than before, greeting Fontaine as he gazed at her solemnly. It was Memorial Day weekend and the traffic was heavy, but he managed to speed along the highway to a restaurant. She alternated between happiness and worry, because moments came when he seemed constrained, and she wondered if he had lost interest in her company. And then they would become engrossed in conversation, flirting with each other, and she was blissfully happy. When he kissed her good night in her hallway, she clung to him tightly, wanting more than kisses, aching for him.

He leaned away from her, his breathing ragged as he gazed at her with a look that made her tremble. "Cimarron," his voice was husky, breathless, "fly with me for the day to New Orleans tomorrow." She nodded, kissing his throat. "Have you ever been there?" he asked.

"No," she whispered, kissing below his ear.

He groaned and pulled her to him, crushing her in his arms as he kissed her passionately. Finally he released her. "Good night, love," he said softly and walked away.

"What time tomorrow?" she called to him, wondering if he had left so abruptly to control his desire. She hadn't sent him away.

"Eight o'clock."

She watched him drive away before she locked up.

She had a wonderful day in New Orleans, but she had the

same feeling with him that part of the time he enjoyed himself enormously, and part of the time he was worried over something. And then that night he told her he had to fly to California to work for the next week. As she watched him drive away at three in the morning, she realized he hadn't asked her for another date—something he had always done since that first dinner.

There were no phone calls that week and she hurt over Fontaine. Fear began to grow inside her. He had always held back, kept himself under control, limited them to brief good-night kisses. He avoided an affair, avoided any deep commitments, and she suspected the novelty of dating her had worn off quickly. She bit her lips, remembering, memories swirling and tumbling in her mind like snow in a storm.

9

When the next week came and Cimarron hadn't heard from Fontaine, she decided she never would. She tried to concentrate on her job, working overtime, keeping busy to avoid going home to stare at the phone. Wednesday she left on time; it was June and heat rose from the paving as she drove out of the lot just as a gray Lincoln passed.

Sure she was wrong, she twisted in her seat to glance back over her shoulder and her breath caught. Fontaine.

She backed into the lot, stopping beside him. He climbed out, leaving the door open behind him, and she couldn't breathe, as if the sky had lowered and the available air were limited. She couldn't take her gaze from him, realizing it was the first time she had seen him dressed casually in faded jeans and a T-shirt. His arms were muscular, his waist trim and flat, and she wondered if she could ever see him as less than perfect.

"I should have called, but I went from California to Louisiana, and I just got to Love Field an hour ago. Can you go to dinner tonight?"

"Yes, of course," she said, and they both laughed. Suddenly he held out his arms.

She ran to him, feeling his arms close around her and sweep her off her feet as they kissed hungrily and her heart pounded with joy. He was here! She didn't care what lay ahead.

"I missed you so," she whispered when they finally released each other a fraction.

"I'm doing everything all wrong," he said huskily. "I left because I knew I should think things over and give you a chance to think."

"All I could think was that I missed you terribly," she admitted with a candor that made his arms tighten around her. Fontaine gazed down into her wide, guileless eyes, seeing the love he felt mirrored in them.

"I seem to have lost my good sense when I met you," he said, marveling at how wonderful she looked. Her hair was pinned behind her head in a practical chignon, yet tendrils had escaped, giving her a disheveled appeal. Her red dress left her arms bare and he kept running his hands over her shoulders and he didn't want to stop touching her. "I'd like to take you to Tulsa tonight to dinner and show you my home."

"I have to work in the morning."

"I can have you home at whatever time you'd like."

"About two at the latest? I think our motors are still running," she said in a sultry tone.

"I know mine is."

"Shall we do something about it?" she asked and this time her voice was breathless.

"Yes, we will," he answered, bending his head to kiss her, his tongue playing against hers while he molded her body to the length of his.

She heard a car motor about one second before she heard a horn honk. She and Fontaine stepped apart and to her embarrassment she faced Brad Crown who grinned, waved, and swung around them. She laughed at the ridiculousness of getting caught kissing in the driveway like two addled teens.

"How early can we go to dinner?" he asked.

"I can be ready in an hour and a half."

"I'll pick you up at seven," he said, giving her an extra half-hour.

"What'll you do while you wait until seven?"

"I have a hotel room."

"For two hours?"

"Yes, I'll pick you up at seven."

Cimarron floated home, drifting through the empty apartment to dress, coming out of her daze enough to worry about what she should wear. She took a long, hot bath and dressed in a clinging, simple black dress, and when she opened the door to meet him, she walked into his arms again.

Fontaine was in a gray summer suit with a dark tie, his thick hair combed away from his forehead, and all the way to the airport she constantly wanted to touch him.

After a short flight they came in over the Arkansas River and Tulsa, the city spread below, the airport looming up where Fontaine set the Bonanza down in a smooth landing. "I want you to see my home. We'll eat there."

"I'd like that," she said, imagining Fontaine cooking steaks on a grill on a patio. He drove up a sweeping drive lined with tall oaks to a sprawling Tudor-style mansion, half timbers and half red brick, that made her suddenly remember the differences between them, the power and wealth he had.

"You live here alone?"

"Yes. Come see my house." He took her arm and they entered through a back door into a wide hallway with stucco walls and a dark parquet floor that led to a kitchen. Two cooks paused to greet him.

"This is Bertie and Ralph Gann. Meet Miss Chisholm."

They nodded in greeting and the man picked up a tray with two glasses of chilled white wine which he offered to them.

Fontaine steered her through the kitchen, continuing down another wide hall with a black-and-white inlaid terrazzo floor to a formal living room with Venetian glass chandeliers, three sitting areas, one having a white silk damask George IV sofa. One glance at the Louis XV *Aubusson* carpet, and a Modigliani hanging above the limestone Tudor mantel, and Cimarron realized that Fontaine had a deep appreciation for antiques as well as art. She was awed, but not so much by the surroundings as by the man. Fontaine held all her interest and the house was merely an extension of his personality.

They ate roast duckling in a glass-enclosed pavilion, overlooking a pond and flowers in his back yard. Beyond a low hedge was a swimming pool. A greenhouse stood to the west, and she learned he grew orchids. After dinner he reached across the table to take her hand. "Let me show you my orchids."

It was steamy inside the greenhouse, the only sound their footsteps on wide flagstones, the drip of a fountain. Tropical plants grew to the ceiling; delicate pink and purple orchids bloomed in profusion.

"Bertie and Ralph have gone," he said, and she turned around, realizing Fontaine was simply watching her while she had been studying the flowers. He had shed his coat and tie before dinner; now he lounged against a post, his broad shoulders and long frame startling among all the delicate blooms.

"I missed you," he said, pushing away from the post. "You haven't seen the upstairs yet. You haven't seen my bedroom." He held out his hand.

He showed her the other rooms upstairs before going to his, which was at the southeast corner. It was a suite of rooms, a sitting room that opened onto a bedroom with a black marble bath.

Fontaine stood in the center of the bedroom with hand-painted Chinese wallpaper in muted apricots and beige colors, a Matisse and a Van Rijn on the walls, a granite fireplace, and a satin-covered king-size bed. She looked around and finally faced him.

"Come here, Cimarron," he said quietly and she walked over to him.

"You do what I ask so easily," he said, his voice husky.

"That's because it's what I want to do."

"You can't imagine how precious you are to me," he said, each word making her heartbeat quicken as she stood on tiptoe and raised her face for his kiss.

He released her slightly so he could talk to her. "I did a great deal of thinking about us while I was away."

"I was afraid you wouldn't come back. I shouldn't tell you that, but I was."

"You can always tell me anything." He looked at her solemnly. "Will you marry me?"

Shocked, she gazed into his dark eyes, her mouth open.

He laughed softly. "Don't look so stunned. Haven't I given some hint of what I feel for you?"

"Marry?"

He realized then she had never expected a proposal from him. "Cimarron, you little fool," he said gently. "I love you," he whispered, knowing the words were inadequate for what he felt. "I'll ask again—will you marry me?"

"You're sure? You were married to a movie star. I'm just—"

"—wonderful," he finished for her, kissing her. He raised his head and looked into her eyes.

"Yes," she answered, stunned and wondering if he really knew what he was doing, yet never more sure in her life what she was doing. Her heart threatened to burst with joy. "You know how much I love you," she added in a whisper that ended all conversation.

His arms locked around her, and he kissed her long and deliberately, taking his time, using all his expertise to make the night right for her. He moved slowly, willing himself to pleasure her to the fullest. He undressed her with care, his hands constantly brushing over her warm flesh, watching her, shaking with his own need, yet trying to linger. Her dress fell with a whispery rush around her feet, the dainty lingerie followed. She was young and beautiful, golden skinned, taut flesh, long legged. He cupped her full breasts in his hands, his thumb playing over her stiff nipples, watching her reaction until he bent to touch each tip with his tongue.

She reached out to undress him, her green eyes as dark as emeralds, her hands warm, caressing him, running her fingers across his bare chest. He groaned and swept her up to carry her to bed.

Cimarron felt on fire with love and passion. Fontaine was slow and deliberate, loving her with consummate skill. She felt as if she couldn't get enough of him, touch him enough, kiss him enough. He was a marvel to her; his lovemaking sent her into a giddy spiral of burning need as she stroked him and lavished kisses that made him groan.

He possessed her, thrusting into her warmth, bursting with passion, calling her name as she cried out his in ecstasy and they both clung to each other. Fontaine felt in his heart he had made the right decision.

Later, stroking her, his hand drifting over her bare hip, he wondered if he could ever look at her without being aroused, astounded that he had been so lucky to find her.

"Thank God for that oversexed engineer," he said quietly and Cimarron looked up. She ran her finger across his smooth-shaven jaw.

"What on earth are you talking about?" she asked dreamily, leaning down to kiss him, ending his answer.

It was nearly dawn when she lay in his arms and remembered their earlier conversation. She rose up on one elbow, her auburn hair tumbling down, tendrils mingling with the mat of dark curls tangled across his chest. "What did you mean, 'Thank God for the oversexed engineer'?"

"If I hadn't overheard that jerk I employ, I might have hurried right on into Curtis's office and never met you. Never really met you."

"Sure you would have. We were together during the storm. We were together when you prepared the government report."

"It seems chancy. How soon can we marry?"

She sat up, her brow creased in a frown while his hand stroked her lightly. "I can't think when you do that."

He grinned at her. "I can't stop. You're efficient. You'll learn to think."

"You're a busy man. What about your schedule?"

He chuckled and played with her hair. "If you only knew how my work has suffered, how behind schedule I am—"

"Because of us?"

"Because of *you*, love. I'd like our wedding as soon as reasonably possible."

"I want a church wedding. This is June. Is September too long?"

"No, not if you need that much time."

"It takes time for invitations to get printed. How about the second week of September?" she asked, wondering if she could get everything done.

"Fine." He rolled over, opened a drawer beside the bed, and looked at a calendar. "September. Our wedding day. Where would you like to go for a honeymoon?"

She gazed down at him stretched out in bed on the fancy monogrammed beige sheets. He was virile, incredibly handsome, strong. His dark locks were tangled now, tumbling over his forehead, his muscles bulged as he flexed his arms. His body was as well cared for as his business, and she couldn't believe that he really loved her, that he had asked her to marry him.

"Are you there?" he asked, amusement in his voice while he lay back on the pillows. Always his hands touched her, sometimes lightly, sometimes heated caresses, but it was constant, as if he were afraid he would lose her.

"I can't believe you want to marry me."

"I do. And you can't imagine how lucky I feel. I'll talk to Peter tomorrow."

"You don't have to ask permission," she said, laughing, amazed that this marvel of a man was going to be in her bed the rest of their lives.

"I'll talk to him. Did your brother tell you he's going to work for me?"

"Freedom?"

"Yes. I'm glad to get him, but not one-millionth as happy

as I am to get his sister. Now the second biggest question. What about your job? Cimarron, it's important to me—''

"I'll turn in my resignation Monday,'' she answered quietly and he drew her into his arms to kiss her.

Finally, on a fall Saturday with a clear blue sky, they stood in the Methodist church, Cimarron beside Peter, ready to walk down the aisle. Her dress was white satin, her auburn hair caught up, looped and pinned behind her head, the veil giving a gauzy appearance to everything. She moved down the aisle on Peter's arm, only able to see Fontaine waiting for her. He was breathtakingly handsome, and she smiled with joy as Peter placed her hand in Fontaine's and they repeated their vows and were declared man and wife.

The reception was festive, but all of Cimarron's attention was on Fontaine. They left in a chauffeured limousine and flew to Paris for a honeymoon, one day driving to Montluçon so Fontaine could show her the little town where his grandfather was born. The second week, Fontaine took her to his home on the Yucatan Peninsula. As she lolled on the cool white beach in the total privacy of his property, she watched him reading through mail. In Paris he had told her he had given her five thousand shares of White Star stock as a wedding present, and she realized the upheaval he would make in her life.

"Why did we go to Paris for a week when you had this?''

"I wanted something very special for our honeymoon.''

"Everything with you is very special.''

He lowered a letter to give her a smoldering look. "I'm afraid my business will vanish, I'm so in love.''

"It won't vanish,'' she answered softly.

"You're ruining my concentration.''

"Am I now?'' she asked provocatively. He groaned and waved the letter at her.

"I have to tend to this or lose a lot of money. Oh, to hell with it,'' he sighed, tossing down the letter and moving to her molded plastic beach chair that rested in the sand.

"Scoot over," he commanded, his intentions plain to see.

She laughed. "Out here? It's broad daylight."

"Who cares? The help is gone and we're alone," he said, nuzzling her throat, peeling away her swimsuit. She responded eagerly. Hours later after lunch and a swim, he sat down again on the shaded patio, swearing as he read through a letter.

"What's wrong?"

He lowered the letter. "Sure you want to hear? It's complicated."

"Go ahead. I'll tell you if I get lost."

As he began to talk about the small oil company they had taken over in San Diego two years ago, she moved her chair beside his, leaning back, listening. Instead of becoming bored or lost, she became absorbed in what he was telling her. When she didn't understand something, she asked and he patiently explained. The shadows shifted, the heat of siesta hours went unnoticed on the cool patio with breezes blowing in from the Caribbean. Palms swayed slightly, birds circling lazily in the sky, an occasional seaplane roaring overhead or a boat chugging past far out from the beach.

They spent the rest of the day going over figures. While Cimarron had no solutions to offer, she was a good sounding board, and for the first time since the loss of his grandfather, Fontaine found someone he could wholly confide in about business as well as other aspects of his life. Suddenly, he got up and pulled her to her feet to slip his arms around her.

"The more we're married, the more I need you."

"I hope so," she answered, wriggling against him.

"It's more than that. It's that and all this," he said, waving his hand over the paper-strewn table. "You know more than I realized about the oil business."

"I've worked in it since I was eighteen."

"And risen spectacularly. I'm beginning to see why."

"How about some dinner?"

"I want to call Peyton. But before I call him," he said

softly, tilting her chin up, his head lowering. "You make me feel twenty again."

They spent three more days in Cancun, and then Fontaine had to fly to San Diego. Cimarron accompanied him and as the days passed, he began to discuss more and more of his business with her. They flew home for Thanksgiving at the farm. Then on Monday they were back in Tulsa, and he took her to the office with him.

On a snowy December night after work, Fontaine sat behind his desk in their bedroom that had changed only slightly since she had moved into his Tulsa mansion with him.

"Have you ever been on a rig?"

"Yes. James Curtis saw to that. And I've had a refinery tour."

"Good. Here's a report about White Star wells. I thought you might want to read it." He studied her a moment, his gaze raking over her and he crossed the room to sit down facing her. "Remember what you told me that first dinner date?"

"What?"

"That you wanted to marry and have lots of babies."

Her green eyes changed and darkened, a sensuous droop coming to her eyelids. "I remember," she answered softly.

"Still feel that way?"

"Yes," she answered, her heart pounding. She wondered if he would ever have the slightest idea of the extent to which she loved him. There were no bounds to it, no end to the excitement he could stir, and she felt like the luckiest woman on earth. He slipped his arms around her, pushing her back in the chair.

"You'll get nail polish on your clothes. It isn't dry," she whispered.

"I don't care," he answered gruffly, his mouth stopping any answer.

10

DECEMBER, 1977

Tulsa, Oklahoma

Crystal chandeliers sparkled above a crowd equally as glittering. It was December and Marge and Christian Newberry were throwing one of their lavish fund-raising parties for the Tulsa Symphony. During the evening when Nick Kaminski was in a cluster of people with the hostess, he moved to her side. "Sometime tonight, introduce me to Fontaine Durand. I met him years ago as a child and I don't remember him."

"And you can meet his new wife."

"Wives I don't have to meet," he said lightly, laughing as Marge made a face at him.

"I might as well warn you, Laz is in town and will be here tonight."

"I won't misbehave," he said with amusement. " 'Course I can't promise anything for Laz."

"Funny boy. I just thought you'd want to know. He has a new woman in his life. New to me."

"How do you always get all the gossip?"

"I get around. She's your age and not the usual stunner."

"Oh? Dad's slipping."

"They say he's really interested in this one. There's rumors of marriage."

"Not Laz," Nick said, his humor vanishing. "He won't ever marry again. I'll take any kind of bet you want to place."

"Not me, darling. I don't like to lose. But I'm curious to meet her. She's a dress clerk."

"Don't point her out to me. Let me guess."

"You may be surprised this time. I heard she wouldn't turn anyone's head."

"I'm willing to offer a wager on that one too!"

She laughed and squeezed his arm. "You and Laz. You like the lookers."

"What man doesn't?" he teased. "We're no different from anyone else."

"Oh, darling, what a lie! You were asking about Fontaine—there he is, right across the room, the tall, handsome man."

Nick turned as someone said something to Marge, and she moved away from him. A circle of guests stood across the room and it was easy to pick out Durand. There was one man taller than the others and as handsome as a movie star with thick, wavy black hair tinged with gray. He was smiling at a striking woman almost as tall with white hair turned under in a neat curl, and Nick assumed it was Durand's new wife. They were distinguished looking and he had long known what an astute oil man Fontaine was.

Someone spoke to him and his attention returned to the group at hand. He heard a deep, raspy voice and glanced toward the doorway to see Laz enter the room. Laz's gaze met his and they nodded at each other, Nick moving on to drift through the crowd. There was no woman with Laz and Nick forgot about Marge's speculation, having little curiosity about anyone Laz dated. They came and went, an endless stream of women as far back as he could remember.

Half an hour later, Marge caught up with Nick again, linking her bare arm through his. Her red hair was swept around her head in a dramatic swirl, diamond earrings dangling. "Now I'll introduce you to Fontaine. Come on."

Nick saw the direction they were headed, spotting Fontaine, who leaned one shoulder casually against a wall in a corner of the large room. His back was to Nick, but facing him was a young woman with auburn hair falling to her shoulders. She was dressed in a clinging black that was as simple as Marge's was intricate, yet far more elegant. The smoldering looks she was giving Fontaine Durand were scalding and unmistakable.

"Marge, let's not interrupt him now. I'll meet him later," Nick said, slowing his stride.

"Nonsense, darling. He won't mind being interrupted and I'm doing my duty as hostess."

For an instant Nick envied Fontaine, his gaze raking over the woman whose willowy figure was clearly defined in the form-fitting dress. As Nick watched, she reached into Fontaine's coat; Nick realized she wasn't searching for anything, but instead was unobtrusively caressing him. "Marge, they're having a very private talk."

She clamped her arm tighter, squeezing his as she moved forward. "Yoo-hoo, Fontaine."

Nick inwardly cringed, but it was too late now. The tête-à-tête was interrupted. Fontaine must have a mistress on the side, because there had been no mistaking the signals and touches of two people who knew each other intimately. Fontaine turned an impassive face, his brows arching slightly.

"I want you to meet a friend of mine who's in the same business as you—"

"Only on a much smaller scale," Nick added, giving the woman one more sweeping glance, wondering if the new wife had the slightest inkling.

"Fontaine and Cimarron Durand, this is Nick Kaminski. Nick Kaminski meet Cimarron and Fontaine Durand."

Nick shook hands and turned as Cimarron Durand offered her hand in a friendly gesture. Gazing into wide green eyes, he shook hands briefly with her. He had known few wives who looked at their husbands during the middle of a party as he had caught Cimarron Durand looking at hers. Fontaine was a very lucky man. And the name Cimarron was unusual—it struck a chord in his memory and in seconds, he remembered talking to a supply manager at Van Horn Petroleum who had been a woman named Cimarron Chisholm, the only female supply manager he had encountered.

"Have you ever worked with Van Horn Petroleum, Mrs. Durand?"

"Yes. I was supply manager. We've talked on the phone twice, Mr. Kaminski," she said, smiling.

"Enough about oil," Marge remarked. "I want Cimarron to meet some of my guests. You men can talk oil; you will anyway. Come with me, Cimarron," Marge said, taking Cimarron's arm.

"I'll be back in awhile," Cimarron said, giving Fontaine a lingering look. She gave Nick a fleeting glance. "It was nice to meet you, Mr. Kaminski."

He replied politely and for just a moment joined Fontaine in watching Cimarron walk away in leisurely strides that made the material shift against her hips and swirl slightly around her long legs. Her hair swayed with each step and Nick thought again that Fontaine was fortunate.

"You're Laz's son, aren't you?"

"Yes. He's here somewhere."

"You have your own company now."

"And you just drilled in Custer County, didn't you?"

"How's fishing?" came a loud voice and a man joined them who had occasionally played golf with Fontaine. In time they were joined by others until Nick finally moved away. At the door he glanced back later to see Fontaine in a group of people, Cimarron laughing beside him, her arm resting lightly on his.

He moved to the dining room to a table of food, picking up an olive speared on a red toothpick, drifting to a large family room where a man played the piano softly. Two women stood talking behind him and when he heard Laz's name in the conversation, he realized one of them was Laz's date. Casually he turned around. Both were his age; neither one particularly beautiful, yet they were well dressed and attractive.

"Laz bought season tickets this year," the one with her black hair fastened in a bun on top of her head said.

"There's Don now. Excuse me, Raye. I'll be back." The other woman moved away and the black-haired woman looked at Nick, who was caught openly staring at her. He waved his drink.

"Hi. Nice party," he said.

"Yes, it is."

"You know the Newberrys?"

"No. Actually I'm from out of town. My date is a friend of theirs so here we are. We're interested in the symphony and opera."

"Oh? What's your favorite opera?" he asked, thinking she looked young, not too pretty, and he couldn't imagine her being an opera buff. In spite of the slenderness to her figure, her plain features, there was an earthy, sensual quality to her; her mouth was too full, round and pouting. She wore a clinging taupe dress that bared one shoulder. He knew enough about fashion to guess it was a designer dress, something Laz had lavished on her. A dress clerk. She had to be good in bed to hold Laz's attention.

"Puccini, any of his, or *Der Rosenkavalier*," she answered.

"A romantic," he said with a smile, surprised by her answer.

"No one has ever accused me of that before! Do you like opera?"

"I like opera, western, jazz, and rock. It's one of the few things Laz and I have in common."

Something flickered in her eyes and she seemed to really focus on him. He realized he might have underestimated her at first glance.

"You're Nick."

"You win the lollipop. How'd you guess?"

"Your answer, of course. And now that I look at you—"

"Don't tell me we look alike," he said more sharply than he intended, surprised that he enjoyed talking to her, realizing he had approached her simply to see what kind of woman Laz had taken up with this time.

Raye's gaze swept over Nick as she heard the annoyance in his answer, but the gray eyes were unmistakable, the thick cap of curly brown hair. She hadn't recognized him instantly because he was taller, his face longer, his cheekbones more prominent than Laz's, his jaw less square. He had a thin, aquiline nose that wasn't broken and prominent like Laz's, but the gray eyes were the same. "I should have guessed sooner. You're not alike in many ways, but your eyes are the same."

"I can't quite bring myself to say thank you. I suppose he's told you about me."

"Oh, sure. A little."

"I hear you sell dresses."

She laughed, tilting her head back. "You make it sound like standing on a corner with a tin cup."

He flushed, sorry he had let condescension creep into his voice. He gave her more of his attention now. Her laughter brought a glow to her.

"Sorry if I sounded less than considerate."

"A Kaminski apologizing? Will wonders never cease," she said in such cynical tones, he wondered how well she liked Laz.

"I know how to apologize, and don't lump me with my father."

"So it's as bad between you as he indicated."

"I'm sure you've been told what an ungrateful bastard I am."

"In those exact terms," she said, her eyes twinkling. He liked her. She was appealing and intelligent and likeable. He was surprised, because the women Laz dated usually bored him or he actively disliked them. Young or old, they weren't the type to appeal to Nick as either friends or lovers. But Raye Honeywall was different from the others.

"My father's tastes are definitely improving with age," he said lightly.

"Thank you."

"I see him headed this way. I think he's looking for you. You seem like an intelligent, nice woman, so let me give you a little warning. Look out for yourself. My father is iron willed."

Nick walked away and Raye watched him, his last words giving her a chill. An eerie premonition of disaster tugged at her as she watched the younger Kaminski. He was as ruggedly handsome as his father and just as appealing. She could see Nick moving through the crowd and realized he was intelligent, discerning, and likeable. She had expected someone belligerent, spoiled, and just like Laz in many ways. Perhaps they were alike in more ways than either wanted to acknowledge.

"So you met Nick," Laz said, stopping at her side. "I see he escaped without having to talk to me."

"He's very much like you. He's nice."

She was startled at the hot flare of anger in Laz's eyes. His fingers tightened on her arm until they pinched into her flesh.

"Don't ever get the hots for Nick, honey," he said in tones that chilled her as much as Nick's words had.

"Laz. Don't be absurd! I merely met him and had a few words with him."

"Yeah. That's all you had with me before we went out the first time."

"Laz. You're jealous."

"The hell I am. Just stay away from Nick. Nick is trouble."

"Stop getting angry over nothing," she said softly, moving closer to him, gazing up into his eyes and twisting so her hip rubbed against his. "We have a hotel room about ten minutes' drive from here. Want a change of scenery?"

He laughed, desire kindling in his expression. She smiled at him as she sipped her drink, watching him over the rim of the glass. Laz's anger evaporated. He was acting foolish, but it had bothered him to hear her praise Nick. Nick was her age. Maybe he was getting old, but he wanted Raye badly. He couldn't understand what it was about her; she wasn't beautiful or even sexy looking, yet she could convey an earthy sensuousness that was searing. Sometimes he felt caught in a trap she had set, something that in the past had always been reversed. Usually, he took women when he wanted them, left them when he wanted without any qualms.

He had a swift, vivid mental picture of Raye as she had been only forty minutes before the party, naked, her long hair flowing over her shoulders as she sat astride him, her eyes closed, her tongue rubbing her lower lip while she ground her hips and moaned softly.

"Let's go, honey," he said in a raspy voice, and she gave him a knowing smile.

Instead of going to the hotel, they flew back to Dallas in his private jet. Twinkling lights spread endlessly in all directions as they descended to land. Later, as he paused above her, in his enormous, round bed, he thought just once he would make her cry out for him, something he hadn't ever been able to do. Always, he had a feeling there was a part of her locked away, forever unattainable.

She moved her hips beneath him, arching up and grasping his hips to pull him closer.

"You want me, Raye?"

"Yes!"

"Then tell me," he ground out hoarsely, fighting for control over his body, trying to wait. Her eyes flew open only momentarily as she looked up at him and he felt a contest flare between them. "Tell me," he commanded.

She sighed, her hands playing over him, making him shake and groan while he touched and stroked her, each driving the other to a frenzy until he lost control and thrust into her violently, hearing her muffled cry as he moved his hips.

With an effort, he withdrew. She gasped and cried out, arching her back, thrusting her hips up and clutching at him.

"Laz, please . . ."

"Ask for me. Beg for it, baby," he whispered, trying to wait while she pulled at him and whimpered. Finally he took her, moving fast, lost in passion, hearing her cry out. Yet in the depths of his being, he felt as if he had no more reached that inner part of her or caused her to lose all her control than any time previously.

Later she lay next to him, her leg thrown over him while he stroked her back lightly, toying with her hair.

"Raye?" he asked, his voice deep. "Who hurt you?"

Her eyes opened, her hand stroked his chest, thick scratchy curls flattened against her palm. "What are you talking about?"

"Some guy hurt you badly."

She laughed softly. "No, he didn't. I told you. I almost married Bobby Zephyr, but we broke off and that was that."

Laz turned on his side to look into her eyes. "You're lying. What happened? It was a long time ago. What difference does it matter to talk about it now? Does it hurt that badly?"

She looked down at his hairy chest, watching curls flatten and spring back as her fingers shifted. "No. It doesn't hurt like it did. I was young and right off the farm and trying to break into show business, singing in cheap nightclubs in L.A. when I met him. He was new in the city too. He was five years older, twenty-two while I was seventeen. I gave my paycheck to him. He said we'd get married. He pumped gas and was a mechanic and he raced stock cars on the weekend. I told him my ambitions, that I wanted to be an actress. He talked about us singing together. He wanted to be a singer. I thought we were saving to get married. He played the guitar and sang, sometimes making up his own songs. He'd get gigs, playing and singing at night and on weekends at roadside joints. And I was as in love as any woman could be."

"So how'd you get hurt?" Laz prompted quietly when she stopped talking.

"I got pregnant," she said so softly Laz could barely hear. He tugged a long lock of silky hair through his fingers.

"I was ecstatic. I went home from work to tell him."

"And he didn't want the baby?"

"That is the understatement of the day. I thought he was going to beat the baby out of me. Why I didn't lose it that night I don't know. He went into a rage. I'd never seen him like that before. He left that night. The next morning, he came back all apologies and plans. We shouldn't have this baby, because we needed to save our money and we couldn't break into the big time with a baby. He wanted me to get an abortion."

"You didn't want one?"

"No. I wanted my baby," she said, and Laz knew enough about people to know now why part of Raye was always withheld. He suspected she had just made the real understatement of the night.

"We argued and fought. He promised there would be more children, promised everything. One night we went to a bar where he sang, and while he earned money, his friend poured drinks down me. Afterwards, the two of them drove me to a house and said someone wanted to see me. I was too drunk to protest. I didn't want the abortion, but I couldn't fight all three of them, couldn't stop it, and then it was done."

"Can you have children?"

"I suppose. The question has never come up again," she said flatly, and Laz was beginning to understand her better.

"That's why you broke up with Bobby Zephyr?"

"No. Which just goes to show you how dumb I was. Most women would have skipped right then, but not me. Even after the heartbreak of the abortion, I loved him. He made promises and I continued to give him my paycheck until one afternoon I went to his trailer to surprise him and found him with another woman. She was naked as a jaybird, Bobby half-dressed. I ran out and didn't answer the phone for a week while he skipped town with Annette and my savings." She rolled over. "So now you know about the dumb, green farm girl who wanted to be an actress."

He stroked her shoulder, leaning over to kiss her throat. "Someday you may want to get married."

"Not ever," she said evenly.

"Running your own store might not be as much fun as you think. It's a lot of responsibility."

"I keep books for Deborah. I've gone to market for her. That's what's nice about a small store—you get all kinds of experience. Laz, I haven't told you this," she said, and he braced for some dark secret to come forth like a hidden child or a huge debt. Women had a way of springing needs on him when he was naked in their arms.

"I design the dresses we sell at the boutique."

He laughed. "You sound like you're admitting you've got your hand in the till."

She shrugged. "No. It's just that I have more than a

passing interest in the store and in dresses. I want a career there and my designs sell well."

"How come you didn't tell me this sooner? That's impressive, Raye."

"It didn't come up."

He suspected there was more to it than that, but he didn't ask. She was closemouthed about herself. He wondered if she had ever told anyone about Bobby Zephyr before. He studied her, as implications of her latest bit of news settled. Van Loring's sold some of the best dresses in town. His mind began to click with possibilities.

"Who else knows about Bobby Zephyr?"

"My aunt did."

"What men since then?"

"None. I haven't had much interest in men, Laz."

"Until now. Have you ever seen Bobby Zephyr since?"

"As a matter of fact, yes."

He forced her to meet his gaze. "You're not still in love with him are you?"

"No!" She shuddered. "No. Not in any way."

"Where'd you see him?"

To his surprise she grinned. "Same place you see him. On television. He's a country-western singer and rather well-known. He doesn't go by Bobby Zephyr any longer. Heard of the Twisters?"

"Yes."

"He's the baritone. The lead guitar. It's his group."

"I'll be damned," Laz said, staring at her. "Has he seen you since?"

"Not that I know about. I'm not on nationwide television."

Suddenly, Laz caught her face in his hands, holding her tightly. "I don't want to share you with anyone."

"You don't have to," she answered, a sultry lethargy coming into her voice. He leaned forward to kiss her, his lips opening her mouth, his hands slipping down to cup her soft breasts as she stretched out on top of him.

It wasn't until breakfast the next morning while they sat on the patio beside his swimming pool, both heated in the winter, that he thought about their earlier conversation. She read the newspaper while he sipped hot, black coffee.

"Raye, I've been thinking about us."

"Hmm?" she asked, glancing at him across the top of the paper. She was dressed in a striped, hot-pink and yellow T-shirt and green shorts. She had her hair tied in a bandanna, and Laz studied her. In her relaxed moments, she looked like someone caught in a paint explosion, yet at work and social events, she was one of the best-dressed women in the room. At work she was attractive, in bed she was fantastic, but in between the two, her appearance was scary. Her bare leg rested against his leg.

"You design those dresses. You must be damned good."

"Thank you. They sell."

"Which ones are your design?"

"The ones from the shop I wear. The green dress you bought for your friend that time. Occasionally we've seen someone wearing one."

"Why in hell didn't you tell me sooner?" he asked, still puzzled by her. He couldn't figure her out and it bothered him. He was tempted to hire someone to punch out Bobby Zephyr.

"It wasn't anything that involved you."

"Well, that's beside the point. It takes more brains to design them than just to sell them. Who makes them?"

"I have two seamstresses I pay."

"Are you getting a good profit?"

She shrugged. "It's not great, but I don't own the store. I set that money aside so I can own a store someday." She moved her leg against his.

"I have to go to the office. Don't get me off course."

"I wouldn't think of it," she answered in a voice that did exactly that.

"Raye, I'm trying to have a serious conversation."

"I'm listening." Her leg shifted.

"I can tell how much you're listening. You want your own store. Maybe we can have an arrangement."

She lowered the paper. She had steadily refused to move into his place on a permanent basis, always giving him his things to take home so he would have nothing left at her place. He had the feeling an offer of an allowance wouldn't please her, so he had never made one, trying to figure some way to coax her to move in with him and give up her apartment.

"I didn't know you designed dresses. That puts a different light on things. Suppose I set you up in your own store? I take twenty percent interest in it; the rest is yours. If you leave me, you pay a penalty and the store reverts back to me if you can't buy out my twenty percent interest."

"What kind of penalty?"

"I should have something for my efforts. Ten grand."

"Your offer is generous since you'll be putting up the money," she said. She had been hoping something would develop to add to her savings, but she hadn't expected an offer like this, and she barely gave the ten-thousand-dollar penalty a thought. "And in exchange?"

"Damn. Sometimes I think you're the hardest woman I've known. You look like a child sitting there, but you have a heart of stone, Raye."

"You'll turn my head with such flattery."

"In exchange, you live here. You're here when I come home."

"What happens when you get tired of me? You might not be able to get rid of me."

"Sure I can. That's part of the deal. If I leave you, you get the store if you buy out my share. I put up the money and take the risk—I don't think that's unreasonable."

"You're not afraid of a common-law wife situation?"

"With you, never."

"I might change."

He shook his head, asking himself the same question honestly. He hadn't ever asked a woman to move in. It was as close to marriage as he would ever get and he knew he could be setting his financial world in jeopardy. But as he looked into her cool brown eyes, his qualms vanished. There was something about her that wasn't going to belong to another person no matter how much financial gain it might bring. "I'm safe with you."

She agreed. She liked him. He was an exciting man, more so than any she had ever known, but he was a hard man and cold even though he didn't realize it or see himself that way. She didn't want to be his wife. She was satisfied with their physical relationship; the business proposal sounded perfect. She had dreamed about her own store for years, scared it might always be beyond her. It would be worth the price to move in with him. And that was exactly how she viewed it without further questions. It never occurred to her to consider if she were safe with him.

Her gaze swept over the back of the three-story stone mansion, the long blue pool, the fountain and ornate garden to the west of the pool, the landscaped grounds stretching away with the elaborate safeguards and alarms, the pen of trained dogs that were released on the grounds at night.

"Shall I give Deborah notice today?"

"Yeah. We'll go look at locations."

"I know where I'd like to be."

"I'll bet you do."

"If I move in here, I'd like a room where I can put up my easel. A room with a lot of light."

"How about the southeast corner? Make all the arrangements and send me the bills. Have the southeast corner room done over. I suspect my twenty percent will bring a good return."

"I think it will. My designs sell. I'd like to market them beyond the local level."

"Whatever you want to do. Keep track of the business expenses. I'll get a contract drawn up."

He felt excitement bubbling in him at the thought that she would be here all the time. The house always seemed too large and too formal, cold to him, but it wouldn't if Raye were here. It needed a woman and Tess had never fit in. The house had overwhelmed her. He wondered if anything had overwhelmed Raye since Bobby Zephyr. He thought of the singer and marveled.

"You don't want children?"

"No. That desire was violently taken from me one night

long ago. It killed the need for more as well as the one that I was carrying."

As well as part of your heart, he added silently. He had had a tough youth and he was accustomed to bad situations, to loss and anger and unfairness. Sympathy was something long ago ground out of him, and he felt none now, merely realizing this was what caused her to shut part of herself away from others. But then, hadn't he done much the same, trying to block out the war years, the early days in this country when he would do anything to accumulate a few dollars?

"I'd like to have a party. I haven't had a party in this house in years." He leaned back, his gaze roaming over the house while he remembered parties in the early years. His gaze shifted to her, and he recalled how Tess hated to entertain and was intimidated by crowds of society people. "Mind being hostess?"

"I'd love to do it," she said, smiling at him with self-assurance, and he realized that in many ways she was very poised, perhaps because of her acting jobs.

"Good. I'll draw up a list and tell you what I want. Get the invitations printed. I can have my secretary address them."

"Give me the list. I'll address them."

"I want to ask Nick."

"You think he'd come?"

"I doubt it, but he might. He's doing other things he's never done before." His gaze went over the pink and yellow shirt. "Wear one of your designs, Raye. *Carmen* is coming to town. Want to see it?"

"Yes."

"Do you know anyone in the cast?"

Her eyes twinkled and she gave a negligent lift of her shoulders. "I don't know until we go and see who's in it."

"Why do I have the feeling you won't know a soul this time?"

She laughed. "You had a good time at all those parties."

"Come here, Raye," he said in a gruff voice, wanting her suddenly, amazed at how easily she aroused him. He pulled her up, crossed the patio to the cabana, and closed the door.

"Laz. The gardener will be here and the maid is—"

He kissed her, stopping her words, his hands working at the button that held her shorts. In seconds he pushed her clothes away, pushing her back against the wall, wanting to possess her with an urgency that consumed him.

Afterwards, he held her close against him, moving his head to talk in her ear. "I don't know what you do to me. You make me want you constantly."

"Good. You're a sexy man," she said, running her hands across his shoulders that were damp with sweat. He had been bare chested; he pulled up his jeans and fastened them, watching her while she straightened her clothing.

"Come swim, Raye. It's half an hour before I go to work."

"If I swim with you, you'll want to make love again."

"I'm exhausted."

"You never stay exhausted. Can you go with me to look at locations?"

"We'll go tomorrow."

She nodded, heading for the shower.

11

FEBRUARY, 1978

Dallas, Texas

Nick went to his father's party at the Highland Park mansion on a cool February evening. Cars lined the street for blocks as he drove slowly past them.

"You're not parking in the street?"

"There's no need," he answered, glancing again at

Darla. He thought she looked more beautiful than ever in a striking black and white pique dress. "We won't stay long. Just a token appearance."

"Maybe Laz has mellowed. After all, he invited you tonight."

"I'm the one who's mellowed," Nick said with a lopsided grin. "I accepted his invitation. In the past he's always sent orders.

"Why don't you go back with him, Nick?"

"And turn off my brain? No thanks." Nick drove the length of the long driveway, memories assailing him as he slid to a halt beside a magnolia tree.

"It'll be interesting to meet Raye Honeywall," Darla said. "I bought my dress at her new store, but she wasn't there at the time.

"I met her awhile back. She's nice."

Darla laughed. "She must be more than nice to interest Laz."

Nick smiled, linking her arm through his as they went in to the back gate and joined the crowd milling in the spacious front rooms of the mansion. In minutes, Darla left his side, moving off with a cluster of friends. He watched her walk away, thinking she was beautiful and easy company. He had known her since high school. She had married, then divorced, and she had no children. She had inherited a wholesale shoe business and was successful, with accounts in eight states.

"So you came," said a low voice, and Raye sauntered toward him. She was tiny, slender, and young, and it surprised him again that his father was so interested in her.

"Pretty dress," he said to her and she nodded.

"Thank you. It's from my shop."

"I've heard good things about it."

"Thanks to your father. He owns part of the business."

"I can well imagine. If it were anything except dresses, he'd be there half the week telling you how to sell them."

She laughed and he remembered before how pleasant it

was to watch her laugh. "As it is, he barely darkens the door and can't wait to get out."

"That's only because you're selling clothing. Don't ever diversify into oil or tools or sporting goods. My date bought her dress in your shop—it's a black and white . . ."

"Oh, the pique. That's one of my designs."

"You designed it?"

"Yes. I design about half the dresses I sell."

"I'm impressed," he said truthfully, studying her.

"Laz let me make over the southeast room into a studio."

"Maybe I'm going to have a stepmother," he said, teasing her.

"No danger, Nick. I'm not the marrying kind any more than Laz is."

Nick didn't believe her for a second. "I'll have to go up and take a peek at the studio."

"I'll show it to you after all the guests arrive." Raye patted his arm. "You're nice, Nick."

"Not the incorrigible he told you about?" Before she could answer, he said, "I came today to see if you've made any changes in him."

"How could I change your father?"

"This is a change. It's been years since he's thrown a party at this house."

"I don't intend to reform the man."

"You might be enough of a good influence that he'll change," Nick said lightly. "I'll let you know if he has."

"How can you tell at a party?"

"That's easy. If I'm home for an hour and he doesn't try to pressure me into doing something he wants, I'll know you've had a remarkable effect on him."

"Don't count on it, Nick. I'm sorry you two don't get along. I like both of you."

"She gives a good party, doesn't she, Nick?" Laz approached, his eyes on Raye.

"She does at that. I don't remember the last one here."

"Years ago. Go up and look at Raye's studio. She designs some of the dresses she sells. Pretty good, huh?" he asked, pulling Raye to his side. She smiled up at him and for an instant Nick felt a jolt of shock. Laz gazed at Raye with unmistakable longing. Nick couldn't recall ever seeing Laz look at a woman with such affection. Perhaps he *was* changing.

"How's the business going?"

"I'm hanging in there," Nick said in a noncommittal tone.

"I've got new neighbors to the east now. The Whittakers wanted a smaller house. The Leonards have moved too."

"Charlie Leonard works for me," Nick said, relieved and amazed when Laz dropped the subject of business.

"Charlie does? I'll be damned."

"Laz, Nick, if you two will excuse me, I see some guests arriving." Raye left them and Nick saw the Durands appear on the patio. Cimarron was dressed in a pale blue sheath, looking cool and posed, turning to listen to something her husband said. She laughed, gazing up at him, and Nick saw they were as blatantly in love as the last time he had seen them. He turned back to Laz.

"Raye's nice."

"She's a smart woman."

"Here comes another smart one."

"Who?"

"Durand's wife."

"You know her?"

"No, but I've talked to her about propane. She was supply manager with Van Horn Petroleum."

"I'll be damned. I didn't know that," Laz said. "Good-looking woman. I'll go speak to them."

"I'll look for Darla," Nick said, feeling good about coming to the party. He had actually had a conversation with Laz without being hustled and without a bad confrontation. Maybe Raye had really changed him.

Later when he was separated from Darla again, Laz appeared. "Come see Raye's studio."

"Sure," Nick said, moving through the crowd to the wide staircase, remembering the last time he had spent the night at home.

"She has a real head on her shoulders. You'd be surprised. I've known businesswomen before, but she's one of the shrewdest. You wouldn't guess it either. Here, down the hall."

Nick moved around the room gazing at Raye's sketches that were good, looking at material draped on dummy figures, a dress hanging on a rack, bolts of material. "I hear she has her own shop. You own part of the business."

"Yeah. It's a good investment even if there were strings attached. When are you coming back, Nick?"

Disappointment settled like a fog bank rolling into the room. "I'm not. I have my own company. The party's been fun until now," Nick said, heading toward the door.

"You can answer my questions. Why are you running a penny ante business when you can run Kamnick Oil?"

"Because *I* control Laredo Oil. I can never do the same with Kamnick Oil."

"I promise you—"

"You promised before and we both know the results. No thanks. This wasn't why I came today."

"If you keep on, I'm going to take that little two-bit company of yours and stomp it into the ground."

"You'll have a fight if you try."

"I swear, I'll let you do what you want at Kamnick. Come back. I'll give you a division and vice-presidency. That's a better offer than you can get anywhere else."

"And if I agree and sell my company or let you swallow it up, and then find out everything is just like it was last time, what do I do then? Start all over with nothing? I won't give you my time and effort again," Nick said as he walked out.

"Nick!"

Nick didn't slow his stride, moving in long steps, asking himself how old he would be before he would stop wondering if Laz would change.

Forgetting Laz, Nick returned to Tulsa. He had fifty employees now and was bidding for a percentage on offshore operations, headed by Terry Lund, a stocky geologist who had recently joined Laredo. If the three wells came in producers, Laredo Oil would gain substantially. In the meantime, along with Kevin Pitman, Nick studied reports and balance sheets, trying to find a small company with good reserves that Laredo could acquire.

Always he felt the specter of Laz breathing in the shadows behind him, expecting Laz to come out like a fiery dragon and demolish him. He was trying to build Laredo as quickly as possible so that when Laz made his move, Nick would be strong enough to fight. He had just made a prospectus to file with the Securities and Exchange Commission, making a registration statement to go public, a move that would give him more capital.

He moved impatiently to the window. In the distance he could see Star Tower. He thought of Cimarron Durand and the last time he had seen her with her husband at a dance. She was a beautiful woman, easy to watch, easy to remember. Laredo was bidding with White Star on the Gulf leases, and that very week Nick went to a charity auction, where Fontaine Durand auctioned his services as a valet for a day. The bidding rose swiftly while his auburn-haired wife watched with amusement. She was sleekly dressed in a deep-blue wool suit, her hair fastened in a smooth chignon.

As always, all her attention was focused on Fontaine, and once again Nick was fascinated by the lovely Mrs. Durand.

12

JUNE, 1978

Cancun, Mexico

The expanse of sparkling white beach and crystal water was relaxing, but Cimarron was preoccupied with Fontaine. She was thankful he had taken a week's vacation to be alone with her at their villa. He sat working, going over ledgers, occasionally raising his head to talk business to her.

Since their marriage, Fontaine had discussed White Star matters with his wife. He grew to value her opinions and he had drawn her into the business more and more. She was his sounding board.

"Remember when I told you about the problem with the tankers to Japan, and you came up with a solution before our supply department did?" he asked suddenly, putting his pen down and sitting back in his chair.

"That's because I'd faced the problem before."

"And because you're a better supply manager than ours."

"You're biased."

"No. I'm not when it comes to business. I think Ralston Taylor is jealous of you."

She dropped the newspaper she was reading. "That's absurd! He doesn't have any use for women in the oil business."

"No, he doesn't. Did you read these reports?" Fontaine asked, waving papers.

"Yes."

"What do you think? I've got to make a decision on the Canada leases."

"If it were my decision, I'd buy them. It's an undeveloped area and right now the market is down there. You'd get a good price. You said the geological logs and maps look promising." She moved beside him, shuffling through the papers. "Your projected buying price is a bargain compared to U.S. properties."

"We have twenty-one new wells going on-line in the Gulf."

"White Star's lease acquisitions are up thirty percent over last year. You're replacing reserves. What does Peyton Phelps say?"

"He's for it; Ralston opposes it. He thinks it's too risky. Peyton is always ready to gobble up land and leases."

"What do you think the board will want?"

"I think Ralston can sway them to his side unless I take

an opposing view. I wanted your opinion. We'd be going in at a time many are getting out."

"That may be the best reason of all. You'll really get a bargain."

He grinned and dropped his pencil. "It's a crime for a woman to be beautiful and intelligent too!"

"You better get back to work, Fontaine."

He laughed and bent over his papers while she returned to her chair and picked up the newspaper. After a while she realized he was watching her. She cocked her head to one side. "Now what's on your mind?"

"There's something I've been thinking about for several months. Who would take over if something happened to me?"

"Fontaine, you sound as if you suddenly turned one hundred years old."

"I'm having second thoughts about the way I have the company structured right now. Who do you think should take charge if something happened to me?"

"I don't like to talk about it."

"For a practical woman, you're getting silly. This is something we should discuss."

She shifted, feeling a chill and wishing he would change the subject because it bothered her.

"Everyone has wills and someone with responsibility for a company and family needs to make provisions. For a woman who usually has an astute mind for business, you're being contrary."

"All right. If something happens to you, Ralston will take over."

"Why Ralston, other than being president?"

"That's enough reason, but he's also aggressive. He looks as if he would like to take it away from you himself. You let him make many major decisions."

"You're right, as usual. Only I've changed my mind."

"Peyton?"

"What do you think?"

She shrugged. "I don't know. Ralston wouldn't accept Peyton. It would divide the company. Each man has his hand-picked people. Peyton isn't as aggressive."

"That's right. It isn't Peyton."

"So who's left?"

"The one who knows as much as I do about the company and as much as I do about how I like things run. The person who wants this company to succeed as much as I do."

Her eyes widened. "Fontaine!"

"You've been in on every big decision I've made. Some of them have been your decisions. You know as much about this business as any of the executives."

"You know I don't!" she said, sitting up straight and swinging her bare feet to the tile floor. "I could never run White Star. I don't even have an engineering or geology degree."

"You can hire all the engineers and geologists you want. You know this business and I've taught you more about it. I can help you learn as time goes by. I'm talking years from now."

The tenseness went out of her shoulders, and she leaned back in the chair. "I'm glad to hear you say that."

"I want you to learn all phases of it. Just keep your hand in, keep on listening and helping with decisions. You'll inherit my stock, so you'll be the majority stockholder anyway."

"You know I'm always interested in White Star, particularly its CEO and owner."

"You have a head for business that's better than many men I've known."

"Flattery will get you everywhere," she drawled in a sexy tone. He winked at her and she put the conversation out of thought.

When they returned to Tulsa, Fontaine had a board of directors' meeting, and when he walked through the door that evening, Cimarron met him in the hall. They kissed and finally she moved away.

"Right now, I'd like a drink. Come have one with me."

"What's the matter? Was the board meeting a fight?"

"Not too bad," he said. "Let's go outside where it's peaceful and cool." They sat on the pavilion overlooking the pond as sunshine cast long shadows across the water. "We're going to bid on the Canadian leases," Fontaine said, stretching out his long legs. He had shed his coat and tie and unbuttoned his shirt. She stroked his arm while he talked and sipped a bourbon and water. "Ralston fought it; he bitterly opposes it. Peyton was in favor."

"You've wanted those leases for some time now."

"And you helped me make up my mind about it," he said, leaning over to kiss her again. He slid his hand behind her head and looked into her eyes. "Come sit on my lap." He moved back, taking her in his arms and holding her tightly. "I need you, Cimarron."

She clung to him, thinking how fortunate she was, filled with happiness.

The bid was made on the Canadian land and it was purchased at a bargain price. Fontaine planned to go to Canada to set up an office, look at sites, and oversee the start of the operation in September. He wanted Cimarron to go with him.

When they arrived in the province of Alberta, Fontaine rented a Piper to fly over the land they had purchased. Dressed in jeans and a red sweater, she climbed in beside him. The weather was rough, and the plane ride made her queasy until she finally told him she had to go back. As they flew over acres of land, all owned by White Star, she tried to imagine the rigs that would someday be scattered across the ground.

As they flew back toward the small, private landing strip, the turbulence increased. Clouds were rolling in and lowering visibility, causing them difficulty. She looked at Fontaine and saw the tenseness in his shoulders.

"What's wrong?" she asked quietly, knowing from the muscle working in his jaw and his pale color that something was awry.

"We're off course, dammit, and we're low on gas. This damn strong wind has consumed more fuel than I calculated." Fontaine's knuckles were turning white, his fingers tightly gripping the controls.

"I'm trying to find a place to land." His words terrified

her as she gazed down at rough, tree-covered terrain. In minutes he said, "I'm taking us down. I have to. Oh, God, I'm sorry, Cimarron."

"Don't worry, Fontaine. We'll be all right," she said stiffly, the words having a hollow ring as they skimmed above treetops.

"Cimarron," he said.

She looked up and he kissed her swiftly and briefly. "Now put your head down and try and protect yourself."

She shivered with fear, praying silently. Aware the ground was rushing at them with alarming speed, she watched Fontaine descend between trees, heading for a tiny clearing on rocky ground.

"Get your head down!"

Trees popped as they swept across tops. With a violent crack the right wing was clipped. The plane spun, pancaking onto the ground. They had reached the tiny clearing but Cimarron was slung sideways and her door popped open, the seat belt holding her snugly. Her head cracked against something sharp and for an instant she was dazed. Then Fontaine was pushing her out, her seat belt gone.

"Cimarron, get out!"

She scrambled outside, flames shooting up in front of her as she ran. She looked back for Fontaine.

"Fontaine!"

He leaned out of the plane, blood streaming over his cheek. "Run! Cimarron, run!" he yelled hoarsely.

The explosion blew her off her feet and slammed her into unconsciousness. She felt a jagged pain until merciful blackness closed in.

13

She woke up gazing into a stranger's face. He wore a white coat and she realized she was in a moving vehicle.

"Fontaine—"

"We're on the way to the hospital," the man said.

Blackness enveloped her again and consciousness came and went in a blurred awareness of voices and hands and pain and constant fear that made her feel like ice, yet always in the back of her mind she saw the orange flames surrounding Fontaine. Once she stirred and thought she was watching the wheat field burn at the farm. She yelled Pierce's name and then Fontaine's image danced before her eyes.

"Fontaine!" she tried to cry out to him, but it was only a whisper, tears burning her eyes, pain making her shake and moan. She wanted to scream in protest, but only a moan came and then she felt violent chills and strangers trying to soothe her, injections that caused her to drift back to a deep sleep.

The first time she opened her eyes and all was finally clear, she looked at the stark hospital room and then at Peter's face. His eyes were red and gray stubble covered his jaw. He was holding her hand, and she didn't have to ask him, because she knew he wouldn't be at her side if Fontaine could have been.

"How'd you get here so quickly?"

"A White Star plane. You've been sedated. Honey, I'm sorry," he said in a raspy voice and she knew he was struggling for control. She turned her head away, tears flooding her eyes while she cried silently. His fingers tightened around her hand.

She sobbed and he pulled her against his chest, holding her as he had done time and again when she was a child, only this time the hurt wasn't a skinned knee; it would go on forever.

When she quieted, she lay back against the pillows, exhausted, wishing she could drift back into unconsciousness and oblivion to stop the pain that was overwhelming. She lifted her bandaged hand.

"You have a broken collarbone, cracked ribs, and two broken fingers."

"Broken fingers," she repeated dully. "Fontaine is dead and I have two broken fingers. I'll have to make arrangements for the burial," she said, but Peter shook his head.

"You can have a memorial service in Tulsa," he replied, and she knew the explosion had destroyed Fontaine.

"Where are we?"

"At the hospital in Canada," he said and received a flash of green eyes.

"In Canada?"

"Yes. When you're able, we'll move you home."

"You should be at the farm," she said, frowning. She couldn't remember a time when Peter was away from the farm overnight. He hadn't taken a vacation in all the years of her life. "You should go home. You don't have to be here."

"Tim's at the farm. I can leave. Stop fussing, Sunny. Tim can handle everything."

She settled back, fatigued by the brief argument, weighed down by sorrow. In another day she was able to dress and board a company plane that flew her home. Peter and Freedom planned the memorial service and as soon as it was over Peter drove her to the farm.

Her appetite was gone and she was so weak, the slightest bit of activity exhausted her. She didn't care. There wasn't anything left in the world she cared about. Megan and Peter pleaded with her to eat, but she couldn't tolerate more than a few bites.

The second weekend Freedom appeared. She was in her bedroom when she heard him downstairs, his deep voice loud in the quiet house. She hated the pity she saw in her family's eyes, yet everything seemed far removed from her as if she were watching strangers in a play.

Freedom appeared in the doorway. His cheeks were flushed from the cold, his woolen shirt was unbuttoned at the throat. He looked masculine and full of vitality and life and it hurt, bringing home again her loss, that she wouldn't ever see Fontaine come through a door again, wouldn't know that vigor and energy she had loved so much.

Freedom closed the door and she shut her eyes. He sat on the bed and pulled her up in his arms.

He smelled like tangy after-shave and he felt solid and hard as she clung to him and cried. She thought she had her emotions under control and now she discovered she didn't at all. She could only cling to Freedom and cry until she became exhausted.

His voice was hoarse when he placed her back against the pillows. "I'm sorry. I wish there were something I could do or say, Sunny."

"I know."

"They say you aren't eating."

"I don't want anything."

"Look, there's one thing you can do and you owe to Fontaine. He talked to me about six months ago. He told me he had everything set up so you'd take over the business if something happened to him."

She looked back out the window, memories crowding in.

"You owe that to him."

"White Star will go right on."

"Maybe. But if Ralston Taylor takes over, he'll change it and you know it. He wasn't Fontaine, and they didn't see eye to eye."

"With Fontaine gone, there doesn't seem to be much point to keeping White Star."

"Except that he loved it and he wanted it to go on and he expected you to do that for him."

Silence enveloped them while she stared out the window. She could remember all the times Fontaine had talked to her about the future of the company, his hopes and dreams.

She squeezed her eyes shut. "Freedom, I can't stop crying. How can I run a company?"

He held her hand tightly. "I'll help anyway I can. And when you have to cry, lock up the office and cry. But do what he wanted. It's the tiny part of him you can keep."

She gazed into green eyes that were so like her own. "I'll think about it, Freedom."

"No. You have to do more than think about it," he said firmly. He held her hand tightly and waited, watching her and hurting for her. She looked terrible, her eyes sunken and cheeks hollow, her skin ashen, slender fingers bandaged. She looked as if she had lost too much weight and he knew Peter and Megan were worried sick about her.

He felt his throat tighten as he watched her. He wanted to pull her into his arms and hold her and let her cry, but he fought the impulse.

"I just have to think. I can't say yes or no now."

"Every hour you let pass will strengthen Ralston's hold on the company. He's already taken charge. He and Peyton have clashed. He's fought with others. He's asked the board to put the Alberta project on hold."

She drew a sharp breath, and he knew it was devastating to talk to her about Canada, but there was only one thing that might put her back on her feet, so he continued, "If you give him much more time, you won't have a choice to make."

"Freedom, leave me alone. I can't do anything yet."

"I stood in Fontaine's office and listened to him talk about how he could count on you."

"Freedom, please." She turned her head to cry again and he felt terrible, but he persisted.

"Sunny, you're here on the farm insulated from the world, but you can't expect Megan and Peter to shelter you forever."

"Go away, Freedom. My head hurts and I'm exhausted."

"I'll go downstairs and get your dinner. You think about what I said. You think about what Fontaine wanted for you and White Star."

She cried, her face buried in the pillow. She looked at the

empty room, pushed back the covers, and sat up, waiting for her head to stop swimming. She pulled on a robe, brushed her hair, and stared at a reflection she barely recognized. She was gaunt, as bony as a skeleton, ashen colored. Her hair was a matted tangle.

Two days later she said, "Freedom, I'll go back to Tulsa with you. You can take me home."

By the time she had made the drive with Freedom back to Tulsa, she was totally drained. She had kept the servants on so the house was ready when she unlocked the back door and switched off the alarm. Freedom carried her bags inside.

She drew a deep breath as memories assailed her. Everything was Fontaine.

"Sunny, why don't you come home with me?"

She shook her head. "You talked me into coming back, Freedom. I want to be here. I might as well start tonight."

"And tomorrow?"

"I'll go to the office."

"Want to ride with me?"

"If you don't mind, just this once. I'd like that."

"Sure." He smiled at her. "I've put my savings in White Star stock. I guess I can keep it there with you taking charge."

She smiled and he crossed the room to hug her and suddenly all her control vanished and she burst into tears, clinging to him. When she finally regained her composure, she moved away to wipe her eyes, standing with her back to him.

"God, I hope I don't do that tomorrow at the office."

"To hell with it if you do. They would all know why."

"Wouldn't Ralston get a charge out of that. I'd never hear the end of it."

"No, you wouldn't," Freedom said.

"Trying to give me a challenge?"

"No. I'm telling you the truth. Ralston will try and demolish you, Sunny, and he won't be coy about it. You won't have Fontaine to protect you. Frankly, I know he wants me out of there. If it weren't for you, I'd be gone now. I don't like the bastard."

"He's done something?"

"He's pushing, but it won't matter if you stay. He's already made changes. You'll see. Carol resigned."

"Fontaine's secretary resigned? She's been with him for years."

"I think Ralston did it. He can be unpleasant and he wants people out who aren't on his team. One engineer is gone, Jason Carey. What's worse, Leo has changed jobs."

"Leo? Your supervisor?"

"My department is managing without him," he said, and she suspected Freedom had taken charge temporarily.

"What would I do without my family?" she asked, standing on tiptoe to hug him. He patted her shoulder.

"This is a hell of a big house. Sure you want to stay here?"

"It's home and in some ways I feel better here. You can move in here if you'd like."

"Thanks, but it's a little overwhelming for me. Sort of like a museum. See you later, Sunny."

Fontaine's things were all over the house. It was his house more than hers and she felt comforted by the ties that bound her to him.

At work the next morning she felt as if everyone was staring at her. They politely said hello as she entered at Freedom's side and he accompanied her to the office.

"You'll need a secretary. Sunny, there's one in my department, Sandy Yates. She's smart and reliable and the newest in the department."

"Thanks, Freedom. Will you ask her to come see me?"

"Sure. You know where I'll be if you need me," he said.

"I'll send a memo that we'll have a meeting this afternoon. The regular board meeting is scheduled for Wednesday."

"See you at lunch." Freedom left and in minutes Ralston came striding into the office, his dark eyes flashing.

"Good morning, Cimarron. If you've come to box up Fontaine's things, I can get a secretary to do it."

"No, Ralston, I came to work."

"You're moving into Fontaine's place?"

"Yes," she answered coolly, staring at him, seeing the anger in his gaze.

"Leslie will be happy to do your secretarial work."

"That's fine. I'll get a secretary."

"Leslie will know the ropes," he stated firmly. "She'll be much more help than someone new."

"Thanks," she said, smiling at him.

He left and in minutes Sandy Yates appeared. "Mrs. Durand?"

"Come in," Cimarron said, watching a petite blond cross the room and gaze at her with curious brown eyes. Within the hour Sandy moved to the empty office to take over secretarial duties for Cimarron. Peyton Phelps was out until eleven, and she arranged to eat lunch with him so she could be brought up to date on what had happened during the past weeks.

Over green salads, she listened to him. "Ralston brought it up before the board and got what he wanted. The board voted to temporarily close the Canada office, pull everyone back. Of course, he hopes *temporary* will be long lasting."

"Why would he do that?"

"You know he opposed it."

"But he knows that Fontaine wanted it."

"Fontaine is gone. Fontaine told me he had changed things so if something happened, you'd take over. Since you're here, I assume that's what you intend."

"Yes."

"Good. I wanted to hear you say that's what you plan. I knew if you didn't come back we'd lose Freedom too. If you stay, you're going to have a fight on your hands, but I'll back you all the way."

"Thank you, Peyton. I'll need help."

"What do you think are our top priorities?"

"Get the Canadian field developed, sell some Texas properties. Get this company pulled together and rolling again before someone decides to step in and take it over."

"I know. That's why I'm here. Ralston may make it damned unpleasant. Want some advice?"

"Sure."

"You can use my secretary if you want, but you should hire your own replacement for Carol."

"Freedom suggested Sandy Yates. She's already at work."

Peyton leaned back looking pleased. "Good for you. I figured Ralston would try to get you to use Leslie's services. While she's good, she's definitely loyal to Ralston."

"If we're too divided, Ralston is going to have to go."

"Don't make hasty moves." He laughed. "Listen to me, giving you advice."

"I welcome advice. Fontaine always listened to you."

"I didn't volunteer advice until asked."

"You can volunteer all you want," she said. "It helps to think about White Star problems. This has been my easiest day so far, but I'll have to admit, I'm wearing out."

"Go home."

"And let Ralston take charge?"

"He won't do much in one afternoon."

In the car Peyton said, "There's a meeting with the Kamnick people on the leases we have with them. Ralston is going."

"When is the meeting? He didn't tell me."

"Tomorrow morning at ten at the Fourth National."

"He wasn't going to tell me about it, was he?"

"I can't answer for Ralston."

"I wonder what else he's doing that I should know about." She rode in silence, glancing at the handsome man beside her, wondering why he hadn't ever married. At the office, she thanked him and went straight to Ralston's office, rapping lightly on the door after telling Leslie that she wanted to see him.

Ralston motioned to her to have a seat. He was on the phone and in minutes hung up the receiver.

"I hear you have a meeting with the Kamnick representatives tomorrow morning," she said. "I'd like to go along."

"It won't be necessary, Cimarron, and you're not up to date on the latest figures from the field."

"Then please get the information to me, so I can get up to date," she said. She could feel the clash of wills and wondered if they could ever work together.

"I'll tell Leslie, but there's no need and you'll have plenty to do here at the office. There are some letters for you to sign on your desk."

"I'll look them over," she said, standing. "And I'm going to the meeting tomorrow. It's at the Fourth National Building?"

"That's right," he said tightly, and she knew he was angry.

"What's happening in Canada now?"

"The board voted to temporarily close down the operation. It isn't feasible."

"You know Fontaine wanted it."

"Some decisions had to be made, and the board voted to close it. I think if you study data from that area, you'll agree we're going to lose money if we pursue drilling there."

"That's not what Fontaine felt about it."

"You can't understand all the elements involved. In six months I can give you a report that will verify what I say."

"We have a board meeting next week. We'll discuss it then."

"Fine, Cimarron," he said, his face flushing.

She moved out of the room, anger making her quicken her step. He hadn't liked a woman having a job as distribution coordinator. He wasn't going to like having one for CEO at all.

She closed the door to her office and stared at Fontaine's desk, seeing him lounge back in the chair, remembering so clearly, aching with hurt for him. Tears spilled over without warning and she leaned against the door and cried.

She heard a knock and hastily tried to wipe away her tears. She opened it and to her chagrin faced Ralston. His eyes narrowed, and she saw a flare of satisfaction.

"Tears, Cimarron? Why don't you go home? You'll be bombarded with memories of Fontaine if you stay here."

"It isn't any less painful at home."

"No, but a tearful widow isn't going to present a solid front to the world. If this company looks like it's in trouble, the sharks will move in for the kill."

"I'm all right, Ralston," she said stiffly. "You won't see a tearful widow again," she said, hoping she could keep her promise.

"Fontaine's memories are everywhere you look," he said softly. "His office, his company, his car, his desk."

"Did you need to see me?" she asked too sharply. Ralston was needling her, and she was letting him get away with it.

"Yes. Here are the new acquisitions in the Gulf and some prospects."

She took the papers from his hand. "I'll read these tonight."

As soon as he left, she looked at the four letters Ralston had left. None of them were important and she wondered what had happened to the other correspondence that should have been on Fontaine's desk. She wanted to look through Leslie's out basket, but she resisted the temptation. Ralston would realize soon enough she was there to stay.

Wednesday morning she asked Peyton where she could reach Porter Scoggins.

"He's no longer with us. Ralston fired him last week. They had a disagreement about something and Ralston let him go."

"Peyton, is that all you know about it?"

He laid down his pencil and studied her. "I talked to Porter. I wanted to straighten it out, but he was so pissed off at Ralston, he wouldn't listen. Ralston wanted him out and he saw to it that their differences came to a head."

"Fontaine thought Porter had a great deal of potential."

"That may be why he's no longer with us," Peyton replied.

"If I try to reopen the Canada office, who can I send up there to run things? That was perfect for Porter. I want the board to consider reopening the Alberta office and now I find out we don't have a man to run it."

"Don't do anything about it right away. Send John Marks up there."

She thought it over. "I'll postpone it. I don't have a choice." She felt as if everything were slipping out of her grasp; as if she were failing Fontaine. She went to her desk, her mind scrutinizing their engineers and geologists. In minutes she pressed the intercom.

"Sandy, would you find Manning Thompson and ask him to come see me?"

"Right away, Mrs. Durand," came her reply, and within the hour Cimarron had a man to run the Canadian operation. It hurt to think about Canada. If it weren't the best thing for the company, she would let Ralston sell if off. She simply closed her mind about it, trying to keep haunting memories at bay.

The first board meeting was brief, routine, everyone treating her kindly because of Fontaine, but Cimarron knew that first meeting was an exception. By January of the new year, she was ready to bring up Canada again. Three minutes before the board meeting, Peyton appeared. "Ready?"

"You go along. I'll be there in a moment." Her stomach churned because she knew a battle loomed. Beneath her fear over tangling with the board of directors was determination to see that Fontaine's wishes were carried out. Taking a deep breath, she went to the meeting.

She glanced around the room, remembering when Fontaine had shown it to her late one night. His picture hung on the paneled walls along with his father's and grandfather's. She greeted men she barely knew, smiling at Sandy who would take minutes.

They discussed routine matters that were handled with dispatch and finally she led into the Canadian matter by turning to Ralston. "Now to some more old business. Ralston, tell the board about Manning Thompson, the kind of engineer he is."

"He's the best we have. He'll head up the drilling in Texas."

She glanced at Peyton whose brows arched in surprise and he nodded. "He's a good man."

"I want him to head the Canada operation instead," Cimarron stated. "I want to reopen the office and I'd like a vote by the board about it."

Ralston's face flushed. "If you drill in Canada, it'll bleed this company dry. The market is lousy there. This board agreed to abandon Canada,'' he said, looking at the three men who usually voted with him, Dr. Wilson Hayes, Mark Ritchey, and Nathan Whitmire.

''It was a temporary closing according to the minutes. Fontaine wanted to drill in Canada,'' she argued. ''He thought it had good prospects and so did Porter. I want you to reconsider,'' she said, looking at each man, ''to open the Canadian office again. It's a gamble, but so is every well we drill. There are incredible risks in this business; all of you know that. Fontaine and I discussed this several times; he felt it would be profitable and I think it will be. I can't produce conclusive proof that it'll pay, but last summer you agreed to go ahead. Fontaine was highly in favor if it. We're in a good position to do this right now.''

''We've already agreed to scrap it,'' Ralston snapped.

Cimarron gave him an impassive look. ''I recommend we reopen the office in Canada. I know how strongly Fontaine felt about it, and you know how often he has been right in his judgments.''

''That's damned sentiment!'' Ralston snapped.

''I don't have one shred of sentiment about Canada.''

Bob Lowman leaned forward. ''When we voted to close the office, things were in a turmoil. Now Mrs. Durand has stepped into her husband's place. We were all set to go on this.''

''If Manning is such a hotshot engineer, what does he think about it?'' Mark asked.

''He thinks it looks good. He has talked to Porter Scoggins about it. Porter was going to head the Canada office.''

''Fontaine expected to make a good profit,'' Peyton added. ''I'm in favor of it.''

''It can be profitable and I'm willing to stake my future with the company on Canadian development.'' She waited in a tense silence.

''It'll be a damned costly mistake!'' Ralston snapped. ''One or two costly mistakes and this company will be gone. And while you've inherited your husband's place, you have little experience in this area, Mrs. Durand.''

"I gave you Manning's opinion. You know what Porter's was and what Fontaine's was. Peyton favors it," she answered coolly, controlling her anger, hearing the condescension in Ralston's tone.

"Perhaps you should postpone working in Canada until next year," Nathan Whitmire said.

"We need to have a motion to vote," Cimarron said.

"I move we approve of opening the Canada office," Peyton said instantly.

"I second," Bob Lowman said.

"All in favor?" Cimarron asked and heard the assenting answers, Sandy counting quickly. Only four were silent, and she had won.

Because of weather and personnel complications, it was June before they could finally drill in Canada. Work started and in a short time Manning called her. "I think we've made a good investment." She listened to a report on drill cuttings and his projection.

"Call me the minute you know."

"I think Mr. Phelps might want to fly up here."

"I'll talk to him," she said, knowing that Manning wanted Peyton to be on hand. She never wanted to go back to Canada again. "Call me at home if it's night."

"Yes, ma'am."

She went down the hall to Peyton's office to tell him the news. "I think Manning wants you there and Freedom might like to go with you. He knows how I feel about this."

"Good. I'll talk to him. Here's the report you wanted."

"Thanks."

"Ralston intends to present to the board the need to plug and abandon the west Louisiana onshore wells."

"Why?" she asked, seeing a bigger battle looming.

"Not as profitable as he thinks they should be."

"How profitable does it have to be to please him?" She closed the door. "I wonder if I'll fight him on everything."

"You're doing fine. Don't worry about Ralston. Do what you think you should," Peyton said, and she smiled.

"You and Freedom. You're my cheering section."

"You're doing a damned good job, Cimarron," he said.

He stood up and came around to her to put his hands on her shoulders. "The stockholders should love you. We're up eight points."

"Okay, Peyton. Thanks for your support." She went back to her office to call Freedom. He wanted to go to Canada and said he would stop by her office to talk to her about it.

He closed the door behind him. He had shed his coat and tie, his sleeves were turned back, his blond hair tangled, and she knew he was laboring over something that was giving him trouble.

"Can you get away to go?"

"I'd like to go. I don't have another meeting with the investment bankers until the twentieth, and the tax people are coming in then too. I have to get the joint interest billings out and file severance tax reports, but other than that," he said with a grin, "I can go to Canada for a few days. Manning thinks it's going to be good."

"I think he'd like me to be there, but I can't go."

"You don't need to go and you know it. Besides, you better stay and keep an eye on Ralston." He moved restlessly around the room.

"Were you planning on going to the farm this weekend? Megan called last night and wanted to know."

"Yes, but one weekend soon, I'm going to look for a house or condo. I'm tired of pouring money down the drain in rent."

"You know you can stay at my place."

He smiled. "You might cramp my lifestyle."

She laughed. "Still dating Marie?"

"Actually there's Marie and Janet at the moment," he said with a grin.

She shook her head. "So what are you considering?"

"I want a condo that doesn't have one blade of grass."

"I don't know how you can dislike farming so much that it carries over into your everyday life. You won't even keep a geranium."

He grinned. "Want to go with me to look at places?"

"Maybe you better take Marie or Janet. They might have more of a vested interest," she teased.

"Nope, they surely don't and I'm not taking either one of them."

"You know, Freedom, sometimes you're too self-contained for your own good. You won't have live plants, you won't date anyone from White Star. You never want to get entangled with a plant or an animal or a person." She ran her hand across her forehead. "Listen to me, I'm sorry. You've been so good to me. You're definitely entangled with me."

He smiled at her. "I'm not entangled."

"Freedom, call me the minute they bring the well in."

He grinned broadly. "Don't worry. You'll hear me yell."

14

NOVEMBER, 1979

Tulsa, Oklahoma

When the well came in and was named Cimarron Number One, Freedom suspected he felt as much satisfaction as his sister. He had spent weekends house hunting and by November he still hadn't found anything he liked. Although he had an appointment to look at a new listing on the market this afternoon, he wasn't very hopeful.

So when he stepped out of his car and saw the condo complex, he was surprised by his favorable first impression. Of course that may have had a lot to do with the real estate agent Judy Hornsby. He had already learned that she was thirty, divorced, and liked skiing, one of his favorite hobbies. They had a date for dinner and as she moved ahead of him to the entrance of the condo, he watched the slight sway of her hips.

"The door's open," she said with a frown as they

stepped into the empty living room from the short entry hall. "Yoo-hoo," she called.

"This is great," he said, gazing around him at the bay window on the south, the enclosed patio beyond it, and the bookshelves along one wall. The room was airy and light with a wood-burning fireplace and a wet bar behind closed double doors.

"It's the perfect location," Judy remarked enthusiastically.

They heard voices and Judy walked around. "Someone else is here. Yoo-hoo!" she called, raising her voice. "You can see all the possibilities. And the patio is lovely. Complete privacy. Wait until you see the master bedroom."

Two women appeared and it was easy to spot the real estate saleswoman, because she was dressed in neat gray woolen slacks and a gray cashmere sweater. The woman with her was in a denim skirt and a flowered shirt; her hair was fastened in a bun on top of her head. Freedom recognized her because he had met her at the races once with a group of oil men. He couldn't remember her name, but he knew she was Laz Kaminski's girlfriend.

She was too thin, too short, and rather plain looking. Actually, she looked about eighteen years old and he wondered what fascination she held for a man like Kaminski. He vaguely recalled something about Kaminski setting her up in business, but Freedom wasn't sure exactly what she did.

As he listened to the conversation between the two real estate women, he realized that the other agent should have made arrangements with Judy's company to look at the condo. He strolled into the kitchen, running his hand over gray cabinets. Always able to make up his mind quickly, he decided this was the place for him.

"Here's the pantry and this is a Jenn-Air range—"

"Let's look at the bedroom."

"It's right down the hall," Judy said with a sweep of her hand. As she joined him in the bedroom, she whispered, "There's a box with the key to the apartment and other agents can show a place, but if they do, they're supposed to call the agency with the listing."

"I like it," he said, looking at the large bedroom that also had sliding glass doors to the patio.

"Freedom," she whispered, moving close to him. "I think that customer likes it too. We've had two other condos in the area and they've sold instantly. Right now there aren't any others in this area available."

"What's the price?"

"Ninety thousand."

The price was lower than anywhere else he had looked. He could hear the murmur of voices from the front room as he looked at the large bathroom and walk-in closet. He followed Judy across the hall to a smaller bedroom.

"Offer eighty-five," he said, knowing it was perfect. "I don't need to look any longer."

"I think you should go at least eighty-six."

"Okay. Eighty-six."

"If we leave, they may realize you're going to make an offer. Ninety is an excellent price for this place. Why don't I go call and you stay here and look. I'll call my office and get in touch with the owner and come right back and get you."

"Fine."

She left, moving quietly through the condo. With his hands in his pockets, he walked into the kitchen. The other client was there, singing softly, and he realized the voice he had heard was hers only.

"Where's your agent?"

"She went out to her car," she said blandly.

"You don't live in Dallas any longer?"

She looked at him intently. "Have we met?"

"You're a friend of Laz Kaminski. We met at the races in Louisiana one time. I'm sorry, I don't remember your name."

"Raye Honeywall."

"Freedom Chisholm," he said, offering his hand. Hers was cool and dry and touched his only briefly.

"You've moved from Dallas?" he repeated.

"Not permanently. I'm opening a boutique here and this is temporary."

"Permanent home for a temporary stay?"

She shrugged. "I'm thinking about it," she said with such nonchalance, he guessed Kaminski was paying for it.

Freedom sauntered into the living room. No cars were parked in front and suddenly he knew that her agent had also gone to make an offer.

He glanced over his shoulder, glimpsing her bending down to peer into a kitchen cabinet. He went outside, striding to the curb, his patience gone. He looked back at the place. It was perfect, a jewel at the price, and in the right location. He would not be pleased if he didn't get it because some woman was buying it for temporary reasons. He peered down the street impatiently. In minutes Judy's car came into view. She slowed and stopped across the street.

"They've already made an offer of eighty-eight and it was accepted."

"Damnation! Dammit to hell."

"I told the owner that we had the appointment first to show the place; they should have waited until they heard from us."

"Would it do any good to make a higher offer now?"

"No. They accepted her offer. I'm sorry, Freedom."

"Oh, hell. I know you want the sale as much as I do. Dammit, the place is perfect." He glared at the condo, anger rising. "She isn't even going to stay here long. She's opening a shop and going back to Dallas."

"You know her?"

"I've met her before. Let me go talk to her. I don't have anything to lose." Trying to control his temper, he crossed the street in long angry strides. He strode into the living room to find her waiting.

"I hear your offer has been accepted."

"Sorry if this is what you wanted, but I like it very much and we were here first."

"Look, you said you aren't staying here permanently."

"No, I'm not," she answered coolly and his temper frayed more. "But it's just what I want while I'm here."

"This is perfect," he said grimly. "It's the right location

for me. How about a little profit to hunt for another place. You don't want this for years to come."

"I'm sorry, Mr. Freedom."

"Chisholm," he said tightly.

"Oh, Mr. Chisholm. I'm sorry, but it's what I want. I'm sure in all of Tulsa, you'll find something you like."

He clamped his jaw shut, knowing it was useless. He spun around and left, swearing under his breath as he strode to the car. "She wants it all right."

"I'm so sorry. Let me make some calls and see if I can't come up with something else."

"Dammit, you won't find anything for the same price."

"No. I don't think I can find that much square footage. I'm really sorry."

He grinned and ran his hand through his hair. "Sorry if my temper's showing. I hate to lose something I want. It wasn't your fault. You tried."

They climbed into the car, and she pulled away from the curb smoothly, making a U-turn and entering the traffic at the boulevard.

"I'll check and see what else we have. Would you like to look at the place on Sixtieth?"

"Sure. I may as well look."

They looked at three more places, and he didn't like any of them. He tried to be pleasant, knowing Judy was as upset over the lost sale as he was.

During December, Freedom picked up the phone to hear Linda, his secretary. "Mr. Chisholm, there's a Judy Hornsby on the phone who says it's an emergency and she needs to talk to you. I told her you were on your way into a meeting, but she said you would want this message."

"Sure. Let me talk to her," he said, suddenly wondering if the deal involving the Honeywall woman had fallen through.

"Freedom, this is Judy. I know you're in a meeting, but another condo in Partridge Hill just came on the market. We got the listing about two minutes ago."

"What's the price?"

"One hundred and two."

He groaned. "Dammit. What's it like?"

"Exactly the same inside except the kitchen is oak instead of ash and all the appliances are new, the paneling in the living room is lighter and the fireplace is stone instead of marble."

He was thinking about his finances. One hundred and two would stretch him thin. "Think they'll take under one hundred?"

"No. I think it's a firm offer. Those have sold like hot cakes as you know."

He figured on a scratch pad, remembering the condo clearly, mentally calculating if he would have to sell any White Star stock or curtail his regular buying of it. "Okay. offer one, two. Let me know."

He had been in the meeting only minutes when Linda rapped on the door and stepped inside to give him a note. He got up and left to call Judy.

"You now own a condo," she said happily.

"Broke, but a roof over my head. Good deal! I didn't ask. Where is it in the complex?"

"Across the hall from the other one."

For an instant his grin faded. "Damn. I live across the hall from that bitch."

"You might not ever see her. You won't care. This place is gorgeous from what they say."

"Good. I get off at five. Can we go look?"

"Sure. I'll pick you up."

"I'll come get you. It's on the way."

Two mornings later he told Cimarron as he paused at her office. "I own a home."

"Do you really?" she asked, her brows arching. He leaned his shoulder against the jamb, watching her as she moved away from a file cabinet to her desk. His gaze flicked over her and he realized that she was looking more like her normal self. She was far too thin, but her coloring was better, the dark circles beneath her eyes were gone. She had cut her hair short, combing it away from her face, giving her a businesslike appearance. She had changed, becoming more withdrawn, and he knew she seldom went out, never dated.

"I'm glad. For a time there I thought you were going to have a breakdown over losing the other condo."

"Yeah. Well, I don't like to lose something I want."

"Once you make up your mind, Freedom, it's forever. Tell me about this one."

"It's the same place," he said grinning.

"The woman—or as you call her, the bitch—moved?" she said, laughing at him.

He grinned. "No. I wish she had, and this cost me a hell of a lot more. I'm going to live across the hall from her."

"The same place?"

"Yes. Another condo came on the market. That's why I left the meeting the other day."

"How nice. I can't wait to see it."

"Come eat lunch with me and I'll show it to you. I already have a key because the people moved out."

She glanced at the calendar on her desk. "Sure. Okay. I don't have anything planned."

At noon she left with him, going into a blustery day. A walk led up to a red-brick building, windows trimmed with white shutters. Inside the wide front hall were two doors to condos opposite each other. Already the place had changed. The front hall had pots of greenery in corners and along the walls and a hanging basket was in front of one of the long windows at the front. Freedom unlocked his condo and as he did, the front door opened and Raye Honeywall entered the hall with a gust of cold air. She stopped, her eyes widening in surprise. "Hello."

He gazed back coolly. "Hello. I'm your new neighbor," he said, irritation returning when he thought of the extra fourteen thousand he had had to pay.

"You're kidding," she said, frowning.

"I'm not going to throw orgies," he snapped, his temper rising. "Hopefully, you won't even know I'm here. I'm quiet. And I mind my own business."

She blinked at him, spots of color rising in her cheeks. Cimarron was amazed at the hostility smoldering in Freedom. "I'm Cimarron Durand, Freedom's sister."

"Raye Honeywall. And I guess I'm his neighbor." She unlocked her door while Cimarron and Freedom entered his condo. As soon as he closed the door, Cimarron confronted him.

"Freedom, you were dreadful."

"Do you know what that bitch has cost me?"

"Stop calling her a bitch. She simply bought a place before you did."

"I'll bet she doesn't stay here six months and then she'll sell it."

"You're dreadful when you want something."

He laughed. "Stop chewing me out. I'll call her Miss Honeywall or Kaminski's broad or whatever you want."

Cimarron laughed. "Miss Honeywall sounds nice. This is lovely."

"Sure you wouldn't like something smaller? I don't know how you tolerate that giant house of yours."

"It's a tie with Fontaine," she said, and he bit back an argument.

"I need to get some new living-room furniture. Want to help?"

"Sure. What was the other place like?"

"Almost the same as this one."

"Where's her boutique?"

"I don't know, Sunny. We haven't talked much."

"Poor soul. Don't glower at her."

"She glowers at me."

"With good reason."

"Come look at this kitchen." He showed her around and that weekend she helped him select a sofa, two end tables and lamps. The deal was closed in two weeks, and the condo was officially his. He didn't see his neighbor again until the first week in January when he opened the front door. A roll of smoke enveloped him and his heart lurched. For an instant he thought the whole building was on fire, but through the smoky hallway, he saw Raye Honeywall waving her arms as she coughed and choked.

He yanked her by the hand and pulled her outside. "Have you called the fire department?"

"No! It's my stove," she said coughing. "I was in the shower."

He ran past her into her place, holding his handkerchief over his nose. Flames raced up the kitchen wall as grease burned in a skillet. Looking around, Freedom swore and yanked up a metal lid, slamming it over the burning skillet. He coughed and choked as he ran to the sink, turning on both faucets, using the spray hose from the sink to squirt water over a burning curtain. A pot holder still burned on the counter and he squirted water over it and the blackened wall. Pushing pots of flowers off the windowsill, he raised the window and ran. His lungs and chest felt on fire. Gasping for breath, he raced to his living room and stretched out on the floor.

She screeched and flung herself down beside him, grasping his head.

"Mr. Chisholm!"

"I'm all right," he tried to say, but it came out a croak.

"Oh, my word! Don't move. I'll get help."

"Hey," he said, sitting up. A wave of dizziness struck him and she was gone, running across the room in her high-heeled slippers, her bottom jiggling beneath the terry cloth. He swore and fell back and shut his eyes, trying to get his breath.

In minutes she was back, kneeling down beside him. "I called an ambulance."

"You *what*!" He sat up, fought another bout of dizziness and gulped for air. "I'm all right," he said in a hoarse whisper.

"You don't sound all right. I'd already called the fire department."

"Call the damned ambulance and tell them not to come."

"I think you need to go to a hospital emergency. I'd feel terrible if something happened to you because of my smoke."

"Do you know what an ambulance costs?"

"I'll pay. I think you need to see if you're okay. Your voice is going."

"It'll come back," he argued persistently, wondering why he had to have her for a neighbor. A siren could be heard in the distance. "Oh, dammit, here it comes. Help me up."

"I think you should be still. It's probably the fire department."

"We don't . . . need them. Put out the fire." His chest hurt with each breath.

"You put out the fire? That's dangerous! I better speak to them."

He swayed and stretched on his sofa, gasping for breath. Too soon she was back. "The firemen are in my place. They said you should have left the fire for them to handle. But thanks. It was brave of you." Another siren whined and he caught her wrist. "I want you to tell those people to go away. I'm not going with them," he struggled to say, gasping for breath.

"I'll ride with you."

"That really isn't an inducement," he said slowly.

She blinked and drew herself up. "I feel responsible."

"There's no way you're responsible for me." With an effort he went into the hall. The front door stood open, firemen moving back and forth. Through the open door Freedom saw an ambulance pulled to the curb, its lights flashing. Two white-coated paramedics climbed out and she hurried to meet them, waving her hands at Freedom. She ran back into her place and reappeared as he argued with the attendants.

"We'll get you to the emergency."

"I don't need to go, dammit!"

"You're suffering smoke inhalation. Mister, that can do something to your lungs. Now come get in the ambulance."

They argued until Freedom gave up and climbed in. Raye spoke to the fire chief and then sat beside him. She sat with her legs crossed, a sweater around her shoulders, looking as calm as if she were in a business suit on the way to the office. After an hour the doctor explained that although Freedom had sustained some lung damage from the smoke, it was minimal and would heal in a few weeks. In the meantime he was not to engage in extreme physical activities.

As Freedom moved toward the door, Raye got up from a

chair in the waiting room. He wanted to put his hands around her skinny neck and shake her.

"I've called us a taxi," she said.

They went outside, and if she were aware of stares from people around them, she gave no indication. They rode in silence and he paid the taxi. A faint cloud of smoke still hung in the air in the hall.

"You went off and left your front door open," he rasped, wheezing with the effort.

"I think the least I can do is offer to take you to dinner."

"Thanks, but no thanks."

"I insist. I feel terrible about your lungs. I'll pay your bill when it comes."

The last thing Freedom wanted to do was spend another hour with her. "I'll send you the bill. That's a promise."

She took his arm. "I need to air my place and change clothes and then we'll go eat."

"No. It isn't necessary."

"I have to. I've caused you pain and inconvenience."

"That's an understatement."

"And I want to make it up to you in some small way and dinner is one thing I can do."

"Do you understand? I do not want to eat dinner with you."

"You need someone to take you to dinner. Come sit down while I change."

"I can wait in my place."

He glanced through the open door at the pall of smoke. "Oh, Lord," he mumbled. "It's too smoky for you to stay in there. Bring your things to my condo. I've got a fan."

He unlocked his door and rummaged in the front closet until he found the box with the fan. He took it to her place. He glimpsed a room filled with plants, antiques, and pictures. He opened windows and plugged in the fan, and then hurried outside to take deep breaths of air while he swore.

The acrid smell of smoke also filled his condo. A bedroom door was shut, and he realized she had gone into his extra bedroom to change. He stretched out on the sofa to wait for her. His chest hurt and the thought of spending another hour with Raye made him grumpy.

"I'm ready," she said, standing in the center of the living room in jeans and a thick blue sweater. Her black hair fell in a shimmering cascade below her waist and for the first time she looked rather attractive. Until he took a deep breath and felt the sting in his lungs. Then he remembered the cause of his pain.

She looked all around. "You'd never know this is just like my condo."

"You don't like it," he said, remembering his brief glimpse of her place with its frilly pillows and doodads and plants.

She gazed slowly around the room at his Danish modern furniture and only picture composed of three broad stripes of red and black paint. "You like things plain."

"And you like them busy."

"I hadn't thought about it looking busy," she said, sounding huffy.

"I'd just as soon skip dinner."

She flashed him a broad smile and it transformed her features. "I know. I don't like you either, but what you did was nice. We don't have to talk to each other but you have to eat. Your girlfriends will be glad I took care of you."

He laughed and shook his head. "Has anyone ever told you how stubborn you are?"

She tilted her head to one side as she fell into step beside him. "I don't recall that they have. Maybe you bring out the worst in me. Has anyone told you what a grouch you are?"

"My sister."

"Ahh. I'll drive. You might pass out."

He was becoming amused by her constantly taking charge. It was new in his life. He settled into her small Toyota. She drove in jerks and quick turns that threw him against the door or toward her.

"You were a taxi driver before you got in the dress business."

"Now why do you say that?"

"Aren't you about twenty miles over the speed limit?"

"What a back-seat driver you are!"

"Maybe we should declare a truce," he said as she spun into a parking lot and slammed to a stop. He braced himself against the dash board and avoided bumping his head on the windshield. "I'll drive home."

"We'll see how your lungs are," she said and stepped out. He half expected her to run around, open the door, and yank him out of the car, but she waited for him and he held open the door to the restaurant. They stared at their menus in silence and ordered as soon as the waiter reached their table.

"I was heating oil to fry a chicken. That's what started the fire. I forgot about it."

Freedom bit back a comment. "Where's your shop?"

"In West Wind Center."

"The new place?"

"Yes. I'm opening a branch. I have a store in Dallas."

"Still friends with Kaminski?"

"Yes." She turned her head and he looked at her shining hair. His lungs hurt and it took an effort to talk. He had no interest in pursuing a conversation with her, so he sat in silence and sipped a cup of hot tea. She did the same, gazing out the window. They ate the entire meal without further conversation and he couldn't recall that ever happening when he was out with a woman, but it was peaceful and in this case, just what he wanted. For long moments at a time, he could almost forget she was present.

She took the check, paid, and they left. He held out his hand and blocked the car door. "I'll drive home."

She looked at him, dropped the keys in his palm, and went around to climb in the passenger side of the car. At home they stepped into the front hall that still reeked of smoke.

"I think you're going to have to call one of those places that gets the smoke smell out after a fire. Look, you might as well bring your things and spend the night at my place," he added reluctantly.

"Oh, thank you, no!"

He grinned at the look on her face. "I won't attack you. I guarantee that."

She laughed then, looking sheepish. "I didn't think you would."

"Get your things. You can stay in the extra room. The sofa makes into a bed in there, and we'll stay out of each other's way. I have some work to do and there's a ballgame on at eight o'clock I want to watch."

He could see her mentally debate whether it was worth a motel bill to spend a few hours at his place. "Go get your things. We got through dinner without a battle."

She nodded and disappeared into her place. He left his door open and in minutes she rushed inside, coughing and shaking her head.

"I'm going to have to call and have someone come and de-smoke my place. Do you want yours done too?"

"No. Mine will air out. The bedroom's yours. I put clean linens on the sofa bed in that room." He moved to his desk and got out his briefcase, removing papers, and she went to the bedroom.

At nine she reappeared. He was sprawled on the sofa, his shirt unbuttoned, shoes kicked off. He had forgotten she was there. She was in men's red pajamas with sleeves and legs rolled up, her hair tied back in a bandanna, her face looking scrubbed and shiny.

She wore pink high-heeled slippers that were incongruous with the pajamas. "I'm going to bed. I like a cup of hot chocolate at bedtime. Do you mind if I fix it?"

"No."

"Do you want some?"

"No, thanks."

"What schedule shall we follow in the morning? What time do you get up?"

"I get up at half past six. I jog for twenty minutes and then shower and eat breakfast."

She frowned. "They told you no strenuous physical activity."

"I'll walk fast."

"Maybe you shouldn't."

He gave her a look and she bit her lip. "I exercise thirty minutes, bathe, and eat breakfast, so I guess I should exercise, eat, and then I'll bathe. By that time you'll be through."

"Wow. Watch this replay."

She moved around to watch the television, sitting down near him. She gasped as she watched the tricky play with a jump shot behind the goal that sailed over the board and through the basket. The teams raced down the court and the team in red stole the ball to race back up court again.

"Who's playing?"

"Oklahoma against Texas."

"Oh, my goodness. I bet my employee that Texas would win."

"Oklahoma will win."

"You don't know that! What's the score?"

"Right now Texas is ahead—"

"Aha! See."

"Texas is ahead one point. Watch!"

"Now they're ahead four points." They watched as both teams raced down the court and there was a jump shot. "Good shot. He's good at stealing the ball."

Texas shot and missed. "Get the ball!" Freedom snapped, sitting up a little straighter. "Ahh," he said in satisfaction as Oklahoma got possession. They missed, Texas scored, and Oklahoma raced down the court, Texas pressing them until an Oklahoma player hit a three-point basket. "One point difference."

"Oh, no!"

Texas lost the ball and Oklahoma shot, making another three points. One of the Oklahoma players fouled and they lined up for the free throw. A time out was called with Oklahoma ahead one point.

"I'll get the hot chocolate," she said and went to the kitchen. The smell of chocolate assailed him, and he went to help. She moved around the kitchen leaving milk on the counter, spilling chocolate on the stove. He wasn't surprised she had set her kitchen on fire. He wiped up after her until she looked at what he was doing.

"You're particular, aren't you?"

"As finicky as an old maid," he said, becoming irritated with her again, tempted to mention something about slobs, but he restrained himself.

In minutes they were settled in front of the television, Freedom with a cup of iced chocolate milk instead of hot like Raye's. He sipped carefully, feeling the cold liquid soothe his raw throat.

They clapped for their own teams, until the last minute when the score was tied with fifty seconds to go. Freedom sat on the edge of the sofa, whispering for Oklahoma while she jumped up and down cheering for Texas. He stood up as Oklahoma raced down the court.

"Throw!" he whispered, unable to yell.

"Miss! Miss! They won't make it!" she cried.

"They will!"

The ball sailed through the air, danced on the rim, and dropped through the net as the buzzer sounded.

"Oklahoma won," he said smugly.

"So it did." They stared at each other, and suddenly he felt sheepish.

"I think you bring out the hostility in me," he rasped.

"You're not always this way?"

"Nope. Believe it or not."

"I guess I'll go to bed now. I was going when you got me interested in the ballgame. Good night."

"Good night," he said. She left him and he looked down at the empty cups of chocolate. With a sigh he gathered them up and carried them to the kitchen to rinse them out and place them in the dishwasher.

He went to bed and was asleep in minutes. When the alarm went off he pushed the lever and climbed out of bed, yanking on his sweat pants. He stood up and ran his fingers through his hair, working his feet into sneakers. He staggered to the bathroom and then stepped into the hall and ran into Raye.

It knocked them both into the wall and he reached out to steady her. "Oh, sorry!" he said, blinking in surprise.

"You forgot I was here," she said, staring up at him. A turban was on the side of her head, her hair spilling out in tendrils.

"I did forget. Sorry. I'm going to jog."

"How are your lungs?"

"My lungs? Better I think," he said in a whisper.

"You don't sound better."

"I am. I promise."

"I don't think you should jog."

"I told you, I'll walk."

"I better come with you in case you collapse."

He was too sleepy to argue so he merely nodded. He drank a small glass of orange juice, pulled on a sweat shirt, and pocketed the key to the door. She ran to get a sweat shirt and caught up with him.

"You're jogging."

He slowed to a fast walk and she ran beside him. He stretched out his legs, knowing she was having to jog to keep up with him. When he returned to the apartment, he was as out of breath as she was.

"I don't think . . . you should have done that."

"I'm okay," he lied, his lungs feeling like they were on fire.

"You get your shower now and I'll eat breakfast."

He showered, shaved, and dressed in gray slacks. Pulling on a white shirt, he went to the kitchen.

"Oh, you're out," she said. "There's your toast."

A charred piece of toast stuck out of the toaster, a glass of orange juice beside it.

She left and he threw the toast away. While he sipped orange juice, he cleaned up crumbs, rinsed her bowl, and threw away the empty instant-oatmeal envelope.

"Bye. I'm off to work. Thanks for the place to stay."

He looked up. She stood in the doorway with her hair in a bun on top of her head, a red and white striped silk blouse and red skirt, her feet in high-heeled red shoes. She was attractive, and he marveled at how she could look nice one minute and a disaster the next.

"Don't forget to send me your medical bill."

"I won't," he said and grinned.

When the bills came, he slipped them into her mailbox without a qualm. His lungs healed and he only saw her as he came and went from the condo. Sometimes she was dressed for business, looking tailored and attractive. Other times, she was in flowered shorts or polka-dot and striped slacks, or going out to get the paper in the rolled-up pajamas.

In late January, Texas played a return match with Oklahoma in Texas, and again the game was televised. On a whim, Freedom stepped across the hall and knocked on her door.

It opened and she stood there in a terry coverup, her hair in two braids looped and fastened to either side of her head.

"Texas and Oklahoma have a return match. I thought you might want to watch."

She blinked and laughed. "Sure. I'll get some hot chocolate. Do you have any popcorn?"

"It's already in the microwave."

"I'll be right there. I don't need to change do I?"

He grinned. "No. You look fine. Same as ever," he said cheerfully.

She flashed him a big smile. When she came to his place, she was carrying mugs of steaming cocoa.

"I made this at home."

"Good. You missed the opening shots. Oklahoma is ahead by five points. The score is twelve to seven."

"Shall we make a small wager?"

"Sure. Name the price."

"You have to turn down your stereo on the weekends."

"It's too loud?"

"It's rather loud."

"I didn't think I played it very loudly. I'll turn it down if Oklahoma loses. If Texas loses, you get those plants out of the hall."

"You have something against plants?"

"They crowd things."

"You're crazy, you know." She looked around the room. "That's why you like it like a jail cell."

"You think my place looks like a cell," he said, looking at his glass and steel desk that cost nine hundred dollars.

"It's a little stark."

"I guess it would be to someone who lives in a jungle."

"Is it a bet?"

"Sure. You'll move the plants."

"Texas is going to win this time. They're picked by three points and Smothers hurt his hand."

He looked at her in surprise.

"I read the sports page," she said with a lift of her chin.

"It's a bet."

By half time he was on the edge of the couch and Texas led by five points. She cheered as they made a basket. Popcorn littered the chair and floor around her and her eyes sparkled.

"Half time. Texas forty-nine; Oklahoma forty-four."

"That's close," he said grimly. "You spilled your popcorn."

"Oh! I forgot how neat you are."

"Is Laz Kaminski a slob?"

She sent him another brilliant smile, and Freedom's anger melted. He watched her pick up popcorn.

"There. All neat and tidy. Maybe you're compulsive about neatness."

"No," he answered carefully. "Just your normal degree of tidiness."

"I'll make more hot chocolate."

"You can make it here." While they worked, she seemed lost in her own world, oblivious of his presence part of the time, and he was amused. He stopped to watch her, thinking he had never known a woman like her. "When are you going to Dallas?"

"This weekend."

"How'd you meet Kaminski?"

"He came into the store where I worked and brought a friend to get her a new dress. While she was trying on dresses he asked me out."

"Are you engaged?"

"No. Laz won't marry."

"What about you? You're happy with that arrangement?"

"Yes. I like Laz."

"Did he open this shop for you?"

"You don't mind asking direct questions, do you?"

He shrugged. "We get on each other's nerves anyway, so it didn't seem necessary to be polite and careful."

"True. He's put up the money and he owns part of the store. It's a wonderful arrangement for me. I design some of the dresses I sell."

"Do you really?" he asked, surprised, instantly imagining flashy dresses with big flowers, bows at the neckline and waist, little ribbons hanging off the sleeves.

"Do I hear skepticism in your voice?"

"No. I believe you."

"But you think they must look dreadful. Like a jungle."

He felt his cheeks flush with heat and she laughed. "I'll show you one sometime."

"You're here more than Dallas right now."

"I want to see that this store gets started right and I have excellent help in Dallas looking after things. Also, I have two new seamstresses here and I'm working with them on designs. It'll take awhile before we get our signals straight. Who's the latest lady in your life?"

"Ginger."

"You have a rapid turnover. Is it you or the women? I guess you can't really answer that."

"Sure, I can. I don't want to settle down."

"Why not?"

He shrugged. "No one is that interesting. I'm a grouch," he said lightly, making her laugh and he found he liked to make her laugh. "Shall we go back?" He bumped her and cocoa sloshed in cups.

"Whoops. Sorry," he said, looking down into pale brown eyes that had flecks of gold in the center. Her mouth was too full, her lips actually sensual, and for a moment he felt a flicker of desire. She moved ahead of him and his gaze lowered to the slight sway of her hips. The terry cloth rendered her shapeless, but he knew from seeing her in shorts that she had long, thin legs. Following her back to the television, he drew a deep breath as if he had just stepped close to a precipice.

They both were on their feet cheering and yelling for the last ten minutes of the game. He jumped in the air as Oklahoma won by three points.

"Whoopee!" He faced her, laughing. "Sorry. The plants have to go."

"A bet's a bet, but it's going to look bare in the hallway."

"You don't stay out there much anyway. It'll look neat."

"Okay. The plants go. It was fun."

"Yeah," he said, looking at her full mouth again. She blinked and gathered up her mugs to head for the door.

He stood in the open door as she crossed the hall. She paused at her door. "Good night, Freedom. Come by my shop sometime and I'll show you my dresses."

"Sure, Raye. Good night."

After she was gone, he moved around the empty room, straightening up cushions she had dropped on the floor, picking up popcorn she had spilled. He paused and looked at his living room. It did not look like a jail cell. He could imagine the dresses she must design. He shook his head and went to the kitchen to wash dishes.

15

JANUARY, 1980

Cancun, Mexico

No food, live animals, or seeds. Cimarron checked the customs list and returned it to the man behind the desk. She had flown to Cancun on the company jet for her first vacation since Fontaine's death over a year ago. Sometimes she would go days without hurting, and then suddenly something like a song on a radio would bring back memories with aching freshness. She wasn't sure how she would feel about being on the island without him, but she needed a rest.

The second night she sat on the beach watching moonlight play over the water. Far down the beach a party was going on, fires flickering, the music of steel drums carrying clearly, laughter occasionally ringing out. She stood up, strolling along the water's edge toward the flickering bonfires. The slap of waves against the sand was steady. She let it wash over her feet unaware of someone watching her.

Nick leaned back in the chair, peering through the darkness, his gaze raking over the slender woman's silhouette that was outlined against the moonlit water beyond her. She shouldn't be wandering around alone on the beach in the dark, but she looked as if she intended to join the party. She was willowy, tall, and long legged, moving with a graceful sway of her hips. He watched the solitary figure move down the beach and stare at the dancers. His curiosity stirred, because she didn't join the others, but merely stood back in the darkness watching them. He wondered if she lived in one of the big houses along the beach. He had never gotten to know his neighbors since he usually flew in for a weekend and then left. He had been in his present villa only once since buying it.

Cimarron stood quietly, her hands in the pockets of her shorts. Ahead, orange flames shimmered on the black water and she could make out dancers moving around the fires. She drew closer, hearing voices and laughter drown out the sound of the ocean. She stood in the dark shadows beneath a palm and watched the hypnotic golden-red flames raging in the night, sparks spinning into the darkness. The sounds and moonlit Caribbean gave a festive ambience to the night that lifted her spirits until the fires reminded her of the crash and she turned abruptly to saunter back toward her home.

She saw she had come much farther than she realized, passing two more beach houses on the way. She meandered in and out of the water, letting it splash through her sandals. Picking up a pebble, she skipped it across the water. It splashed and jumped and splashed again before it sank.

"Good throw."

She spun around as a man moved in the shadows. He was bare except for shorts, seated in a beach chair. He stood up and approached her.

"Did you want to join the party? It's people from one of the hotels. It isn't private."

For a moment she felt a sense of danger. His voice was deep and his outline revealed broad shoulders.

"You saw me go past before," she said warily.

"Yes. If you're lonesome, I'll walk down there with you."

"No, thanks," she said, wondering if she should join the party simply for safety. She realized how vulnerable she was. Her servants were gone for the night and she shouldn't have wandered down the beach alone. She drew a deep breath, walking past him. He stepped beside her and she stiffened.

"Hey, don't be afraid. I was just going to walk with you. I'm Nick Kaminski."

"Oh. Mr. Kaminski," she said, relaxing, the tenseness going out of her shoulders. "I knew you had a home here, but I didn't know where."

"Mrs. Durand. I didn't realize it was you when you went past." He tilted his head to study her. He knew about Fontaine Durand's violent death a year ago last fall; recently Laredo had clashed with White Star. "You're the white knight who came to Denco's rescue in our buyout."

"They were glad to see us step in."

"Your people used our information handily," he said, and she wondered how many enemies she had made managing White Star.

"I'm on vacation," she said sharply.

He laughed. "And you don't want to be hassled. That was fancy footwork, and we were caught napping. I learned a few things. Some of that sharing of information is just a chance you take."

"Denco didn't want you on their board."

"No, I'm sure they didn't. Their stockholders might have welcomed me though."

"It's all done now, Mr. Kaminski," she said serenely, and he laughed.

"Maybe we'll cross swords again," he said, and she detected the challenge in his voice. "And call me Nick, Mrs. Durand."

"I'm Cimarron," she said coolly, preferring to keep him at a distance. He had been a tough opponent and only quick moving by their accountants and Freedom had secured the Denco deal for White Star.

"Hello, Cimarron," Nick said softly, holding out his hand. His fingers were warm and firm, closing around hers, making her acutely aware of him. Drawing a sharp breath, she moved away. Nick felt the fleeting touch of her cool hand and the abrupt withdrawal. She walked away and he didn't want her to go.

"Want to go to the party?"

"No. I just wandered down there and listened to the music a minute. I'll walk back to my place."

"You haven't been here in a long time, have you?"

"No," she answered, wondering how he knew. She didn't remember seeing him on the island before. They walked in silence along the beach. "Here are some more rocks," he said. "Let's skip them." He handed her one and threw his, muscles flexing as he stretched out his long arm. Moonlight caught glints on the ripples where his rock bounced as it slid over the surface of the water beyond the breakers.

"I can't throw that far," she said, giving hers a toss.

"That's the best throw I've ever seen a woman make," he said. "You must have brothers."

She laughed. "I do. They're all older and I played ball with them."

"I don't have a peace pipe to offer, but how about a margarita?" he asked, remembering asking about her once after Fontaine's death. It was Kevin Pitman who had given him an offhand answer. "She's a hermit, since Durand's death." Now after watching her stroll down the beach alone, he remembered how in love the Durands had seemed; he thought about her being alone and felt a stir of sympathy for her. "I have all the mixings there on the table."

"I shouldn't—"

"Come on. There's no reason to spend the whole evening alone. One margarita, a stroll on the beach, and we won't mention business." He took her hand and led her to a table that held bottles and glasses.

"You're prepared," she said with amusement.

"My old Boy Scout days weren't a loss." He mixed drinks. "Come on, we'll walk down and listen to the music again. We won't join them."

She strolled beside him, sipping the bitter margarita while steel drums played a familiar song. Nick took her drink from her, set it beneath a palm, and faced her while he danced to the quick, Latin beat.

"Come on, Cimarron."

"Oh, I can't," she said, feeling a sense of alarm as he moved around her.

"It's just a dance. Come on."

She moved with him, sand filling her shoes, her body swaying to the music, trying to keep her mind numb, trying so hard not to remember the tall man she loved more than anyone else on earth. She twisted and turned, feeling good moving with the music. When it ended, she laughed. "I haven't danced in a long time."

"I didn't think you had. It wasn't so difficult, was it?" He handed her drink back and picked up his.

She looked at the fires again. "If you don't mind, I'd like to go back now."

"You're scared and there's no need to be. I'm harmless."

"I don't do so well with people," she said quietly. "It's just easier to be alone."

"You don't mean *people*, you mean men," he corrected her gently. "You have to get back out into the world sometime."

"I'm into it enough," she said sharply.

"Hey, listen, there's a switch."

She paused and heard the steel drums change to a slow,

old piece as American as hot dogs. Nick Kaminski set down her drink again, his voice cheerful. "Just this once. We can't pass this up." He pulled her hand. "You can't slow dance in ankle deep sand. Come up here," he urged, walking to a wooden picnic table.

"On top of the table?"

He laughed and swung her up, stepping to the bench and then to the table top with her, holding her away from him and dancing.

"We'll fall off this!"

"I promise, I won't ever let you fall," he said, the words suddenly seeming to echo in his mind with a double meaning. Nick watched her, her auburn hair a pale swirl as she moved around, thinking he had never seen such sadness in someone's expression, wanting to make her laugh, wondering at himself, because rescue work wasn't his nature. She followed his lead solemnly staring up at him, and he felt as if he were dancing with someone in a cocoon, unaware of life around her. It seemed the most colossal waste because he could remember times he had seen her with Durand and she had been vibrant, alive, amazingly sensual.

She followed his lead as they moved on the table, their feet faintly scraping on the rough boards, the ridiculousness of dancing on a picnic table making her smile. Moonlight played over his features and she gazed at his tangle of brown curls, a slight smile curving his mouth.

"Nice," he said when the music ended and they reverted back to a fast island number. He held Cimarron's hand and began to dance. "One more. Just one."

She laughed and danced with him. It was so fast, it was mindless, her feet keeping time to the music, her body swaying. She shook her head to fling her hair away from her face. Nick was a good dancer, moving his body with ease, keeping perfect rhythm. His chest and shoulders shone with perspiration, but his breathing was steady.

He watched her, seeing her move with a sensual grace, her tight shorts and shirt making it easy to imagine her without the clinging garments. Her short hair looked silky, the color of flames. Cimarron Durand looked as if she had energy to burn, an intensity to her movements, and he realized she was having fun. For the moment she had shed her cloak of loneliness and sorrow.

The music ended and he jumped down, his hands closing on her waist as he swung her to the ground and laughed with her. "That's better," he said softly, aware of the narrowness of her waist beneath his hands.

He stood too close, his voice was deep and soft, his gaze too intimate. Her laughter vanished as she stepped away. He caught her arm and she looked up at him.

"You're scared to come back into the world."

"I don't want to," she answered, knowing exactly what he was saying.

"You're too much alive."

"I'm fine. I'm going home."

He let her walk away, mentally telling himself to leave her alone. He wasn't a white knight in the boardroom or on the beach. Saving forlorn ladies was not in his repertoire and he didn't want to start now. In spite of his arguments, he picked up both margaritas.

"Hey, I'll bet you can't do this," he said, and she turned around as he caught up with her in long, fast strides, balancing both drinks without spilling a drop.

She had to laugh at him. He set the drinks on the sand and held her wrist lightly. "Let's wade out in the water. I'm hot from the dancing." He wondered if he could get her to swim, what she would do if he simply pulled her down into the water.

Cimarron didn't want to wade with him, but he had a cajoling way of leading her into a dance or the water without waiting for her to consent. It swirled around their legs, warm as the night, sparkling in the moonlight.

"Come on. One quick swim."

"Suppose we get eaten by an alligator?" she asked lightly, knowing the nearest alligator was a thousand miles away.

"I promise. No alligators, jellyfish, or sharks."

"You can't promise that, except the alligators," she added, feeling lightheaded, dreading going back to the empty house.

He scooped her up and marched into the water.

"Hey, wait!" she gasped, having to cling to him, and suddenly one of those moments assaulted her when memories came vivid and clear. It felt so good to be in a man's arms. *Fontaine*. "Oh, please," she said, her throat constricting. She was always afraid that she would lose control in front of people, that longing for Fontaine would strike and she wouldn't be able to hide her feelings. It was four months and a year later; the loss shouldn't hurt so badly still, but it did.

Nick's heart lurched because he heard the note of distress in her voice.

"Here we go, hang on," he said, lunging into deeper water and tossing her away.

Cimarron hit the water and wriggled to go to the surface, having to swim or sink. She felt a hand lock in the back of her shirt and tug. Then she realized he was pulling her along. She surfaced beside him and swam, glancing back over her shoulder.

"Twenty yards and we'll go back."

"I'm going back now. Dammit."

"No, you're not," he said. "I'll pull you out or you'll come willingly, but you're not going back now."

He was solemn, his voice filled with conviction that shocked her. She blinked and glared at him as she kept up with him. "You son of a bitch," she said softly, angry that he was forcing her to swim. She plunged ahead wanting to leave him behind, knowing he meant what he had said. Swearing at him silently, determined when she got back to shore to tell him goodbye, she thrashed through the water and then began a steady stroke. He swam beside her in silence.

"We're over twenty yards," she said, suddenly stopping and treading water. She looked back at the shore. It looked a hundred yards away and fear gripped her, because she realized she hardly knew the man beside her. She swam away from him a few yards and looked at him. "Damn you. Look how far out we are."

"You'll sleep good tonight. Old Doc Kaminski's cure for bad nights. I'll race you in."

"I don't have bad nights."

"Liar," he accused lightly. "Get ready—I'll give you a head start—get set, go!"

She swam for all she was worth, wanting to beat him in and go home and never talk to him again. Her muscles ached as she pulled for shore, and she wondered what was swimming around her in the inky water. As he caught up and swam beside her, she wondered if they had gone too far out. With the shore still yards away, her muscles ached and she was tiring.

She slowed, realizing if she stopped, he would tow her in. Exertion ate away anger and by the time her feet hit the sand, her good humor was restored. They stood up and waded ashore and she flopped down on the beach to pick up the margarita and take a long drink. She gulped for breath and lay back on the sand. He sat beside her, wondering if she had forgotten him.

Her shirt was wet and clung to her, molding to the outline of breasts that were full and firm and tantalizing. Her ribs showed, her ragged breathing pulling the wet material tighter. She sat up and shook her hair that was plastered to her head.

"Still ready to throttle me?" he asked, scooping up a handful of sand and letting it trickle along her thigh, wondering if she was even remotely aware of him as a man.

"That was a dirty trick," she said, and they both laughed.

"You'll sleep better."

"I guess you're right."

"I'm right. And you didn't get bitten by a single alligator."

She smoothed her hair away from her face. "I'll get even sometime."

"Idle threat. You couldn't get even if you thought about it from now until this time tomorrow."

"You're offering me a challenge."

"No. I meant it. You can't get even. Probably part of why you were so angry. But now you're not. Let's have one more margarita."

"Okay."

"We're closer to your house. Do you have the mixings or shall we walk back to my place?"

"I have everything," she said, jumping to her feet. He moved beside her, matching his steps to hers and they walked down the beach to her house. It was three times the size of his, lavish and comfortable as he followed her inside to the bar where she switched on a soft light that was reflected in rows of glistening crystal and bottles. "You can mix them. I don't know anything about margaritas."

"It's simple," he said, moving into the bar with her, working quietly, occasionally brushing against her while he explained how to mix the drinks. He paused and looked at her. She stood only inches away, her top wet and clinging. Her eyes were a shade of green faintly tinged with blue, a color he knew he would never forget. He wanted to touch her, to lean closer; most of all he wanted to make her smile.

She looked away, getting out ice and he still watched her. Her arms were slender, slightly muscular, her neck long and slender, a brown mole on her shoulder.

He forced his attention to the margaritas, working in silence because now he didn't trust his voice. He was aroused, and more—he wanted to get to know her better. He took the drinks and left the bar ahead of her.

"Let's go out on the beach," she said, and they strolled onto the moonlight beneath the shadows of a palm. They sat down to gaze at the water. "How long have you had your house here?"

"Only five months," he answered. "It's relaxing. I heard you had success in Canada."

"Yes, we did. And you've had success with your offshore drilling."

"Your stock has increased twelve points in the past year."

"So you keep up."

"I need to keep up. Laredo is expanding fast. I don't want to be taken over and lose my company."

"I'm surprised you're not with Kamnick."

"It's a pretty well-known fact that my father and I don't get along."

"I've heard you don't, but I've heard he wants you to take over the business and you don't want to. That's a little peculiar for a man struggling to build his own so quickly."

"That's the reason I'm struggling to build my own," he said casually.

"You want to do it your own way."

"Very much," he said, beginning to suspect she was more than a mere figurehead for White Star. "Laz wants it all his way."

"You're scared he'll buy you out," she said. "That's why you're acquiring other companies."

"You figured it out with about one minute's thought. Some people can't grasp the simplicity of it. Actually, I'm a plain guy with rather simple tastes. What do you want for White Star?"

"To keep it going; to make it grow. It was Fontaine's dream and his life's devotion. Sometimes it seems pointless when he's gone, but then it's a tribute to him, to his memory and it's the one tangible way I can cling to part of him."

"He was a lucky man."

She smiled at him. "Thank you. I think we were good for each other. What do you want for Laredo Oil?"

"To be big enough to fight Laz," he answered with acrimony. "All I want out of life is a good business, and someday, I hope, a happy family. Nothing much, just Utopia. Something that doesn't exist."

"It exists—if only briefly," she said, and Nick detected the sadness coming back to her voice.

"You've been coming here since you married. How long ago was that?"

"Since September, 1977. We were married a year."

"Sorry," he said quietly. In a moment he asked, "Have you had chicken at *Mama Maronda's*?"

"No."

"Your life on the island isn't complete. Go with me tomorrow at lunch. This is the best chicken in the world.

The place doesn't look like much—actually it's scary, but I promise you, the chicken is the best. How about half past eleven? And you can close your eyes and we'll order it to go if you want, because the place looks like hell."

"All right," she said, laughing, realizing moments later when he was talking about another restaurant that she had a date, the first one since Fontaine's death and it had happened so simply that she hadn't given thought to it.

"Do you like the sunfishes? The little sailboats?"

"Fontaine wasn't into sailing. He liked deep-sea fishing. He wanted a boat to take him some place to do something and he didn't care about in between, so I don't know anything about them. I never saw the ocean until I knew Fontaine."

"I'll give you a lesson in the morning. Are you an early or late riser?"

"I come from a farm. I'm an early riser. It's a habit I can't break."

"I'm no farm boy, but I like to be out early. Meet me on my beach—how early?"

She shrugged. Another date. Yet it didn't seem important enough to argue and it might be fun to learn how to sail the small craft. "Seven."

"Half past six and I'll feed you."

Breakfast and lunch. A little stir of apprehension came. She didn't want involvement or even to be touched by a man. She had withdrawn into a shell and she wasn't ready to come out. She was still so in love with Fontaine, it was impossible to think of someone else and she saw no reason to change.

"Look, there goes a shooting star," he said. "Make a wish."

She glanced up in time to glimpse a silvery streak in the sky. "Why do they always seem so special?"

"They're out of the ordinary. They're beautiful. When they happen, they're one in billions, the spectacular exception," he said in a deep, quiet voice that made her tingle. He watched her intently and she drew a deep breath, her profile to him as she leaned back in the chair, her long leg bent at the knee.

"Did you make a wish?" he asked.

"No. Wishes are for children."

"No. Wishes are for people who have hope."

"I haven't lost hope in a lot of things. White Star for one."

"What do you do to relax, Cimarron?"

"I read, I swim, I go home to the farm."

"How many brothers?"

"Two now. One died when I was in high school. Tim is at the farm and he's twenty-eight. Freedom lives in Tulsa."

"Freedom Chisholm? He's your brother?"

"Yes. You know him?"

"Yes. I've met him at oil meetings and I met him at the Denco deal."

"He has a condo across the hall from Raye Honeywall."

"Really? I knew Raye was opening a shop in Tulsa. Are they friends?" he asked dryly.

"Actually, they're not. My brother is usually nice, but they got off on the wrong foot and I don't think they speak."

"Raye? She's a peach. In spite of the fact that she likes Laz."

"Freedom's usually a nice guy too. It was just one of those things." She told him about Raye beating Freedom to the condo, buying it minutes before he made an offer. Nick was a good listener, paying close attention to everything she said and she found it was nice to have someone to talk to because so many hours had been empty.

He listened to her talking about her brother and her family and suddenly he felt as if he knew the people and farm she was describing. He stared at her, trying to think what was nagging at him and then he remembered. He had met Freedom Chisholm, but had always seen him in a business environment. Or had he? As he listened to her talk, he remembered a wheat fire years ago and a boy named Freedom and the auburn-haired young girl called Sunny who rode on his bike. She had just mentioned a brother had died years ago. Nick stared at her, unable to match her up with that girl, but a name like Freedom was too rare and everything else fit. The beautiful, sophisticated Cimarron Durand was also the young farm girl, Sunny Chisholm.

"Sunny Chisholm," he said softly, and her head snapped around.

"How'd you know my family calls me Sunny?"

"I remember the day your brother died, the fire, the thrown rod. I had a nickname too, then—Rebel."

She turned to stare at him. "*You're* the biker?"

"Yes. My father had given me such a hard time when I worked for him, I quit and just roamed." She kept staring as he told her about those years, and he finally smiled. "We've both changed."

"You helped fight the fire. I didn't think I'd ever see you again."

"I'm surprised you remember."

"I've always remembered. You frightened me at first."

"You got over your fright," he said dryly.

She blinked and looked away. "Yes, I did," she replied. She stood up. "I better go inside. I think it's really late."

"It's been fun," he said lightly, coming to his feet. "See you on the beach at half past six."

She nodded and gathered up their glasses to go inside. On the darkened patio, she glanced over her shoulder and saw him walking along the beach, his hands jammed in the pockets of his shorts. He followed the water's edge, meandering along much as she had earlier in the night. Fires still burned far down the beach, but the music had stopped. She saw the orange flames and went inside.

When she was in bed, she remembered dancing with Nick Kaminski, a slow dance on top of a picnic table. She smiled in the darkness. Tonight was more fun than she had had in a long time.

It seemed only hours until she stirred and saw pink light glowing, a hush on the beach when she moved to the window. She didn't want to see Nick this morning. Now she wished she hadn't agreed to breakfast and lessons and lunch, but it was done. She sighed and moved around the room to dress.

It was cool and marvelous outside. Wearing black swim

trunks and a T-shirt, he was waiting for her and she climbed broad plank steps to a wide patio and a table set for two. A servant brought steaming plates of scrambled eggs, pink slices of papaya, green melon, pineapple, slices of limes, and bananas. The coffee was hot, black, and strong, and she found Nick charming company.

He gave her a lesson on handling a sunfish, sitting close beside her and reaching around to hold her hand as she unfastened lines. He let her take charge and they sailed in a zigzag course until he took the tiller from her and steered them around to head back to the island.

"I didn't realize how far we had come!" she exclaimed.

"Be careful if you're alone. We are a long way from help. I'd hate to have you call from Cuba."

She turned her face into the wind, her hair tumbling loose from the clip that held it behind her head. He couldn't resist and reached out to pull a strand away from her cheek.

"Can I see if I can take it in?"

"Sure. Change places." He stood and held her as they shifted seats, catching a whiff of familiar perfume, getting a quick, impersonal gaze from wide, green eyes.

She lost control, and he reached back, his hand closing over hers.

"I'm okay," she said and he moved away. As they came in, they headed straight for the dock. He sucked in his breath and hoped she didn't wreck his boat. He curbed the urge to yell and grab the tiller, clamping his jaw shut, waiting until the last possible second. They came within three inches of the dock, sliding past with a hissing sound. Thick wooden pilings raced past his face. He braced for her to hit the beach and jumped out swiftly, splashing in the water.

"We're here!" she exclaimed, laughing, and he grinned. "You have nerves of steel! I almost hit the dock."

"But you didn't," he answered, glad she didn't know that was exactly what he expected.

"I brought it in all by myself!" she said excitedly, looking enormously pleased.

"Good job. You'll do better tomorrow morning." He tied the end of the rope.

Cimarron wondered if he was as unaware of her sexually as he acted. He had made another date without asking, simply assuming she would sail tomorrow morning. Her gaze went over his long, muscular body, his well-shaped legs. He was younger than Fontaine had been, his body rippling with muscles, the flesh taut. Every time she could recall seeing Nick in the past, he had had a beautiful woman with him. He was appealing, and she couldn't understand why he would spend his time with her, but maybe he was bored or getting over an affair. She dismissed the question and hopped out of the boat.

"That was fun," she said with sincerity.

"Good. It's early and cool. Let's go for a bike ride and then we can snorkel and by that time we'll have worked up an appetite for the chicken."

He had four bicycles in his garage and they pedaled down his brick drive to the bicycle path that circled the island. It was refreshingly cool with air blowing against them and she followed him in single file until he slowed to ride beside her. No one else was on the path, so they had room, gliding smoothly beneath the overhanging branches of almond trees and red poinciana trees. Nick ducked, but too late and his head struck a low branch. Scarlet blossoms showered in his dark hair and he laughed, shaking his head, blossoms falling to his shoulders.

They pedaled to the point, passing new shops and hotels that were under construction. By the time they returned to Nick's house, she was hot, ready for a swim. "I understand why they have siesta here."

"Sleepy?"

"No, but it's getting hot and it's only ten o'clock."

"You'll cool off when we join the fish." They snorkeled, drifting through the clear water, gazing at bright blue chromis and yellow butter hamlets. A pink jellyfish moved along the bottom and she swam in the opposite direction, seeing Nick moving ahead of her. His body cut through the water with ease. He had shed his T-shirt; the narrow black trunks were tight on his slim hips and she was more physically aware of him today than before.

Afterwards, he drove her to town to eat in a tiny thatched-roof building with thick walls and open windows. The floor was dirt, the tables leaning on uneven legs. Nick spoke in Spanish to a woman who grinned and talked to him. He introduced Cimarron who could follow their conversation and answered a question in Spanish.

"*Hable español. Muy bueno,*" Nick said.

"I speak it when I'm here sometimes. I'm not very fluent."

"What else do you do when you're here?"

"Not much. Read, swim, relax. Now I'd like to get a sunfish. Want to help me buy one?" she asked on a whim.

"Sure. I'll show you where I got mine."

They spent the week swimming, snorkeling, and sailing. Nick was friendly, keeping a distance that made her relax, touching her in a casual, impersonal way. If he were aware of it he didn't give the slightest indication. She could have been part of the beach furniture for all the sexual attention he gave her. She liked his company. He was fun, sometimes relaxed, sometimes energetic.

Thursday afternoon they picked up her new sunfish, put it into the water, and had a christening ceremony.

"*El Capricho,*" was painted in bright blue letters on the side and she tried to break a bottle of Tequila against the bow, but when the bottle wouldn't break, Nick took it from her and smashed it over the boat and they pushed off, laughing.

As they walked home later, he draped his arm across her shoulders. "Change your clothes and I'll take you to eat. Another island specialty."

She agreed and left him, promising to be ready in an hour. He appeared at her back door, knocking lightly, and she came out to meet him. She had changed to a red cotton skirt and blouse and he wore jeans and a pale-blue T-shirt. His skin had darkened with each day in the sun, and she realized he was handsome. She had barely noticed before. Most of the time on the island, he was relaxed, but she had watched him when the boat was caught by the wind and she could see the quick flare of determination in him, the sudden hardening of his jaw, and she suspected in business he could be a tough, formidable opponent.

They ate at a restaurant that doubled as a marina and had a dance floor outside. Lights sparkled on the water in the lagoon, on boats, and on wires strung above the dock. There was a cool breeze and the beat was fast. Cimarron enjoyed dancing with Nick. His body was hard, muscular, moving with a masculine grace when he danced. He watched her with a faint smile. During the week he had become a friend, someone she could relax with, yet tonight she became aware of each brush of his shoulder or touch of his hand. He seemed more handsome than when she had first seen him, and he seemed sensitive to the slightest change in her emotions.

While traffic sped past, they walked home along the boulevard, and then sat on her patio for a late-night drink. They talked, watching palms sway, listening to the steady slap of waves on the beach.

"How come you didn't like working at Kamnick Oil?" she asked, vaguely recalling talking to him about it before.

Nick gave a dry, bitter laugh. "My father wants complete control. He would smother me if he could."

She twisted around to look at him, leaning forward in her chair. "You sound bitter."

"I am," he said, tenseness going out of his voice. "It's do it his way or else. If he would just leave me alone. But he won't, so I intend to get big enough to meet him on his own terms."

"You're out for revenge."

Nick was quiet a moment. "I just want him off my back. I want to lead my own life. In order to do that, I have to make Laredo Oil strong enough that he can't destroy it. I'm surprised he hasn't tried, except I think I know what he's doing. He's hoping I'll take over Kamnick or come back to Kamnick, because I like the oil business."

"And you won't?"

"I don't want Kamnick Oil as long as he has anything to do with it."

"Doesn't he realize that he's alienated you by trying to hold you?"

"He's a powerful man who's accustomed to taking what he wants. For me, it's a matter of survival, Cimarron, not revenge, just survival."

She was astounded by the anger in his voice. "I'm sorry because that's foreign to me. And sad if you love him. Can't he see what he's doing?"

"He sees he is giving me Kamnick Oil. He's giving me money, and power. He can't understand that I want to have one independent thought. I can't give up my mind and become Pinocchio. Laz needs a wooden boy."

She stared at him, saddened to think about someone as intelligent and nice as Nick having such a difficult time with his father, a man he must love. "Our family is close. The older I grow, the more I realize it."

"Then you're very lucky."

"Well, I was about that. I didn't stay so lucky about husbands. I guess we all have our hurts." She smiled, thinking Nick was one of a kind. "I'm lucky here. I have a new friend."

"Actually, sweetie, I'm lusting after your gorgeous body, but I know when to make a pass and when to pass on making a pass."

She laughed. "You're absurd."

"The absurd beachcomber, friend, and companion of sad ladies and beautiful farm girls."

"Handsome, fun, reliable. You've made this week so much better for me."

"Handsome, huh?" Nick asked, teasing her, but surprised and pleased if she even half meant it, because he didn't think she had noticed him at all. "I hope when we get back to T-town we don't square off in business."

"I hope not too, but if it happens, it won't be anything personal, Nick."

"Said by the beautiful lady shark whose business is growing monthly. Ah, well, if I have to be devoured, better you than Kamnick Oil."

"I'm sorry you have trouble with Laz. My family is so compatible," she said, returning to the topic.

"I'll bet they are," he said, remembering the wheat field fire so long ago.

"I have a nine-year-old half brother, Jerry. My older brother Tim lives on the farm with my folks. He's building a house on a farm near them and he works with Dad. You know Freedom. That's all of us." She gazed at millions of stars scattered overhead. "What do you think about when you look at stars?"

"I remember sitting on wells."

"Where did you do that?"

"Texas and Oklahoma." In the quiet of the night, his voice was soft and deep. He told her how he got started, funny moments in the oil patch. A little about his bull riding.

"You're kidding!"

"No. I have some trophies."

"Tim did that for a time until he broke his leg. Now he enters calf roping. I rode in the barrel racing one summer."

"I'll bet you were good."

"No. The only prize I ever won was a rag doll at the state fair in the kids' contests."

They talked for another hour. He stood when she did. "I should go inside now, Nick. It's getting late and tomorrow I go back to the States."

Suddenly he was facing her, his arm stretched out to the stucco wall behind her head as he braced himself casually and blocked her from leaving. "Will I see you when we get back to Tulsa?"

She shook her head. "I don't think so. I don't go out much."

"I've had fun this week," he said quietly, putting his other hand on the opposite side of her head, hemming her in and moving closer.

She felt a sense of panic. She didn't want him moving closer; she was aware of him, aware of her vulnerability. "Nick, please don't. I can't. All I want is Fontaine—"

"Cimarron," he said in such gentle tones she thought she

would lose control. He placed his finger beneath her jaw and lifted her face. "Let me just hold you."

She didn't consent or refuse. He put his arms around her lightly, moving closer while she stood with her arms at her sides. He placed his cheek against the top of her head and stood quietly. It felt too good to be in his arms. She could become involved with someone for all the wrong reasons and she really didn't want anyone else in her life.

"I don't know when I'll lose control," she said so quietly he had to strain to hear her. She was soft and warm and his heart thudded with need. She had seemed only half alive all week—part of her hidden away from the world while he was growing more acutely conscious of her every day. He ached to kiss her; he knew he couldn't until she was ready. "I'm sorry, Nick. Find someone fun. The world's full of whole people who aren't in mourning."

"You're not always in mourning. Go ahead and mourn when you want to. I can cope with it."

She relaxed, her head against his chest, her arms at her side. "I can't do this."

"Do what?" he asked with amusement, leaning back to look down at her.

She gazed up at him; his face was so close, his mouth wide, well shaped, lips slightly full. "Don't be afraid," he whispered.

"It's just physical. Nick, I loved him so," she said, her throat closing in a knot. "See. Now I can't keep control and I hate that. I hate to get so weepy—"

"Cimarron, shh," he said softly, running his thumbs beneath her eyes, wiping tears away before they fell while his lips brushed hers so lightly. "Shh. You're doing fine and I know you were in love. I'm not doing anything much. Nothing at all actually," he said, brushing his mouth over hers again, a feathery touch, yet it stirred physical needs into life. She was aware of what he was doing; it was an amalgam of ambient tenderness and a physical reawakening. She stood with her eyes shut while his mouth moved on hers again in another feathery kiss.

He shifted, his arms sliding around her waist. "This is

easy,'' he whispered. ''It won't hurt you or me. Put your arms around me.''

''No,'' she whispered in return, looking up at him. A smoldering, hungry expression on his face seemed to consume her, making her forget sorrow; making her aware of him as a man, because he wanted her badly and it showed in his eyes. She wanted to be kissed. As if she had fought the urge and finally lost, she stared at him. He pressed closer, watching her intently.

Nick's lips touched hers, opening hers so lightly, the slightest touch of his tongue against her mouth. Desire flashed white-hot in her, bursting up from her loins, rippling inside her like a taut bowstring just released. She clung to him.

For a second Nick felt her body change, the laxness left her; her hips thrust against him, her breasts strained against him as her arms tightened around his neck. Her lips opened, fiery petals beneath his, and his tongue thrust into her mouth deeply probing, getting a scalding response that made his body harden, that brought a hard erection. His arms crushed her to him; he bent over her, running his hand along her back. And he realized she was the most sensual woman he had known.

Suddenly she spun away from him. ''No!'' she gulped as if she had been suffocating. She turned her back, and he suspected she was crying. He moved closer, touching her gently, rubbing her shoulders.

''All you're having are perfectly normal feelings and you're fighting it. Sorrow, regret, guilt, maybe some of all three. That's normal, Cimarron.'' He spoke gently and she turned around to cling to him and cry with her head against his chest.

''See. This is dreadful. I shouldn't be out with you. I shouldn't—I can't keep control. Nick, I'm sorry that—''

He tilted her head up and she had to look at him. ''Don't ever apologize because you're human, because you loved your husband, because you know sorrow over your loss.''

He gazed into her eyes while he talked and he saw the battle she was waging between emotions and desire. He looked down at her mouth. Her lips were parted, red from his kisses, wet from her tears.

"You want this," he whispered. "I can see it," he added, brushing her lips with his. She gasped and leaned her head back and closed her eyes and he brushed her lips again with his.

Cimarron fought the heady reaction his kisses caused. She trembled. She wanted to be kissed until she couldn't think. It felt so good to be in a man's arms, to be kissed, and Nick was gentle, patient. "Oh, Nick."

"Let go, honey. Stop thinking. I'll stop the minute you ask."

He kissed her, moving close again, fitting her to him and holding her tightly as his kiss changed from tender to wildly passionate and demanding.

Tremors raked her as she began to respond to him, her tongue thrusting against his, her hips moving against him. She moaned softly, running her fingers in his hair, feeling textures so different, a body that was more muscular than Fontaine's, arms that held her tighter, kisses that were wild.

Thoughts stopped; her body gained control of her emotions and heart. Yearning burned through her. Nick shifted, holding her tightly, his hand sliding down over her breast. She moaned and trembled, aching badly.

Finally, she pushed against him and he released her instantly. "I have to stop now."

She knew how badly he wanted her; his hard erection had pressed against her. "I can't go any farther, Nick." Her breathing was ragged. "I'm not a tease. This is the only time, the most—"

He put his fingertips on her lip. "You don't have to explain to me. Tomorrow night you'll be in Tulsa. Go out with me then."

"I can't."

"Yes, you can. We can have dinner just like we've had here."

"If I do that, others will ask me out."

"I swear, I'll take you to such a hole in the wall, it'll be like Mama Maronda's and you won't be seen by anyone you know.''

She had to laugh. ''Oh, Nick. How come you're so patient?''

''It's just my lovable, charming nature,'' he answered flippantly, thinking what an effort this week had cost him, but it was beginning to be worth all the aching restraint, because her icy reserve was melting. Her kisses had been well worth the wait. He caught a handful of her silky hair and let it slide through his fingers. ''Let your hair grow again, Cimarron. I remember it long.''

''How on earth would you remember when I had long hair? We've hardly ever seen each other.'' She received such a smoldering look of desire that her heart seemed to miss a beat. ''You noticed me?''

''Yes, I noticed you. You're a very beautiful woman.'' Heat flooded her cheeks, and amusement seemed to sparkle in his gaze. ''Surely you've been told that many times.''

She shrugged. ''Fontaine did after we were engaged, but he was biased.''

''I'm not biased. I'm enough of a stranger to be coolly objective.''

She laughed then and Nick curbed the urge to reach for her. If she only knew how badly he wanted her, how badly he wanted to just touch her. ''Okay, lady, will you go out with me to a hole in the wall tomorrow night?''

''Yes.''

''Ah. Hurdle number one over.''

''You don't really have hurdles. We've done what you wanted all week long.''

''No, we haven't,'' he said in a husky voice.

''Oh, Nick, thanks for tonight.''

He nodded and brushed her throat lightly. ''How about six tomorrow night?''

''Fine. I live at Aimsley Drive. Want me to write down my address? Actually, it's in the phone book.''

''I'll find you,'' he said easily. He caught the back of her head to pull her forward suddenly, kissing her long and hard. He released her and walked away, jamming his hands into his pockets.

"Night, Cimarron. See you tomorrow."

"Thanks for a fun week. It would have been so lonely."

"It would have been for me too."

"Liar," she teased, making a face at him and he laughed.

"It was fun." He walked away and she watched him go. If she wanted, he would come back and make love to her. The thought made her ache with desire, yet she wondered how much of it was a deep feeling for Nick and how much of it was simply physical need. She shouldn't have made the date for Sunday night. Once she was back in Tulsa, everything would be so different. She watched Nick stride away in long steps and remembered how his body had felt pressed against hers.

16

The morning paper rested on the kitchen counter while Freedom ate a slice of toast and drank orange juice. His gaze raked over the page and he saw an article about the All-College Wrestling Championship. He read swiftly, knowing Oklahoma was third, Texas fifth. It would be televised on cable tonight, and he wondered if Raye was in town.

That evening when he returned from work, his gaze swept the hall, and he grinned, remembering their bet. The morning after he had their basketball bet the plants were gone, and he had been happy with bare walls, a happiness that had lasted three days until he came home to find a note from Raye saying she had returned to Texas, leaving behind a hall filled with papier mâché animals. Two parrots roosted on bars hung from the ceiling, a dog and a cat rested beside Raye's door. A six-foot gorilla filled a corner, and they were all lined up on her side of the hall. She hadn't been back in town since she had placed them there.

The aroma of something bitter assailed him and he paused, sniffing the air, wondering if something was on fire. He took several deep whiffs and moved closer to her door.

Sauerkraut. He stared at the door, glancing at the menagerie, and was tempted to confront her about them now. Instead he went home. Inside the kitchen as he put away groceries, he glanced at the paper and saw the article about the wrestling match.

With a shrug, he crossed the hall and punched the bell. The door swung open and she stood there in a bright red, yellow, and orange jumpsuit made of material he didn't recognize. Her hair was looped and pinned on her head, little tendrils escaping as they always did.

"You left me with a zoo. I should have let you keep the plants. I should have guessed you would retaliate."

"My animals? *Quid pro quo?* No, not at all. I thought it would keep things from being so stark, so cold."

"Oh, it isn't cold out here. You've ruined one date's evening with me. The gorilla terrified her."

"No kidding? Gorilla phobia?"

"No. She thought some mugger was lurking in the corner."

"L.T. doesn't look like a mugger."

"L.T.?"

"Sure. They all have names." She took his arm and moved beneath a flaming parrot. "That's Polly."

"Not too original," he said, noticing Raye had smooth skin.

"The dog is Will. The cat is Isabelle. The other parrot is Bebee."

"How long are they going to be here?"

She shrugged. "It's my side of the hall."

"I know that. How long?"

"I suppose as long as there aren't any plants."

He laughed. "I could complain to the condo board."

"You won't."

"Why not?"

She smiled. "You're sorta nice."

"Gee whiz, thanks," he said, suddenly enjoying himself. She was grating, but interesting. "'*Quid pro quo?*'" he quoted her. "Sure you dropped out of high school?"

"I'm sure. Why?"

"The All-College wrestling matches will be televised in twenty minutes. Want to come watch?"

"Do you mind if I bring my dinner?"

"I'll feed you if you'll eat spaghetti. I haven't eaten either."

"Sure. I'll bring a salad."

"Bring the fixings and mix it at my place," he said, and then remembered her messiness.

"Sure. I'll be right there."

He went home and put water on to boil, cutting up green peppers and onions to make sauce. Raye came in and began making a salad, littering the counter with lettuce leaves and bits of radish and peppers. She went back to her place to get the dressing.

"Freedom," Raye called, walking in with three people behind her. "You have company."

He faced three friends, Thad Ketcham, one of his accountants, Jeannine, Thad's girlfriend, and Ava North, a friend Freedom had dated off and on for several years.

"Hi," Freedom said, introducing everyone, realizing Ava looked embarrassed and annoyed to find Raye.

"We came by," Thad said, sounding awkward, "to see if you wanted to go with us to the concert. I have four tickets. I didn't think you'd have company."

"Sorry. We're watching the wrestling match. Raye's a neighbor. She's a Texas fan."

"Oh? Did you go to Texas University?" Ava asked.

"No. I live in Dallas part of the time, so I cheer for Texas."

"Oh? Where'd you go to college?" Ava persisted.

"I didn't," Raye answered in a level voice, glancing at Freedom. "You go on with your friends. The wrestling match isn't important."

"No. We have a bet and I have to see if I win or lose," he answered with a smile, moving closer to drape his arm across her shoulders.

Raye was startled, looking at Freedom. He smiled at her and his arm tightened around her shoulders, pulling her closer.

"Sorry we interrupted you," Thad said, sounding sincerely regretful.

"Hey, stay and watch," Freedom said, having no gripe with Thad. "If the wrestling matches weren't on, I'd go."

They declined and left quickly, Ava giving him a fiery look that meant it would be a long time before he had a date with her again, but at the moment, he didn't care. When the door closed behind them, he looked down at Raye.

She stood pressed to his side, his arm still around her as she gazed up. His green eyes drifted over her face, down to her mouth, pausing there as his expression changed.

She became acutely aware of him, feeling the strength in his long arm. Her heart began to drum to a faster beat, stirred by hungry eyes that shouldn't have noticed her presence. His golden hair curled over his forehead, his eyes were intense and curious, his lips slightly parted. His mouth was sexy and appealing, the look he gave her made her hot. She lifted her face, closing her eyes when he leaned down and kissed her.

Relishing his kiss, she felt a hard young body press against hers and bend over her. When he released her, she moved back. He frowned, and she felt as if he must be having the same reaction she was.

"Let's forget that happened, Freedom," she said in a breathless voice.

He nodded, studying her as if he hadn't really looked at her before. "We'll go watch the match."

They ate in front of the television and within half an hour the edgy awareness they had of each other seemed to dissipate and they could cheer their respective teams with their old enthusiasm. "You have to remove the animals if my teams win," he said at one point.

"No way! Your team will probably win."

"I'll spot you eight points."

"No way. I won't bet the animals. I'll bet cooking dinner for you, putting the plants back, taking out the gorilla or one parrot."

"The gorilla is a deal."

"And eight points."

"Deal."

"And if I win what do I get?" she asked.

"What do you want?"

The words didn't sound the same as they had before. There was an innuendo to them that held a double meaning. "A trip to the zoo," she tried to say lightly. "I love to go to the zoo."

"You've got to be kidding! I haven't been to a zoo since I moved here."

"The zoo and my gorilla and eight points."

"Deal." He grinned and shook his head and she remembered too clearly his kiss. There were moments she caught him studying her and her heart seemed to lurch. Oklahoma won, but only by six points.

"I win!" she yelped as they both faced each other. "We get to go to the zoo."

"Oh, Lord. I can't believe they lost. They were supposed to win by a big margin."

"A deal's a deal. Of course, if you want to change it and let me put my plants back—"

"When do you want to go to the zoo?"

"I go back to Dallas Saturday. How about Friday afternoon when you get off work."

"The animals will be going to bed. I can't believe that I have to go to the zoo and live with B.T. too."

"L.T."

"L.T., B.T., what difference does it make?"

"Freedom, Schmeedom—you want to be called the right name."

"I'm real. That's a paper monkey. You must not have had any toys when you were little."

"I didn't have *anything* when I was little," she answered

quietly. Instantly she laughed. "And I don't need your sympathy!"

"I didn't give you any," he answered just as lightly, wondering about her background. "Late Friday the animals will be going in for the night," he repeated.

"We can see the monkeys. I'm happy with the monkeys."

"That figures."

"What do you mean by that?" she asked. She knew he was teasing her. His eyes sparkled and a smile hovered around his mouth. He shrugged.

"I'm going home now," she said. "Thanks for the game and I'll see you after work Friday."

"Sure thing," he said, following her to the door, watching the sway of her hips as she moved ahead of him. "Actually, Raye, it's early."

"I better go home," she said, all playfulness evaporating. "Thanks, Freedom. Thanks for staying home tonight."

"It was fun," he said, his gaze devouring her. Her breath caught and she turned away quickly because she saw him moving closer. He caught her arm. "Raye—"

"No," she whispered.

He drew her to him, ignoring the slight push against his chest as his arms tightened, and he kissed her long and hard. When he released her she stepped away.

"Don't do that. I'm the same as married." She hurried across the hall into her condo and locked the door behind her.

He stood scowling at the brown wood, knowing she was another man's woman, knowing he shouldn't want her. They weren't compatible. All they did was fight from the first moment they met. His gaze swept over the animals and in anger he picked up an ashtray from a hall table and threw it at one of the parrots that grinned down at him.

It hit the paper bird squarely in the chest, knocked him off his perch, and struck the wall with a bang. The parrot fell to the floor, wire feet sticking into the air. Raye's door flew open.

"What was that bang?"

"I killed one of your damned birds!" he snapped, went into his condo, and slammed the door.

Raye stood staring at his door and looked around, spotting the parrot. She frowned and stared at Freedom's door, and then went over to pick up the bird. It had a tear in its chest. She picked up the gleaming brass ashtray and stood with both items, staring at Freedom's door again. She set the ashtray outside his door and took the parrot home with her.

The next morning as Freedom left, he glanced up. The parrot was back on his perch with a bandage wrapped around its chest. Freedom stood glaring at it, embarrassed, feeling ridiculous for losing his temper, remembering why he had lost it, finally laughing at Raye's bandage. He thought about her that morning, struggling to keep his mind on his work. He thought about her during lunch until Thad said, "Hey, you there. Where's the mind?"

"Sorry, Thad."

"What are you thinking about?"

"The Louisiana offshore wells," he answered absent-mindedly.

Thad gave him a dubious look and ate in silence.

After lunch he went to see Cimarron, taking a report to her. "How's it feel to be back from the Caribbean?"

"Busy. I forgot how many problems can crop up in one day. It was nice to have a week away."

"You had a good time?"

"Yes, I did."

He watched her closely, decided she was telling the truth and thought she looked better. "You're tanned now. I think Mexico agreed with you."

"It did. Let's see what you have." She stood up to come around the desk and his gaze raked over her, taking in the sleek navy dress with a simple narrow white band four inches from the hem. "Wow, Mrs. CEO, you have a new dress. Nice."

"Thanks, Freedom. You always notice women's clothes."

"Actually—"

"I know. You always notice women."

He grinned. "Best thing on earth to look at, bar none."

She smoothed her skirt. "As a matter of fact, this came

from your neighbor's shop. I hate to patronize the enemy, but she's nice, Freedom. And she's a marvelous designer." Cimarron spun around to show off her dress. Freedom's brows arched, and there was a scowl of disbelief on his face.

"Raye designed *that* dress?"

"Yes. You're too hard on her. I know you. When you don't like someone, you don't like anything about them. This is a good design and you have to admit it."

"I'll be damned."

"You sound terribly surprised. Give her credit for a brain."

"Do you know what she wears around her house? Things with big glow-in-the-dark flowers and old ratty bathrobes and purple shoes and red socks."

"Maybe she doesn't design the things she wears at home."

"She couldn't design that and wear what I've seen her wear."

"She didn't look loud and flashy when I saw her. She had on a red skirt and white blouse."

"Yeah, I've seen her wear them."

"You should be a little more tolerant."

He gave her a sudden intense look that startled Cimarron and puzzled her.

"I'll try, Sunny. I promise, I'll try." He spread the report on the desk and they both bent their heads over it, but once during their conversation, his arguments tapered off and she looked up to see him studying her.

"Freedom?"

"Oh, I was just looking at your dress. It's really nice."

"I know. You were telling me about the cost on this."

"Hmm?"

"Freedom, are you all right?"

"The cost. Look, here are my figures."

They both returned their attention to the report, and later after he left, she sat at her desk staring after him, wondering what was the matter with him, if something was wrong he hadn't told her. He seemed preoccupied and worried, a little angry. She sighed and went back to work.

Raye changed clothes four times before she decided on new white jeans and a navy sweater. She caught her hair up by fastening it at the top of her head, holding it with a flat navy bow, and letting it tumble down the back of her head. It hung straight in a shimmering fall. She sang as she dressed, excitement humming in her, trying to think of the zoo, instead, thinking of Freedom.

The doorbell rang and she frowned, glancing at the clock. He was thirty minutes early. She didn't have on any makeup and she had just polished her nails. She rushed to the door, glancing once at the mirror. She flung open the door to face Laz.

"Hi, baby," he said, taking her in his arms to kiss her. For just a moment she didn't respond. In seconds he pulled away and frowned. "Hey, you act as if you aren't glad to see me."

"Of course I'm glad," she said, pulling him inside, praying Freedom wouldn't come home. "You surprised me. That's all."

"Yeah," he said. "You look great. Were you going out?"

"No, oh no! Maybe now I am," she said, smiling at him, feeling a sense of panic. If he found out she had a date with Freedom she was frightened of what he might do.

"Yeah, we'll go out to dinner," he said, shedding his coat. "In a little while. First things first. I've missed you."

He reached out to fondle her breast and she wanted to step away. She caught his wrist. "Laz. I want you to see the store."

"Sure. We'll go down there."

"Now, please. Let's go first. Before dark. It looks different in the daylight."

"In a minute, Raye," he said, taking her in his arms. He kissed her throat, peeling off her sweater and she changed her tactics, suddenly sagging against him, running her hands over him wildly and moaning.

"That's more like it," he murmured, unfastening her jeans. She peeled away his trousers, stroking him, pushing him toward the sofa.

"You're a wildcat," he murmured as she straddled him. In minutes they climaxed, and she relaxed on him. She shifted slightly to look at the grandfather clock. Ten minutes before six. Freedom could knock at any time.

"I'm starved, Laz. Take me out to eat." She sat up to smile at him.

He studied her and she felt another moment of panic. "That was fast," he said.

"Since when don't you like fast? I didn't get breakfast or lunch today. I was just leaving to pick up a hamburger, but now that you're here, let's have a steak, look at the shop. We have lots of time," she said seductively, kissing his shoulder.

"Okay," he picked up his clothes. "Where's the bathroom?"

"Straight through that door," she said, pulling on her sweater. He left and she yanked on jeans and scribbled a note. Racing across the hall, she propped the note against Freedom's door and ran back, her heart pounding crazily. She picked up her underwear and went to her bathroom to shower quickly, praying Freedom saw the note.

Freedom slowed and parked at the curb, his anticipation growing. The zoo. He smiled and started to get out of the car when the front door of the building opened and Raye came out with a man.

He had his arm around her waist and she walked close against him, laughing at something he said. They headed toward a Lincoln parked at the curb. Laz Kaminski. Freedom knew him and felt a flash of dislike that was burning and unreasonable. He had never cared for Laz Kaminski and his heavy-handed tactics in bidding on leases, but now he hated him.

Raye looked directly at him, her eyes meeting his. Without acknowledging Freedom's existence, she looked up at Kaminski. They climbed into a car and drove away. Freedom stared at the black car until it was out of sight and then he realized his hands were knotted into fists and his chest ached.

"Son of a bitch," he said. "Damned son of a bitch." He climbed out and went inside, spotting the white paper propped against his door. He closed the door behind him, pausing in his entryway to read it. It was in cramped handwriting almost as unreadable as his own.

"Freedom: Sorry. Laz is in town. We'll do the zoo another time. You can't get out of your bet. Raye."

He crumpled the note and threw it. He shouldn't care. Laz Kaminski's kept woman. His mistress. She would sleep with Kaminski tonight. Freedom swore and picked up the phone, dialing a number.

"Janet, this is Freedom." He listened a moment and laughed, some of the tenseness going out of his shoulders. "Want to go out to eat?"

When she accepted, he felt a wave of relief engulf him. "Sure, I can go to the ballet," he answered when she told him she had to go for her paper and write an article about it.

"Pick you up in twenty minutes," he said, thankful he wouldn't have to stay home and think about Raye and Kaminski.

That night as he held Janet Grant's hand and watched dancers spinning across the stage, he thought of Raye. He shouldn't care. She was messy, unpredictable, not his type. She lived with Kaminski, and he opened stores for her. It was high-class prostitution. Freedom argued with himself and none of his logical arguments changed the anger he felt. He spent the night with Janet, trying his best to please her, to forget other women. At two as he lay in the darkened bedroom with Janet wrapped around him, sleep wouldn't come and he stared at the clock, wondering what Raye was doing.

She was probably sleeping like a baby in Kaminski's arms, he thought angrily. He stared at the ceiling, images taunting him of her with Kaminski. Freedom swore and extricated himself carefully, climbing out of bed to go to the darkened living room.

"I don't care," he whispered aloud. He hadn't ever cared about anyone except Janie Winters. Women were alike and easy to find, someone fun like Janet tonight. His arguments were hollow and he sank down in an easy chair, falling asleep there to wake at seven o'clock to find Janet tiptoeing around him.

Wednesday when he went home, he found Raye standing with her arms full of groceries, trying to balance them and unlock her door. Without a word, he crossed to take the key from her hand and unlock the door, pushing it open.

"Thanks, Freedom," she said, sounding subdued. "I'm going to Dallas tomorrow."

He followed her inside. "Is he here?"

"No. And I have a dinner date in just a few minutes."

"Kaminski?"

"No, he's gone back to Dallas. No, it's a buyer who wants to show me a new line of clothes. I'm sorry about going to the zoo. I won't be back from Texas for a long time."

He watched her move around him, setting down the bags of groceries and putting lettuce in the refrigerator, talking too fast, avoiding looking directly at him. "I may put this condo up for sale. I should have let you have it that time."

He argued with himself. Walk out and leave her. Let her go back to Dallas where she wants to be. He felt as if something were pushing against his heart, cutting off his breath. "Yeah, well, good luck, Raye," he said. He walked out and slammed the door behind him, crossing to his door and hunting for his key. He looked back, his gaze sweeping over the paper animals. He didn't want her to go. He crossed the hall and knocked on her door. It opened instantly and she looked up at him.

He pulled her into his arms, losing all his finesse. He kissed her hungrily, his mouth opening hers, his tongue thrusting deep, playing over hers. She stood stiffly resisting him, trembling in his arms, pushing against his chest until he held her too tightly for her to push away.

He bent over her, not caring if she lost her balance. She clung to him, her arms tightened, and then she responded as if a dam had burst. She kissed him, holding him, wanting him.

Raye was torn with conflict. For the first time since she was seventeen and so green, she wanted a man desperately and she knew exactly how disastrous it was to want this particular man. She knew she shouldn't. She belonged to Laz. She was committed financially, physically. Yet . . . she moaned and held Freedom and kissed him back and stopped thinking.

He picked her up and carried her into his condo and kicked the door shut. She knew what he was doing and she wanted him. She wanted his young, virile, golden body. She wanted his kisses. Freedom Chisholm. Just this once. One time, she wanted to be his, to love him in return.

He set her on her feet in his living room, his hands drifting slowly down her sides.

She opened her eyes to meet his burning gaze. "Just this one time, Freedom. Otherwise I really belong to him. I'm on the pill."

"Damn him to hell," Freedom said quietly with such force, she drew a deep breath and stood on tiptoe to kiss him, letting her mouth savor his, running her hands over him as if she had found an infinitely important treasure.

Freedom held her, trembling with need, knowing just this once wouldn't do. Not the way he felt about her. He twisted tiny pearl buttons and pushed away her blouse. His heart seemed to stop. She wasn't wearing a bra. Her breasts were full and high and firm. He bent his head to kiss her, teasing her, his mouth closing over a dusky nipple, listening to her moan as he peeled away her jeans and lacy bikini. She was small waisted, her hips flaring out, long legged, and he wanted to kiss every inch of her, to make her burn with the same desire he felt.

When he finally moved between her thighs, he paused, fighting for control as he gazed down at her. "Raye, this is special," he said gruffly, his forehead beaded with perspiration.

She gazed up at this incredible golden body. He was muscular, tanned, fit. His chest was covered with a golden mat of curls, his body breathtaking, his belly flat, his buttocks firm, his erection hard and ready. She raised her hips to meet him, giving herself to him as fully as possible, knowing how he was fighting for control until they both cried out and clung together and it was a once in a lifetime moment.

She held him tightly, stroking his back, no words of love passing from either of them because she was frightened and sad and suspected he was angry. He couldn't love her. She had annoyed him too much and too often, yet he wanted her, no mistake there. But she loved him and she knew it. And she wasn't free to do anything about it.

"I love you," she whispered and he raised up to look at her.

"Do you mean that?"

She looked away. "I have to stay with him."

Freedom swore and moved away, gathering his clothes and leaving her. When she dressed, she returned to find him standing beside a window.

"Freedom, I've made commitments to him, I might as well be married to him."

"You're not married. What do the stores cost? Can I buy out his interest?"

"No. He's poured an enormous amount into them." She moved restlessly. "I'm bound to him."

"Dammit, you could get free if it were a marriage. People divorce, people break contracts—"

"No. I went into this with an agreement. I have to pay him to get out. I never expected this to happen."

"Tell me how much money you're talking about. I have investments."

"I'm legally bound. Maybe someday. If he tires of me or—"

"Or what?" Freedom snapped, trying to control his rage. His gaze raked over her and he wanted her again. She was too hippy, too long legged, but none of it mattered. She looked gorgeous to him. He moved to her to put his arms around her. "I want you, Raye. I want you to leave him."

"I can't," she answered stubbornly.

"Tell me you love him."

"You know I don't, but I'm not leaving him," she answered, every word like a knife thrust. "I don't want to lose my stores," she said. "If I leave him, he gets my stores. I've dreamed of them for years and they were beyond hope until Laz."

He drew a sharp breath as if she had slapped him. His eyes narrowed and he moved away. "I hope to hell your stores give you a lot of happiness," he said, storming out and slamming the door behind him, leaving her in his condo.

He stood in the hall with the paper animals and he wanted to smash every one of them, to vent his rage and frustration. He strode to his car and left with a squeal of tires, having no destination, heading out of the city.

Raye watched him leave in stony silence from the front door of the building. She went back to his condo to look at it one last time. She would go to Dallas and put the condo up for sale and not come back to Tulsa unless she had to. She wanted Freedom. She had kept a wall around her heart, but she had let her guard down with Freedom.

She left at ten o'clock that night for Dallas, leaning against the cool window of the plane and looking down at the sprawling city with sparkling lights, knowing Freedom was there somewhere, that she was leaving him. Freedom. A funny name and how she wished she had him.

She was in Dallas for only two days. Friday she left for Tulsa with Laz; he had business there and insisted she accompany him. They didn't see Freedom and she was relieved, but the moment she walked into the hallway of the condo, she wanted him as she had never wanted anything before.

17

In the blue waters of the Gulf of Mexico, twenty-eight miles offshore Louisiana on the Grand Isle acreage, the West Pass Block Number Six logged fifty-two feet of net oil pay. A confirmation well just logged forty feet of net oil pay and Laredo Oil had a sixty percent working interest in the property. The only cloud cast was the fact that Nick had to leave Tulsa for two weeks. He had another date with Cimarron, but he was afraid the long absence would make her more wary. He had promised to go back to the same hole-in-the-wall place and his pulse drummed with anticipation as he stood in front of her door.

A maid ushered him inside and he waited, barely giving notice to surroundings that reminded him of the home he had grown up in. His full attention was on the staircase as his gaze drifted up over her jeans and pink shirt. Her hair was a fraction longer now, swinging slightly with each step.

Cimarron smiled at him. "Welcome back to Tulsa. I've been hearing about your new offshore well."

"We did all right."

She laughed. "Always given to understatement?"

"Only when I'm with my competition," he retorted, tucking her arm in his. They drove to Papa Luigi's and one of Papa's sons, Tony, greeted them.

"It seems odd to think of you living in this neighborhood and playing with Tony as a child," she said when they were eating.

"We moved to the bigger house when I was seven, but I still played in sports with Tony."

"The food is marvelous. I wonder why they haven't moved."

"They do a good business. Tony has a nice big house in an older part of town. This works, so they stayed with it."

"They could do more," she said, gazing at the cracked walls, the plain wooden floor.

"Some people are content if they have enough to get along. They're not out to own the world like Laz. You're pretty ambitious yourself, so this is probably difficult for you to understand."

"I don't know that I'm so ambitious. It's just a way of keeping a tie with Fontaine."

"Come on, Cimarron, admit it. You like the challenge." A fleeting look of distaste crossed his features. "Well, hell. I promised we wouldn't see anyone you know, but I forgot the one person we do know who eats here. Here comes Laz."

Nick stood up as Laz and Raye stopped at the table. "Hi, Raye. You know Cimarron. Cimarron, this is my father, Laz Kaminski."

"Of course," Laz said. "We've met. White Star Oil. The Kaminskis still come back to eat spaghetti at Papa's. I suppose Nick told you he grew up with Papa's boys. They played on the same baseball team and on the same football team."

"That's what he said," she said pleasantly, noticing more than ever the resemblance between father and son in their smoke-colored eyes and curly hair. "How are you, Raye?"

"Fine."

"Good to see you two," Laz said. "Go ahead and eat." He took Raye's arm and they moved to a booth at the back. Nick sat down, staring at Cimarron over glasses of red Chianti.

"Tell me again about Raye and your brother. I remember your saying something about them."

"They own condos across the hall from each other in the same complex," she said, looking at Laz who leaned forward to talk to Raye. "They don't get along."

"Is that right?"

She focused on Nick. "You sound doubtful."

"How long since you've heard him mention her?"

"A long time. I take that back. He did the afternoon I came home from Cancun. Freedom usually isn't so hostile. It's too bad, because Raye is nice and they're neighbors, but I don't suppose it really matters."

"It's none of my business, but I would be willing to stake a small wager that they're not quite the enemies you think. Which is interesting. And maybe sad. Laz is possessive."

"What on earth are you talking about? Freedom doesn't think she has any taste, he thinks she's sloppy."

"It would be humorous if it were any other situation except the one she's in. If she's madly in love, Laz won't let her go until he's good and ready."

"You're crazy. Why would you think something like that?"

They sat in silence while Tony placed steaming white platters of spaghetti covered in thick red sauce before each of them. He refilled wine glasses and left a basket of golden-brown garlic toast, and after a few bites, she returned to the conversation. "Why do you think they're friends?"

"Your brother and Raye? You should have seen the look she gave you. It couldn't have been you; I'll bet it's because there's a resemblance between you and your brother."

"How could you notice something like that?" She stopped eating to study him. "What makes you that way?"

He sipped his wine. "Maybe it's because I grew up an only child in a volatile household. I had to learn to read the signals early."

"When you talk about Laz, you change completely," she said, hating to hear the smoldering anger in his tone. "Maybe he's changed, Nick. How do you know he hasn't?"

"That's exactly what I hoped the last time I accepted an invitation to one of his parties. I hadn't been there an hour before he started talking about my coming back to Kamnick. He hasn't changed and he never will."

She placed her hand on his. "I'm sorry," she said, starting to withdraw her hand swiftly, because the touch changed the moment and awareness sparked between them.

She could feel it and saw a flickering response in his eyes. Nick was a handsome, exciting man, and she was becoming more aware of it each time she was with him. In the car after they left the restaurant, he drove to his place.

"Come see where I live."

"Nick, I just don't want to—"

"All you're doing is looking at a house," he said offhandedly, driving to the fringe of Tulsa, a wooded hilly area where he owned twenty-five acres. He took a gravel road to a stone ranch-style house nestled in oaks. Holding her hand casually, they walked through rooms that were so different from Fontaine's formal mansion with its flawless decorator interior, priceless antiques, and fine art. Nick's living room was chintz and leather and lived-in furniture. The paintings were animals in western settings, a cougar on a snowy branch, an eagle above a craggy peak. A gun rack lined the wall to the east of the fireplace. She learned he owned three horses and rode as often as he had a chance. "Tim, my oldest brother, would love this house."

"And Freedom?"

"Freedom is Danish modern and doesn't want to think about trees, land, animals, or plants. He wants as far from a farm as possible." A piano stood in the corner and she looked at him in surprise. "You play the piano?"

He grinned. "My mother's influence. Laz likes music, too. Music and sports—football and basketball—are our two common grounds. I don't play the piano for company."

She laughed as they moved through the room and stepped down into a large den with a stone fireplace, a sofa and chairs, a pool table, and a bar.

"You have a nice home, Nick."

"It's comfortable. Play pool?"

"A little," she said, moving to the cue sticks.

He knelt down to build a fire, his jeans pulling tightly on his long legs. As soon as it was roaring, he poured them each a brandy and handed her a cue stick. "Want to play eight ball or rotation?"

"Eight ball is fine."

He racked the balls and waved his hand. "Go ahead."

They played in earnest; Cimarron lined up her shots with care, seeing that Nick was good, wondering if he was letting her keep up with him or if she was just being lucky. She sunk the eight ball first and gave him a victorious smile.

"This time let's wager," he said, tossing balls on the table.

"Depends on the wager. What do you want to bet? I don't go in for high wagers. I'm a two-dollar bettor at a race track. That was how Raye Honeywall lost all her plants."

"How's that?"

"She bet my brother that Texas would win a basketball game. She lost and had to move her plants out of the hall they share."

Nick laughed. "And that made him happy?"

"Not really, because she replaced the plants with papier mâché animals," Cimarron said, bending over to line up a shot. Her hair fell forward, a shimmering red-gold beneath the soft glow of the brass lamp hanging over the table. "I think there's a whole side to Raye she keeps to herself. Her shop is extremely tasteful. Unless that's all your father's doing."

"I doubt it. Laz probably gave her the money and told her to do what she wants simply because it's dresses. A boutique would bore him." Nick set down his brandy and bent down to study a shot. "Paper animals," he said softly, laughing. He didn't shoot, but instead stood up. "I'll make you another wager—I'm right about Raye and Freedom."

"I don't think we can get an answer to that one easily. My brother hasn't given any indication he likes her—" She frowned and stared into space. "I hope he doesn't get hurt. If she loves your father . . ." Her voice trailed away. "People in love lose all sanity."

"Do they really?"

She glanced at him. "Haven't you ever been in love?"

"No. Not a lasting need for someone for the rest of my life."

"Well, good sense goes when it happens."

He smiled at her, thinking he had lost all good sense where she was concerned. "Want to bet?"

"No. Only on pool. I won't bet on my brother."

"Okay," he said cheerfully. They moved around the table and she was aware of his strong hands, the tangle of his thick curls, his concentration. He paused and squinted up at her. "How about betting a date tomorrow night if I win?"

"Agreed!" she said, laughing. "You could just simply ask, you know. And if I win?"

"Nope. I want to bet you a date tomorrow night against whatever you'd like."

"A date tomorrow night. I'd win then too," she said quietly, and his heart lurched. She went on and he wondered if she had been flirting, openly honest, or simply lying to him about tomorrow night. "I suppose I'll wager you take me to Papa Luigi's once again."

"Done. I win either way."

As he moved around the table, she began to think he had set her up and let her win the first game, because he stayed ahead of her, winning handily. He sank the eight ball while she still had four balls on the table—he had had only one at the end of the last game.

"One game for you and one for me. Let's play one more. This time if I win, you go with me two weeks from Friday night."

"Where?"

"I'm riding in a rodeo in Nowata."

She straightened up to stare at him. "You actually still do that?"

He grinned and shrugged. "It's a way of relaxing."

"This I'll have to see. I'll go win or lose."

He laughed. "Good. I should have known an old farm girl like you would be happy at a rodeo."

She laughed and tossed her head and her hair swung back from her face. Desire scalded him. He wanted to throw down the cue stick and go around the table to take her in his arms, but he knew he would ruin things if he did. He sighed and bent over to line up the balls for a shot. He won again;

it was closer this time with only two balls left on the table. "Rodeo it is," he said as the eight ball dropped into the pocket. "I'll take you back to Papa's too. Bring your drink and we'll sit by the fire."

He sat down on the floor, patting a spot beside him. "Come down here. You'll get warmer."

She came down, leaving a space between them. "I'm not cold, but this is nice."

The phone rang; Nick answered and held out the phone. "Peyton Phelps. He says it's important."

She took the phone and Nick moved back in front of the fire, listening to her talk softly about a well. Finally, she replaced the phone. "Too bad I can't ask your advice."

"You can."

"Sure. I seem to remember you have your own company and we're in the same business."

"Depends on what it's about. There are things I'd be happy to help; other problems, no way."

"They've had a blowout on a well in the Gulf."

"Jesus. Where?"

"It's offshore Texas. We have the working interest, so it's White Star's responsibility. They'll call to report on it, so I may get another call, but Peyton said they already have a specialist they've flown in, and he thinks he can get it under control quickly. They're working on it now. No men were seriously hurt, which he said was a miracle, and they're optimistic about controlling it. He'll keep me posted. There's nothing I can do at this point. This is where I miss Fontaine. I'm not an engineer or a geologist. I have good ones who work for White Star, so it's all up to them."

"That's the best thing to do. Peyton Phelps has a reputation for being a good man. If you need any of my people to help, they're available."

"Nick. You're the opposition," she said, teasing him.

"Not on a blowout and never where you're concerned," he said gruffly, his gaze moving to her mouth.

She felt desire flare; an aching awareness that made her wish he would reach for her. She wanted to be kissed. Nick made her forget problems and have fun again. He looked at her with blatant desire, and it made her breathing slow.

He slid his arm around her waist and pulled her closer. "Cimarron," he whispered. His mouth touched hers, his lips opening her mouth. He moved, kissing her deeply and long. She held him a long time before she pushed away and sat up with a dazed expression.

"Nick, don't. I'm ready and then I'm not."

"I'd call that progress," he said softly, touching her ear.

She stood up. "I should go home."

He took her home right away, asking her to call about the blowout no matter what the hour.

At three in the morning, she called him as she had promised him she would. He sounded as alert and awake as ever.

"Nick? Haven't you been asleep?"

"Yes, as a matter of fact. How's the well?"

"They have it under control." Her voice was sleepy and instantly Nick was taunted by visions of her.

"Good! I'm glad you called."

"They said you sent some equipment and men from one of the Laredo rigs."

"We're close."

"I hate waking you, but you made me promise and I always keep my promises."

"I'll bet you do," he said softly. He lay back on the pillow, his body aching with desire for her, longing stirred simply by the languorous sound of her voice on the phone. "Have you seen the rigs in the Gulf?"

"Yes, when we flew to Cancun."

"Let's go back to Cancun this spring," he said in a husky voice.

"Maybe so, Nick. It was fun."

"Honey, I think you better hang up the phone now before you fall asleep."

"I'm sleeping better. Maybe that's thanks to you."

"Good ol' Doc Kaminski. Good night, Cimarron. I'm glad you called me."

"Sure, Nick," she said sleepily and replaced the receiver, leaving Nick to stare into the dark.

They went out every night for the next three weeks. Friday, the rodeo night, was a balmy first week in March, the air chilling as the sun went down. Nick picked her up at half past five and they drove north out of Tulsa, stopping on the road to eat at a truck stop.

At the rodeo Cimarron sat in the center of the bleachers and Nick said he had to leave her. "Give me something for good luck."

She laughed and kissed his cheeks. "How's that?"

His eyes sparkled, and he winked at her. "It's great! Cheer for me." He jumped down to stride away. He wore boots, faded jeans, a wool plaid shirt, and a broad-brimmed black Stetson and he looked as handsome as he had in a navy pin-stripe suit. Excitement churned in her along with a thread of fear for his safety.

She watched the first two bull riders with mounting tension. One was thrown the second he left the chute, the other clinging almost until the buzzer sounded. And then Nick. The announcer read his name, telling the last win and the riding time. He directed attention to chute three and Whirlwind. When the chute burst open and Nick clung to the bull, she was torn between watching and hiding her eyes.

The buzzer sounded and she cheered with the spectators as Nick dropped to the ground to scramble over the fence. With seventy-five points, he came in second and everyone applauded. Bull riding was the last event; people were leaving when he met her as she climbed down the bleachers. She hugged him wildly. He smelled of dirt and leather and his shirt was dusty, but she was so thankful he was all right, she didn't care. "Nick, I was so scared! That was terrifying."

Nick held her tightly against him and thought he would ride a bull every night if it would get her into his arms. "Let's go get a beer. There's a place down the road." They walked in long strides to his pickup that he had kept from oil-patch days. It had a wide front seat, and he could pull her close against his side.

"I was so frightened you'd be thrown and stomped on," she said, holding him around the waist. He didn't think she was aware of what she was doing, but he loved it and intended to make the most of it. They pulled in alongside a row of pickups at a rustic log building with a sign over the front that proclaimed: *Tumbleweeds*. Another sign read: Beer, Food, Snooker.

As Nick led Cimarron to a table, couples doing the two-step circled the dance floor, boots shuffling on the planks. He ordered two beers and asked her to dance.

Keeping in step, they gazed into each other's eyes through the dark, smoky interior. Nick thought she was the most beautiful woman he had ever known. He had always thought she was beautiful, but the feeling was stronger after getting to know her. Tonight she had let down more barriers, her spontaneity showing. She had been carefree enough to give him the kiss on his cheek. She gazed back at him solemnly, and he wondered what ran through her mind. It was becoming more difficult to practice restraint around her.

Later he took her to his place. "Come in and have one more beer or a brandy and play a game of pool and I'll take you home."

Laughing she climbed down, and he held her close as he walked. He put on a tape, got them both another beer even though she protested, and played pool with her. They each won a game, and he took her hand to sit down in front of the fire.

"You're good for me, Nick. I've had fun tonight."

"Good. Ol' Doc Kaminski, bull rider and pepper-upper extraordinaire," he said, pulling her back against his chest. As he talked, his breath fanned on her cheek. He stroked silky locks of auburn hair away from her face. As they sat quietly talking, he wanted to kiss her. He turned her to face him, and she was only inches away, the expression in her thickly lashed green eyes changing to a languorous sensuality that didn't hold protests.

It was dusky in the room and Nick was masculine in his western clothes. His hair was tangled, his eyes filled with longing, desire burned in their depths. She wanted him to hold her. She wanted his kiss. He drew her to him slowly, sliding his arm around her waist, his hand behind her head. "How I've wanted to do this all evening," he whispered. When he bent his head to kiss her, she slid her arms around his neck and pressed against him as his arms tightened while he kissed her deep and hard, his tongue playing over hers, Cimarron returning his kiss.

Desire made her tremble. She wanted Nick. His arms were strong around her, his body hard, bending over hers. He wanted her and she wanted to be loved. He was careful, sensitive, and solitary, and she felt safe with him. She ran her hands over his muscled shoulders, unfastening the buttons of his shirt to slide her fingers across his warm, muscular chest. He was virile, more energetic than Fontaine had been, more demanding. She felt his fingers at her buttons and she shivered with delight, wanting him to make her forget everything, to make her lose control, to drive her to abandon.

He pushed her blouse off her shoulders, peeling it away to drop it on the floor with his shirt. She tugged free his belt and dropped it and he stepped back, holding her, looking at her with smoldering, hooded eyes. She drew a deep breath beneath his scrutiny that made her react as much as if he had caressed her.

Nick held her waist, unfastening her jeans, looking at her full, thrusting breasts that were beautiful, covered with scraps of pink lace that he removed. He burned with need for her, but he wanted to look at her and relish the moment. He was in love with her. Passionately, permanently. And he didn't think it was mutual. She liked him, she had fun with him, she was lonesome; she wanted his kisses tonight, but she wasn't in love and it frightened him, because he wasn't sure he could ever win her love. She was a marvel to him in so many ways, her body dazzling.

"I'm protected, Nick," she whispered, her fingers running through thick soft curls at the back of his head. He cupped her breasts, filling his hand with her warm, soft flesh, teasing each nipple with his lips and tongue. She gasped and moaned, her head tilting back, her eyes closed.

He peeled away her jeans and pink bikini, stripping off the last of his clothes.

"Touch me, Cimarron," he whispered, inhaling deeply when she did. Her fingers moved over him intimately until he caught her hands, because he wanted to take time with her and he couldn't if she continued to stroke him. Nick's hand moved over her smooth skin, down the curve of her hips to her thighs. He pulled her down on the thick carpet as he held her and caressed her. She was wild in his arms, passionate, demanding, moving over him to explore his body as much as he had explored hers, kissing him until he shuddered. He rolled her down on her back and moved between her thighs.

She clung to him, raising her hips to meet him. Her gaze raced over him, his hard, long, lean body that was taut flesh and muscles and throbbing, blue-veined erection, so masculine, so virile. He cupped her hips, pulling her up, pausing to caress her and make her gasp with need.

Words of love rose to Nick's lips as he thrust into her softness. Instead, all he did was murmur her name over and over while his fingers tangled in her hair and he kissed her deeply, moving in rhythm that built to a climax. Wanting her, he cried out her name, hearing her soft cry, hearing her say his name in return.

Spent, his weight came down on her as he rolled on his side and held her close against him, their legs entwined.

"You're wonderful, Nick."

"That's mutual admiration, love." He slid his hand over her heated flesh, feeling the indentation of her waist, the slight flare of her hips, the smoothness of her thigh. She was a marvel, and his desire was far deeper than purely physical. "I could hold you forever."

"I think I want you to."

"You're good for me, Cimarron."

"And you for me," she said, twisting to gaze at him. Her eyes looked darker, her lips swollen and red, a sensual languor to her expression that made it evident she had just made love.

"You're so beautiful," he said in a husky voice, cupping her breast and feeling her softness.

"My, we are a mutual admiration society, because I rather like to look at you," she said with fatuous satisfaction that made him laugh.

"Look all you want. Everything you see is yours." They talked lazily, Nick stroking her lightly all the time. He wanted her in his arms all night. He couldn't stop letting his gaze drift down over her body.

She kissed his shoulder. "I should shower."

"And so should I, so why waste the water?" He stood up. "We'll do this together. No protests. This isn't a night for protests. They're permitted on Mondays, not Fridays." He led her to the shower, turned the water to a steamy warmth, and joined her beneath the spray. Her golden and pink and ivory body glistened in the water as he soaped her, moving his hand in lazy, sensuous circles, seeing her nipples harden, feeling desire rekindle in him as her hands slid along his thighs and she looked at him with passion burning in her gaze. He continued, turning her, his hands gliding over her, rubbing and stroking until both of them were gasping with need.

"We'll slip and break our legs."

"Never," he whispered, kissing her breasts. He picked her up. "Put your legs around me," he said, easing her down his hard, wet erection, entering her easily, and bracing his legs as she moved her hips. He trust into her warmth and both of them cried out as they climaxed. He held her, water hitting him between the shoulders, unaware of anything except Cimarron's marvelous body, her head on his shoulder, her slippery arms and legs wrapped around him. Finally, she raised her head to gaze into his eyes and they both smiled with satisfaction and joy.

"You're pretty fantastic, lady," he said in a husky voice. He let her slide down, her feet touching the floor again and they both washed off, climbing out and drying each other.

At dawn they lay in each other's arms in his bed, his leg thrown over hers.

"What a perfect night," Nick whispered.

"Do you ever wear out?" she asked sleepily.

"Not when I'm with you. It's impossible. All I have to do is look at you or brush my hand over you like this, or rub my leg against you like this—"

"Or have me put my hand on you like this?" she asked softly, teasing him as she stroked his thigh. "Lord, you're oversexed, Nick."

"No. That's not the reason," he answered solemnly, and her breath caught at the hungry look in his eyes. He pulled her close to kiss her.

Midmorning, she stretched and yawned and rolled over to find him watching her with that intensity that was beginning to become familiar. "Haven't you slept?"

"I dozed a minute or two. Mostly I want to look at you."

"You're crazy."

"No. I know a good thing when I see it."

"I should be home doing something constructive."

"No. You're right where you belong. And you're going to be back here again."

She studied him, seeing complications arise, wanting the night left like it was with no strings attached. She played with a lock of his hair. "I do need to go home."

"Okay. I'll take you home. Will you go to dinner tonight?"

"Yes. That would be nice."

"Can we come out of hiding yet and let men know you're going out with me? It shouldn't make a whole lot of difference, because I intend to monopolize your time."

"Sure, Nick. We can come out of hiding," she said, smiling at him, her voice filled with affection and he ached to hear more than affection, to see something besides desire in her gaze.

They dressed and he drove her home. "See you tonight at seven, Cimarron."

"Sure." She bent down to kiss him again and it was a long kiss. Both were breathing hard when they pulled apart.

"If I thought you'd go back home with me, I'd pull you down in this car right now."

"No. I really do have things I have to do today. I

promised Freedom I'd go with him to get a new chair for his living room."

"Okay. See you tonight." Nick drove away and she stood and watched him. It had been a marvelous night. She didn't know what she felt for Nick or what he felt for her, but the night had been fun and Nick was wonderful. She realized she might be a little in love with him and she almost missed a step as it dawned on her. She paused, gazing back down the drive where dust was settling from his car. She didn't think she would ever love again, but Nick's unassuming charm could slip up on her without warning.

She thought about his battle with Laz as she climbed the stairs to her room. That was a dark cloud on Nick's horizon. She suspected both Laz and Nick would lose when a showdown came. She wondered if Nick could give up his determination to destroy Kamnick. If he loved Laz deep down, he would ultimately destroy part of himself.

She didn't understand the kind of fighting and clash of wills father and son had, because it was foreign to her family. Peter had raised each of his children to be independent, to think, and to act on their decisions. They also had been raised to help each other and pull together. She and Nick were different breeds.

18

In twilight before dark set in, Laz stood in the empty Tulsa boutique. "Very nice, Raye. Damned nice. You think this woman can manage it now with you in Dallas?"

"Yes."

"I'm going to be in Tulsa more often."

"Why?" Something seemed to constrict her breathing and she felt as if something dark and terrifying loomed ahead.

"I'm going to buy out an oil company here." His voice held anger, and she knew instantly it had something to do with Nick.

"You're going to take over Laredo Oil," she said, trying to think how this would affect her. She liked Nick. He was pleasant, intelligent, and sometimes more likeable than Laz. For a moment she studied Laz, who was wearing his new double-breasted, cream-colored, wool-and-silk suit by Verri. He wore a striped monogrammed shirt and enameled vermeil cuff links, a silk-twill tie by Luciano. She thought of Nick last night dressed in jeans and a sweater, so different from his father. Laz was successful, but he needed all the trappings that went with it, and right now she guessed that the clothes he was wearing, including the cap-toed calfskin shoes, would tally over two thousand dollars. He didn't need the ten thousand she had contracted to pay him if she walked out, but he would demand it.

"No, it's not Laredo I'm after. Not yet. I want Kamnick to grow. It's good business. I want Kamnick to be there when Nick decides he wants to do things my way, because I think that's where he's headed whether he realizes it or not."

"Laz, Nick is intelligent, successful. Why don't you make peace with him before you're an old man and it's too late?"

"Shut up, Raye. You don't know a damned thing about it! The kid is a smartass who has to run things without listening to his old man who made it all possible. Just shut up about it!"

"You're going to lose a fine son who really loves you—"

"The hell he does. If I thought he did—"

"You can't see anything except what you want!"

Laz slapped her hard, his palm hitting the side of her face, a crack in the silence of the empty boutique. She cried out and moved back, looking at him with loathing.

"I told you to shut up about it," he said, his voice tinged with rage. "You don't know a damned thing about Nick and me."

Her jaw hurt, her skin stung, and fury made her clench

her fist. But along with fury was fear. Laz was a strong, violent man. She knew if she angered him further, he would beat her. If she left him now, he would take the stores. She tried to breathe deeply, to calm her stormy emotions. "So what are your plans, Laz? What oil company do you intend to buy?"

"At the moment that's a secret," he said. "Only a few people know, but I can trust you. I want White Star Oil. White Star has been put into play by Fontaine Durand's death. It's in a weakened position with a change in leadership, internal problems in personnel. His widow is managing and at the rate she's going, she can withstand a hostile takeover before long. I want to act now."

Her mind raced over his secret. *Freedom's* company. Cimarron Durand's actually. Would a takeover hurt Freedom?

"How can you keep it a secret?"

He moved restlessly around the boutique. "I made a toehold purchase long ago. Once a purchaser owns five percent, they have to make a public disclosure to the Securities and Exchange Commission. What we're doing won't be secret much longer. This is the fourth of March. I expect to file with the S.E.C. within two weeks, no later than the middle of March. We have brokers in New York buying up shares of stock for us. We've put the money in a dummy account."

"And now Cimarron Durand is seeing Nick."

"That was an interesting development," Laz said with satisfaction. "It will make the whole deal more fun. It opens up new possibilities. I can make her a promising offer to stay."

"What kind of promising offer?" she asked, hearing a sly note in his voice.

"She likes Nick. She can keep an important position, vice-president, if she gets Nick to cooperate."

"I don't think they're that friendly."

"If she was at Papa's with Nick, they're more than friendly. He doesn't take everyone there. That's a private place to him. As a matter of fact, I hope she is important to him. Nick needs to marry and she's a classy dame. Real class. She's a good businesswoman, and she's damned beautiful. One of the best-looking women I've ever seen," he said, idly bending down to look into a case displaying jewelry. "Is this stuff expensive?"

"Yes," Raye answered with antipathy, wondering what she meant to Laz, and if he had any respect for her.

"Good. I don't want to invest in trinkets."

"What about the others at White Star. Would you keep them on?"

"I doubt it. The company needs to be overhauled." He looked at her intently. "Come here, Raye."

She knew what he wanted. She heard the change in his voice and she suspected he wanted to make her aware of his power. He had done it before when something had annoyed him, only this was the first time she had angered him. She crossed the room to him and put her hands on his shoulders, uncertain what he would do.

"Undress."

She knew better than to protest. Anger rose in her, but there was no way to fight him. She smiled at him and tried to be seductive as she unzipped her green dress and pushed it to the floor. She stepped out of it, flicking the catch to her bra. His eyes lowered and his chest expanded with a deep breath.

She tried to stop thinking, to move and obey him, to survive the moment, because she suspected it was a test of sorts to see if she would cooperate, to find out if she were still angry.

She hated him with a burning rage, but she was smart enough to know she had bound herself to him and she would have to pay the price. She unfastened a stocking from her garter belt and slowly drew it off and then did the same with the next one. She peeled down the narrow yellow bikini and stood naked in front of him. She wouldn't have been surprised if he had hit her. Instead, he gathered her to him, pushing her down on the floor and moving between her legs.

"Laz, we're in the store!" she blurted.

"It's dark and empty and mine," he answered, and she

suspected what he wanted was to remind her of his power. He unzipped his pants, his throbbing cock ready as he jammed it into her. He climaxed swiftly before she did. She clung to him; her eyes were squeezed shut and she wanted to scream with frustration and anger. As soon as he was through he moved away.

"Get your clothes on and we'll go eat."

She knew she should try to get him into a better humor, but she didn't care and she didn't want to make the effort. She was well aware she was running risks. Her thoughts were filled with worry about Freedom, because Freedom had invested heavily in White Star.

Over dinner she tried to show interest in Laz. Several times she caught him watching her with a puzzled expression.

"Still angry because I hit you, aren't you?" he asked once.

"My face hurts."

"You didn't answer my question."

"I'm trying to forget it. It wasn't like you."

"Yeah. Well, let's see a little life out of you, Raye. I don't like temperamental women."

"Sure, Laz."

They went back to the condominium. She glanced at Freedom's door and felt a sharp stab of pain.

To her relief, Laz was busy every day, gone before she left for the boutique, late coming home. She wished he were seeing another woman, but she knew he wasn't. When he came home, he told her about his business meetings and she listened closely. One thing she could do for Freedom was warn him what Laz planned. Yet if Laz found out there was a leak, he would be wild until he found out who had done it. She was torn with the choices, worrying about Freedom, terrified she would encounter him in the hall sometime when she was with Laz. If Laz suspected she hadn't been faithful to him, that would bring down his wrath as swiftly as a business betrayal.

One day she came home and Freedom was bending over to unlock his door. Her heart slammed against her ribs and she looked at him as if she wanted to memorize every detail about him. He looked marvelous. She wanted to walk into his arms and beg him to run away with her. Only he couldn't and she couldn't. All she could do was stand and stare.

"Hello, Raye," he said solemnly. He looked thinner as she studied him.

"Freedom," she answered and her voice was weak and breathless. His eyes narrowed and he came closer.

"You're staying here with Kaminski now aren't you?"

"Yes. He has business in Tulsa."

Freedom kept walking closer and her pulse began to pound, blocking out all sounds. He stopped inches from her, his gaze raking over her features, longing plain in his eyes.

"I miss you," he said, and she closed her eyes.

His arms went around her and he bent his head and they kissed desperately until she pushed away.

"Don't do that! I'm bound to him. I did it. He didn't. I won't leave him."

"You're scared of him."

"I made a deal. I'm going to stick by it."

"Bullshit. You don't love him. Tell me you love him."

She hurt so badly, yet she was terrified Laz might return.

"Tell me you don't love me."

"I don't . . ." She couldn't say it. She loved him with all her being. He was golden, handsome, exciting, marvelous, and so unattainable. "Leave me alone, Freedom. Just leave me alone!" She tore away to run to her door and jam the key in the lock. Freedom's hand closed over hers.

"Raye, let me fight him for us," he said quietly.

"Can't you understand, I'm his, Freedom. My body is his. I'm his kept woman."

With each word he looked as if he were receiving a blow and for the first time in years, tears came to her eyes.

"Get away from me before he walks in and catches us." She unlocked the door and stepped inside. "If you don't want to make things harder for me, leave me alone."

She locked the door and sagged against it, slipping down to the floor to put her head in her hands and rock back and forth. "Freedom," she whispered repeatedly, wanting him, wanting more than one kiss, aching for him, loving him, needing him, and knowing it would never be.

Two days later after living in torment, knowing she was making Laz impatient with her because of her preoccupation with problems, she slipped a note beneath Freedom's door. She had written she would come home for lunch the next day and she asked Freedom to come home so she could talk to him about business.

Just the thought of seeing him, being alone with him, made her dress with care. She let her hair fall freely over her shoulders, wearing a simple red dress with a white collar. She waited in the hall, watching for him. He came up the walk in a long stride and entered the hall.

"You wanted to see me," he said.

"Yes. Can we go in your place?"

He unlocked the door and ushered her in, following her inside. "Where's Kaminski?" he asked tersely, tossing the key to a table and shrugging out of his navy suit coat.

"In a meeting, I hope." Freedom's gaze drifted down over her and back up and she felt as if he had mentally stripped away her dress.

"How long do we have alone?" he asked, his gaze scalding.

"I need to talk to you and go. I never know when he'll change his plans."

"All right, Raye. What is it? We don't have any kind of business together."

"If he ever finds out what I've done—" she said, but all she could really think about was Freedom. "He's buying up shares of White Star," she said fast.

It took a second for her news to register with Freedom. He hadn't expected anything concerning White Star, expecting something involving the two of them. He stared at her, dumbfounded. "*White Star*?"

She nodded and started moving around him. "I've risked everything I have, and Freedom, you can't understand what poverty I came from, why I have to keep my boutiques, but I don't want you hurt,'' she said, moving toward the door.

''You're leaving?'' he asked in a pained voice.

She gazed into eyes filled with longing and she couldn't take another step toward the door. As if invisible bonds were fastening around her, she stood motionless, knowing she should go, unable to move.

Freedom reached out and drew her to him, her brown eyes widening. Desire rocked him; he forgot White Star and Laz Kaminski. His mouth covered hers to stop any protest, but none came. She clung to him, moaning with longing, kissing him wildly in return. Her hands raked over his shoulders, down his flat belly, feeling his hard erection that came so swiftly. He moved his face inches. ''How long do we have?''

''We don't have any time,'' she said, hurting because she wanted him. ''I can't let him find me here or learn that I've been loved by another man.''

''Oh, hell,'' Freedom murmured, kissing her passionately, moving his hands over her, sliding up the skirt of her dress to caress her and in minutes her dress lay in a heap on the floor. They made love frantically, desperation making them hurry, yet how marvelous it was to her. Her heart seemed to burst with joy and rapture, blanking out all the horror of a future without Freedom.

They lay spent in each other's arms on the floor and she moved away from him, pausing to kiss him tenderly. ''I love you. I never thought I'd say that.'' She rose swiftly and pulled on her clothes. ''I have to get home.''

Watching her, he sat up to pull on his shorts and slacks. He followed her to the door. ''Raye, we have to do something.''

''We can't. I won't.'' She hurried across the hall while Freedom closed his door. When he was dressed he phoned Lars Griffen at the New York brokerage firm used by White Star. It took only a few minutes to relate his problem to Lars, to ask him to check on the trading of White Star stock and to see if someone was trying to put the company into play.

He had appointments for the first two hours after he got back to the office until half past three when he went to Cimarron's office. "Hi, what's going on?" he asked as he closed the door and sank down on a chair.

"The usual. Ralston is hot because of the equipment expenses last month in Canada."

"Going out with Nick tonight?"

"Yes, as a matter of fact."

"Is he still crossways with his father?"

"Yes," she answered, slanting a curious glance at Freedom as she put away a folder. "I wish he didn't feel the way he does."

Freedom had been worried lately, his temper short, and she had tried to leave him alone. She hadn't seen him this way in years and she didn't know what was wrong. Right now his eyes were stormy, his hair tangled.

"Cimarron, do you discuss business with Nick?"

"Nothing I shouldn't. What's happened?"

"Laz Kamnick is going to attempt to take over White Star."

Her first reaction was a protest that such a thing was absurd. The protest died when she looked at Freedom and when she thought about Nick. Had he been using her? She frowned. "We haven't been informed of any heavy trading. The price of shares is the same."

"I'm checking into that, but if it was done quietly enough, the price might not change."

She wondered how Freedom had heard the rumor. "You think your source is accurate?"

"Very."

She stared at him with a feeling of dread in the pit of her stomach. "I've never heard Fontaine talk about fighting off a takeover."

"They're not too common. Particularly a hostile one, but there are beginning to be more of them. And this is a bad time for us, because of the commitments to exploration and drilling we've recently made." He didn't add because of Fontaine's death and battles between Cimarron and Ralston.

She stared out the front window. "Freedom, I swear Nick

can't be in on it. He and his father are bitter enemies." She noticed the tight lines around Freedom's mouth that she couldn't remember seeing before.

"Raye Honeywall told you this," she said, suddenly wondering if Raye were the reason for Freedom's irritability recently.

"Jesus!" He paled, giving her a shock. "If you guessed so easily how I learned, it won't take Laz Kaminski a full minute."

She was astounded, realizing for the first time what was the matter with Freedom. *"You're in love with Raye Honeywall?"*

Freedom's eyes filled with fiery anger and unhappiness, and Cimarron closed her eyes in pain. "Oh, Freedom!"

"Yeah. I can really pick 'em, can't I. Maybe I have some kind of hang-up—always wanting the impossible."

"She can leave Laz."

"She won't leave him. He gave her the boutiques, and she won't give them up," he said with bitterness. "I'll call you the minute I hear any further developments from Lars."

"I'll call a meeting. Peyton is out of town, but he'll be back tonight."

"I have a call in for Bruce Flagstaff, one of the bankers. Don't worry prematurely. At least we know what they're trying to do. Cimarron, I had to ask about Nick. Your instincts are probably right about him."

"I don't know. I thought so, but if someone's quietly buying up shares, I don't know."

"I think you'd know. Don't worry. Believe what he says; you'll know without a doubt soon enough."

19

The black ball rolled across the smooth green felt, struck the orange to sink it in the pocket with a thud. Nick straightened up to gaze across the table at Cimarron. His tie was loosened, the top button of his collar was unfastened, his cuffs were rolled back. He watched her line up a shot and miss. She glanced at him. "Your turn."

He put down his cue stick, walked around the table to take hers from her hands and place it on the table. He led her to the bar and climbed onto a stool facing her. He spread his knees so hers were between them. "Okay, what's wrong?"

Something flickered in the depths of her eyes and he could feel trouble coming. Her gaze slid away from his. "Sorry. I didn't know it showed. Business problems."

Silence drew out between them as he studied the top of her head. He wanted to pull her into his arms and try to get her to share her burden with him, but he knew how fiercely independent she was. "And since I'm competition, I can't share the worries with you or try to help?"

She gave him a look of despair. "That's right, Nick. You can always figure things out."

He ran possibilities through his mind, wondering what could be so bad at work that she couldn't unburden herself on him. "We don't have any mutual leases at the moment, no competitive bids that I know about—and I would know."

"If we can't drop it, Nick, we'll have to avoid each other for the time being. I have to keep my personal life and my business separate."

"In that case I'll drop it like a rock. But I hate to see you worry. It gets to me that I can't help in any way."

"Maybe in a few days. Right now things are crucial and it's important that I don't discuss it. See—already you know something is going on at White Star that's secret. That's enough to make any oil man perk up his ears."

She smiled, but it didn't reach her eyes and he guessed that he was directly involved even if he didn't know why. "How about a movie? A comedy that will make you forget White Star for maybe five minutes tonight."

"Okay," she answered in a preoccupied voice.

He sat next to her in the darkened theater and laughed when the audience did, slipping surreptitious glances at Cimarron.

When they were parked in the car on her driveway, she faced him. "Sorry I'm such poor company. I really shouldn't go out, Nick, until we get this settled."

"We can't discuss it?" he asked, watching her closely. He wanted to do something to stop the barrier that was rising again between them; he had worked so carefully to tear it down. He loved her and wanted her and was trying to give her time. They hadn't made love since that once even though he wanted to more than ever before in his life. The slightest touch by her could ignite desire that seared him like a torch.

"Have I done something?" he asked gently, groping for a way to reach her. He frowned and studied her, knowing it was something he had done inadvertently, because he had no inkling of what the trouble could be. "Honey, can't we talk about it?"

Cimarron listened, hurting. She had spent more of her emotions on Nick than she realized and the thought that he had been winning her friendship, making love to her for financial gain hurt. Yet she knew she was naive and vulnerable. There was something trusting in her nature; she instinctively expected people to be good and was shocked when they weren't.

She looked at Nick in the darkness and she wanted to know the truth. "Let's go inside for a minute."

Without a word he came around to hold the door. Inside, she turned off the burglar alarm and entered the large kitchen where a light burned over the stove.

Cimarron faced him, finding it hard to ask, half wanting to avoid knowing. He looked so handsome and she wanted him to kiss her until she forgot business. Worry showed in his eyes, a tenseness in the set of his shoulders. "Nick . . ."

"Go ahead. Ask whatever you want."

She looked down at the smooth cherry-wood cabinet and ran her fingers along the edge. "Please don't lie to me." Her voice was flat. "Isn't that a ridiculous request!"

He drew her to him, tilting her head up to gaze into her eyes. "You think I'm about to do something to hurt you. I swear to you, that is the last thing I'd do. I can't imagine what I've done to cause you trouble. Honey, I wouldn't knowingly—"

"I can be so gullible."

"Lord, Cimarron, I won't hurt you," he said. His eyes darkened and he bent his head to kiss her passionately. His arms tightened around her and he kissed her as if it were his last kiss for the rest of his life. He leaned over her until she had to cling to him. Finally she responded, letting down the barriers, yielding, returning his kisses.

When he stopped, he raised his head. Argentine eyes, thickly lashed, intense, focused on her. "Want to tell me about it?"

"I promised Freedom I wouldn't discuss it with anyone except Peyton."

"You promised Freedom, yet it's something I've done?" Nick was more perplexed than ever.

"It's your father," she confided finally. "He's trying to take over White Star."

"Jesus!" Nick moved away in agitation, his fists resting on his hips while he swore. He turned around to stare at her with an intensity that made her draw a sharp breath. "You think I'm in it with him! God, Cimarron! You should know better than that! I wouldn't hurt you—"

"I know I'm vulnerable right now, and there's always the part of me that's a trusting farm girl."

"Oh, hell. Cimarron, I swear to you, I don't have anything to do with Kamnick." He met her searching stare. "You'll see," he said gruffly. "Time will prove the truth. There's no way I'd side with Laz against you."

Wanting to believe him desperately, she closed her eyes and rubbed her forehead. "I feel so uncertain. I don't want to lose White Star."

"Damn Laz." Nick rubbed the back of his neck while he mulled over possibilities. "Who're your lawyers?"

"Randall, Segura, and Thompson."

"There's a firm in Houston, Baker and Botts—one of the best. We use a New York firm and New York investment bankers. It means traveling—I meet with them in New York—but they're experienced at this."

"Fontaine always used R.S.T."

"Have they made suggestions?"

"Yes. We've talked and we have another meeting tomorrow."

"You have a line of credit established?"

"Yes."

Nick paced the room while she made coffee. "It's not my decision, but I wouldn't resort to greenmail. Don't pay Kamnick to withdraw their offer; that's poor use of stockholders' funds."

"Greenmail isn't one of the options we're studying right now. They've talked about several possibilities—a proxy fight. A lollipop tactic where certain current shareholders can tender shares."

"At a premium price," he said. "But only if an undesirable bidder acquires a number of the outstanding shares. It makes the hostile takeover unappealing. What about your board members? If there's a proxy fight, will you have them solidly behind you?"

"No. I'm afraid Ralston will oppose me. I think if there's a proxy fight, three, possibly four directors will vote with Kamnick and they can influence shareholders."

"Have your lawyers suggested a phone campaign, try to reach stockholders for their proxies?"

"Yes. It's one choice."

"I'm asking the questions here," he said dryly. "You don't have to answer or you can just tell me to shut up."

"I may be a sucker, but ask away," she said solemnly, deciding to trust him completely. His eyes darkened a fraction and he leaned forward to kiss her. When he pulled away, he ran his fingers through his hair, raking tight curls.

"Have they suggested making an offer for Kamnick?"

"I think that's out of the question, but Freedom doesn't."

"It shouldn't be out of the question. If you need a partner, Laredo would be willing."

"I couldn't pit you against your father! I'll take other partners, but not Laredo Oil."

"Surely, you would use our help to save White Star!"

"I hope it doesn't come to that. We've invested heavily in exploration and refinery improvements, we're still expanding because that's what Fontaine had projected and that's what seemed best, but now, it may put us in a precarious position."

"Once again—you can have Laredo for a partner if you need one. I can probably line up other partners for you. If Kamnick makes a tender offer for White Star stock, or vice versa, I suppose you know it means the bidder has to wait twenty business days before paying for the tendered stock."

"Yes. Kamnick's stock is around forty-five dollars a share right now."

"White Star's is slightly lower, isn't it? Forty?"

Cimarron pushed away a curl from his forehead. Her suspicions of him evaporated. "Nick," she said, her voice changing, "thanks for your help." She ran her hand across his shoulder. Instantly, his gaze swung to meet hers, and desire fanned to flame in his expression. The look he gave her was as potent as a caress, heating her, making her forget White Star.

They made love on her dining room floor, clothes strewn around them and when they were exhausted, holding each other, Nick rose up on his elbow. "I love you, Cimarron," he said in a husky voice.

A tremor shook her and she clung to him. "Nick, I'm so

scared that what I feel is a mixture of loneliness and sorrow and love."

"Honey, we have time," he said, stroking her head. "We have lots of time. You're the only woman, today, yesterday, tomorrow and tomorrow."

She ran her finger over his jaw, feeling tiny stubble, letting her hand drift over his chest. His body was a marvel. He excited her until she lost all reason. As his hand moved lazily across her full breasts, she leaned forward to kiss him.

Much later she said, "Nick, I owe you an apolo—"

"No, you don't. You've only known me a short time and Laz is my father."

"I should have known better."

"Forget it," he said gruffly, smoothing her hair back behind her ears. "I'm glad you're letting your hair grow. I like it long. How the hell did you find out about Kamnick? When Laz wants to do something sly, he's careful."

"Freedom learned it."

"Freedom knows?" Cimarron knew what was going through Nick's mind. "I hate to say I told you so," he added quietly.

"You were right. Freedom is in love with Raye, and she won't leave Laz."

"She's a little money-grubber then," Nick said. "I'll have to admit I'm disappointed because I like Raye."

"Freedom loves her and with my brother, it's serious. Freedom said she made a deal with Laz."

"She's made a bargain with the devil."

"Oh, Nick, I wish you didn't hate him!"

He studied her and slowly smiled, pulling her closer to kiss her. "Let's talk about love, instead of hate," he whispered.

When he kissed her goodbye it was dawn. "If I can do anything, I will."

"You're good for me, Nick," she said softly. It wasn't what he wanted to hear, but he was glad to have made as much progress with her as he had. He had won her trust. Hopefully, love would follow.

"I'll call you today and we'll go to dinner tonight."

"Thanks, Nick."

He strode to his car and drove away with her watching him. He ached to hear her say, "I love you," just once. It rolled off the tongue of so many women so easily, but he knew when Cimarron said it, she would mean it. His jaw tightened when he thought about Laz. He had to try and stop him. If she lost the company now, Cimarron would suffer another loss almost as great as the one she had been through. It was vital to her at this stage when she was slowly recovering from her tragedy.

"Damn him," Nick mumbled in anger. He clamped his jaw shut, his mind racing over the problem.

Freedom stared at financial data. White Star oil reserves were evaluated at one hundred and sixty-two million barrels, natural gas reserves at nine hundred and seventy billion cubic feet. Oil production increased forty percent, gas production increased seventy percent during the past year. Crude oil prices climbed and were projected to continue to climb in the coming year. His mind shifted to Kamnick Oil and the strategies presented in the White Star meeting. He tossed down his pencil and swore, thinking of the man behind it all, trying unsuccessfully to keep from thinking about Raye.

He was determined to thwart Laz Kaminski in every way possible. He ached for Raye and tried to avoid seeing her, hating the few times he had seen her arrive at the condo with Kaminski. Another meeting was scheduled for Monday morning. White Star intended to make a tender offer for Kamnick stock, but the Kamnick tender offer had already been filed, and time was on Kamnick's side. Even so, White Star lawyers were drawing up the tender offer document to file with the Securities and Exchange Commission. Laredo Oil had lined up Jason Sutter's company, Thorson Petroleum, as a partner, and also, White Star had Braden Petroleum. Cimarron wouldn't accept Laredo's help, refusing to come between father and son, but with Nick getting

Thorson's help, it didn't matter. Freedom would have enjoyed joining with Nick to crush Laz.

Freedom stared at the figures in front of him. If they saved White Star, it would be due to Raye's early warning. He ran his fingers across his eyes. His head throbbed and memories of Raye tormented him constantly. If she had risked so much to tell him, she had to care.

Freedom folded papers, filled his briefcase, and went home. A late spring storm had blanketed the state with cold air and he hunched his shoulders in the chill.

On Monday night, the tenth of April, Cimarron ate an early dinner with Nick. He said he had a meeting with his lawyers and kissed her goodbye at half past six, saying he would call her later. Ten minutes after Nick left, Freedom called to ask her to attend a brief meeting; Peyton was already there as well as two of the Thorson and Braden lawyers. Their meeting broke up at nine. Cimarron now left each meeting feeling solemn and tense, knowing the battle would take time, aware White Star was in a struggle for survival. Kamnick had filed their tender offer on March seventeenth, White Star filing four days later, giving Kamnick an edge. Now White Star's team was busy contacting shareholders to persuade them to give their loyalty to White Star. Nick had been a constant help, contacting people personally, working with the Thorson lawyers while Jason Sutter was in Scotland.

She drove home to the empty mansion that had become too empty. She would always love Fontaine, but the clarity of their time together was beginning to blur.

Remembering Nick tonight, thinking about his gray eyes and curly hair, his easygoing personality that was becoming more important to her, she moved to the bedroom window and pulled back the drape. Winter seemed to be having one last fling. She let the satin drape fall back into place, longing for Nick's house that was informal and cozy and his arms that were strong. She glanced at the clock and the phone, feeling an urge to call him, but he had said he wouldn't be home until ten or eleven. In bed she rolled over to look at Fontaine's picture.

"I love you," she whispered. "I can't stop crying over you, but you're not here."

A smiling likeness of Fontaine stared back at her. She wiped her eyes and gazed at him, kissing the cold glass of the picture, hurting, replacing the picture. "Fontaine," she whispered, "I'm beginning to love Nick. It doesn't make me love you less."

There was only silence. When she called Nick, he wasn't home. As the hours ticked past and she tried to no avail to phone him, she wondered where he was. He wasn't home at one in the morning, and she worried about him, wondering if he were still in a meeting. She dozed with the light on and a book beside her. At ten minutes after two the phone rang and she answered it groggily.

"Sunny," Freedom said, and she came awake at once, because she knew his tone of voice. "I have bad news. I'll come pick you up. The fire department just called me. Star Tower is on fire."

20

"*Whirlwinds of tempestuous fire . . .*" The old quote from Milton lingered in Cimarron's mind. She watched Star Tower burn while police cordoned off the block, pushing the ring of spectators back. She pulled the collar of her coat higher, chilled to the bone in spite of a mink and a thick sweater. The glistening mirrored windows popped from the heat, glass shattered and crashed on the concrete below and she remembered the first time Fontaine had shown her the building, the note of quiet pride in his voice, the excitement she had felt.

Black smoke billowed skyward, and the roar of the fire intensified. As she watched the building slowly being destroyed, she knew this would give Laz the strength he needed. The fire would financially and psychologically weaken White Star. Laz was here, of course, and she wouldn't be surprised if he and some others linked hands and danced uproariously around the burning funeral pyre.

Yards away from her stood Peyton, his blond hair tangled by the wind, his mouth open slightly and his eyes wide as if in shock. He was hatless, wearing only a jacket, his shoulders hunched forward as if to ward off a blow, disbelief clearly written in his features. His disaster might be as great as hers.

A slender figure swayed slightly, her hand raised to her mouth. In a red silk evening dress and a short sable jacket, Raye Honeywall had also come to watch the destruction.

Another siren screamed and died as a truck stopped close behind Cimarron. Men burst into action around her, hauling more hoses toward the fire. Only a few feet from Peyton stood Tim, yet neither man spoke to the other. Tim's broad-brimmed Stetson was pushed to the back of his head. He studied the crowd, and she knew he was looking for her. He would find her soon enough, and she made no effort to catch his attention. Cimarron was surprised that Tim had heard about the fire and had arrived so soon.

Since Freedom had invested heavily in White Star, Tim might finally be able to persuade Freedom to go back home to the farm.

Freedom appeared at the edge of the crowd. He spotted Tim first and went to him, the two brothers barely acknowledging each other as they watched the fire. Then Freedom turned and started walking toward Raye.

Cimarron's gaze drifted over the crowd as she searched for a head of curly hair . . . If everyone else was here, Nick had to know about the fire. *Why wasn't he here?*

Once she glimpsed a tall man with tousled locks, and her heart seemed to stop until she realized it was a stranger. She needed Nick and his strength now; he was as deeply involved in White Star's future as she. So why wasn't he here? She knew that if he really cared for her, he would be here. Puzzled hurt stirred in her and she wondered if she had misjudged Nick's motives. Perhaps he had worked with Laz after all.

The fire chief, Adam Worth, introduced himself to her. "We're doing our best, Mrs. Durand. You'd be safer if you'd get back aways."

"I'll be careful. Do you have any idea what the cause was?"

"No, ma'am. We'll have to have an investigation, although there are some indications of arson. We'll have to have a lab analysis to know."

Arson. A fire set deliberately to ruin her financially. There were dozens of people who knew Star Tower's fire would tip the scales in the takeover, including Nick.

She had never told him she loved him; never acknowledged it herself, but there was no mistaking the symptoms now, because she hurt as badly as she would have had he thrust a knife into her.

Nick had to know about the fire, and he had to have a reason for not coming. In Cimarron's mind, there could be only one reason.

Flames glittered against the inky sky, shouts of firemen, the crash of windows, and the rush of the powerful, silver jets of water mingled in the night. She was too numb for tears.

Cimarron wanted to get away from all of them, their problems, their victory, the others' losses. She walked through the darkness back to her car to sit in solitude.

Raye looked around to face Freedom who stood only yards away. His hands were jammed in his jeans pockets, his jaw raised defiantly, and when she met his gaze she felt as if she had received a blow in her midriff. Rage burned in Freedom's eyes and suddenly she wondered if he blamed her, or by blaming Laz, she was also guilty. She moved closer, hurting for him, for herself, and wanting to change things.

"Don't glare at me," she said quietly. "This will hurt Laz."

"How in sweet hell did you come to that conclusion?" he snapped, and she drew a sharp breath in shock.

"The building is insured, isn't it? Now there's not as much for Laz to gain."

Freedom didn't know whether to laugh or swear. "Raye, now he's won it all. This is a setback. We'll lose stockholders' confidence. We'll lose time, records—oh, hell. We lose."

She blinked and stared at him and suddenly he hurt so badly. "The damned building doesn't even matter," he said gruffly, striding away from her.

Raye shook violently, watching him walk away. Laz was ignoring her, watching the fire avidly. She hated Laz in that moment more than she had ever hated anyone. She loved Freedom when she had thought she would never love a man again. And she had hurt him terribly.

She stood on the edge of the crowd, her mind racing. There was a rumbling noise and suddenly the roof crashed through the top floors. Firemen yelled and ran, yanking hoses away, glass shattered and sparks shot into the sky, flames roaring with a new surge of life.

Cimarron drove away easing into the dark street and winding her way home at less than twenty miles per hour. She went into the empty mansion. She was alone. She had lost White Star. All of Fontaine's dreams and hopes, and a great deal of blame rested squarely on her shoulders.

She felt foolish for trusting the one man who hadn't bothered to show up to witness her ultimate destruction. And deep down she knew her hurt pride was only half the reason she ached so badly. She loved Nick. She put her head in her hands and wept.

21

Winging over the Atlantic in the dead of night in the Falcon jet, Nick headed for Aberdeen, Scotland, and the North

Sea. As he studied reports spread in his lap, he paused, staring into darkness, thinking about the North Sea. Its oil had few impurities, so it was bringing a good price and Laredo had an interest in one of the best wells.

Jason Sutter long ago had asked Nick if Laredo would like a percentage of the deal and Nick had jumped at the chance. Then Thorson's vice-president in charge of the operation had suffered a heart attack, and Jason Sutter had flown to Scotland to step in.

Nick hadn't been away from Cimarron for more than thirty minutes when he had received a call from one of his New York lawyers asking him to fly to New York to talk with the Thorson lawyers about the Kamnick takeover. As soon as he finished talking with Charlie Leonard, Nick tried to phone Cimarron. When she didn't answer, he called Freedom and finally Cimarron's secretary, Sandy, to tell her about the meeting he needed to attend in New York. At the Tulsa airport, however, Nick was paged and learned he was needed more desperately in Scotland and the North Sea site. He arranged for one of his executives to fly to New York to the meeting.

Nick knew Sandy would relay word to Cimarron that he had gone to New York; he didn't expect to be gone more than two or three days and Charlie would notify him if any emergency arose with White Star. While waiting in the Tulsa airport he tried to call Cimarron. He couldn't understand why she wasn't home, but finally he gave up and reset his watch to the time in Aberdeen, Scotland, six hours ahead of New York.

They stopped in Manchester, England and he tried again to call Cimarron, a frown creasing his brow when she didn't answer. Concerned, he stared at his watch, because according to his calculations, it should be almost three in the morning and she should be home asleep. He tried to call repeatedly until it was time to board the plane.

In Aberdeen he changed to jeans and a sweater, pulling on a heavy parka and trying again to call Cimarron. When they called him to the chopper, he stopped once more at a phone, knowing he was holding up the flight. The weather was worsening, but he wanted to talk to Cimarron. Nick swore and ran to the chopper.

A brisk wind was blowing, rain falling in Scotland, the morning dark with storm clouds as the chopper swept up over slate-colored foaming water.

The chopper flew in over a seventy-thousand-dollar-a-day jack-up rig that stood eighty-one feet above the surface and could be moved later when the drilling was finished. Nick looked down at the derrick, a crane, the living quarters, stacked drill pipe and equipment. Seventy men worked on the rig in three-week shifts.

They landed on a helicopter pad on the production platform. Thankful they had reached the rig, Nick climbed down, wind buffeting him as Sutter came out to meet him, shaking hands, his sandy hair hidden by a hard hat. His dark eyes sparkled. "I know what this means to you, and with Dan in the hospital, I wanted you here. You've got a knack for fixing trouble," Jason said, raising his voice above the clank of machinery and the howl of the wind and sea.

Nick nodded, thinking what success here in this remote, wild place would bring not only to him, but indirectly to Cimarron. Thorson, because of Jason Sutter, was giving all the help possible in the White Star battle with Kamnick. Nick was doing what he could without directly involving Laredo, something Cimarron forbid. This well could give Thorson and White Star the protection against Laz that Cimarron needed.

Nick, Jason, and the crew worked in the foulest of weather, hoping their instincts had been right. Damaged machinery and a diminished work force due to illness left them all tense and irritable, but when at last the well was flowing at the rate of fourteen thousand barrels a day, they celebrated. Nick was anxious to get off the rig, to get to Scotland and start home, but weather had locked them in. His men were busy lining up stockholders for Cimarron, so he felt better about waiting out the storm one more day on the rig. He knew Cimarron would wonder what had taken him so long, but he couldn't wait to share his good news with her. It would most likely secure White Star's future in her hands.

The morning after the fire, Raye pulled the belt of her flowered bathrobe tight as she read the newspaper headlines. With every sentence her fury increased. When Laz appeared in the kitchen doorway, she flung the paper at him.

He caught the paper and his eyes narrowed. "What the hell?"

"You set that fire."

"The hell you say! It helped me, and I'll benefit from it, but I didn't set it."

"Oh, I know *you* didn't! You'd hire it out."

"I don't know why you'd give a shit, but I didn't. I'm as innocent of causing the fire as you are."

She stared at him. She knew him well by now and she knew he didn't mind admitting when he did something underhanded. If it worked, he usually bragged about it. All was fair to Laz. What counted were results.

"It's nice to know what kind of guy you think I am."

"I know what kind you are, Laz." He grinned. She knew he was in a good humor this morning because soon White Star would be his. "The paper says arson," she persisted.

"It could have been a bum. Who knows? I wonder where the hell Nick is and why he wasn't there?"

"Maybe they don't date any longer. Laz, what about Cimarron Durand? She lost her husband in a plane crash. Don't you have any compassion?"

"I'm going to see her this week. First things first. I'm going to make her an offer. Provided she's still dating Nick." He frowned, "And I hope to hell she is."

Raye set a plate of bacon and eggs in front of Laz, frowning as she sat down across from him. "You're going to interfere in Nick's life again. Every time you do you create a bigger gulf between you."

"It's funny, Raye. I've been hard on the kid, but he's turning out to be a damned good businessman."

"You sound proud of him, yet you turn around and hurt him!"

"I think we can work together if he'll just give it a try. There may be a good reason why Nick wasn't there last night. They had a date last Saturday, so it can't be too big a rift."

"You're offering her vice-president if she'll bring Nick into the fold," she guessed.

"Vice-president and a little more."

"I wouldn't think this week would be the best time to try and wring favors from Cimarron Durand."

"Shock and desperation is always the best time." He ate quickly, scanning the paper, and then left the kitchen. In minutes he stood in the doorway in his tan, double-breasted, wool gabardine Gianni suit with an Aboud brown-and-black silk tie. He looked successful and powerful; she wished she had never met him. "I'll pick you up at the boutique tonight, Raye."

She nodded as he left. She went into the living room and watched Laz stride along, his walk full of confidence, his shoulders moving slightly with each step, looking like he owned the world.

Raye studied her contracts with Laz for the boutiques. She had mulled over her plans and this morning she had an appointment at a bank. She was thankful beyond measure Laz had been generous enough to put the condo in her name.

At eleven she walked into the small lobby of one of the new suburban banks miles from her home. The young and friendly loan officer, Rand Smith, had brown hair, gold-rimmed glasses, and pearly teeth. He sat down facing her and asked how he could help. She told him briefly about her stores, placing a balance sheet in front of him.

"I have an eighty percent interest in both boutiques, and a businessman has a twenty percent interest. The stores are running in the black. I don't have any debt."

"Who's the businessman who owns twenty percent?"

"Laz Kaminski. He owns Kamnick Oil."

There was a studied look from Rand Smith and more

interest in his eyes. "Looks like you have a good business. So how can we help you?"

She smiled at him. "I need a car and I don't want to ask my friend Mr. Kaminski for a car. As I see it, my business is doing well enough that I should be able to get a loan—fourteen thousand dollars. The shops are eighty percent mine and that includes all the fixtures, the inventory, the location in Dallas, the furniture and inventory here. I'm in the black. I own my own home and have a good credit standing."

He studied the figures. "We'll need a financial disclosure from you. What kind of car did you have in mind?"

They discussed cars, her loan, the possibility of her moving her business account to his bank. Rand Smith gave her a financial statement form to fill out.

"Thank you, Mr. Smith."

"We're a new bank and we welcome your business."

Two days later she picked up the check. She took it to another bank where she deposited the money in her account and sighed with relief. She would have the ten thousand to repay Laz to get out of the contract, because the condo was sufficient collateral, and she would have four thousand left for herself until she could find another job.

She made appointments for the next day and spent the afternoon calling on four other boutiques showing them her designs and telling store buyers that she no longer wanted to sell them exclusively in her own boutiques. She took orders for dresses, sold six during her calls, and pocketed cash that went straight into her new account.

Raye knew Laz would be busy getting the deal settled with White Star and she intended to use her free time to her best advantage. That night after Laz had gone to a meeting, she dressed as plainly as possible and left home at eight, driving to a popular singles' bar, watching crowds, knowing what she wanted.

She spotted a likely prospect, a beautiful young woman perched on a high stool at the bar. Her legs were as shapely as a model's, her hair a shimmering fall of silky gold. She had a wide mouth, giving her a sensual look, and dark eyes.

The tight red skirt and top revealed a better than average figure. Within seconds a guy moved in beside her, but Raye didn't want to lose this chance, so she got up and went to the bar to squeeze between the woman and a stranger.

He glanced at Raye and she smiled. "Excuse me, I won't be here long. I'm meeting someone, and he's late." She flashed him another smile and turned toward the woman. The man beside the woman was gone, but his beer was still on the bar, so Raye expected him to return. "Hi. I'm Raye Honeywall," she said. The woman gave her a vague smile.

"Will your boyfriend be right back?"

"Yeah. He's not my boyfriend. He's coming back."

"Can I ask you something?"

Suspicion clouded the woman's face. "Okay," she replied.

"Where do you work?"

"I sell cosmetics."

"I own a boutique and I need someone who looks like a model."

The suspicion and frown vanished. "Gee, thanks. You think I look like a model?"

"Yes, you do. Have you ever modeled?"

"No!" She smiled at Raye. "What store is it?"

"It's Honeywall's in West Wind Center."

"Oh, classy place, huh?"

"It's nice. I'm looking for someone really special."

"Sorry. Modeling would be nice, but it's not steady."

"This could be very steady."

"Yeah? Tell me about it."

The man returned and said something to her and she turned her back to Raye for a minute, and then introduced them. "Ray, meet Tom. Tom meet Raye. We want to talk just a minute," she said to him, and faced Raye while he took his beer and walked to a video machine.

"I just met Tom, but I don't know your name," Raye said.

"I'm Sherry Banks."

"Is Tom a steady boyfriend?"

"No. I just met him ten minutes before you did."

Raye fingered the diamond drop around her neck. It

sparkled in the dusky light of the bar. "Would you like to meet an interesting man? He's handsome, wealthy, likes beautiful women."

The suspicion was back instantly. Sherry's voice sharpened. "Are you setting me up or trying to hire me for something dirty?"

"No. I'm looking for someone who would like to meet the man I just described."

"Well, sure. I'd like to meet a guy like that."

"Even though you and I have just met, I need a friend. Can I confide in you?"

"Yeah, sure." Sherry's brown eyes were full of curiosity.

"You see, the man I described gave me ownership in two dress boutiques. I run them, and he gets part of the money."

"Yeah?"

"I'm tired of him."

"Well, then tell him and walk."

"I can't walk because the stores make it complicated. See, he's very rich." She waved her hand so it caught the brilliance of the huge zircon on her finger, dangling the diamond drop in front of Sherry's nose. Sherry looked at the drop and the ring. "He gave me this," Raye said, waving the drop.

"No kidding!"

"And the car I'm driving is his."

"And you're tired of that?"

Raye's hopes rose a notch. "Yes. Actually—" she leaned closer to Sherry—"I'm in love with another man. You see, the rich man is older than I am."

"How old? You said he was good-looking."

"He is and he's got the energy of a nineteen-year-old. He's forty-two I think. I don't know exactly," she lied, knowing Laz looked younger than he was. She waited, sipping her beer.

"So why do you need a model?"

"Well, what I'm actually looking for is someone who might like a boyfriend like my friend. A fun man to take them places, give them gifts. He gave me a mink this year."

"Yeah, but shouldn't he be the one looking?"

It was the question Raye had been waiting to answer. She took a deep breath, her pulse racing as she answered carefully. "He's got me. I want out. If I find a beautiful woman who can interest him, I think he'll leave me and I can keep my shops. If I leave him, I lose my shops."

"How can you want to leave this guy?"

"I've really fallen for another guy. We like the same things: basketball, jogging." She smiled. "My friend isn't into jogging. He likes horse races and yachts and fancy parties and flying to Vegas."

"He isn't rough is he?"

"No."

"And you want to introduce someone else to him?"

"Indeed I do." Raye relaxed while eagerness gripped her. She had Sherry's undivided attention. "This is what I planned. I'll find the best-looking woman I can find in a bar—which means she likes to meet men, right?"

"Yeah, right. I like to meet men."

"Okay, let's say it's you. I hire you at a good salary to work in my store. This man often comes to my store. When he does, you can meet him and flirt with him and in no time, if all goes well, he'll leave me for you."

"I'd have to quit my cosmetics job."

"Well, now, I'd be willing to pay you the same salary if possible. I mean I really want out of this relationship, but I couldn't live with my conscience if I left him unhappy after all the things he's given me. A mink coat, diamonds, dresses, presents, the car to use, nightgowns. You should see the lingerie—"

"No kidding!"

"No kidding. If you'll come by on your lunch hour I'll show you my store. Sherry, this man is a well-known man. If I told you his name, you'd know him."

"You got a picture of him?"

"As a matter of fact, I do." Raye was ready and pulled out a publicity photo of Laz. It was a good picture, probably taken three or four years before, but an accurate likeness and he was smiling at the camera.

"He is good-looking. Quitting my job, though. That's a risk."

"Well, if you want to tell me what your salary is, we might be able to work something out."

Sherry leaned close to tell Ray, who realized it was more than she wanted to spend. "That's a lot." She studied Sherry, seeing the fall of white-gold hair, the big, wide eyes. "You think you could interest him? He's a sophisticated man."

Sherry smiled, her eyes sparkling. "I do all right with men. I'm here tonight because I broke up with my boyfriend. He was getting serious and I wasn't ready to settle down."

"Is that right? Suppose I offer you exactly what you're making at your job now and you come to work selling dresses? We're both taking a risk."

"I'll come to your shop tomorrow. I can get away at five."

"Okay. Here's my card. See you tomorrow after five."

"Yeah. Thanks, Raye."

"I'm the one to thank you." She left the bar, marveling at how easy it had been and thankful Sherry had been interested after seeing Laz's picture.

The next day on Saturday afternoon at five, just before the store closed, Sherry appeared. She wore jeans and a T-shirt that was skintight, outlining her full bust and long legs. Raye smiled in gratitude as she greeted Sherry. "We close in another two minutes. If you can wait in my office, I'll be with you."

Raye waited until they were alone and her employee Margo had gone home for the night. As soon as they were alone, Raye said, "Let me show you around."

It took only minutes and then Sherry faced her. "I gave notice today. I can start next week."

"Good!" Raye's heart missed a beat. Sherry wanted the job. She wanted Laz. Raye intended to deliver him on a silver platter. Everything in her cried out to run tell Freedom her plans, to tell him she loved him, but she couldn't. She had to be careful. Laz was a shrewd, powerful, vindictive man. And she didn't want to have to pay him ten thousand dollars or lose her shops.

"Do you think you ought to tell me his name?"

"It's Laz Kaminski."

"I don't recognize him," Sherry said with obvious disappointment. "You said I would."

"He owns Kamnick Oil Company."

"Jeez! No kidding!"

"Look, your clothes may be fine, but for the time being how would you like to have some of my dresses to wear? Let's pick out a few things, an evening dress, a cocktail dress."

Sherry was staring into space, her jaw agape. "The head of Kamnick Oil. I don't think I can interest a man like that."

"Oh, yes, you can. I picked carefully."

Sherry focused on Raye. "Jeez. And you want a guy who jogs and likes basketball. Does he own an oil company too?"

"No. At the moment, I think he's unemployed, but he'll get work soon."

"No kidding. That's crazy, but if that's what you like. He must be some looker."

"He's nice. He's very tidy."

"Yeah."

"I'll tell you about Laz. I don't have to tell you how to flirt."

Sherry grinned and shook her head. "No. You don't have to tell me. You just watch me."

"If you want you could come after work and hang around here at night. I can say I have to work late to train you since you're new and then you might meet him sooner."

"Sure. I'm willing. My feet get tired after all day, but I don't guess you have tons of customers at night."

"I don't have any. The shop will be closed. We'll just sit and talk in the office and if he comes, we'll move dresses and rearrange things and put tags on new things."

"Sure. Raye, this is great. Really great." She studied Raye. "Raye, tell me the truth. Is he kinky? Does he have anything bad about him?"

"Nothing unusual. He snores. He wants his own way. He fights with his son."

"That's nothing. Will he come in tonight? I didn't dress to meet him."

"You look good," Raye said, her gaze running over Sherry's figure and skintight clothes. "You look very good."

"This is like a dream come true."

"That's what I keep thinking," Raye said dryly. Now that the possibility dangled, she was growing more anxious to be rid of Laz. "You get him interested fast, really fast, like the first month you meet him—I'll throw in a two hundred dollar bonus," Raye offered.

"Gee, you bet! I'll give it my best." Sherry nodded her head, her eyes sparkling in anticipation, and Raye was filled with hope. Half an hour later she spotted Laz.

"Sherry! Here comes Laz. Here's the key. You unlock the door and tell him I'm in back, that I'll be here in a minute."

"Sure thing, Raye." She tossed her head, her hair swinging behind her shoulders as she headed toward the door.

"Go get 'em baby," Raye whispered and hurried to the back.

Laz walked through the door and paused. "Is Raye here?"

"Hi. Yes, she's in the back. I'm Sherry."

Laz's gaze swept over her and he closed the door behind him. "Hi, Sherry. I'm Laz Kaminski."

"You have a key to the shop?"

"Yeah. Are you working here now?"

"Yes, I just started. She wants someone who can model."

His gaze raked over her at a leisurely pace. "You should be able to do that damn well."

"Thanks. I don't know a thing about modeling. Of course, I don't think women dress for women. At least, I don't. I think of a man when I pick out a new dress."

"Do you?"

She shook her head, her hair shifting across her shoulders

while she smoothed his tie. "That's a really nice tie. I always notice ties. There's something about men with curly hair and the right kind of—" She smiled. "You're a friend of my boss."

Laz smiled back at her. "Yeah, but tell me about ties."

She glanced over her shoulder. "Maybe I shouldn't. But curly hair is really *nice*."

"Yeah, Sherry. You have a regular boyfriend?"

"Not too regular. It depends."

"On what?"

"Just depends," she said smiling again.

"Want to go to dinner tomorrow night?"

She glanced over her shoulder. "Yes, I'd like that."

"I'll see if I can find a good tie."

On Wednesday in her cramped, new temporary office, Cimarron faced Freedom. The tiny room was cluttered, folding tables lining two walls, the place rented hastily and equipment moved as soon as men could work in the lower floors of Star Tower. Soggy papers were stacked on the floor.

"Laz Kaminski called," she said. "I have an appointment to see him Friday. He's taking me to lunch."

"Want me to come along? You don't have to see him alone and we don't have the situation completely assessed yet. Stock trading has been temporarily suspended because of the fire."

"I'll see him," she said.

Freedom moved around to put his hands on her shoulders. "Sorry, Sunny, you've had a tough time."

"This is getting as tough as farming, Freedom. You thought you were going to do something easier."

"With all the ups and downs, I'll still take bookkeeping to farming. I'd rather sit behind a desk than behind a horse."

She smiled at him. "When did you ever sit behind a horse?"

He couldn't smile. "Sunny, I'll help any way I can. We'll

pull through this. I can't find out where Nick is,'' Freedom said gently. ''Sandy said he left word he'd be with Thorson lawyers in New York. When I talked to one of them, he said Charlie Leonard was there in Nick's place and he didn't know where Nick was.''

''Stop trying to find him.''

''I'm going to find out if he's in this with his father.''

''I don't think so,'' she said, but her voice lacked conviction. Every hour that passed without word from Nick shook her trust more. ''I think they're truly at sword points. But I'm beginning to think he helped us fight Laz, not because he loved me, but because it would give him revenge,'' she said stiffly, finally facing the fact that had nagged at her since the fire. ''He may be doing it without even realizing what he's doing, subconsciously trying to get to Laz,'' she said, rubbing her arms.

''I think you're right. He wants Kamnick and White Star was the way to get it,'' Freedom said, agreeing with her suspicions.

''Sometimes I wonder what I've done wrong.''

''You didn't do anything wrong. You could have been as conservative as hell and Kaminski still would have managed a takeover. By the way, I meant to tell you, Tim's staying in town for awhile. We better get to the meeting. Are you ready?''

''I'll be right there.''

Freedom closed the door behind him. She hurt all over and she didn't know whether it was Nick or White Star that pained her the worst. She opened her purse and took out a picture of her with Nick on the sunfish. He was laughing, gazing down at her, wearing only cutoffs and sneakers and looking so handsome. She tore it into tiny pieces and dropped it into her wastebasket, shaking papers so the pieces would settle out of sight at the bottom. She gathered up papers for the meeting, squared her shoulders, and left.

The day passed in a blur and she spent the evening with Tim and Freedom. Both of them stayed at the mansion with her, and she knew the reason Freedom gave her was nothing more than a flimsy excuse so she wouldn't be alone.

On Friday before she was to leave for lunch, Freedom appeared at her door. "Sure you don't want me to go with you?"

"No. I'm not scared of him now. All we're doing is having lunch. I don't know what he expects to accomplish."

"Nick's out of town."

She paused from getting her lizard purse out of the drawer. "How'd you find out?"

"He's in Scotland. Laredo and Thorson are drilling in the North Sea."

She drew a deep breath, seeing the rage in Freedom's eyes, because news about the fire would have reached Nick even on a North Sea rig. There was only one conclusion she could draw—he had used her either to get at Laz or to aid Laz. She had been wrong about Nick, and although she hated to admit it, that hurt more than the loss of White Star. "I better go."

"I wouldn't put anything past Laz Kaminski. God, I hope they nail him for the arson."

"Let's not be too quick to accuse him wrongly, Freedom."

"You be careful," he said as he went out the door.

Taking one last look at herself, she wanted to be certain she looked her best. Laz may have defeated her, but she didn't want to look it. She studied her two-piece, double-breasted beige Hermès suit with a brown Armani washed-silk blouse. A thin gold Ebel watch from Fontaine circled her wrist and her hair was smoothly combed and fastened in a chignon. Satisfied, unable to find the tiniest bit of lint on her suit, she left the one-story brick building serving as the temporary headquarters for White Star. She drove to an elegant new restaurant nestled in wooded hills that had once been a home for an early-day Tulsan.

"Mrs. Durand," Laz Kaminski said, stepping forward and offering his hand. She greeted him coolly and he held her arm while the maitre d' ushered them to a private room.

Laz's gaze swept over her as she moved through the door ahead of him. Her suit was exquisite, her appearance as regal as royalty, yet the sea-green eyes and flame-colored hair gave her a fiery sensuousness that her cool manner couldn't hide. For a moment he envied Nick. If he could take her away from Nick, he would try, but after the business conflict, he didn't think it was possible. Laz moved across the table from her while the waiter held her chair. They were next to a large window with a view of the sprawling wooded grounds. Sunlight splashed through the window behind her, catching golden glints in her auburn hair and Laz enjoyed looking at her. He had won, he could see everything he wanted falling into his hands, and he felt magnanimous. He always loved to be with a beautiful woman.

"We're eating alone," she observed when they were seated. "Are you taping our conversation?"

"No," he answered with a smile, surprised at her forthright question. "First, let me say, I read in the papers that the fire was caused by arson. I swear to you, I didn't pay someone to set it or have any knowledge about it until I was called and told Star Tower was burning."

"I've reached a point in life where I'm finally learning to be not quite so gullible where people are concerned," she said, remembering her admonishment to Freedom to avoid jumping to conclusions about Laz Kaminski's involvement, but now that she was in Kaminski's presence, she felt as if she had her back to the wall and she resented his blatantly heated glances.

"In other words, you don't believe a word I just said."

"No."

"You're refreshingly candid, Mrs. Durand. No wonder you and Nick like each other." She raised her chin and a flash of anger showed in her wide eyes. Laz had a moment of uncertainty. Something he said had angered her. As instructed, the waiter brought two glasses of imported Kobrand *Pouilly-Fumé*, dry, pale wine. He placed long red menus in front of them, and they were silent a moment.

"What would you like?"

"The shrimp cocktail."

"That's an appetizer."

"And that's all I have an appetite for today."

He knew enough about people to know when he heard a decisive statement and he nodded, realizing dealing with her was not going to be easy. He ordered shrimp cocktail for her, steak and red wine for himself. When they were alone again, he sipped his wine and watched her. She gazed out the window, her long, slender fingers holding a glass of tea. She looked composed, impassive.

"It won't stop anything, but I'm sorry the way things had to work out. I'm not sorry about the business part, but I'm sorry a beautiful woman is getting hurt."

"I can hardly find it in me to say thank you graciously."

"You don't need to. There are things to work out, our lawyers will get together, things you and I can't solve now."

"But you have an offer to make."

Startled, he realized he had underestimated her. She was smarter than he had expected, more composed, unemotionally frank, and he shifted in his chair, studying her, reassessing his opinion and mentally changing his offer. He would have to offer far more than he had expected. She was too shrewd to settle for a desk job and title and no responsibility.

"Yes, I do. You're going to lose your company. There aren't a lot of places for you to go where you can acquire the same executive level. Liberation to the contrary, in our industry it's against you that you're a woman. You know I'm right."

"Go on."

Now she sounded amused and he was drawn to her. He wanted to put his hands in her silky hair and pull it free of pins. He wanted to try and make her smile, to see what it would be like to get her to melt. The thought of her responding to lovemaking made him draw a sharp breath and he pulled his thoughts away from erotic fantasies. Beautiful women who were intelligent appealed to him. They offered an extra challenge.

"I'd like to offer you a vice-presidency, a division, a job with responsibility."

"You can't be serious!" she said, lowering her fork, her mouth open and staring at him with such amazement, he felt as if he had made a terrible mistake.

"That's not so unlikely," he said with a little annoyance.

She put her fork on her plate and stared at him. "It's astounding. Of all people, the Kaminskis understand revenge."

He received another small shock. "You wouldn't."

"It hasn't even crossed your mind, has it, that I would take your offer and use it against you? Of course," she said with cynical amusement, "if it's merely a token responsibility and I suppose that's exactly what it is, you're quite safe. Well, thanks, but no thanks."

"It wouldn't be token. You're too intelligent to waste. And frankly I made the offer in good faith and expected the same from you. It would be White Star even if it's called Kamnick—"

"It will never be White Star if it's called Kamnick."

"You wouldn't wreck your own company to cause me trouble," he continued.

"Oh, come now, Mr. Kaminski. Talk about gullible and naive—I'm not your child. I don't owe you loyalty."

"There's an excellent reason you would give me loyalty."

"Oh, this should be interesting."

"Nick," he said flatly, and was surprised again to see anger in her expression. He leaned forward over the linen-covered table. "Mrs. Durand, this is why I asked you to lunch. If you'll marry Nick and give me an heir, I'll set up a trust for your son for ten million dollars and I'll set up one for you for half that much. Fifteen million in all. You can work for Kamnick, and you can have responsibility. Until you get pregnant."

She burst out laughing, and he felt as if he were grappling with sunshine. She was elusive, quick-witted, unpredictable. And he couldn't remember a woman giving him as much mental challenge.

Cimarron saw the anger in his face and beneath her amusement was hurt and shock. "Haven't you forgotten one thing?"

"What?" he asked, a muscle beginning to work in his jaw and she wondered if he had expected her to fall into his arms with gratitude for his proposal.

"Nick."

"You're going together. You're a beautiful, intelligent, desirable woman. Get him to marry you. That shouldn't be so hard."

"Nick has never been married," she said, for just an instant forgetting her problems, because she was dumbfounded and amused by Laz Kaminski.

"That's all the more reason. Hell, I'd marry you myself if you'd say yes," he said suddenly, startling her because he sounded as if he half meant it.

"I'm afraid I can't say thank you. All I can say to that offhanded proposal is no."

"I'm that repulsive?" he asked, his anger momentarily leaving, and she saw he could laugh at himself.

"I don't know that you really want me to answer you."

He grinned and leaned back in his chair to toss his napkin on the table. "You're quite a woman, Mrs. Durand." He smiled and studied her. "I envy Nick now, frankly. I wish I'd gotten to know you sooner and better."

"And I'm glad you didn't."

He laughed. "*Touché*. All right, let's get back to the offer. You can get Nick to marry you if you want. If there was ever a man determined to avoid a second marriage, it was Fontaine Durand, yet he wed you. Nick should succumb easily."

She gathered up her purse and sunglasses and pushed her chair back a fraction. "I need to get back to the office. No, I can't get Nick to marry me. I don't want your vice-presidency. Now I understand Nick a little better. You're going to lose him completely with your attempts to control his life. He's a grown man and an intelligent one. I pity you both. At the same time," she said with a slight lift of her chin, "I hate you both for what you've done. Neither of you care whom you hurt when you're trying to get at each other. I'm going. The lunch wasn't all that good."

She left the room and for an instant he stared at her back. He started after her, slowed his steps, and stared at her as she walked down the hall away from him. He would take over White Star and he would see to it that Cimarron Durand couldn't get a job with any oil company. Anger shook him as he strode down the empty hallway. The waiter met him.

"Sir, I didn't realize you were finished. I'll—"

"Give me the Goddamned check," he snapped, his anger growing when he thought back over the luncheon. The bitch. God, she was a cool one. He was going to take pleasure in buying her out and he wasn't going to agree to any concessions. She'd regret her insolence and remember his offer for the rest of her life.

Cimarron drove carefully, trying to keep her fury in check and concentrate on traffic until she reached the office. She swept into her office and shut the door, throwing her purse across the room. Damn the Kaminskis!

There was a rap and Freedom thrust his head into the room. "Hey, okay?"

"That bastard!" She let loose a string of names she had heard Peter and her brothers use and Freedom's look of worry changed to anger as he came in and shut the door.

"Did he hurt you?"

"Hurt me! No, he didn't hurt me. It must be hell on earth to have a bastard like that for a father! I don't blame Nick for hating the son of a bitch! He proposed to me. He offered me millions to marry Nick. He offered me millions to give him a son by Nick."

Freedom's jaw dropped. "He *proposed* to you?" he asked in shock.

"Yes. Probably just to see what kind of reaction he—" She turned to stare at him as she thought of Raye Honeywall for the first time. "Have you seen Raye lately?"

"No," he said so abruptly, Cimarron decided to drop it. "Sorry, Freedom. I should have thought before I opened my mouth."

"That's all right. It's okay to talk about it. I know the bastard's a womanizer."

"Father and son—what a pair they are!" She turned away. It was Nick that made her hurt, not Laz Kaminski and his cavalier manipulative offer. "Nick never has called," she blurted, the real hurt surfacing. "Not even a phone call, Freedom!"

"Sorry, Sunny. We're not lucky in love."

Silence lengthened until Freedom reminded her of their two o'clock meeting with the lawyers and insurance representatives. "Remember too, we meet with the Kamnick people at eight o'clock Friday morning. Laz, their lawyers, their investment bankers. We have a suite at the Sheraton."

"I'll feel like I'm going to a funeral."

"Eat dinner with us tonight. Tim and I will take you out."

"Sure. Peter called me this morning. I think he and Megan are taking the fire hard," she said. "He sounded torn up."

"He's just worried about you. I need to see Peyton before the meeting," Freedom said, and left her alone.

Her world was topsy-turvy and lunch had made it more so. She shouldn't have told Freedom about the proposal, but in anger she forgot Raye. If Raye had left Laz Kaminski, she wasn't running to Freedom. Cimarron didn't think Laz expected anything of the proposal. Probably an offer to see what kind of reaction he would get.

The telephone at her elbow buzzed and she jumped as she picked it up to hear her secretary's voice: "Mrs. Durand, you have a call from Nick Kaminski."

"Go ahead," Cimarron said, suddenly gripping the phone tightly and turning the chair so her back was to the door.

22

In a cramped booth in the Aberdeen airport, Nick shifted impatiently, waiting for Cimarron to answer the phone. His fist was knotted as he stared at the second hand moving on his stainless-steel TAG-Heuer watch.

"Hello."

"Cimarron. I just found out about the fire." He hated the distance between them, the static in the poor connection that made it more difficult to communicate.

"Nick, it's headlines. Where are you?"

"I'm in Scotland. We have a rig in the North Sea we've brought on stream. Charlie called yesterday, but gale winds were up and there was no way to get to a phone until now. I've been calling for an hour."

"I've been out to lunch," she said, doubting his reasons. She couldn't believe he really hadn't known; that his men hadn't contacted him the night of the fire.

"Did you see that I called?"

She looked at the notes on her desk. "I just got back."

"I'm on my way home as soon as I can make arrangements."

As soon as he could make arrangements. When would that be—another few days? She gripped the phone and felt as if she were on the verge of losing control. "Nick, finish your work. There's nothing you can do here."

Nick held the phone away to stare at it, frowning. "Cimarron, don't you want me there?"

"Freedom said you had a meeting in New York with the bankers."

"I sent someone in my place because Jason needed me here. Things weren't going well until yesterday. I'm coming home," he said stiffly, realizing things were more amiss than he had imagined.

"You stay in Scotland on your well, Nick. I don't need you here, and your bankers can't do anything now. I have a meeting." She replaced the receiver. She couldn't believe he hadn't known, that his men hadn't called him in Scotland. It seemed more likely that he had been using White Star to get at Kamnick. It fit all his plans. She gathered up her things.

"Sandy, if I get any calls, I'll be in the meeting until about four. I don't want to be disturbed."

"Yes, Mrs. Durand."

Nick stared at the phone in anger. He placed another call to White Star and was told Cimarron would be in a meeting until four o'clock. He slammed down the receiver. For the first time in his life, he felt defeated by Laz.

The eight-hour flight to New York seemed interminable. Looking harassed, Charlie met Nick when he landed. He apologized for not calling Nick, saying they were in meetings, fighting to save White Star. He had made a mistake and realized it, but Nick's rage was beyond its limits.

Nick fired Charlie on the spot for not calling him sooner and briefing him on the disaster. He should have been with Cimarron, and he would have given up the North Sea find to have been at her side the night of the fire.

In the proxy fight, Kamnick had now garnered enough stock to succeed in the hostile takeover, and the twenty-day waiting period with the Securities and Exchange Commission was over. Laz's offer had been accepted. Cimarron had no choice now. As the jet lifted off the runway at La Guardia and circled over Manhattan with lights twinkling below in the tall buildings, defeat swamped Nick. For years he had fought Laz, been frustrated and angered by him, but now he felt overwhelmingly defeated by him.

He vowed he would get Laz for what he had done to Cimarron. Nick's nerves felt raw; he wanted to be home, his feeling of disaster increasing.

In Tulsa he drove straight from the airport to the hotel where the Kamnick lawyers and White Star people were still conferring even though it was in the early hours of Saturday morning. Cimarron and Laz left twenty minutes before Nick arrived, and papers were being drawn up for a transaction of stock; by next Friday afternoon, April twenty-first, White Star officially would belong to Kamnick. A verbal agreement had already been reached.

When he was unable to find Cimarron, Nick's feelings of disaster mushroomed. Suspicions stirred by his phone conversation with her now became convictions—she blamed him for failing to save White Star and she didn't want to see him.

Freedom wasn't home, Cimarron wasn't home. Peyton was gone. Cimarron and Laz were not needed until the scheduled meetings on the following Friday. Nick swore and paced his room, trying her number again. Laz would soon own White Star. It made Kamnick Oil an international giant.

Nick knew Laredo Oil would be next on the list and there would be no way to fend off Laz unless a white knight could be found fast and it would have to be a bigger one than Thorson Petroleum. He paced the house restlessly, energy boiling in him, defeat tearing at him until he went down to his stables in the pink and gray splash of dawn. He didn't bother to saddle a horse, but mounted the chestnut and rode away, winding through trees, urging the horse to a gallop when he reached a dirt road. He was too upset to stay shut in his house, feeling as if Laz had delivered a killing punch.

Nick returned home from riding and called Cimarron again to no avail. He sprawled on his bed and in minutes he fell into an exhausted, troubled sleep.

He tried again to call her at noon, calling Freedom as well, unable to find either one. Frustrated and worried, he walked for miles in the woods and down back roads, hurting, knowing Cimarron was angry and he had probably lost her. He paused once at a weathered wooden fence over a small stream, gazing down at the trickle of muddy water while he thought about Cimarron. He felt he had failed her simply by being out of the country.

Most of all he hurt for her. She needed White Star. Her life was beginning to stabilize; she was beginning to come back into the world and out of mourning, and now she was hit with another bad blow. Nick wasn't going to give her up, because he loved her too much.

And then Nick realized what he had to do. He would take over Kamnick for Cimarron. He would buy back White Star for her.

The moment the idea came, he latched on to it like a drowning man grabbing at a lifeline. He didn't know how he could do it, because Kamnick was a giant, but he would find a way. He would have to make Laredo Oil's attempt to take over Kamnick Oil succeed. Cimarron hadn't wanted Laredo Oil involved in the fight before, but now the harsh reality of losing all Fontaine had built would give her a different view of Laz. It wasn't power or shares or stockholders that Nick thought would win Kamnick for him. It was Laz himself.

If Laz thought Nick finally wanted to run Kamnick, he might give it to him. Nick knew that was a gamble, and if Laz didn't, if Nick misjudged him, Nick wanted to be ready to buy out Kamnick without Laz's cooperation.

More important to him at the moment, he had to find Cimarron. He spun around and began to jog for home, breaking into a sweat in minutes as he raced the few miles back. He went straight to the phone. There was still no answer at her place or Freedom's. He tried to think where she would go, and then he realized she was probably at the farm. He picked up the phone to call and see, was half through the number when he thought about it, and replaced the receiver. He hurried to shower and change to drive to western Oklahoma.

The Chisholms were at the supper table when Nick arrived. They heard a car and Megan got up to go to the kitchen window. "Looks as if we're going to have company."

Since her arrival, Cimarron knew they were all trying to cheer her up. Peter had come in early, Tim staying all day. She tried to be cheerful for their sake, and found it easier at the farm to forget the loss of White Star. When Megan said company was coming, Cimarron guessed it was a neighbor.

"Who is it?" Peter asked. "Leroy said he might come by tonight, but he wouldn't come this early."

"I don't know who that is. It's a man in a BMW."

Cimarron glanced up. "What's he look like?"

"You can see for yourself," Megan said as there was a rap on the back door.

"I think that may be one of my friends," Cimarron said, standing up, unaware of her family's curious stares. She opened the kitchen door and stepped out on the porch. Her heart missed a beat as she saw Nick on the other side of the screen. He wore a sweatshirt and jeans, and his hair curled over his forehead.

"Hello, Nick," she said, trying to keep her emotions under control.

"I had a difficult time finding you. Am I interrupting anything?"

"Well," she glanced back over her shoulder at the closed kitchen door, "we're having supper." She didn't ask him in; she didn't want him to stay. Silence stretched between them.

"Can we talk?" he asked. "I drove a long way to see you."

"For a minute."

"Can you come out here?"

"I don't think I need to. We can talk here."

He opened the door and took her arm. "Come here, Cimarron."

She stepped outside, drawing a sharp breath when he touched her, something deep within her responding in spite of her hurt and angry feelings.

He was solemn, his gray eyes intent on her as he placed his hands on her shoulders. "I'm sorry I was in Scotland."

"It really doesn't matter now."

"Oh, yes, it does. I let you down."

"Nick!" she tried to move away, but his hands tightened on her shoulders.

"Are you angry because you blame me for letting Laz succeed? Are you angry because I wasn't here? I want to know, Cimarron. Which is it?"

"It's been five days since the fire and this is the first time I've seen you. There are phones, Nick. If you—" Her head came up and her eyes blazed. "You just used me to try and get at Laz, didn't you? That's all you really wanted. I was gullible. You wanted Kamnick Oil, and White Star was the way to do it and you sweet-talked me into believing you were trying to save my company for me! You charmed me into believing it was me you were interested in instead of Kamnick Oil!"

He was astounded, the conviction in her voice shaking him. It hadn't crossed his mind that she would think he was merely using her in a play against Laz.

"No! I've never used you to get at Laz. I wouldn't. I told you that before."

The back door opened and Megan appeared. "Excuse

me, Cimarron, but supper will get cold. Bring your guest inside."

"Megan, this is Nick Kaminski. Nick, meet my stepmother, Megan Chisholm."

"Mr. Kaminski, come join us."

"Thanks." He glanced at Cimarron, seeing anger burning in her gaze, but he wasn't leaving until they got matters settled between them. They followed Megan inside and he met the rest of the family.

"This is Peter, my dad, Tim, and Jerry. This is Nick Kaminski." Tim pulled up another chair across from Cimarron's.

"I don't want to interrupt your dinner," Nick protested.

"Nonsense," Peter said, smiling at Megan. "Mama would be insulted if you didn't eat."

"Yeah, if you just ate five miles down the road, you better eat again now or the whole evening will be ruined," Tim added, teasing Megan.

She blushed and glanced at him. "Stop that! Mr. Kaminski—"

"It's Nick, please."

"Nick. Would you care for milk or water?"

"I'm a milk drinker," he answered, "and I can't remember when I last ate."

Cimarron glanced at him, saw he looked thinner, and wondered what kind of problems he had faced overseas.

"You came to the right house if you're hungry," Peter said. "Best food in the whole U.S.A."

"Will y'all stop it!" Megan said lightly. "He'll expect a paragon of a cook now. All we're having is meat and potatoes."

The aroma of the thick, brown roast and fluffy whipped potatoes made Nick realize how long it had been since he had eaten. He looked at Cimarron who was carefully avoiding meeting his gaze. Her hair was tied behind her head with a ribbon, tendrils escaping because her hair was too short to be tied. She wore a pale-blue sweater and jeans that hugged her figure. She looked gorgeous to Nick, but the worry in her eyes made him impatient to be alone with her.

"Your name is Kaminski," Tim said, studying Nick.

"I'm Laz Kaminski's son," he said quietly.

"But you're not connected with Kamnick? You have another company?"

"That's right," he said emphatically, watching Cimarron. "I own Laredo Oil. I don't have any connections whatsoever with Kamnick Oil. Only a relative who owns it."

Cimarron's cheeks became pink and she refused to look at him. Nick wondered how long it would be before her family realized how strained conversation was between them.

"This is about the best food I've ever eaten," he said, meaning every word, knowing he couldn't settle anything at the table with her family present.

"Thank you," Megan answered with a soft laugh.

"I've been traveling from a North Sea rig and I'm not sure when I last ate."

"How was the North Sea?" Peter asked.

"As bad as I've always heard as far as the conditions, but oil is there to find. That's the good part. That's what makes it worthwhile. How's the farm?"

"We've had a good year with the crops," Tim said. "We're trying a new type of wheat now. Ever been on a farm?"

"Very little."

"He rides bulls," Cimarron said. She had meant to keep quiet and let the conversation drift around her, wanting to send Nick back to Tulsa as soon as dinner was over, but without thinking about it, she spoke up about his bull riding, and everyone looked at Nick.

"It gets my mind off other worries."

"It does at that," Tim said. "I don't remember seeing you around here. Where have you ridden?"

Nick listed rodeos and soon he was in a discussion of the rodeo circuit with Tim, who was into bronc riding and bulldogging. Cimarron noticed Nick had a second helping of everything and she wondered if he had gone for days without eating. He had two full glasses of milk and finally moved away from the table. As she picked up dishes to help Megan, Nick carried his to the counter.

"Go talk to Tim. Megan and Jerry and I'll do this."

"I can help."

"No. You'll ruin family tradition if you stay in the kitchen," she said with the same solemnity she had shown since his arrival. He wanted to fling down the dishes and pull her out to his car where he could talk with her privately. Instead, Nick followed the men into the family room while Jerry cleared the table and Megan and Cimarron scraped and loaded the dishwasher. By the time Cimarron joined the family and Nick, they had prevailed on Nick to stay the night.

As the family sat in the den and talked, Nick guessed it took about half an hour for them to realize something was amiss. And he suspected they all went to bed hours earlier than usual. Tim told him good night and took Jerry upstairs to read him a story. Megan and Peter said good night and silence descended as they left the room. He waited, wanting to be sure they were alone. Sometime since his arrival, Cimarron had combed her hair and removed the ribbon that had held it tied behind her head. Her auburn locks were glossy, catching glints from the light. His gaze roamed over her and he wanted her in his arms. He hated that he had inadvertently hurt her. Cimarron got up to stand beside the empty fireplace. Waiting to talk, wanting to be sure they were alone, Nick lounged back on the sofa, watching her, his legs stretched out in front of him. He had had time during dinner to think about her accusations and he had no intention of going back to Tulsa until he had laid them to rest.

"Can we talk now?" he asked.

She crossed the room to close the door and turned to face him. "We really don't have anything to discuss."

"Yes, we do. Come sit down."

"I'm fine."

"I didn't know about the fire until Thursday night. I got to Scotland as fast as I could when I heard the news."

She moved away impatiently, going back to the mantel to stand with her back to him. "I find that difficult to believe. It was headlines." Finally, she faced him, her green eyes fiery with anger. "Tell the truth, Nick. You hoped White Star would crush Laz."

"It occurred to me that would be nice," he said, "but if you think I've been using you to get at Laz, you couldn't be more wrong."

Cimarron heard his admission and couldn't believe his denial. "I'm sure you can find a motel room in town. I'd rather you did."

"I tried to call you the night I left Tulsa. I couldn't get you and left word with Sandy I had a meeting in New York. I didn't know until I was at the airport that I needed to fly to Scotland. I changed my plans at the airport, sent Charlie in my place to New York, and I flew to Scotland. We ran the drill stem test Wednesday. Gale winds had set in and I couldn't get off the rig and Charlie didn't radio me about the fire until Thursday night."

"Come on, Nick. You usually do better than that."

"If all I wanted was to get at Laz and to get Kamnick, why would I be here now?"

"I've been wondering why. I can't figure out what you stand to gain." He stood up and crossed to her. She drew a deep breath, raising her chin.

He reached around her, bracing his hands against the mantel and hemming her in. "Answer my question, Cimarron. What do I stand to gain?"

"I don't know." She started to duck beneath his arm and he lowered it so she couldn't. Her head snapped around, and she gazed at him angrily.

"Cimarron," he said softly, "I can't tell you how sorry I am I wasn't here the night of the fire, or that I didn't get here the next nights, but I didn't know about it. When I knew, I did all I could to get in touch with you and to get home."

She listened to him woodenly, finding it difficult to believe, wondering what he wanted from her, still hurt and furious with him. He stood too close, his voice was too gentle, and she found anger slipping away.

"Now, answer my question. What do I stand to gain by being here?" he asked in a deep, quiet tone.

She stared at him, wondering again. White Star was gone. Nick no longer could use her. He no longer needed her. "I don't believe you," she whispered, hurting, knowing she was going to believe whatever he told her.

"You have to believe what you know to be true. There's only one possible reason to be here."

"You could have called, Nick," she whispered.

"I did as soon as I knew and could."

She had been so angry and so hurt, it was difficult to dismiss it in a moment. And she was scared she was doing something foolish.

"I fired Charlie for not getting in touch with me sooner."

"You *fired* Charlie?" Cimarron stared at him in shock. "He's one of your best employees, you've said, and he's a friend. You've told me you confide everything in Charlie."

"I have and he knew what a calamity the fire was. If he had enough brains to run things in my absence, then he should have had sense enough to know to contact me instantly, to get me home."

She was astounded, shaken by his news, slowly letting go of anger and realizing she had jumped to the wrong conclusions.

Nick watched her and waited, seeing her expressive eyes change, knowing she was mulling over all he had said to her. She looked away and rubbed her forehead. "If you're using me, Nick—"

"I'm not."

Her head was still turned away, her voice subdued. "I kept watching for you and wondering why you didn't come."

She sounded agonized and his chest constricted. He drew her to him, folding her arms around her, stroking her head, feeling her arms slip around him. "I wanted you there so badly and when hours passed and then time passed and they said you were just in New York—if you were in New York, you had to *know*."

"I'm sorry I wasn't there or couldn't get there. I'm sorry I couldn't stop Laz in time."

She stood stiffly in Nick's arms, her head against his

chest. "I could think of only one reason you wouldn't be there. You didn't really care. And if you didn't—"

"It doesn't matter now. I care, I'm here, and I'm sorry I wasn't in Tulsa when Star Tower burned."

"Nick, it hurt so badly," she whispered and his arms tightened around her.

"You'll survive, Cimarron. You're strong."

"But I lost all Fontaine had built."

"Not really. It will go on under another name. Things change. The outcome might not have been different if Fontaine had been in charge."

He tilted her face up and she gazed at him. "It hurt to think you hadn't really cared."

"I care. More than you can begin to guess." He looked into wide green eyes that gazed back with uncertainty. Her eyes searched his.

"Nick, if you're here for any other reason—"

"I've told you before, and I'll tell you again. I'm here for only one reason," he said gruffly, his gaze dropping to her mouth as desire intensified. He lowered his head, watching her closely. "I'm here because I love you, because I want you, because I don't want you hurt or alone or to lose—"

"Nick—"

His lips stopped her words. He felt as if he would drown in her kiss. He wanted her, and all the hours and days of missing her, of longing and loneliness made him bend over her and kiss her hard and deeply, his arms crushing her against his chest. His erection throbbed against the constraints of his jeans, Cimarron's hips moved in a scalding way.

"I've wanted you so damned badly," he whispered once, kissing her throat. He paused and glanced at the door. "Are we alone down here?"

"Yes. They've gone to bed and the door is shut and locked," she said, gazing into smoky eyes that seemed to devour her.

"Cimarron," he whispered gruffly, and desire uncoiled within her, curling up from her loins, spreading heat in her body. She wound her slender arms around his neck, her fingers playing in his soft curls, letting anger and fear and mistrust go, believing him, hoping she wasn't being a fool, but wanting him so badly.

Nick could see questions and uncertainty still in her eyes and realized her doubt ran deep. He would convince her; time could do that. Time and love. He wanted to pour out his love to her, to unleash passion until all uncertainty was obliterated.

Nick kissed her throat, peeling away her shirt and dropping it, his hands moving over her full breasts slowly, drawing his fingertips over her in leisurely, tantalizing caresses as he stood back and looked at her. It took an effort, but he raised his eyes to meet hers.

"I wouldn't use you or desert you."

She felt sheltered, loved, and for the first time in days, no longer alone. She ran her hands across his chest as he flung away his shirt. Her fingers drew down to unfasten his belt and jeans, shoving them away while he peeled hers off. She stood before him in wisps of lace while he looked at her and kissed and caressed her until finally he picked her up to carry her to the sofa and love her.

Later as they climbed the stairs, he asked, "Are you going back to Tulsa early in the morning?"

"No. I'm to meet with your father and his lawyers on Friday. I'm taking Tuesday and Wednesday off too. I'll go back to Tulsa, Wednesday night."

"Good," he said, knowing it was easier for her at the farm. When she got back to Tulsa, she would be constantly busy.

"Can you stay tomorrow?" she asked.

He thought about all the things awaiting him, but none of them were as important as Cimarron. "Yes, I can."

They tiptoed through the darkened house and she switched the light on in the room where Nick was to stay. "I'm next door."

"I haven't seen your room." She suddenly had a feeling of *déjà vu*, remembering Fontaine staying so long ago, remembering his wanting to see her room too.

"What is it, Cimarron? Did I say something I shouldn't?"

"No, of course not. Come on." He draped his arm around her shoulders as they went to her room. He gazed around, studying everything that still looked as if it belonged to a girl in high school, not a grown woman and CEO of a giant corporation. And then he didn't care how the room looked.

Leaning back against the closed door, he drew Cimarron to him, spreading his legs and pulling her between them, fitting her close against him as he bent his head to kiss her.

Nick hadn't been in bed five minutes when he heard a rustle and saw her move across the room, her gown a white blur in the darkness. She slid into bed with him as he folded her against his length, his legs entwining with hers.

"I have to go back to my room in just a few minutes."

"Wonderful," he said in a husky voice, kissing her, rolling her over on her back as he straddled her and fondled her and thought he could never get enough of loving her.

In the morning he stirred and rolled over, searching for her. An alarm went off and he pushed the button to stop the buzz. The bed was empty, but he felt a piece of paper and sat up, turning on a light beside the bed and reading her neat, legible writing: "Nick. If you want to go with Tim and Dad today, Tim said they would like to have you. Get up before five and go down to the kitchen and tell Tim."

Nick groaned and looked at the clock. He had had so little sleep in the past week and it was only half past four in the morning now. He bent back over the note.

"If you'd rather sleep in, go back to sleep. (We won't have any privacy, so don't sleep in on my account. I'm sleeping in. See you about nine or later. Hugs and kisses. C."

He stared at it. *Hugs and kisses*. She didn't even sign "love" in a casual closing. Yet today was better than yesterday. He had cleared up mistaken notions and hurts and anger. He couldn't undo what was done, but she was beginning to decide he hadn't been using her and he would have come sooner if he could have. He pushed back the covers. He wanted to get to know her family and a good way was to go with Tim and Peter.

Nick showered, shaved, and dressed in fresh jeans and another sweat shirt. As he stepped into the hall, he gazed at the comfortable farmhouse and thought of the contrast between it and her palatial Tulsa mansion. He suspected Cimarron would be happy with whatever surroundings she had, luxurious or simple. Her happiness was an inner one, an enjoyment of people.

Going downstairs, he followed the drifting, tantalizing aromas of coffee, bacon, and eggs, and by the time he reached the kitchen, the enticing smells had created a hearty appetite. Tim and Megan greeted him, Megan in a fuzzy bathrobe, her hair caught behind her head in a clip, her eyes puffy, looking older than she had last night.

"We're getting machinery ready for harvest," Tim said when they sat down to eat. "I'll take the combine to a dealer for an engine overhaul, but right now, I'm doing what I can here, replacing hoses and belts, replacing bearings. I've been working on that and I'm getting the grain bins ready."

"How much can be harvested in a day?" Nick asked.

"We'll cut about one hundred and twenty-five acres. We have our own combines now and hire them out."

Nick listened to Megan and Tim talk about problems while they ate a breakfast of eggs and sausage and oatmeal, and then Nick went upstairs to brush his teeth. He opened Cimarron's door quietly and went to her bedside. She was curled up, her hair tangled over her cheek, her breathing deep and even, one arm flung outside the covers of the bed. He bent down to kiss her lightly on her temple. He ached with love for her, wished he could hand her White Star, give her everything, and wondered if he would ever win her love. He tiptoed out of the room and closed the door.

It was cool and crisp, the first pink rays of dawn spreading on the horizon. A rooster crowed as Tim and Nick walked together, their boots crunching the grass. "We've got a tank that sprung a leak. I patched it yesterday, and I want to check and make sure it's holding. I'll show you around a little and then we'll come back. I need to work on the grain bins."

"Sure," Nick said, lifting his head and deeply inhaling fresh air that seemed to smell sweeter in the country than in town. He glanced over his shoulder at the house, thinking about Cimarron upstairs asleep. When they climbed into a mud-spattered green pickup, Tim headed for the barn, driving south.

They turned onto a road that was little more than two wheel tracks. "We only have a fourth of the cattle now. We sold most of them last month. We buy steers in the fall, graze them, and then sell them in the spring. I work at my place all week, usually helping here on the weekends."

Nick followed Tim as he looked at his patchwork on the tank. Satisfied it was holding, he climbed back into the pickup and they headed farther south. Tim slowed beside a green field that spread far in the distance. "Here's our wheat. Harvest is about seven weeks after it heads out. We've had to spray this spring because green bugs can eat it up and we've had some patches destroyed."

"What kind of wheat do you plant?" Nick said, curious about the farm.

"This is Early Triumph. It withstands drought, has lots of foliage."

"How's the crop this year?"

"So far, so good. We've had good moisture this winter." Tim cut the motor and hunched forward, his hands gripping the steering wheel. "You and Sunny must be good friends."

"I don't think she knows how serious I am. I'm waiting. She isn't ready for another marriage yet."

"I know she's not, but I sure as hell don't want to see her hurt more."

"The last thing I want to do is hurt her. She's damned independent," he added.

Tim sighed. "Yeah, I guess we were raised that way. Just keep on being a friend. Right now she needs friends and family."

"Sometimes I wonder if your sister has really ever needed anyone," Nick said softly, thinking about her and how she had weathered each crisis. "I still don't know the particulars of the fire."

"She knows more than I do." Tim turned the pickup north and drove back to the barn to get his tools to work on the grain bins. "Look, you don't have to help with this."

"I'd like to see what you do," Nick said. "I'll be better helping check motors than fixing a grain bin. I know a little about motors. And frankly, it's good to work with my hands and forget about hostile takeovers and production expenses. I should be in Tulsa now, but it's nice to get to know the Chisholms and I need time with Cimarron."

"Okay. We'll get to the motors when Peter comes down." As they strode to the silver corrugated-steel bins, Tim talked. "We have to get the old wheat cleaned out first. After that I'll check for water leaks, and treat with an insecticide to kill weevils that get into the grain."

"How much do the bins hold?"

"About fifteen hundred bushels," Tim answered. Nick worked in silence beside him, trying to watch what Tim was doing, cleaning a bin while his mind was on Cimarron.

That afternoon in the cool of the barn, they worked on equipment, checking bearings and belts. Nick was on familiar territory, one he enjoyed, and he was hot and dusty by the time he started in with Tim and Peter. As they approached the back porch, Cimarron appeared. She was bathed, dressed in a clean cotton skirt and blouse, her hair softly curled under. Tim and Peter went on inside.

"Hi," she said, coming down the steps to meet Nick.

He draped an arm around her and held her away. "I'll get you dirty," he said, wanting to crush her in his arms.

"You've had some phone calls today."

"Here?" He scowled. "Damn. I'll probably have to go. I told them not to call me unless it was an emergency."

They heard a car and Freedom pulled into the drive. He got out as Nick and Cimarron went out to meet him. When he saw Nick, he stopped yards away.

"What are you doing here?" he asked in a cold tone.

"Freedom!" Cimarron snapped, becoming bristly, and Nick wondered if she had already forgotten that less than twenty-four hours ago she had been angry with him.

"That's all right," Nick said easily, facing Freedom who looked ready to fight. "I can't blame him."

"He's Kamnick Oil, Cimarron, whether you realize it or not."

"No, Freedom, I'm not."

"Stop it, Freedom," Cimarron said. "Nick and his father don't work together."

"You didn't feel that way in Tulsa!" Freedom shot a long, searching look at Cimarron and relaxed his stance. "Sorry. I'm wound up tight. You're a Kaminski and right now that isn't a good thing to be."

"Freedom, please."

"It's okay, Cimarron," Nick repeated. "Want me to go?"

"No!" she answered before Freedom could say anything. She slipped her arm around Nick's waist.

"Sorry," Freedom said and offered his hand. "I know about you and Kamnick Oil, but it's been a bad week."

Nick shook his hand. "Actually, I just got back into the country. I don't know exactly what's happened and Cimarron hasn't wanted to talk about it yet."

"And I don't now," she said. "Come in the house and Freedom, stop being a surly bear."

"Sure."

Nick returned his calls, but was unable to locate Kevin. By dinner Freedom was more relaxed, still slightly reserved with Nick. Occasionally, Nick looked up to see Freedom studying him with speculation. They carefully avoided talk about the fire or the oil business, conversation revolving around the farm instead. As Tim and Peter and Nick discussed equipment they had worked on during the afternoon, Peter said, "Son, you sure you haven't lived on a farm before?"

"No, sir," Nick answered. "I've worked out on rigs, but never on a farm."

"You go at it like my oldest son, Pierce."

"How's that?"

"Work here was as natural as breathing to him. He could fix any machine."

"Maybe I missed my call," Nick said, grinning at Cimarron. "I always liked it out on the rig. I like working outside. Sometimes I feel like I'm in a cage when I'm inside an office."

"If you aren't careful, you'll have a new job here," Cimarron said dryly, and the men laughed, except Freedom who continued to study Nick with a wariness that Nick hoped would fade with time.

After dinner Nick got his phone call. He stayed shut in Pierce's room for twenty minutes and when he came out, anger burned in him. He found Cimarron downstairs and took her arm. "I'd like to talk to you alone."

"Sure. We can go for a ride."

They left and he drove down a dirt road that led to a creek where he parked. "I hate to pull you back into the real world, but I had a call from Kevin. I have to get back to Tulsa tonight instead of enjoying the company at the farm."

Cimarron didn't want to think about the problems awaiting her in Tulsa. For once in her life, she wanted to shut them out and put them on hold for a few more hours.

"My family likes you."

"I'm glad. You have a wonderful family."

"I'm sorry yours wasn't so good. Dad is really impressed with you. He says you're a farmer and don't know it."

For just a minute Nick's anger diminished a fraction as he thought about the past two days. "I like it here. It's so damned peaceful and I like the work."

"It's a never-ending task. It's ruined a lot of men."

"Name something that hasn't."

"I'll be in town Wednesday. I told you, Friday I sign the papers and White Star changes hands."

"I'll go with you if it'll help."

She squeezed his hand. "Thanks, Nick. I want to say yes, and cling to you and use your strength, but this is something I have to do on my own. I'll be all right."

"If you change your mind, the offer is open. That's one thing I won't have to worry about—Laz will be very courteous to a beautiful woman. I'll pick you up afterwards."

"I'd like that," she said, grateful to know he would be there.

"Cimarron, Kevin said that according to the first indications from the firemen, it was arson. Is that right?" he asked, his anger flaring up again.

She stared out the front window at the muddy creek, the water was silvery where it rippled over rocks. She told him quickly about the fire. "I'll come out of this with a nice bundle of money and no job, no company. I lost Fontaine's company."

"*Arson!* I have to get back to Tulsa right away because of other matters, but I wanted to hear what the fire chief told you. I swear I'll get Laz for this."

"No! Don't do something to him in revenge for what he did to me. I think the hate between the two of you warps your judgment where Laz is concerned. It comes between us, Nick."

"You want him to take everything you have, take it in an unethical, illegal way—"

"You don't know that!"

"Someone set the fire in Star Tower."

"There have been other cases of arson in Tulsa. You're jumping to hasty conclusions."

"Have the other fires occurred in the middle of a corporate takeover? Do you want Laz to hurt you and then get away with it? Do you want me to say, 'Oh, too bad my father did that'?"

"Your father denied having anything to do with the fire."

"What in the sweet hell would you except him to do? He may be vicious, but he's not dumb!" Nick gazed at green fields that seemed so far removed from corporate takeovers, yet even here, the results were felt.

"Nick, don't retaliate. I couldn't live with it. This part of you scares me."

"This whole family calls you Sunny. You're a starry-eyed optimist looking at the world through rose-colored glasses. After all that's happened to you, you're still charitable, you can find some happiness, you pick up the pieces and go on without looking back—"

"And you think that's bad?" she asked, hurting because she knew there was a chasm opening between them that was going to be unbridgeable.

"You're too conciliatory. Except where your love life is concerned," he said, thinking about her doubts concerning him. "I can't sit by and see him get away with this. I've built up Laredo to protect myself. I'm big enough now to help you."

"It won't help me if you destroy Laz or Kamnick Oil."

"*Why?*"

She drew a deep breath, suddenly seeing that they couldn't understand each other on this subject. "You'll destroy part of yourself. You can't live with hate and not have it eat away part of you. Part of the good that's in you. Hatred is deadening."

"Oh, to hell with that!" he snapped. "You'd let him walk away from this, taking what's important to you?"

"If it meant ruining a part of you, yes, I would. Hate burns in you, Nick, and you should let it go."

"Wouldn't you like White Star back?"

"Well, of course, I would, but—"

"There. Just stop right there. Of course you would. You said it all. You know he set that fire."

"I don't know that and neither do you. You were in Scotland. There have been several cases of arson in Tulsa. I asked Chief Worth. We're arguing uselessly," she said with regret, looking into his thickly lashed eyes and suffering a fresh hurt.

Nick pulled her to him and kissed her long and hard and she returned it passionately, but with sadness because she suspected it was a farewell kiss.

"Nick, if you do something to retaliate, it'll come between us," she said, hating the anger that burned in his eyes.

"You're too soft and sweet and loving for your own good. Laz will survive. You'll feel differently when time has passed and you stop and think about it." He didn't add when she realized she was without a job or prospects of another with as much challenge and responsibility. He drove her back to the house, thanked everyone and told them goodbye.

Worry plagued Cimarron as she watched Nick drive away. She couldn't reconcile his hatred of Laz with a future with Nick. Nick had finally broken down all the barriers and she was in love with him, wanting him, caring about him. She stared at the diminishing cloud of dust and turned to walk down the road.

In minutes Freedom caught up with her. "You look worried."

"I am. Nick's gone back to fight Laz."

"Well, good for him."

"Don't say that!" she snapped and Freedom's brows arched. "He's consumed with hatred for Laz. I don't want him fighting his father because of me."

"Laz has it coming."

"Anger and hate aren't good things to live with."

Freedom frowned and studied her. "Sunny, that's a normal male reaction. You get slugged, you slug back."

"You wouldn't destroy Dad."

"No. But Dad wouldn't treat me the way Laz has treated Nick. He's been a bastard to Nick."

"Nick is tough and survived it and made his own life and built his own company. He ought to be able to grow out of a childhood hatred."

"Yeah. You two will work it out. I'm sorry I flew off the handle at him when I got here."

"He understood. That's one thing he understood completely." They fell into step together, passing the barn and strolling down the road in the quiet of evening. "I love him, Freedom."

"Does he know it?"

"I think so. I didn't think I would love again." A shuttered look came to Freedom's face, and Cimarron remembered Raye and lapsed into silence as they walked back to the house.

23

Nick met with a battery of lawyers Tuesday morning. He was given reports and figures to study and he shut himself away in his office. Two hours later he pulled a stack of newspapers in front of him to read. His anger mounted as he pored over accounts of the fire. He talked with Adam Worth about their investigation. It was set by gasoline and rags on several floors—the fifth case of arson in Tulsa in two years that had been set that way.

"Were the other cases written up in the papers?" Nick asked.

"Yes, Mr. Kaminski, they were."

"Thanks for your time," Nick said and replaced the receiver, staring at it and swearing softly. Nick's secretary buzzed that Peyton Phelps was waiting to see him.

He stood and shook hands with Peyton and motioned him to a chair. "I just got back in town," Nick said.

Peyton glanced at the paper-strewn desk. "I suppose you know everything that's happened."

"I saw Cimarron over the weekend. I drove to the farm and stayed two nights."

"Good. I'm sure she needs all the support she can get."

In spite of his natty appearance and elegant tailor-made gray worsted suit, Peyton looked drawn and haggard, his boyish good looks faded.

"Can I ask your opinion on something?" Nick asked.

"Of course."

"The fire was arson."

Peyton gave him a wintry smile. "And you want to know if I think your father was behind it?" He looked Nick directly in the eyes. "Sorry, but since you asked—I do. It came at too critical a time."

"That's what I think," Nick said grimly. "Laredo Oil is young and growing. It's not White Star or Kamnick. Not yet. I could use a man with your knowledge."

"Frankly it's good to hear I'm wanted. I know when Kamnick takes over, I'll be the first to go. I've heard Ralston and Laz are friends."

"You think about my offer. Get back to me when you decide. I'd want you in the same capacity you had at White Star, and I think I can increase your salary."

Peyton smiled with a flash of even white teeth. "I don't have to think it over. Laredo Oil has a good reputation; it would mean staying right here in Tulsa where I want to be, and I think I'll like working with you."

"Good," Nick said, genuinely pleased. "How soon can I put you on the payroll?"

"I'll have to give notice. And I'd like a vacation."

"At another point in time, I'd say, of course, but right now, if you come to work for me, I need your brains and help right away."

"It sounds as if you're a man with a mission. Some new leases? You're getting quite a reputation for finding oil where others haven't."

"I want some men I can count on. I intend to get Kamnick Oil and give what I can back to Cimarron."

Peyton's jaw dropped for a moment and then his features became impassive. "Another battle. Kamnick is—"

"—more than five times the size of Laredo Oil. But I think I can pull it off. I can get the partners I need, the financial backing if necessary."

"You sound as if you don't think it will be necessary."

"I think Laz will accept Laredo's offer. But I want to be prepared if he doesn't."

"Why would he take your offer?" Peyton asked, frowning. "I've heard you've fought for years."

"We've fought because he's tried to get me to work at Kamnick for him. He may take an offer, because he'll figure I'll be working for him."

"You won't be working for him if it's a buyout."

"That isn't the way Laz's mind works. I'm the kid, and he'll expect to do as he pleases. I'll be ready if he fights though. I want that company for Cimarron. I want to give control of White Star back to her."

Peyton eyed Nick. "You have a reputation for succeeding where the odds are against you. Of course, I'd be happy to see Cimarron come out with something more than cash in the bank. She was dedicated to the company, feeling a bond in it with Freedom. She was doing a good job. None of us was prepared for the takeover. I don't think Fontaine would have been prepared."

"He might have fought more fiercely. It's not her nature to fight. Can you put off your vacation for a few months? If you can, I promise you, you can take off weeks."

"I think I'm going to like working for you, Mr. Kaminski."

"You continue calling me Nick," he said with a grin. "I don't have to stand on protocol." Nick came around the desk to offer his hand again. "Welcome aboard. Let's find you an office. As I said, we're a small operation in many ways, yet we've outgrown this office space. You might be in a closet."

"I'll manage. Just a desk, a file cabinet, and a light."

"I can do a little better than that."

Nick called a meeting and included Peyton along with his trusted men, Kevin, Moss, two lawyers, one banker, and Peyton. As they debated financing sources and strategies, Nick listened, asking questions, giving his opinion. Against all possibilities he weighed personality. He knew Laz, knew the directors and officers of Kamnick, and he could guess reactions.

Finally, he leaned back in his chair. "We have several possibilities. I'm in favor of a bearhug. I want to take an offer to the Kamnick board."

"You think that's the best approach?" Kevin asked.

"Won't his directors flatly refuse? They're handpicked, loyal to Laz Kaminski."

"A bearhug will appeal to the stockholders even though it won't be the best deal. The directors are damned if they do, and damned if they don't. They're loyal to Laz, all right," Nick said in cynical affirmation. "They'll do exactly what he wants and every last one of them knows he's been trying to get me back in Kamnick since I left."

They argued about it for another hour, Moss adamant that whatever Nick did, Kamnick would come back with an offer for Laredo—one Laredo couldn't fight.

"You're gambling this whole deal on your father wanting you back at Kamnick," Peyton said at one point.

"If he doesn't, I want to go after Kamnick and win," Nick said. "At the same time, I'm the only person in this room who knows how much time and money he's spent trying to get me back at Kamnick. I'm his only son and that's important to him."

"He could come back with a poison pill defense—he could spin off White Star."

"I'm gambling he won't."

It was agreed they would go with the bearhug, and if that were turned down, be ready to tender a bid for stock.

"Get Al Nordstrom at the paper and draft a press release so the stockholders will know about the offer," Nick said, standing at the window, thinking about Cimarron. He wanted to give her the world, and White Star would come close. He thought about her at the farm, wanting to get out of the meeting and call her.

She had stayed one more night on the farm. When Nick was in bed, he called and talked for hours to her. He didn't mention the offer, because he didn't want to discuss it until he had accomplished his purpose and knew he could give her White Star.

Thursday morning Nick took an hour off work, telling Ginger he would be back without leaving word where he was going. Nick went to Tiffany's and spent an hour talking to a jeweler, finally deciding on the ring he would like to have made for Cimarron. He knew it was far too soon to ask her to marry him—she hadn't yet told him she loved him—but after last weekend, he was more certain about her feelings, suspecting it wouldn't be long before he could propose. And when the time came, he wanted a ring. He didn't want to wait for a piece of jewelry.

At three that afternoon he received a call from Laz. They agreed to meet at the Hilton at eight o'clock in the morning a week from Friday, April the twenty-eighth. As Nick replaced the receiver, he thought how simple it had turned out to be; no long drawn-out battle like Kamnick had just waged with White Star, no bids and counterbids. And he didn't think there would be, but if it came to that, he would fight. He called Cimarron, talking only twenty minutes because she had a meeting.

Friday, Nick waited downstairs at the Sheraton while she met with Laz to sign the papers that would give him White Star. She emerged from the elevator surrounded by lawyers and bankers with Peyton holding her arm. Nick crossed the lobby to her. He led her outside into the deserted area behind the building and pulled her into his arms.

"I feel like I failed Fontaine."

He hurt for her, and he held her tightly, suspecting she was crying quietly, waiting until she signaled she wanted to go. Finally Cimarron moved away, climbing into the car, and Nick took her home with him. That night he drove her to the farm for the weekend so she could be with her family.

During the next week both of them had long hours of overtime, Cimarron getting ready for the transition at White Star, providing information for Kamnick while Nick was busy running Laredo as well as attending meetings to get ready for the takeover strategy.

Nick talked Cimarron into taking time to meet him for lunch Thursday. He swung to the curb and held open the door to the BMW. She was waiting for him, her blue dress blowing around her long legs. Desire made him forget everything else.

He leaned across the car to kiss her while someone behind him honked. Laughing, she pulled away. "Nick, move. Traffic is piling up behind us."

"They can wait for one kiss," he said, easing back into the stream of traffic. "I promised lunch, but I'd rather whisk you off to my place."

She placed her hand on his knee and he drew a sharp breath, wondering if she had the slightest idea of the effect she had on him.

"Want to go to my place?" he asked in a husky voice.

She gave him a heated, intense look filled with consent, but she shook her head. "I have to be back promptly at one."

"Maybe you better take your hand off my knee. I might embarrass you when we walk into the restaurant."

"I've missed seeing you."

He groaned. "You're not helping me." He slowed for a red light and pulled her close for a quick kiss.

"Nick! You'll get a ticket!" she scolded, laughing and gazing at him with sparkling eyes. "Keep your eyes on the road and hands on the wheel, mister."

"I'll give it a try."

"I feel buried in paper at the office. It's amazing how much paperwork is involved in this transaction."

"Want to take some time off?"

"I shouldn't, but that's exactly what I'm going to do. I'm going to the farm for the weekend. Do you think you might see your way clear to be there too?"

"I'd love it if I can get away. Maybe on Sunday I can. Megan may not be so overjoyed."

"Yes, she will be. I promise."

He whipped into the parking lot of Papa's, driving to the back and parking beneath an elm. It was the twenty-seventh of April and the weather was balmy. There were new leaves on trees and flowers in bloom; sunshine was hot on his shoulders as he hurried around the car. She swung her long legs out and he reached down, pulling her up against him, turning so he could lean back on the car and pull her hard against him. His erection throbbed and he bent his head quickly, stopping her protests, not caring that they were in public. No one had been in sight and he was starved for her kisses.

She melted against him, clinging to him, temporarily forgetting everything. Finally she pushed away, gazing up, wanting him badly, knowing that her need for him was growing daily. "Nick, someone will come along—"

"Let them," he said gruffly.

"Nick," she said, studying him, looking at his gray eyes and brown curls as if she had never seen them before. "I should have told you before now. I'll always love Fontaine. Part of me will always belong to him and his memory."

Nick felt as if his heart had stopped beating as he watched her search for the right words.

"You understand that, don't you?" she asked. When he nodded, she continued, "I have to be so sure about my feelings. Love and family is the most important thing to me. I just had to be sure—"

"Cimarron," he urged in agony, knowing what she was leading up to, having to hear her say it now.

"I love you," she said quietly, and Nick thought he had waited a lifetime to hear her say those three words.

"God, you tell me in Papa's parking lot," he said before he kissed her.

His heart pounded with joy that he hadn't believed possible. He had never known love such as he felt for Cimarron. And the thought of spending the rest of his life with her was dazzling. Never would he have to worry about his sons growing up with hostility and infidelity. He couldn't think of anything he really wanted besides Cimarron. He crushed her to him, kissing her hard until he raised his head a fraction.

"You're sure you have to be back at your office at one?"

"I'm sure." She twisted to glance at her watch. "As it is, we're going to have to inhale lunch!"

"Suppose we skip lunch and find a motel on the way back to your office?"

She put her head against his chest to laugh softly. "No. I'd never get back at one."

"In that case, I'll feed you." He tilted her chin up to gaze into her eyes. "I've wanted to hear you say that since the week in Cancun."

"You couldn't have," she whispered, her eyes searching his.

"I can remember watching you at parties. You impressed me before I knew you. After the first few days—I was all yours, honey. I've just been waiting."

She gazed at him solemnly, her arm tightening around his neck. "Thank you, Nick, for being so incredibly patient. You helped me over rough times." She closed her eyes, standing on tiptoe to kiss him.

They had less than half an hour in which to eat lunch, and Nick barely knew what he ate. He held her hand all through lunch and couldn't keep from watching her.

On the way back to the office, he got lost and stopped at two green lights, prompting Cimarron to turn to him. "Nick! Do you want me to drive? What's the matter with you?"

He grinned and kissed her knuckles, and she laughed. "You can't be that smoozy about one little 'I love you.' "

"Smoozy?"

"That's my word. Watch the light. You stop at another green and a car will plow into us! Take a left at the next corner."

"Keep telling me directions," he said happily. "I'll try and concentrate on getting you there on time, but it's damned difficult to think about oil or mergers or stuck pipes or pressure valves or leases."

"Is it really?" she asked in a tantalizing drawl and he swore lightly.

"You're making it harder."

"Making what harder, Nick?" she teased. He clamped his jaw shut, gripped the wheel, and hunched forward as if trying to give all his attention to driving. She smiled, feeling excitement and love bubble up in her. She was happy, so happy with him. Her world was crumbling on one hand, the last stages of the White Star takeover taking place daily, on the other there was Nick who gave her joy with his charm and appeal and sexiness. He made her feel alive again.

He pulled to the curb in front of the long brick building that had become the temporary headquarters of White Star. He caught her wrist as she started to get out of his car.

"This has been one of the best days of my life," he said softly. "I won't ever forget today."

"Oh, Nick!" She kissed him until they heard whistles

and claps and turned to see two White Star bankers standing on the sidewalk watching them. She laughed and climbed out of the car and Nick drove away, whistling, trying to concentrate on traffic.

Work kept them apart that night, but Nick talked to her a long time on the phone. He felt as if he could never run out of things to talk about with her, wanting to tell her about Kamnick and White Star, but also knowing he should wait.

Friday morning Nick reached the Hilton suite at six, having a thirty-second argument with a desk clerk because he was two hours early. He settled to wait along with an unusually nervous Peyton, two silent lawyers, Kevin, a banker, and Moss. Only Kevin had agreed that Nick was right in assuming Laz would take the offer. The others expected the next few hours to be unproductive. He stood at the window at seven when Laz and his entourage arrived. The suite overlooked the front of the hotel and Nick saw the black limos pull into the lot.

"Here they come," he said, wondering if he had guessed wrong, if Laz would produce a giant defense.

Laz and his men entered and from the look on Laz's face, Nick knew he expected to get there first and settle his men, to act as the host, a narrow psychological edge.

"Come in, Laz," Nick said in as friendly tones as possible. Laz gave him a flash of anger and Nick knew better than to be elated. It was difficult to best his father and he had rarely done so. Introductions were made where necessary. Laz had brought three investment bankers, five lawyers, four accountants, his finance officer, a secretary, and three of his vice-presidents.

"There's a suite right across the hall," Nick told Laz. "Step over there with me."

Laz nodded, and they went across the carpeted hall to a room where they could be alone. By prior agreement, they had decided to discuss the offer alone before calling in the lawyers.

"Can we discuss terms?" Nick said, stopping in the center of the room to watch Laz, who sat down on the beige sofa. He pulled out a cigar, carefully lighting it, seemingly a man in control, happy with events. Laz's manner made Nick more cautious.

"The board has authorized me to accept the fifty dollars a share with the written agreement you're CEO, and I remain on the board."

In spite of expecting Laz to eventually accept, Nick experienced a ripple of shock because he hadn't expected it to be this simple or this cheap. He had expected Laz to raise the price or to fight. And he never for a second expected the condition that he become CEO.

"You're shocked."

"Yes," Nick said, studying Laz.

"Why in hell would you be shocked? This is what I've wanted all these years," Laz snapped.

"No, it's not," Nick argued. "You wanted me under your thumb. You would have stayed CEO. You never wanted to turn everything over to me." Nick was dazed by Laz's offer, wariness holding back his acceptance that otherwise would have been forthcoming immediately.

"I'm older now, and you've proven yourself. You were a green kid right out of college before."

"Bullshit. You're bullshitting me."

"No. I get what I've always wanted. You run Kamnick Oil. You'll do a good job and I'll be on the board."

Nick didn't believe a word of praise. Laz thought it was a way to get him back under control. "I'm reinstating Cimarron."

"She's a very intelligent woman."

Nick received another shock. Laz laughed softly, his voice filled with cynical amusement. "Don't look so damned skeptical, Nick. I know a good deal when I see one."

"A shark can't change into a dolphin."

Laz shrugged. "Hell, I'm older. I want you running things. I always have. You want to do it your way. Do it. You've proved with Laredo that you can manage an oil company and you can find oil. I could have used more geologists like you."

Nick drew a long breath. Stunned, he stood mulling over the past few minutes and his easy victory. "What about Ralston? I've heard you're friends. I won't keep him."

"Nick. It'll be your company. Kamnick Oil, Nick Kaminski. Fire Ralston now if you want."

Never in his life had Nick seen his father so cooperative unless a woman was involved. He stared at Laz who smiled. "Shall I call in the lawyers to draw up papers?" Nick asked finally. He still felt a fight would come and he had no intention of celebrating.

"We're ready."

Nick nodded and went to the door.

They sent out for lunch while Nick carefully and slowly waded through all the legal documents, looking for a trick, trying to find something that Laz was slipping past him, but he couldn't. It looked exactly like Laz had said. Occasionally, Nick would stop and look across the room at Laz who reclined in a chair studying *The Wall Street Journal*.

At lunch they took a break and parted with their own men to eat and it was all Nick could do to keep from calling Cimarron and telling her she would soon be president of White Star. It would belong to Kamnick, but it would be Cimarron's to run and they could work out an agreement. She would have her job and her dream and he would be through fighting.

After lunch, Laz didn't return, but had told his men to call him when they were finished. Nick continued studying papers until ten o'clock that night. None of his men could find anything in the agreement contrary to what they wanted. As soon as it was signed, Nick and Peyton left.

"I can't believe he delivered me this victory all tied up in silver ribbon. I feel like we've taken in the Trojan horse. Laz doesn't change."

"Your lawyers have gone over it repeatedly," Peyton said.

"As soon as the ink dries we start getting rid of Kamnick Oil. We'll put it up for sale, retain the White Star part for Cimarron and when I'm through, there will be no Kamnick Oil."

"There isn't anyway."

"Oh, yes. It's still Kamnick. It's what my father built. And as long as it exists, he will be waiting in the wings."

"Does he know what you plan?" Peyton asked as they emerged from the hotel into the cool night.

"Hell, no! You think he'd do this deal if he did?"

"You want Laredo to grow. Why not just absorb Kamnick?"

Nick's voice was filled with grim satisfaction. "I'm going to send Kamnick into nonexistence, like pressing the button on a bomb."

"It's your baby now. Didn't he see the danger of this?"

"He can't believe I'll do it. I know how his mind works. The company is so big now. Nope, this is the last thing on earth he'll expect. He's gloating constantly because he thinks I'll run Kamnick. I won't do anything with it except get rid of it. For a good price."

"You should get that. He had a good operation."

It gave Nick a feeling of satisfaction to hear Peyton speak about Kamnick in the past tense. "I just want Cimarron to have back what she had before."

"That's quite a gift."

"She'll probably want you back. You'll have to choose between us, but if she needs you, as much as I hate to lose you, I'd rather see you go with her."

"And if you two merge?"

Nick shook his head. "She needs to be independent of me. I want to be in Enid before the morning paper so I can tell her."

"That's great, Nick. Really great. I think I can stop worrying so much about her."

They parted to go in separate cars. Nick felt keyed up, excited over the prospects of restoring White Star to Cimarron. Still going over their lunch date in his mind, remembering her declaration of love, he clung to it like something precious he had to examine often.

Her arguments about his acquiring Kamnick had diminished in his mind to nothing. As soon as they came back from the farm, he wanted to take her out to dinner and propose.

During the warm April morning alfalfa fields smelled sweet as he whipped along. The drive to the farm seemed longer than usual; eagerness to see her made him want to get there.

When he reached the house, he hit the horn lightly and climbed out. She came across the porch and stepped outside, hurrying to meet him, and his pulse hammered with joy. Her hair swung with each step, and in cutoffs and a blue hair ribbon, she looked as much like a kid as she had the first time he had seen her.

He had all he wanted: Cimarron, Laredo, victory over Laz. He caught her up in his arms, swinging her around, kissing her while he held her inches off the ground. She returned his kiss, holding him. She smelled sweet and fresh, like a bouquet of flowers. When they paused she raised her head and her green eyes focused on him.

"I didn't know you were coming."

"I couldn't call in the middle of the night. Well, early morning. Am I barging in at a bad time?"

"No. Don't you want to put me down? I must be getting a little heavy," she said, smiling at him.

"Never. I could carry you around with me always."

"Oh, sure. By ten o'clock you'd be staggering."

"You make me sound like a wimp."

She ran her hand over hard biceps. "Yeah, some wimp." They both laughed and he kissed her again, a long kiss that made them gasp for breath when they stopped.

"The family has gone to town—Saturday grocery buying and all that."

Nick thought he would remember this moment with perfect clarity forever. The sky was blue behind her, the leaves of the cottonwood moving slightly in a breeze that also caught tendrils of Cimarron's hair, pieces that would never stay pinned down. She had a faint smile on her face, a curious questioning in her eyes. She wore a simple blue cotton shirt open at the throat and he wanted to reach out and unfasten the row of buttons down the front. He was tempted to carry her into the empty house to bed and talk later.

"What is it, Nick?" she asked, tilting her head to study him. Cimarron wanted his arms around her and it was wonderful to have him here. She realized he was happy and excited and must have some news.

"Honey, I got White Star back," he said. "It's yours again," he said.

It took seconds to register. "What do you mean, you got it back?" she asked quietly and all her joy disintegrated like a broken bit of crystal.

"I made an offer to the board at Kamnick and Laz accepted it. It's mine now, all mine."

"He went along with it just like that?"

"Yes. He thinks he's won. He thinks I'll run Kamnick now. I'm CEO. The only concession he wanted was to stay on the board. It never occurred to him I would destroy Kamnick and give you back White Star, but that's what I'm doing."

She shivered with a chill as she listened to the harsh note of anger in his voice. "And so the enmity is perpetuated," she said, beginning to hurt.

Nick blinked and frowned, staring at her.

"I don't want White Star that way, Nick."

"God, I can't believe what you said!" he exclaimed in shock. His eyes widened and he stared at her, momentarily thinking of the men and money and careers involved in the transaction. "I did this whole thing for you!"

"No, you didn't," she said slowly, regret, hurt returning as she remembered clearly their last time together. She took a step back away from him. "You did it to hurt Laz."

"The hell I did! I want to give you back White Star."

"Nick, you know how I feel about your taking Kamnick from Laz. If you drop this and go to Kamnick—"

"Hell, no!" He swore and walked a few paces away to stare in the distance and then came back. His face had darkened with anger, but she couldn't accept what he offered. "I can't believe this! You'd turn down *an oil company*—Fontaine's company—your precious Fontaine—"

"That's enough, Nick!" she snapped, raising her chin. "You're going to destroy your father if you do this. He's willing to let you run things your way. That's what you said you always wanted. I don't want Fontaine's company when it means destroying the man I love."

"It sure as sweet hell isn't going to destroy me!"

"Yes, it will. I don't think you can live with hate and anger and revenge and not be destroyed or twisted."

"Laz has lived with it and survived. *I did this for you!*" He was stunned by her reaction, unable to understand it.

"If you did, you haven't listened to what I've said. And you really don't know me at all."

"I did this for you. I love you. You said you love me."

"I do, but I can't love the part of you that is filled with hatred and I don't want to be deeply involved with a man whose life is governed by anger. If I marry again, I want children. I don't want my children hating their grandfather and seeing their father live with anger."

"That's a Pollyana way of viewing the real world," Nick snapped, hurt and stunned.

"Maybe it is, but it's the only view I can live with."

"You're going to let White Star go, because I hate Laz?"

"Yes. I don't want to be part of what you're doing," she said, hurting because in all other ways, Nick was wonderful. He was a man with a blind spot where his father was concerned, and it could be fatal to other relationships.

"Jesus. I can't believe you! No one else will either."

"If I didn't love you, it might be different."

He glared at her. "Dammit, Cimarron, you're a bullheaded, stubborn woman who has a heart too soft and too sweet for the business world. You're not going to accept White Star?"

"No," she said, knowing she would lose Nick in this moment, but knowing if she had to live with a man filled with hatred, it would be an impossible future.

In angry strides he crossed to kiss her. He bent over her, his tongue playing in her mouth. His kiss was passionate and long, insistent and in seconds, she couldn't fight him and returned it. He released her. "You're going to give up what we've found between us?"

"I don't want to, but I have to," she said quietly.

"All right, Cimarron. If it gives you any satisfaction, I

bought an oil company for you. If Laz had wanted to play hardball, he might have been able to crush me on this deal. I took enormous risks to put this together. I took the risks for you. You're the only woman I have truly and deeply loved."

They stared at each other, a gulf of anger between them. With a stormy expression he spun on his heel and climbed into his car, slamming the door. The motor roared to life and he shot backwards, spinning around, scattering gravel behind him and stirring up a gray cloud of dust that shimmered through the tears she no longer had to control.

"Nick, I love you," she whispered, knowing it was useless now and knowing he was gone.

She went back to the house to sit down on the step and cry. Finally, she got up to go inside and do her jobs, but she hurt all over and moved stiffly as if she had bruised all her muscles.

Nick sped away, rage and hurt making him drive too fast and grip the wheel too tightly. He spun onto the county road, tires squealing, skidding across the asphalt and spinning off on the shoulder. He gained control and shot back onto the asphalt leaving a cloud of brown dust behind him. Oblivious of what was happening, he pushed the gas pedal to the floor. He loved Cimarron deeply, and he felt as if someone were slowly turning a knife in his chest.

He couldn't believe what she had just done. Twenty minutes later he shot across a bridge and realized his speed, easing his foot off the accelerator. Pain came in waves; Cimarron was the woman he loved. Forever. There never had been a woman who had stirred as much reaction in him, one whom he cared about as much, one he needed as much.

The more time that passed the worse his agony became, because he realized the finality of it. Cimarron was not one to vacillate or soften once she had taken a stand she felt strongly about.

When he reached home, he sat in his driveway in silence. He hadn't stopped to eat on his way home, all his appetite was gone. He stared at his house that seemed so empty now. He wanted her and he wanted her always, his wife. Sunny. He swore and climbed out of the car, leaning against it as if he were in pain while her words ran through his mind again as they had all the long drive home. He went inside to pour himself a large glass of bourbon and gulp it down.

After jogging himself into exhaustion, he spent a miserable, sleepless night and knew that the next nights weren't going to get any better.

Freedom carried his trash out through the patio to the cans in the alley. He couldn't help but notice Raye's overflowing trash cans. Her papier mâché animals were stuffed into a can, the gorilla lay in the dirt. Freedom dumped his trash and strode back inside. He moved around the kitchen and finally stared into space, his fists on his hips.

He want back to retrieve the dog and cat. The dog's nose was torn, the cat's leg broken. He picked up one parrot and untangled the wires of its perch. The parrot was ruffled and torn; Freedom looked at the bottom of the can and pushed aside newspapers. The other parrot with the bandage on his chest was smashed flat beyond repair and Freedom left it. He picked up the gorilla that had splotches of dirt on it now.

Pulling the gorilla behind him, he wondered how Raye had managed to move it around. He studied his living room and put the gorilla in a corner. Satisfied, he went to the kitchen to sit down with glue and scissors to repair the parrot. He worked patiently, his mind on Raye while he came to a decision.

While Freedom worked on the tattered paper animals, Laz sprawled on Raye's sofa with a stiff bourbon and ice. He sipped the drink as she poured a glass of soda. "I have a meeting tonight. I won't be here for dinner."

"Oh? I had steaks."

"Yeah, well cook yours and put mine in the freezer. Sorry." He glanced at the television. "Can you turn that off?"

"Sure. Rough day?" she asked as she punched the button on the remote control and the picture vanished from the screen.

"Haggling over fine points with the lawyers. Raye, this isn't my style."

She looked at him. "Yeah? How so?"

His chest expanded as he took a deep breath. "This condo. I'm cramped. I'm going back to Dallas. I'm through with business here anyway."

Raye tried to keep her features solemn. "Sure, Laz."

"I'll be around, and you'll be in Dallas soon. If I didn't have a damned appointment—"

"But you do. What time are you supposed to be there?"

He glanced at his watch. "In twenty minutes. I'll be back late." He kissed her, set down his glass, and left.

He was moving out. She had suspected for two weeks that he was interested in Sherry. He came to the boutique several times after their introduction and then he stopped coming, but for two weeks Sherry had been quiet, withdrawn, and Raye suspected she was seeing Laz often. He wasn't around as much, coming in late, leaving early for business appointments the past week, not coming in at night, telling her he slept at the hotel where meetings were held. Part of it actually was time taken by the Kamnick, White Star, Laredo deals, Raye knew, but she suspected part of his time was taken by Sherry because Raye was seeing him very seldom now to her relief, finding it increasingly unpleasant to pretend with him, praying Sherry earned her bonus. Raye decided to raise the bonus another hundred. Sherry loved a dollar.

Her thoughts shifted to Freedom, remembering every detail of how he looked. Her throat tightened and she tried to shift her thoughts to something else.

A week later on a Wednesday afternoon in May, she was showing dresses to a customer and glanced through the plate-glass windows at the sunshine on the flower beds and parked cars in the lot. Raye held two dresses, a green silk and a burgundy velvet as a man outside caught her attention.

Heading for the store from the curb, walking in long, purposeful strides, his jaw set, was Freedom. He was dressed for work in a navy pin-stripe suit, the jacket open and swinging with his stride. She took one look at his face and hung the dresses on a rack.

"You think about it, Mrs. Knolling. I'll be right back."

Freedom was closer and he looked enraged. "Sherry, I'm not here. I'm just not here!" She rushed into her office and shut the door as the tiny bell tinkled at the front.

Raye's heart pounded. All she could hear was a murmur of voices. She started toward her desk when the door burst open beside her and Freedom barged in.

"I'm busy," she said, gasping as if she had run a marathon. His blue eyes blazed with fury and determination. He caught her and spun her around to pull her into his arms.

"Freedom, there are customers—"

He kicked the door shut behind him as he pulled her against his chest. "Tell me you don't love me," he commanded, looking at her with a scalding, searching look.

All she could think was that it was too soon to tell him and it was the most wonderful thing in the world to be in his arms.

He saw his answer and bent his head to kiss her and she felt as if she would melt with joy and agony.

He stopped kissing her to look at her solemnly. "You have to leave him. I'm not going to take no for an answer. You love me. You can't tell me you don't, and dammit, money is only just so important. You can't have children with money, you can't grow old with someone you love if you throw everything away for dollars—"

Her heart pounded with fear and joy. She put her fingertips on his lips. "Freedom, I love you."

"You'll leave him? Today?"

"Will you listen to me? I'm on the verge of leaving him. Just a little more time—"

"Do you know what it's like for me to think about you in his arms at night?"

"It won't be long before he tells me goodbye."

"I'll be damned if I'll wait and let you love him—"

"It'll save me ten thousand dollars that I have to pay back if I leave him."

Freedom's eyes narrowed and fires of rage burned in his eyes. "Dammit, I'll pay the ten thousand! Why didn't you tell me that was what was holding you?"

"Ten thousand is a fortune!" she said, stunned by his offer. She couldn't believe what he said. She didn't dream he had money available to be able to pay off such a sum without a qualm, and she was overwhelmed he wanted to. Her throat constricted. "That's so much money! There were other things at first. I've been working on those."

"You're breaking it off tonight, Raye."

He looked ready for a fight with his hands on his hips, his jaw thrust out stubbornly, spots of color in his cheeks, a lock of hair tumbling over his furrowed brow. Her heart pounded and for a second she thought of the boutiques she had dreamed about for so long. But they were empty comfort in a life without the man she loved.

"I can't let you pay ten thousand dollars to Laz."

"I can and I will. Since the White Star deal, I don't have a job, but I have money. I want you and I don't—"

"All right, Freedom," she answered quietly.

"Dammit, you're going to—" He blinked, just realizing what she had said. "You agreed!"

"Yes," she said, hoping he really could pay Laz without hardship, growing more sure of her answer with each minute.

"You *agreed?*" he asked, the tenseness going out of his shoulders, his voice changing, a light coming to his eyes that wasn't stirred by rage. "Raye, just like that, you'll leave him? Why didn't you do it sooner if you're willing now? The damned ten thousand?"

"Yes. I've been doing my best to get things set up so I can leave him. I don't want him angry with you. He's iniquitous and bullheaded and I don't want him angry with me, making me repay him, taking my stores."

"Listen, that's something else," Freedom said, the inflexible note returning to his voice. "I don't want my wife running a store that was bought for her by another man. I'll buy you another boutique."

No one had ever loved her enough to do half of what

Freedom was offering. With Laz there hadn't been a shred of love, only a deal. And in her childhood and early romance, she hadn't received love, but she ached with it for Freedom. At the same time joy made her feel as if she would burst. She flung her arms around him, sending him staggering back. He caught his balance and leaned against the door to gaze down at her and both of them looked at each other as if they had been desperate for this moment forever.

"Sometime I'll hear about what you've been doing, but not right now." He reached behind him to lock the door.

"There are curious women only yards away waiting to see what's happening in here."

"They should be able to guess," he said in a husky voice, bending his head to kiss her neck.

"Freedom, they're waiting for me."

"Yeah. So am I." He kissed her long and hard while his hands unzipped her dress and pushed it down on the floor. Soft music from Muzak played and Raye was lost, forgetting her employees and customers, thinking only of Freedom as her hands roamed over him while he pulled her down on the soft carpet.

"Freedom, you're wicked," she whispered. "And wonderful."

"I want you always. Will you marry me?"

"Of course," she whispered before she kissed him.

She shifted and moved against his bare chest. "How will I ever go out and face them?" She sat up. "They'll know what we've been doing."

He grinned and put his hands behind his head. "Naw, they won't. Just get gussied up and tell them we've been discussing a merger." He chuckled, and she wagged her head at him.

"It's embarrassing."

"It isn't embarrassing to be in love."

"Well, this isn't something for spectators or speculation. I'm embarrassed. It's like you're so—so—"

"Sex starved? I am. I haven't been able to look at another

woman in a long time and when I looked before, they came up pretty short."

"Did they really?" she asked, suddenly pleased. "I used to annoy you and you weren't impressed with my looks."

"Believe me, Raye, I was impressed," he said, thinking of her zany polka dots and flowers. "You annoyed hell out of me, but I can't live without you. You made me fall in love with you."

"That's sweet. Oh, dear. The longer I wait, the worse it'll be. We're going to dress and act dignified and leave."

He grinned and got up, moving around quietly until they both were dressed. She tried to comb her hair and twist it back around her head. "Look at this. Pins are all over the floor and it'll take me another fifteen minutes to get my hair back where it belongs."

"Leave it down. Raye, they all know what we did. Putting your hair up isn't going to convince them we've been having a business discussion."

She was busy studying herself in the small oval mirror behind the file cabinet. "It might. It takes me a long time to get it up neatly."

He whistled a tune and moved around her office. "I'm astounded. Your shop isn't like your home."

"I know what women like." She combed her hair and caught the ends to twist them into a long roll. "This is the best I can do!"

"You don't dress like this at home."

"No. My last year in high school I owned two pairs of jeans, some T-shirts, and one brown skirt. That's all. I love flowers and colors and paper animals and toys. I know I look crazy at home, but I never could have anything pretty. I wear fashionable clothes when I go out. I design attractive clothes. At home I have fun."

He crossed the room to hold her. "Let's go to Hawaii for a honeymoon, and I'll get you a hundred Hawaiian shirts and flashy mu-mus!"

He pulled her to him to kiss her tenderly, a kiss that changed to passion until she pushed away. "Uh-huh. Not again!"

She opened the door and they emerged. Three women looked at them. "I'm going out for awhile, Sherry. Would you handle things. If you ladies will excuse us . . ." She took Freedom's arm and steered him out the back door and he burst into laughter.

"I thought I carried that off rather well."

"You were three shades of red. And now that we're in the alley, what are we going to do? My car is parked right in front of your shop."

"Oh, no! I'm not walking back through there. We'll go around."

He glanced down the long line of doors and brick walls. "It's quite a hike around there."

"It'll be good for you," she said, striding away. He chuckled and caught up to walk beside her, draping his arm across her shoulders and pulling her close.

She wondered how many times they declared their love while they strolled around to his car. She thought she had never seen a more beautiful day. Sunshine was brighter, purple periwinkles and red geraniums more colorful, the air fresher.

"Freedom, Laz is on the verge of leaving me," she said as Freedom pulled away from the curb. "If he does, it would save you money—"

He stopped the car and turned to her. His voice was mild, his eyes filled with love, but the unmistakable, inflexible note was back in his voice. "Raye, don't ever bring up Laz Kaminski again. If you have to pay ten thousand, I'll pay. You're through with him. I want you to move in with me tonight."

"Yes," she answered emphatically, throwing aside worries and giving herself over to absolute joy.

They went to Freedom's and as soon as she stepped inside the living room, she stopped. "Freedom, you have L.T.!"

"It's goofy to name something made of paper."

"I threw my animals away."

"I didn't think they should be discarded. Not yet," he answered solemnly.

"But you hated them," she said, spinning around to

study him as if she hoped to find her answer for his behavior in his expression.

"I guess I kind of grew to like them. They were part of you; you seemed to like them so much. Hell—they were just something of yours, and I didn't want to see them go."

"You don't have to explain," she said softly. "I cried all the time I put them out there." She went to the gorilla to hug it, her arms spread wide around his large girth. "Good old L.T."

Freedom grinned. "L.T.! Raye, that's a stupid paper gorilla and ugly to boot!"

She looked at him smugly. "Then why is he in your living room?"

They both laughed and Freedom held out his arms. She crossed the room to walk into them and hug him. "I want you to meet my folks," he said. "How soon can we have a wedding?"

"I don't have any family. I lost contact with all of them years ago, so I'm free. So free," she said, feeling as if lead weights were dropping from her. "Can you forgive me?"

"For what?" he said softly.

She looked up at him. "For Laz. I didn't think I was capable of loving again, so I settled for other things."

"Would I be marrying you if I couldn't forgive you? There's nothing to forgive, Raye. It's over. And it won't have anything to do with us from now on."

"Honey, I have to tell him," she said gently. "I can't walk out without telling him it's goodbye forever."

"I don't like Laz Kaminski. I never realized how much I had to be thankful for the father I have until this last month, watching Nick and his dad. I don't want you to tell Laz if you're in any danger."

"I won't be in any danger. I think he's going to welcome the news. Actually, in just a short time, I expected him to dump me. See, I found him a new woman."

"You what?"

"I know Laz likes beautiful women. And I'm no beauty."

"That's what you think!" Freedom said, kissing her throat.

"You didn't think so when you first saw me! But anyway, I hired her and offered her a bonus if she could interest him in her within the month."

Freedom leaned back to stare at her. "How the hell did you find her?"

"In a bar. She was the one at the store today."

"I saw only one woman in your store."

"Well, she's very attractive and she wants Laz, and I think that's why he moved out—"

"I didn't know he had moved out."

"Oh, yes. He's going back to Dallas or her place or somewhere. I'm on the verge of getting out of my contract."

"Damn, you have a written contract?"

"Yes. I don't think it will be any time at all before he settles Sherry in with him."

"How long have you been working on this?"

"Since I decided I couldn't live without you."

"We've talked long enough," he whispered. She stood on tiptoe to kiss him.

A week later Freedom flew to Dallas with Raye. He waited at a hotel while she went to see Laz at his office. As she crossed the room and sat down facing him, she felt calm. She had a check for ten thousand in her purse.

"You've never been to the office before."

"No. I just got back in town."

"Have you been to the house?" he asked, frowning, and suddenly she realized Sherry might have some of her belongings there, because Laz looked uncomfortable.

"Not yet."

His chest expanded and he glanced away and back. "We haven't seen as much of each other lately as we used to."

For a moment Raye was tempted to try to bluff her way to save the ten thousand if she could, but she thought of Freedom and wanted a clean break with Laz before she walked out of his office. She opened her purse and placed the check on his desk.

"I'm paying the penalty named in our contract and the stores will revert to you, because I can't buy out your shares."

Shock reflected in his expression fleetingly, and then anger replaced it. He stood up to face her. "Why are you doing this?"

"I think there's another woman in your life," she stated coolly.

"The hell there is!" he snapped. "I've been busy because we've been bought out in a hostile takeover. I needed to come back to Dallas." He came around the desk and she faced him as he gripped her shoulders. "Is there another man?"

"When have I had time for another man?"

"You wouldn't walk in here and hand over the stores, your dreams and hopes wound up in them. You couldn't have gotten the money on your own."

"I used the condo for collateral. There's your ten thousand and you have the stores. Not a bad deal, Laz. I want out."

"You little bitch!"

"You won't miss me," she replied calmly. "I've seen you out with someone else. I saw you in Tulsa."

He clamped his lips together and a muscle worked in his jaw. "So because of one time with one woman, you're leaving?"

"Do you really want me to stay?" She watched a brief mental debate. "You don't have to say it. I just got my answer."

"Get out."

She turned and walked across the thick carpet and closed the door behind her. If she had waited another month, Freedom could have kept his ten thousand. He had paid off her bank loan and she had taken the ten from the money she had put away, but now it was done and she was free to marry.

Freedom and Raye had a small wedding at the farm with only the Chisholms and their close friends attending. Cimarron stood close beside Raye as matron of honor, watching them and thinking Raye looked beautiful in a pale-blue silk dress, Freedom handsome in his navy suit. She felt a pang, missing Nick so much it took her breath. She studied

Freedom as he looked down at Raye, and it was obvious Freedom was deeply in love.

Freedom and Raye left for a long honeymoon in Hawaii and as Cimarron watched them drive away, she felt an empty ache for Nick that seemed to grow with time instead of diminish.

24

Nick suffered over Cimarron's rejection while he made arrangements to sell parts of Kamnick and eliminate staff. As time passed and worries and hurt assailed him, he gave more thought to her arguments, trying to see things as she did. Slowly, he began to reassess his ruthless destruction of Kamnick. The Chisholms were a close-knit, loving family, something that had always eluded him. It was hopeless to expect that from Laz, but Nick realized he should give more thought to what Cimarron had said. Now Nick wondered if the destruction of the family business wouldn't be a hollow victory. He spent restless nights, mulling it over, rethinking things, knowing no matter how much he tried, there were some things Laz would never be. A loving, understanding father was one. But perhaps it wasn't too late to gain some tolerance and respect for each other.

Moss was handling some of the fact-gathering data and stopped in Nick's office Tuesday morning. His wheat-colored hair was parted in the center, steel-rimmed glasses perched on his thin nose. "Nick, this south Texas division is in charge of the Gulf wells for Kamnick. There are more men in that division than any other except the Dallas one. We're getting two offers on that division." Moss laughed. "I've heard Laz is still celebrating our deal."

Nick had been thinking about Cimarron; he swung his

chair around and stood up. "Yes. I'm going to drop a bomb. I want to put all the plans for Kamnick on hold."

"You have another buyer?"

"No, I don't have another buyer, but I'm having second thoughts about what I'm doing. I may keep Kamnick."

"Jesus, Nick." Moss had known Nick since the first year of Laredo Oil and he knew Nick seldom reversed decisions. "Has something happened?"

"I need to give it more thought."

Moss shrugged. "You're the boss."

"So far," Nick whispered as Moss left the office. He asked his secretary to make an appointment for him with Laz the next morning at eight.

When he walked into Laz's lavish office, his father came forward to shake his hand. "I'm glad you're here. I wondered when you would take charge. I've got some things lined up for you that you'll like."

For an instant, antagonism flared as Nick listened to his father tell him what land he should try to lease next, what to sell, the executives to get to know first. And then as Nick sat back in the chair, he studied Laz and tried to see only a father, not a manipulative, aggressive businessman. Anger dissipated and he realized that his father's age was showing more now. There were more lines in his face, a puffiness beneath his eyes he had never had before, a thickening in his waist.

"Nick, are you listening?"

"Sure, Laz. Go ahead."

Laz stared at him, smiling, a look of triumph sparking his eyes. "Nick, I always knew you'd come around and see it my way. Kamnick was too big a plum for you to ignore. When I dangled it, you took the bait right down to the hook. We'll work together well. You can do whatever you want."

"Thanks, Laz," Nick said mildly, knowing Laz hadn't changed, and wondering if it were possible for him to change or if he were as molded in concrete as his father. It wouldn't help him with Cimarron, because she wouldn't believe or accept it until he had proved it, and by the time he convinced her, some man could come into her life, but

Nick was going to try and salvage this one thing, because she had wanted it badly enough to throw away love and career.

"Nick, I heard some rumors, that you might be selling part of Kamnick."

"I was going to, but I changed my mind."

Laz stared at him, a puzzled expression on his face. "Why'd you change your mind?"

"I decided to see if we could work together."

"It would be a damned dumb thing to sell that southern division. It's a moneymaker."

"That it is."

"Are you taking my office?"

"No. That's part of what I came to talk to you about. I know you're not ready to step down. So I think we need to draw territorial lines. You take charge of Texas. I'll take Louisiana, Oklahoma, and Kansas. You take California and I'll handle Canada and the North Sea."

"How come you're giving me all this power, Nick?" Laz asked, a frown creasing his brow. He leaned forward in his chair, shoulders hunched, reminding Nick of a linebacker getting ready for the play to be called.

"You don't really want to step down, do you?"

"Since when did you start worrying about what I want?"

"Since a short time ago."

"What the hell brought that on?"

Nick moved to the window to gaze down at the traffic. At the moment he almost didn't care if he gave everything to Laz. But he knew he would care someday. "I met a family—and they were a real family who cared about each other."

"What the hell does that have to do with the oil business?"

"Very little. But it made me see you're my only family."

Laz stared at him. "You sound like you're on something."

"Because I'm trying to be cooperative? You think I'm high, because I'm acting like a son." Cars sparkled in the sunshine on the LBJ Freeway while silence stretched in the room.

"I don't know if you're getting tricky or what."

"How does the territory sound?" Nick asked, getting back to business, wondering if Laz would understand in the next twenty years what he was saying. "I get final approval on all sales and purchases."

"Yeah, that's fine. You don't want this office? I figured you'd be here."

Nick looked at the office that would hold three the size of his. "No, just give me another office. I never did need anything fancy. I'll make my headquarters in Tulsa."

"In that dump? This whole building is Kamnick's."

"I like Tulsa. I know the people there and I don't want to move," he said good-naturedly, determined he wasn't going to let Laz get under his skin.

Laz stared at him, his jaw thrust out. "You move here. This building has everything you'll need. It's known everywhere as the headquarters—"

"Okay. Keep it headquarters. I'll come one week a month and work here," Nick said pleasantly, finding it wasn't so difficult once he put his mind to the task of getting along with Laz, if he just let the bluster pass.

Laz leaned back in the chair. "That's better. I'll put you next door to me. Don't expect me to come to Tulsa, Nick."

"That's fine."

"I don't understand you," Laz said, a querulous note in his voice. "You've changed."

"I hope I'm still young enough to change if I try."

"What do you mean by that? You think I'm too old to change?"

"I didn't say a word about you. I brought some papers about restructuring White Star."

"Give them to my lawyers first. You need to get your signs changed to the red and green of Kamnick Oil."

"We're doing that."

Suddenly Laz laughed and leaned back. "Hell, I don't know why you're worrying me. You're doing it my way. I won, Nick, just like I always knew I would."

"I wish we could have both won," Nick said, thinking of Cimarron.

"You ought to give Cimarron Durand a vice-presidency. I

guess that's who's keeping you in the Tulsa office. Can't say I blame you. Are you marrying her?''

''No. There are no plans of marriage.''

''If she's bitter with me, she'll get over it. You name your first son Lazlo after me, and I'll put a million in a savings account for him.''

''Then we can make his middle name 'Million'—Lazlo Million Kaminski.''

''I don't know about that, Nick,'' Laz said with a frown that vanished as he smiled and he stood up. ''Go to lunch with me.''

''Sure, Laz.''

Laz beamed. ''Let me show you the changes in the place since you worked here. We have the finest equipment in this office you've ever seen. Wells are on computer now. We've put cameras on some wells so we can monitor the drilling right here in the office and make big decisions quickly.''

''Sounds good,'' Nick said and meant it, wondering why he hadn't thought of monitoring wells by computer.

Laz clamped his hand on Nick's shoulder and they walked down the hall, pausing at an office while Laz talked to someone, and then joined Nick again. ''Come look.''

From Laz's office on the tenth story to the ground floor they toured, and the building was impressive. Kamnick had made money and spent it lavishly. When they went back upstairs, two of the maintenance staff were moving furniture down the hall. Laz led Nick into the office next to his own where a new desk and file cabinet were being placed.

''You can have one of our secretaries or get your own. Here's your new office. I told them to get a desk and file cabinet for you—I know it's only temporary. You'll want to redecorate, but how's this?''

Nick gazed at paneled walls, a wide view of Dallas from the glass floor-to-ceiling windows, doors opened to a bar, and a door to an adjoining bathroom. ''Did someone just vacate this place?'' Nick asked, noticing books and papers stacked on the floor.

''Yes. He moved to another office. One of our vice-presidents. Do you like it?''

"Yes, it's nice."

"Hell of a lot better than the box your office is. Come on, I'll take you to lunch."

Nick drove Laz to a country club for lunch. Laz had a martini, trying to order steaks for both of them, but Nick ordered a sandwich and milk.

"What do you plan to do with White Star?"

"It's in the report I brought. Some people will have to go, but I hope we can make changes with a minimum of upheaval."

"Upheaval is the oil industry. You'll have to meet Sherry."

"Raye married Freedom Chisholm."

"The bitch. I sold the stores."

"She's a smart, talented woman. You're bitter. What did she do? Walk out on you? You got the stores."

"Hell, yes. And a ten grand penalty she had to pay."

"You still love her?"

"Oh, no. I have Sherry. But sometimes I wonder. . . I think Raye set it up so I'd meet Sherry."

Nick's respect for Raye mushroomed for outwitting Laz and extricating herself from a possessive relationship.

"A little dress clerk . . . I didn't expect a challenge. 'Course she wasn't so damned smart. If she'd bided her time, she wouldn't have had to pay the ten grand. If I'd walked out on her—and I was getting ready to—she could have kept her money."

Nick listened, amazed. "Maybe she didn't want to wait."

"Hell, I'm glad she's gone. Sherry's a looker."

Nick didn't want to listen to Laz discuss his women. "I expect to bid on four more leases in the Gulf this month."

"That North Sea well you have an interest in is great."

"Thanks. We've got an interest in another one."

"Kamnick is a giant now," Laz said with satisfaction. "We've done well, Nick. I always knew you'd grow up like me."

Nick laughed softly, looking at Laz, thinking of the years of struggle between them, thinking if he had a son, he intended to be a different kind of father, so different. And then he thought of Cimarron and the possibilities of sons faded. He wondered where she was right now and what she was doing.

"Nick?"

"What? Oh, sorry. There's a lot on my mind—"

Laz chuckled. "Bogs your mind to suddenly find yourself at the top, doesn't it?"

"A bit."

"When I came to this country, I didn't have a dime, Nick."

Nick listened to a story he had heard many times as a child and his thoughts drifted back to Cimarron.

He spent the week in Dallas, lunching with Laz, sometimes going to dinner with Laz and Sherry. It wasn't difficult to be cooperative. He knew there would be a fight again when they crossed on company policies, but his desire to crush Laz had gone. He hoped Cimarron heard about it, because she would know why. He knew she wouldn't expect it to last, and only time would tell, because right now Laz was in the magnanimous glow of victory. Time would come when they would disagree violently. But Nick thought he could cope with Laz, because the burning hatred he had felt had gone, evaporated by Cimarron's love—yet he had lost that love. His animosity was gone, and along with it went his need to have complete control. Laz and his cavalier demands no longer seemed important, just another obstacle to deal with. What was important was the love of his life.

On Friday he worked through the lunch hour and at two Laz entered his office. "You missed lunch. Lori said you didn't send out for anything either."

"I didn't think about it. I'm not hungry. We've got some new leases in western Oklahoma that look promising."

"Turn it over to one of our landmen, Hartshorne."

"You're doing Texas, remember?"

Laz waved his hand. "Assign it over to him anyway. He's the best."

Nick nodded, having no intention of turning it over to Hartshorne.

"Nick, why don't you come out to the house and stay the weekend? We'll do something fun. Fly Cimarron here—"

"I don't see Cimarron any longer."

"What happened? Hey, is it because of the merger?"

"Somewhat. And disagreements."

"Oh. Well, Cimarron Durand is an icicle. Brilliant and cold," he said, and Nick wondered what had happened in the battles between White Star and Kamnick.

Laz left and Nick walked to the window to look at the tall buildings, the round Reunion Tower and Hyatt Regency Hotel, the old Mobil Building dwarfed now by taller towers in downtown Dallas, the treetops and busy arteries of highways between the Kamnick Building and downtown. To the north in Tulsa was Cimarron, only an hour's flight away. Close, and yet she might as well be in Cancun. He closed his eyes, remembering her in Cancun, remembering the first time with her, thinking about her until he physically ached.

It was in the scorching heat of late August before Nick returned to western Oklahoma to the Enid office that was now Kamnick Oil instead of White Star. He spent three days there, one day looking at wells, and Friday, looking over prospective leases.

Monday he was back in Dallas for only a few hours, the company jet waiting to take him to western Oklahoma. Dressed in a new burgundy suit with gold cuff links gleaming, Laz entered the office. One look at his face, and Nick sat back in the chair, bracing for trouble.

"I hear you're bull riding in rodeos."

Nick laughed and relaxed. "I'm going to ride the last week of September."

"You can't! Dammit, don't you realize the responsibility you have? You're president and CEO of Kamnick Oil. You can't ride a bull."

"Why the sweet hell not?" Nick asked with amusement.

"That's the most dangerous sport in existence. You could get gored to death."

"Laz, a million things can happen to me. If anything does, the transition would go as smooth as water running through a pipe."

"Dammit, you have responsibilities!"

Laz stood across the desk, fists on his hips, his jaw thrust out belligerently, and Nick's amusement vanished as two ideas assailed him. He wished Cimarron could hear their exchange. He realized he was succeeding in dealing with Laz, because eight months ago, Nick would have been ready to fight Laz if he had this same conversation. He had always felt he didn't have Laz's love, but now he realized that Laz cared, that he may have always done so, but that he was incapable of expressing it in a way Nick could understand.

"What difference does it make to you?" Nick asked quietly.

"It's important that you're here to run this company! Bull riding is stupid for a man in your position."

Nick stared at him, seeing another side to Laz, pitying the man because he was unable to declare his love. He hoped that if he were ever a father he would remember to tell his children he loved them. Nick had grown up hearing the rags-to-riches story of Laz after he immigrated to the U.S., but there was a curtain of silence about the earlier war years, and he wondered about Laz's childhood in Poland. Perhaps they had been so bad, all expressions of love had been stunted and twisted forever.

"Laz, it's a challenge. I'll be all right."

"You've got a giant oil conglomerate to run! Isn't that enough of a fucking challenge?"

"Bull riding is something physical," Nick said. "I'm flying to Enid today. Look at these leases and see what you think would be a good bid." Nick handed files to Laz who stared at him with anger flashing in his eyes until finally he reached out and took the folders.

While he was in Enid, Nick heard of a ranch for sale, seventy miles southwest of Enid, and he made an appointment to meet the owner and look at the land.

He talked to real estate people, and from lease work knew the prices of acreage. It was hot, wind-swept prairie, stretching for miles to meet the horizon, cottonwoods lining a meandering river. The ground was the sun-baked red earth of Oklahoma except to the south where the dark North Canadian bottom lands lay. Nick felt a sense of peace as he walked around it. He had a big income and simple tastes, so there was no problem with finances. He bought the ranch outright with cash, and his spirits lifted. He tried to look at it without picturing Cimarron there.

Back in Enid, he worked the rest of the week and on Friday as he was finishing lunch in a cafe, he glanced out the window and saw Tim Chisholm striding across the street.

Nick tossed down his napkin, calling across the counter to the waitress that he would be right back. In hot sunshine, he yelled at Tim, who turned and came over to shake hands with him.

"Let me buy you lunch."

"I'll have a cup of coffee, thanks," Tim said.

When Tim had ordered coffee, Nick asked, "How's everyone?"

"We're doing pretty good. I hear you bought land around here."

Nick grinned. "News travels fast. I'll have to hire someone to run the place. If you hear of a good man who's looking for a job, tell him to call me."

"I might know someone. Alec Burnside."

"Does he know wheat and cattle?"

"Yeah. He's reliable, levelheaded, hard-working. He can play the fiddle, too. Best bluegrass you ever heard. Do you square dance?"

"No."

"Too bad. Alec Burnside calls a lot of dances around here."

"How's Cimarron?"

"She's okay, I guess. Right now she's in Tulsa. Sometimes she stays at the farm."

Nick looked down quickly and drank his coffee.

"Sorry, Nick."

"That's all right. I didn't know it would show so badly."

"I bought a horse today. You'll have to look at him. I'm riding in a rodeo the last of September."

Nick's head came up and he grinned. "Maybe our paths will cross again. I've signed up for a September rodeo. September thirtieth here in Enid."

"I'll be damned. I've signed up for bulldogging. I've got this new horse and he's a honey."

"At least I don't have to buy a bull!"

"I hear you're spending time in Dallas and changing everything to the name Kamnick. You're working with your father now."

"That's right," Nick said, realizing if Tim knew, Cimarron would also know.

"Want to look at my horse?"

"Sure," Nick said, paying for their lunch before walking outside.

"Thanks for the coffee," Tim said, setting his broad-brimmed hat squarely on his head. They went across the square to a pickup and trailer while Tim talked about the roan gelding.

"What are you going to do with your farm? Is it an investment?" Tim asked, his arm propped on the shiny black truck.

"I want it for a place to live part of the year. Kamnick is big enough that I don't have to be there all the time and I can afford a farm."

"I guess you can," Tim said dryly.

"With Laz still active, I know I won't be missed when I'm gone. I like it in the country. It's something I need."

"Amen to that. I don't know why Freedom doesn't like the farm. He hates it down to the last little grain of wheat. Raye's been good for him. He's happier than I've seen him in years." He extended his hand and shook with Nick. "Thanks again for the coffee."

"Tell the fiddler, Burnside, to call me. I'll see you at the rodeo if not before, Tim. Tell your family hello. When you see Cimarron, tell her—tell her I asked about her," Nick said, controlling himself, seeing the faint family resemblance between Tim and Cimarron in the color of their eyes and hair.

Nick drove back to the Tulsa office and that night he drove out to the ranch that was now his. He had a new tent and sleeping bag and found a deserted spot beside the river where he camped beneath a cottonwood. He fished, sitting in solitude, his thoughts on Cimarron. He wanted to call her, but he knew it would be useless. She wouldn't change this quickly, and a few months with Laz didn't prove much. But he could call Cimarron sometime in the future, and knowing that made him feel better. Three months from now, if all was going smoothly at Kamnick, he would call her. By then it would be six months since he began trying to work with his father rather than destroy him.

"Cimarron," he said softly. Nick set his pole down and changed his boots to jogging shoes, getting some weights out of the trunk of his car. It helped to work mindlessly, doing something purely physical.

By the middle of September White Star was absorbed into Kamnick, the employees cut by ten percent. More changes were ahead, but Nick moved carefully, listening to Laz's suggestions. After working several months with his father, he saw that his father was an astute businessman, good at dealing with management problems, while Nick was better at overseeing drilling operations and lease acquisitions. To Nick it was ironic that they made a good team. Kamnick and Laredo would profit by the merger.

Nick hadn't been back to his ranch in western Oklahoma since the night he camped there. His time in Dallas and Tulsa consisted of long hours and working weekends. His desk was constantly piled high with papers and he looked forward to the weekend of the rodeo. He intended to take Saturday and Sunday off and spend the night on his farm and relax.

Nick still took time to work out each night no matter how late. He lifted weights, exercised, and got up an extra hour early every morning to jog. Every Sunday, he spent some time riding his chestnut, finding it relaxing, trying to constantly keep busy to combat his longing for Cimarron. He had his calendar circled with the dates when he intended to call her, the days seeming interminably long, now moving the initial date to October first.

When the last week of September came, the week of the

rodeo, he found business he could do in western Oklahoma at the division office. He was switching the territory of the Enid office to include Kansas. He changed his schedule to go to Enid on Tuesday and stay the rest of the week.

Wednesday night, he worked until midnight, finally closing up, the only person in the empty office. It was Indian summer, the nights were still warm, and it was the best time of the year to him. He drove to his ranch and pulled out a sleeping bag and camped out again, seeing the lights about half a mile away where Burnside lived in the house that came with the property. Nick had picked out another place to build his own home, a knoll with a view of the river and fields. He wanted a big, one-story ranch-style house, but he hadn't had time to talk to any contractors or architects yet, so it was only a vague plan.

Cimarron left for the farm on Wednesday evening for the weekend. Her house didn't feel the same anymore. It was lonelier, too big, too empty. She forced her thoughts away from Nick. Tim would be at the farm because Freedom and Raye would be there Wednesday and Thursday while Freedom had business in Enid. He did accounting for Baker, an engineering firm in Oklahoma City. She tried to think about her family, but it was Nick who was constantly in her thoughts. Everyone said he was working with Laz.

Several times she had reached for the phone to call him, but caution told her to wait. She didn't see how years of bitterness could evaporate overnight and she wouldn't put it past Freedom to exaggerate, because he thought she was making a mistake.

Maybe she put too much emphasis on family, but then when she thought about children, she couldn't bear to live with a man who was constantly at war with his father. And if he wasn't at war with Laz any longer, she would have to give it time to see.

Thursday evening as they ate leftover ham sandwiches, Tim said, "I saw Nick in town, Sunny."

"In Enid?" she asked in surprise, feeling as if every

nerve had been touched merely by the mention of his name.

"He's been at the White Star office here. He bought some land southwest of here."

"For wells?" Freedom asked. "Is Kamnick going to drill some more in this area?"

"No. He bought a ranch."

Cimarron felt something constrict and there was a long, stiff silence that was broken when Jerry began to talk about wanting a horse of his own. Conversation swirled around her, and once she caught Freedom studying her with a frown. She looked down and tried to get her thoughts away from Nick.

As Megan placed a plate of cookies in the center of the table, Freedom leaned back and put his arm around Raye. She smiled at him, and Cimarron was thankful he had found Raye. He needed her, and from the look on Raye's face, she adored him. As Cimarron watched, some silent message seemed to pass between them and Cimarron felt another ache. During the first lull in the conversation Freedom said, "We're going to have to head back to Tulsa now." Freedom grinned happily, and Cimarron couldn't help envying them. Raye wore jeans and a T-shirt, her hair hung below her waist, pinned on both sides of her head with clips. She looked prettier and younger than she had when Cimarron had first seen her.

"Before we go," Freedom said, "Raye has an announcement."

Raye's brown eyes sparkled as she looked around the table. "We're expecting."

Megan and Cimarron gave cries of joy and Megan hugged Raye who looked radiant while Peter and Tim congratulated Freedom. The baby wasn't due for eight more months, but everyone was too excited to let them go, so they sat back down and talked for another half-hour. Finally, they said they had to leave and Freedom went upstairs to get their things. He called Cimarron, and she saw him lean over the bannister. "Come up here a minute."

She went up, thinking he wanted a hand with suitcases.

Instead, he was leaning against the wall, waiting for her.

"Want some help?"

"No, and Raye's waiting so I have to go, but I saw you when Tim was talking about Nick. Why don't you pick up the phone and call him?"

She raised her head, and suddenly he grinned. "Don't blow your lid. I see the smoke rising, and you don't have to tell me to mind my own business."

"I'm sorry. I do miss him."

"Then dammit, call him," he said, going into his room to get two suitcases.

"Freedom, I can't get along with him and I can't get along without him."

"Since when can't you get along without him?"

"I've told you. I can't love a man who set out to destroy his father."

"Sunny, Nick is working every day with Laz. He works in the Dallas office every month."

"How do you know?"

"I hear things."

She barely heard his answer, her thoughts were on Nick. She missed him more than she would have dreamed possible. His easy-going nature, his slow, steady winning of her affections had been so subtle, she hadn't realized how thoroughly he had succeeded until he was gone.

"Freedom!" Raye yelled from downstairs.

"I'm coming," he called. "Forgive me?"

"Yes," Cimarron said, feeling a knot in her throat. She wanted to call Nick, but she had to be sure about what he was doing. It occurred to her that the more time that passed, the less likely it would be that he would want to hear from her. She followed Freedom to the car and they all discussed when they could get together again.

After Freedom and Raye drove away, Sunny saddled Tim's horse to ride, letting the wind blow her hair that had grown shoulder length now. Nick owned a ranch southwest of theirs. He hadn't ever tried to call her; she thought about calling him, wondering if there was another woman in his life, wondering where he was and what he was doing. Was his feud with Laz really over?

Back at the house she studied the calendar in the kitchen and drew a line under October fifteenth. She moved her finger on the calendar. October first. Why wait longer than that? Her finger slid to today's date. It was one o'clock in the morning, Friday, September twenty-ninth now. Slowly, she reached for the phone and her heart began to pound. She punched the buttons, closed her eyes, holding her breath for seconds while she listened to Nick's phone ring. She could be interrupting him. He could have a date. Cimarron squeezed her eyes closed, gripping the phone until her knuckles were white. Now that she had called Nick, she wanted to talk to him desperately. All the feelings she had tried to withhold came surging forth and she ached to hear his voice.

After more than two dozen rings, she replaced the receiver, wondering where he was, knowing she had sent him away. She tried at half past six the next morning, calling until eight, trying his office and not leaving a message when she was told he would not be back until next week.

The rodeo was on the west side of town, held outside with bleachers on two sides of the oval arena. When Nick arrived there was already a field of pickups and horse trailers parked on the hard, bare ground. Excitement mounted in him as he went in back of the chutes to get his rope ready, greeting cowboys he had met before, watching for Tim. He heard a familiar voice and turned to see Tim, the ever-present black Stetson squarely on his head.

"Did your parents come?" Nick asked, shaking Tim's hand.

"Yes. Peter and Megan and Jerry. I told them you'd be here. Meet us afterwards and we'll go get ice cream. I promised Jerry we would."

"Sure. Listen, thanks again for sending Burnside. He's just the man I hoped to find."

"Glad to. Good luck, Nick."

"Thanks. Same to you."

Tim moved on, leading his horse while Nick smoothed more resin on the rope.

They went through the events, Tim came in fourth and received a good round of applause. Nick had moved to the fence to watch, glancing at the crowd for the Chisholms, thinking about Cimarron in Tulsa.

He had drawn Thunderbolt, an unfamiliar bull. He climbed the side of the chute and saw a smoke-colored Brahman. "Okay, Thunderbolt," he said, easing down on the bull's broad back.

"Take it easy," he said softly, talking to the bull, hoping to calm the animal slightly while cowboys helped him wind the rope around his hand in a loose wrap. He heard them announce his name and Thunderbolt's, tell the audience he would come out of chute five. Taking a deep breath, Nick nodded he was ready. The buzzer sounded, the gate was swung open, and Thunderbolt burst out into the arena.

Nick raked his heels back and forth. His right hand was high in the air, his left tight beneath the rope as the bull bucked and twisted, the arena blurring. The crowd's roar became louder; he was riding, gripping with his hand and legs, knowing he was going for the prize money when he looked up. Faces were a blur, but even in a blur, he could see Cimarron.

Startled, Nick forgot Thunderbolt, staring at Cimarron as she jumped to her feet.

Suddenly he was flung off, his arm wrenching, pain exploding and oblivion enveloping him as he tried to push away from slashing hooves.

When Nick regained consciousness his head swam and pain stabbed him. Groaning, he tried to focus and gazed into Cimarron's eyes.

"I'm dead and in heaven," he mumbled.

"No. But it's a wonder you're not." Her eyes were brimming with tears and she squeezed his waist, putting her head against his stomach. He started to reach for her and pain made him gasp and lie still.

"What's wrong with my arm?"

She sat up and wiped her eyes. "You're too old to ride bulls, Nick Kaminski!"

He stared at her intently, suddenly feeling as if weights

had been lifted off his heart. Pain became secondary. "What are you doing here?"

"Trying to find out if you're going to live and if you'll have an arm."

"An arm? What about two arms?"

"You've pulled ligaments."

"It feels worse than that."

She shook her head and he suspected she was on the verge of tears again. He turned his head carefully. "Where are we, Cimarron?"

"In an ambulance."

"Do I have to go to a hospital?"

"Yes. You should be X-rayed."

"It doesn't feel as if we're moving."

"We're not. The ambulance can't leave until the last bull ride is over in case someone else gets hurt."

"Did you know I was going to ride?"

"No!"

"Your family," he said with a sigh. "Tim knew I was going to ride. He didn't tell me you would be here."

"Tim *knew?*"

"Yes. Maybe they thought you wouldn't come."

"Oh, Nick!"

The door opened and two attendants came in and in minutes they were on their way to the hospital. Nick was X-rayed, his arms and ribs taped, stitches taken in his forehead and leg, and finally he was released. By that time Cimarron had a car and was waiting for him. He waved a paper at her. "I have to get a prescription filled. They gave me a shot for pain but I'll need some pills later. And my car is still at the arena."

"No. Tim said he would drive it to the farm. He and Dad drove my car here and they're going to get yours now."

She seemed restrained, and he didn't know if she wanted to be with him, if she was still worried, or if she was angry. "We're going to the farm?" he asked quietly, trying to decide what she felt, thankful she was with him.

"No."

"Cimarron, I can't drive back to Tulsa." Suddenly, it

dawned on him she must not want him at the farm. "I can stay in a motel."

"That's exactly what I thought," she said firmly, taking his arm and holding the door open for him.

The shot he had received blurred reality. His speech slowed and he tried to maintain a steely control of his emotions, knowing he might do something maudlin and foolish. He couldn't understand why Tim had taken his car to the farm if he was staying in a motel, but he wasn't going to ask yet. He was busy thinking of what he would say to her at the door of the motel, because he had no intention of letting her drop him off, say goodbye, and leave without a chance to talk to her.

She got his prescription filled and climbed back behind the wheel without conversation while he continued to think what he would do at the motel.

He intended to tell her how well he was working with Laz. He glanced at her profile as they sped along the four-lane boulevard and then whipped into a sprawling new Sheraton Inn. "I can register for you."

"Here," he said, pulling out his wallet and tossing it to her. He watched her walk into the lighted office. She wore tight jeans and a cotton blouse. The jeans hugged her hips and long legs and he swore at his injury. He felt dazed, his arms ached, and he wanted to break through Cimarron's icy reserve.

Beneath bright neon lights, she came striding back out, a sexy sway to her hips, and he began to feel more normal. He noticed how long her hair had grown. It hung below her shoulders, a red-gold silky cascade that bounced with each step. He took the room key from her and sat back until she stopped in front of the unit.

"Here we are." She came around to hold his door and opened the door of the motel for him. His fingers closed on her arm. "Cimarron, come inside. I want to talk to you."

"I'm coming inside, Nick."

They entered a room done in shades of blue with a thick carpet, new furniture, and a king-sized bed. One small lamp burned over a table. Nick barely noticed the room as he faced her. While she closed the door, he said, "We need to talk."

"We certainly do!" she exclaimed and faced him. "Nick Kaminski, you scared me senseless tonight! I thought you had been killed!" she accused, coming toward him with her eyes flashing. "Are you dating anyone else?" She snapped the question at him.

"No."

"You have to promise me you won't ever ride a bull again!" she said, her cheeks turning pink. She reached up to unfasten the top button of her blouse. Nick's jaw dropped, and then he realized it. It hurt to grin, but he couldn't keep from it.

"Don't you laugh! Dammit, I saw you fall and that bull kept kicking and stomping—" Anger filled her voice, but she was down to the third button and tantalizing pink lace was peeking through the V of her open blouse. Tears filled her eyes and she wiped at them angrily.

He moved forward, sliding his good arm around her, wincing as it hurt and sent pain shooting up his shoulder, but he didn't care. "Cimarron," he said tenderly, drawing her to his good side. "I'm in pain. I can't use my arm."

"Promise me, you won't ever ride again," she said, her fingers working at his belt buckle.

"I promise, absolutely. Look up at me," he commanded and gazed into green eyes that confirmed what he had already guessed.

"You didn't decide you loved me because I fell off a bull. And I fell off because I looked up and saw you in the stands."

"I've been trying to call you for a long time."

"How long?"

"Since yesterday."

Suddenly he smiled at her. "You know I'm incapacitated."

"Your arm is," she replied solemnly, and his smile vanished. She was here to stay. He pulled her against his side and bent his head to kiss her. "It's about time," he said gruffly, kissing her long and hard while she slipped her arms around his waist and held him tightly.